Dot —
Hope you end
The book! Good stuff in
it

Jerry Cahn

# Hunt of the Kite

Jerry Coker

**Pocol Press**
**Punxsutawney, PA**

POCOL PRESS
Published in the United States of America
by Pocol Press
320 Sutton Street
Punxsutawney, PA 15767
www.pocolpress.com

Publisher's Cataloguing-in-Publication

Names: Coker, Jerry, author.
Title: Hunt of the kite / Jerry Coker.
Description: Punxsutawney, PA : Pocol Press, 2019.
Identifiers: LCCN 2019936211 | ISBN 978-1-929763-87-0
Subjects: LCSH World War, 1939-1945--Fiction. | World War, 1939-1945--Underground movements--France--Fiction. | France--History--German occupation, 1940-1945--Fiction. | Women spies--Fiction. | Survival--Fiction. | Historical fiction. | BISAC FICTION / War & Military | FICTION / Historical
Classification: LCC PS3603.O3963 H86 2019 | DDC 813.6--dc23

Library of Congress Control Number: 2019936211

Front/rear cover art: Kay Cassill.

# Author's Note

*Hunt of the Kite* is a work of fiction, with the story threaded between real events in wartime France during 1940-1944. I used the movement of actual military units based on historical records of their operations, specifically those of the German Army 'Das Reich' SS Second Panzer Division, the British Special Operations Executive, the U.S. Office of Strategic Services, the special operations U.S. Army Air Corps B-24 squadron from the 801st/482nd Bombardment Group known as the 'Carpetbaggers', and the Number 75 (New Zealand) Royal Air Force Bomber Squadron. The characters portrayed in the story never existed and are entirely from my imagination.

My special appreciation is extended to Al and Susan McLemore and George Rooks for their thoughts and suggestions during the initial drafts of the manuscript; to Kay Cassill for her interpretations in the cover art and her love of France; and for the love, support and guidance from my wife, Jan.

For Verlin and Kay Cassill

The kite is a raptor, a bird of prey from the Falcon family found all over the world.    In the Bible the Hebrew term is *ayyah*, although in some translations the word used is *ayet*, which means a vulture.

# Prologue

*September 16, 1974. Police Prefecture, Ile del la Cite, Paris, France.*

The policeman in charge of the bomb investigation was a young detective supervisor who specialized in homicides named Guy Metzger. A tall, intense young man, Guy was pulled off his current cases and put in charge 12 hours after the bombing because his boss suddenly took ill and was hospitalized. The attack, which actually involved the tossing of a single live hand grenade into a crowded drugstore on Saint-Germain-des-pres, killed two and injured 34. The incident was determined to be a terrorist attack linked to the Popular Front for the Liberation of Palestine (PFLP), and was now reported on every newswire worldwide. Guy was not surprised there were dossiers of every victim on his desk only a half a day after the attack, nor surprised to have messages forwarded to him from the offices of the new President, Valery Giscard d'Estaing, and the new Prime Minister, Jacques Chirac. He was dismayed at his own tendency, despite his signature self-discipline and iron focus while sifting the initial information gathered in a crime, to keep returning to two of the dossiers of the victims.

As could be characterized for all good investigators, Guy was a natural hunter with a sixth sense when something was not right. But the sense also triggered an alarm on a personal level that a piece of a puzzle, unrelated to the grenade attack, had suddenly revealed itself. His professional discipline told him to ignore the alarm and focus on the crime investigation at hand, so he visited the crime scene, re-read the witness statements, and began visiting the injured at the various hospitals they had been sent. But before he did this, he re-skimmed the dossiers of the victims, saving two of them, a husband and wife, for special attention. He saw them last.

The dossiers were generally thin, the results of the hasty gathering of information that could be compiled from police, school, employer, tax, military, prefecture and in the case of tourists, passport and INTERPOL records. Most of the victims, including the two dead, were French nationals and residents of Paris. Every indication at this preliminary level pointed to the attackers choosing the location for its prominence in the heart of Paris, and the late afternoon timeframe because it guaranteed the drugstore would be crowded. The grenade thrower, as described by witnesses, appeared to be alone. Nothing about the 36 victims seemed to point to them individually or as a group as particularly special targets for the PFLP. Due diligence and normal criminal protocols demanded a careful look anyway for any potential associations, but there was just a bit of guilt and not much justification for the extra time Guy spent on his married couple.

As with all of the victims of the attack they were separated from other patients in a room by themselves. It was unmarked, with their location known only to select hospital staff and not available to the general public or the press. There was no policeman stationed at the door, but there was one assigned to the hospital as a rover 24/7 for the duration. The couple each had a concussion from the blast and injuries from flying shrapnel, and reported as heavily sedated. Guy checked in at the nurse's station, showed his ID then knocked gently on the door. Upon not hearing a response, he entered cautiously.

It was a large room prepared for four patients, but the two beds on the right were both empty. A subdued light, dodged behind a divider of some sort, lit the room with a diffused glow highlighting the cracked paint in the corner of the ceiling. Guy stood still only a step away from the door, feeling foolish and guilty. The two sedated victims were motionless and there was no way he could question them. But he stood there anyway, defiant to the knowledge that it was not the reason he was there.

If it wasn't for the attack he would not know of their existence, and if he wasn't a policeman in charge of the investigation, he wouldn't be allowed in this room. But here he was, and after a long moment, he walked quietly up to the foot of the bed of the wife and examined her face carefully. Even under sedation with her mouth partially open, he could see she was and still remained, a handsome woman, with delicate features and full lips. Her hair was light with no streaks of gray. She looked like what she was, the well-cared for wife of a prosperous American businessman.

The records reported her age as 57. Born in Aix in 1917. An American citizen born in France, now living in Carlsbad, California. Her passport information stated her occupation as a 'retired teacher'. Her name was Anna Metzgen-Markham. French records on a high-priority search revealed this Anna Metzgen born to her Polish father and mother in Arles in 1917 was an enrolled medical student in the Sorbonne in the late 30s. She left the Sorbonne and Paris in 1940 to never return. The war years were a blank, although there was a Ministry of Defense notation specifying Anna Metzgen and an Anna Metzger who served in both the British Special Operations Executive and the American Office of Strategic Services. No dates of service noted. It was noted the Limoges Municipal Police listed a prostitute named Anna Metzger who worked in a brothel during 1940, but no photograph or fingerprints were available. It was also noted in the record the prostitute named Anna Metzger was wanted for questioning regarding the murder of a German officer and two Aix Prefecture officials in Limoges. She had simply disappeared in 1940. The case was never resolved and closed the same year.

The Paris hotel the victims were staying in stated the Markham's had booked the hotel for two and a half weeks. This coincided with their Pan American Airways return tickets to Los Angeles. For the sake of the investigation they appeared to be what they were—tourists, who were in the wrong place at the wrong time. For his own personal inquiry—some things fit and some things didn't. His instinct was wrong, it was that simple. There was no proof this woman was ever in Limoges. It was only a casual statement made by a nun in his orphanage that his mother was a medical student from the Sorbonne that set his nose on the prowl, nothing more. He had asked if he was given his father's name or his mother's, and the nun had said his mother's. *I have told you too much, Guy,* she said.

Guy had glanced at his hands when he realized she was awake. But she was more than awake, she was staring. Anna Metzgen-Markham lifted her head slowly as her eyes widened. She was recovering from the sedation. She gasped and moaned softly, blinking her eyes rapidly. A genuine confusion in her eyes slowly dissolved and some recognition appeared, but she held back, not quite believing what she was seeing. She lifted an arm clumsily, hand open, fingers reaching out toward Guy.

"*Karl?* --", she asked timidly, "is that really you?"

Guy could see the woman thought he was somebody else, but who could tell for sure, since she was so heavily sedated.

"No *Madame*," he said soothingly, "I'm a policeman. You've been through a great deal of stress. There was a grenade thrown in the drugstore you were in, and you and your husband were injured. You are very fortunate. Go ahead and rest. Maybe tomorrow one of my men will come back and ask you some general questions. Purely routine. Hopefully you can extend your stay and enjoy your time in Paris. Forgive me the intrusion. Hopefully your recovery will be quick."

The woman simply stared at him, her mouth moving but no words came out. Guy waved and slowly backed out of the room. *Time to focus on the job at hand. Enough of these distractions.*

# Coming Back

## Chapter 1

*May 5, 1944.   30 miles off the coast of Bordeaux, France.*

The bomber was cool and drafty, although the pilot said they weren't going to climb much over seven or eight thousand feet.  She laid astride a canvas bench/casualty stretcher affair installed specifically for people in her condition, that is, someone who could not bend enough to sit down.   The last time she had entered France it was under the auspices of the British Special Operations Executive (SOE).   She landed like a lady, formally clothed in a dress and a raincoat.   The Lysander thudded down in a small field in Brittany west of Rennes in the brilliant light of a partial moon, and as she and her radio operator pulled out their suitcases, they waved the pilot a kiss.   The ground was partially plowed but firm.  Her carefully fitted French shoes, not too stylish and deemed still available to French women if they had the money, didn't even get dusty.  They followed the shadows of the tree line per instructions and waited for the recognition signal from a flashlight.   A Renault was waiting for them at the end of the field under a tree.

Now after four months of constant training in the English countryside after transferring to the Americans, the Office of Strategic Services (OSS) had determined she was mission-ready. The long-distance flight deep into the heart of enemy-held territory required a big airplane and a parachute insertion.   Because of recent experience with agents not finding all their air-dropped equipment pods, the OSS now stuffed a ton of gear directly on the agent, shrouding the poor soul entirely in an experimental jumpsuit.   The purpose was to enhance agent survivability by landing with his/her minimally necessary clothing, weapons, code books, bags of money, or anything else the pencil heads could think of.

The result, for Anna, was preposterous.   At five feet, eight inches she was tall for a woman, but her lithe, athletic  body now weighed closer to 170.   She didn't walk to the airplane.   She waddled with assistance.  The jumpsuit was designed to keep everything intact and close by after being hurled from an airplane and dropped to the ground at 20 feet per second.   Anna worried about what she would do if she broke her ankle colliding with the hard ground.   The pins had never been removed and it was a fact her right was not as strong as the left.

Her weight, even with all of her attached equipment, was less than the average for a basically-equipped American paratrooper without his full combat load, which the T-series US Army parachute was designed to accommodate. *You will have no problem*, the trainers said. Anna was skeptical, having injured her legs and ankles on every jump she made at night. And they had never done one with this much equipment in training. Despite her mastery of the parachute landing fall techniques, she could not see the ground coming up at night. She could only sense it. They practiced as low as 500 feet, falling straight through the *Joe hole,* their body sucked out by the slipstream a second before the lanyard attached to the airplane jerked the parachute open.

Despite the careful fitting of the parachute harness straps around her by the ground handlers, her body was too slight for a truly tight fit and the parachute opening was always painful, the harness slapping her breasts hard. She never remembered the pain on opening until later, when the bruises would be felt because her focus and her fear was the ground coming up so quickly. The trainers drilled them to glance up, confirming a full canopy above them, then immediately tucking their knees together, legs slightly bent, hands up gripping the risers, their elbows inward protecting their face. *Start counting… one thousand one…one thousand two…* having fallen 70 feet in two seconds just getting the parachute canopy fully deployed, then dropping 20 feet per second with it open, the ground was 20-25 seconds away. *Look down, prepare for impact…*

When Anna first came over to OSS, she was more than a little concerned the organization was filled with rich, highly-connected amateurs who didn't know what they were doing. The SOE seemed more professional, with a clearly defined intelligence gathering side and separate special operations side, both with decades of experience. When SOE recruited her she was desperate, running away after living with a resistance leader who she suspected was a traitor to his own *tireurs et partisans* (FTP) *maquis* group in the Limousin. He was a Communist who played the fiefdoms against each other, and in the end revealed himself as no patriot of France. He was a criminal and a terrorist at heart, responsible for many senseless deaths among loyal French men and women whose only crime was in trusting him with their money, livelihood and families.

Luckily for Anna, her innocence was known to the SOE, who had several agents working directly with the FTP *maquis.* The agents provided arms, money and intelligence support only to be disappointed again and again with the treachery and lack of cooperation between the groups. The SOE agents suspected her lover as a traitor; set him up to confirm it, and within a week of Anna's departure he was outed, captured by a rival *maquis,* tortured, tried and shot. Once he was dead, Anna had no choice but to come out of hiding or be forever suspected as a traitor herself. At first it was tense and her future was uncertain, but SOE,

2

recognizing the opportunity, decided to vouch for her. They recruited her on discovering her fluency in four languages, including English. With nowhere to go she agreed to join them with the other Free French in England. Within two weeks she made her way south, departing on a moonlit night on a fishing boat out of the Calanques west of Cassis. Once in Gibraltar, the British flew her and two other Frenchmen to London.

In England she was sequestered in what appeared to be a grand old estate somewhere outside of London. Used to living a lie, she was appalled how quickly the SOE and Free French interrogators unraveled her story. She expected strong questioning, had been through dozens of intense interrogations when meeting with other untrusting, highly suspicious *maquis* groups in the Limousin for the first time, and understood she was an unknown to the SOE. Born in Arles and raised in Aix en Provence in formerly Vichy-controlled Southern France, her loyalties, family connections and political associations would be carefully sifted. After an initial meeting where a Free French Army officer, a de Gaullist, had sat across the large table and simply stared at her in silence for nearly ten minutes while a British officer examined her documents in equal silence, Anna demanded to know what was going on.

The British officer simply lifted his head. His blue eyes brilliantly clear without a trace of emotion. He gave instructions as if Anna had not spoken. She was to write down, right now, a detailed history of her life, from birth to this very moment purely from memory. She could not retrieve any notes and must list dates, names and places of all major events and places she had lived. There was paper and pencil in the drawer under the left side of the table. Take as long as you like. Some refreshments would be served around supper time. With this statement both officers rose and left.

Anna, confused and annoyed by the stone-walling and cool treatment from her own countryman, decided she would stick to her basic story with details omitted she was sure the SOE or even her transplanted countrymen would have no resources to confirm. Her deception, using only small alterations to her own name and family history, had survived nearly 3 years under the intense scrutiny of French police, minor French bureaucrats, the German police and secret police, and even the scary, slippery gray world of the *maquis*. Her documents were, for the most part, legitimate in that they were real issue documents, not carefully done copies, with appropriate stamps and up to date. The deception kept her status at such low social levels she survived in the shadows. She felt, at times, almost invisible. The gnawing fear always present, her natural tendency to trust no one and her casual, but purposeful ability to sense danger had served her well. Her antenna was already up. Her purpose

3

now, she told herself, bracing her resolve, was to survive, and in doing so help France and the Allies defeat the Germans. Trust, she learned early in this war, was a reward given only after a long, careful courtship.

The interrogators were polite to her, with the exception of the Free French officer, but it was very apparent she was going nowhere until she cleared this initial "debriefing", as the British officer characterized it. Her accommodations in the evenings were spartan, but there was a comfortable reading chair, desk, and a small bookcase filled with, of all things, English story books for a middle-schooler. It occurred to her the first evening the room was formerly the bedroom of a child, and the British government was either donated the estate property by the owner for the duration of the war, or it was simply confiscated. She didn't know English laws or common practices, but was certain the French government would have had no qualms to walk in one day and kick out the owners, all for the good of the government, all for the good of France.

It took one full day to complete the life-history, and a large part of this time Anna spent committing what she wrote to memory. She knew what was coming. Police and intelligence services everywhere use the same techniques to break down the story of a suspect, and initial statements were the fuel for the combustion. What she didn't expect, once she called for the British officer was to watch him carefully place her statement, or life history, in a large manila envelope without glancing at it. She knew she was in trouble when the British officer handed the envelope to the French officer, who placed in on the table in front of him. The Frenchman lit a cigarette and nodded to the Brit, who stood up and went to the door and knocked. A moment later a British Wren stepped inside just long enough to hand another large envelope to the British officer. He placed it, unopened on the table between Anna and the French officer. For the first time, the Frenchman offered a thin smile. He tapped the insignia on his chest, and nodded to Anna in some vaguely familiar way.

"Do you know who I am, Anna?" Anna resisted the urge to lean forward to get a better look at the man, who she considered as some form of enemy, and therefore had avoided looking at him. He was in his early 30s, darkly handsome in an odd fashion, his hair cut very short. Examining him without appearing to do so, she realized he was disfigured on the right side of his face, the skin unusually taut and smooth where there should be a dark beard line. He had been burned. She recognized the French Air Force uniform, the wings of a pilot, but not the man. She had an excellent memory for faces. If she met him, it was years ago and no impression was made.

"I don't believe I know you, Captain. Have we met?"

4

"Yes, we have. I'm Captain Jacque Denon. It's been a long time."

Anna waited for him to continue but his glance shifted away, his eyelids lowering, almost closed. The name didn't mean anything to her. Captain Denon drew hard on his cigarette, the tip flaring briefly, the embers almost at his knuckles. He pressed the stub hard into the glass ashtray, exhaling the smoke down into his lap. Sitting up erect, he pulled his chair closer to the table and lifted the envelope. He opened it slowly, looking carefully inside before withdrawing a large photograph, image down, and placing it on the table.

His eyes opened wide, straight at Anna. "We don't know what you have written. Hopefully it will correspond with what we know of you.

"Is your name Metzger, Metzgen or Metzenbaum?"

Anna's lips parted involuntarily but she did not gasp. Self-discipline forced her to breathe slowly, not be drawn into speaking too soon where her words would be artificially high, but not as high as the shriek of terror clutching her heart. She narrowed her eyes and stared back at the French officer.

"My name is Metzger—Anna Metzger." She said as slowly as she could.

Denon continued to stare at her before slowly nodding his head.

"Not Metzgen?"

"No."

"I am not the only one who knows who you are, Anna. You declare you are Anna Metzger. It says so on your papers, true. A *domestic*. So, are you a milkmaid, house servant, cook—what are you?" Anna kept her eyes on Denon, following his hand as it reached towards the photograph on the table. He lifted the photograph with his finger and stopped.

"Or Anna, are you a prostitute? Or were, in a well-known *maison* in Limoges? Which is it?"

Anna knew the records would be there somewhere. The French police keep excellent records, which the Germans appreciated when they confiscated them. She lifted her head in defiance, her eyes shining.

"If you think you already know who I am, why are you asking me this?" Denon leaned forward and flipped the photograph over. Anna glanced down at it immediately, not knowing what to expect. She could see a very clear head and shoulder official photograph of a German Army officer, a major. His blond hair was closely cropped, the billed officer's cap set at a jaunty angle. The eyes were remarkably clear, the color not apparent in the black and white photograph. Anna gasped and glanced up from the photograph. The British officer sitting three feet from her right was the spitting image of the German major, except the officer across from her had a neatly trimmed moustache. He smiled and nodded courteously.

"Hello again, Anna." He said this in perfect, unaccented German. This time Anna could not control her emotions. Her heart sank as she stopped breathing, her hands trembling. She stared down at the table for a long moment.

"Captain Ericson, formerly of the Royal Fusiliers, has spent some time in the German Army, quite a bit of time as a matter of fact." Denon leaned back and stared at the top of Anna's head, where her long hair was tied into a tight, becoming bun until she slowly looked up.

"He says you were one of the most desired ones at the best *maison* in Limoges. Beautiful and refined, I believe he characterized you. Educated, perhaps an immigrant, but with native language ability. Excellent German. Very hard to get, this Anna Metzger, but this was an old picture, and Captain Ericson was a *Oberstleutnant* (Lieutenant Colonel) by the time he was assigned into the *Haute Vienne*, well connected, and was able to get on your—list, so to speak. At least the list for this one—Anna Metzger. He says without a doubt it was you, is that true?"

Anna was furious she had allowed herself to be led into this situation. She was off guard because she had naively assumed a warm reception among both the English and the Free French who escaped here. The SOE officers who had pulled her from the tentacles of the *maquis* seemed so impressed with her language skills, and so quickly arranged her departure she simply assumed she would be—*rewarded. Recognized. Yes, she was recognized all right.*

Her breathing slowed down as she appraised the two officers, first one then the other. There was only silence in the room for several minutes.

"What do you want of me?"

Captain Denon pulled a cigarette out of his box, offering it to Anna. She ignored the gesture, unwilling to break eye contact with either man. Denon lit the cigarette, inhaling and blowing the smoke out of his lungs forcefully. Anna, a pain in her temple, watched them through the veil of smoke.

"Anna," he spoke so softly she almost couldn't hear him, "you understand, if you're the Anna Metzger Captain Ericson believes you are, you could be considered a *collaborator*, yes?"

Anna lifted her chin slightly, her eyes narrowing as her face flared red. "How *dare* you call me a collaborator, you bastard! You have no idea who I am or what I have gone through!" Anna stared hard back at Denon, her eyes cold as she examined his uniform and his face with contempt. "Who are *you* to treat me like a common criminal, Captain? What have *you* done for France since the capitulation in 1940! For all I know, since we had one of the most modern and well-equipped air forces in the world when the *Bosch* attacked us, you *abandoned* your aircraft and *ran screaming* to Dunkirk and pleaded with the *damned English* to save you! To hell with you! You have no idea who I am!" She spat.

"Then *tell us* who you are, and why we should trust you, *Mademoiselle!*" Denon leaned far across the table, his face twisted in cold anger, inches from Anna.

"This officer, in the guise of a *Wehrmacht Oberstleutnant*, says he slept with you several times in the best whorehouse in Limoges, which means you were professionally in the business of *fucking* German senior officers! Are you not a French citizen? Are you not a French woman?" He spat, "tell us Captain Ericson is wrong! Certainly, you would remember if you slept with this man, apparently several times! Or were there just too many to remember? Tell us those SOE officers who recruited you were not wrong in not letting the *maquis* mob shoot you for being a traitor! For sleeping with the *enemy*! It seems to be a pattern with you, Anna Metzger."

Her only reaction from the verbal assault was a slow retreat, a physical withdrawal barely perceptible because it occurred over several minutes of which not a word was spoken by anyone. Anna's shoulders slumped as her back, arched up and straight in defiance, lowered as she brought her head down. There was no change in her face, angry and flushed, her nostrils flaring as she glared at Denon and Ericson. She brought her hands up from the side rails of her chair to place them, one upon the other in front of her on the table, just inches from the picture of Captain Ericson as a German officer. Her hands, small and well-formed, were chapped and rough, the nails tightly trimmed without polish from the months with the *maquis* both in and out of the bush. They looked like the worn hands of a domestic. Her gaze lowered until she was looking at her hands. Denon, who was also looking at her hands, pulled the picture back and returned it to the envelope, setting it over to the side.

"Anna," he said softly, but Anna lifted her head only when he repeated her name again, louder.

"Anna, we do know who you are, and what you've been doing. And you've had a hard time of it, but France is an *occupied* country, and French men and women have all responded to the occupation in different ways. Coming from a Vichy region, with all intents and purposes directly adding to the comfort and support of the occupying enemy..." Denon lifted his hands in question, the query purportedly obvious. Anna stared back at him with weary contempt.

7

"Fuck you, Captain.  Fuck both of you, and fuck the English, and fuck the Free French if this is how you fight!"  Anna pushed her chair back from the table, and stood up.  There was no window to the outside in this room, so she pointed vaguely away.

"Send me to a prisoner of war camp if I'm an enemy collaborator, if you wish.  I'm done here.  Or dump me off back in France!  I'll take my chances with the *maquis!*  I know where I stand there."

"Anna, sit down."  Anna snorted, and shook her head.  She glanced at the door, realizing, as a de facto prisoner, it was probably locked on the outside.  She walked around the table anyway and neither man tried to stop her.  She turned the door handle and much to her surprise, it unlatched.

"Anna," said Denon firmly, "we have to do this."  Something in his tone stopped her.  Anna closed the door and turned around, leaning her back on it.  She ignored Ericson, still seated but watching her.

"I did what I had to do in Limoges to survive.  I'm not saying anything else.  I have plenty of regrets, but I'm no *collaborator.  I am not Vichy.*  But who exactly are you, Captain Denon?  Where have I known you in my life?  Why do you think you know me so well you can treat me like this?"

Denon stood up and gestured towards the table.

"I apologize, Anna, my comments were rude and perhaps unnecessary.  Please sit down.  We must establish who you are, what you have been doing, and your motivation to want to work with us.  It is that simple."

"It is not that simple!  You have called me a whore, humiliated me with—this man, and treated me like a Nazi spy.  Am I free to go or not?  Am I truly a prisoner of you people?"

Denon shook his head.  "No, you are not a prisoner.  You are free to go if you wish.  You are a French citizen, a guest of the Allies, the British government.  We can get you vouchers to try to find you a place to stay, places to eat, but finding a place can be very difficult right now with so many Allied troops in the London area."  He gestured towards the door as he shrugged his shoulders.

"It is up to you.  However, if you want to join the SOE and fight the Nazis in France, you will need to cooperate with us during this initial briefing."

Frustrated, Anna shook her head slowly in disbelief.

"Who are you, Captain?"

In the small dining hall, there was an alcove with a surprisingly well-equipped bar.  Numerous Allied uniforms, including Americans, were mixed at the bar.  Denon seated Anna in a corner table as he ordered. In the way of the world, the bar reminded Anna of *Madame* Marchand's in Limoges.  Under the strictest possible rationing, certain privileged individuals and groups seemed to always have access to what is impossible for anyone else to get.  Denon came back with two gins, even though Anna stated she did not drink, and something he called a "lemon squash".  It appeared to be freshly squeezed lemonade, an incredible delicacy in 1944.  He placed it in front of her.  It tasted delicious, the sugary, pulpy texture exquisite on her tongue.  Denon smiled at her obvious delight, and they touched glasses.  Anna wondered about the second gin, but her curiosity was satisfied a few minutes later when another French officer, a major, joined them.  He was older, very tall with cold eyes, and it was obvious from the outset he was in charge.  After the introductions, he got straight to the point.

"*Mademoiselle,* Captain Denon tells me you are not happy with the initial—arrangements, necessary as they are to determine your viability and suitability for our kind of work.  Is this not true?"  At close range, his eyes were even colder, piercing and, Anna could think of nothing else to describe them—frightening. Before she could answer, as if he understood how his eyes affected people, he looked down and reached out to touch her hand, just momentarily, the contact warm but electric.  She reacted instinctively and withdrew her fingers a fraction of an inch.

"Captain Denon is not an intelligence officer, as you may gather, but instead of joining the RAF or the Free French forces fighting elsewhere, he wanted to contribute to the war effort directly in taking France back from the Germans, so he came to SOE.  He screens our countrymen coming to England, and during the vetting and background investigation determined he knew you.  Captain Ericson, who you have met, also believes he knows you, so as you can imagine, we take advantage of such special relationships to cross-reference what we know."

The Major glanced around casually, his cold eyes revealing nothing as they swept the noisy bar, the gesture as ordinary as a London-based officer waiting for a friend who was running a bit late, and expecting to see him any moment.  Anna, who was not an amateur at such subtle tradecraft, wondered if it was all for show.  They were, after all, northeast of London on some estate in Essex run completely by the SOE.  Her own antenna was working but at very close range.  When she looked up herself, she realized with a sudden shock there were 15 to 20 men in the bar alcove, and about a third of them were looking at her at any given moment.  Most of the viewing seemed to be sly, momentary glances from men coming into the bar to get their drinks, perhaps surprised to see a pretty young woman in their midst.  Others were appreciative, wolf stares

9

that left little to the imagination to their intent.  She blushed and became very interested in her drink, embarrassed by the attention.

"Perfect place, isn't it?"  The Major noted, almost out of ear shot. He sipped his gin and placed both of his hands on the table, which brought him several inches closer to Anna.

"I will say this, *Mademoiselle,* so we do not waste each other's time.  You are a Frenchwoman, someone we believe wants to relieve France from the clutches of the Nazis.  Most of us serving here are de Gaullists, and feel he is the best hope for the future of France in the fight that is coming, and after the war.  We have yet to determine your loyalties. You served with the FTP, lived with a Communist *maquis* leader who turned out to be a traitor."

The Major stared at Denon before returning to Anna.

"You were selected because of your language skills, and the unique experience you have had in Limoges and with the *maquis* in the *Limousin.* To survive as long as you have without being arrested by now, you must be either very good, very lucky, or an opportunist who will collaborate with anyone if it is to your advantage.  At this point in the war, there is no clear definition of a loyal Frenchman, or woman."

Anna, steaming inside, squirmed but said nothing, maintaining the casualness of the bar setting with painful awareness of the numerous eyes upon her.

"You have lived in the shadow world, *Mademoiselle,* under the noses of the *Milice,* our own French police, the SS—and the *Abwehr.* You understand what it is to be hunted, outed and betrayed by those you trusted; be they friends, family or lovers.  We have had a very high loss rate among the Resistance fighters who have come to our aid, and sometimes we lose our own agents because of the betrayals."  The Major sipped his gin, his eyes cool and unblinking, never leaving Anna.

"We will train you, equip you with the best tools available, and provide cash in *Francs* for payments and quality weapons for Resistance groups ready to stand with the Allies against the Nazis.  But before we entrust you with this responsibility, we must establish our own trust, between us, yes?"

Anna simply nodded, aware that to the men watching from the bar or other tables, she was attentively listening to a French officer; perhaps her trainer, her boss, or her date.   SOE provided her with reasonably well-fitting, tan gabardine trousers, open-collared khaki shirt and light cotton sweater, well chosen for the fluky English weather, even in late summer.  Her slim but shapely curves were still evident under the quasi uniform.  She wished she could say she looked like all the other women in the dining hall, but there weren't any others.   Anna believed the exposure in the bar was for a reason, she didn't quite understand why just yet. She just didn't know what to think, she needed some time alone to consider this.

"*Mademoiselle,*" the Major seemed to sense her indecision and hesitation, despite his assurances, "you need to understand how much we are aware of your—circumstances. You have lived under a deep veil for a long time, but part of our ability to work together is to realize how we can help each other. We have agents placed everywhere in France, sometimes it's the Prefect himself, or someone very close to him. As you have learned from Captain Ericson, we have infiltrated almost all levels of the *Wehrmacht* command structure, including the *Waffen-Schutzstaffel.* We have copied and photographed lists from the most mundane bureaucratic tax records, to *Milice* transport records of *Juifs* in every district in France. We have birth records, marriage records, death certificates and passports records used to determine the immigration status of practically every citizen of France."

Anna very slowly raised her chin and her eyes narrowed.

"Why are you telling me this, Major? To prove to me without a doubt I was a prostitute in Limoges? To hold this over my head so you could humiliate my family if you so choose?"

"The Limoges part of your past is only a segment of your double life, Anna," said Denon softly, speaking for the first time. His eyes were hooded and sad. "Part of the cover that has served you well. We don't want to humiliate you or your family. But understand we know about them. Most importantly for you, we know where they are."

The color drained from Anna's face and her glass slipped from her fingers. The Major deftly caught the glass and set it aside as Denon stepped in closer, holding Anna up by the arm and shoulder. She had no idea when she collapsed or passed out. Drawing shallow breathes she sensed movement and murmuring as the load was lifted from her feet. Minutes passed, and she sensed, more than felt, she was being carried by her head and shoulders and under her thighs away from the voices.

She realized she was lying on her bed in her room. There was the single water color, somewhat faded, of some obscure castle on the pale pink wall. There was a knock on the door, a hesitation, and the door opened. Captain Denon peeked in, saw she was awake, and came in carrying a small tray. He set a small glass down and poured her a measure of some caramel colored liquid from an unmarked decanter. She shook her head, but he waved her protests away.

"Brandy," he said quietly, "it will do you wonders, Anna." Denon pulled the single wooden chair from the desk and slid it beside the bed, setting himself down on it carefully before bringing the brandy to Anna, holding it in mid-air.   After a moment, Anna accepted the glass and then set it on the little table by the bed.

"I don't drink, Captain."

Denon shrugged his shoulders, pausing thoughtfully before reaching over and taking the glass.   He drained it in one gulp.   Anna slowly pulled herself up and swung her legs to the side of the bed.   She rubbed her neck and thighs, watching Denon carefully.

"Who carried me here?"

"I did."

"Why did you do that?"

"Do what?  Carry you here?  Say something that upset you?  We made quite a scene.  Or do you mean why did we carry you away from 20 guys who wanted to kill us for making you upset?  That's no joke, a couple of those Americans almost stepped in to do a damsel in distress thing.   It could have gone ugly, we covered ourselves by saying we had to tell you a family member was killed in action."

"No, why did you put me in a bar with a couple of dozen men and tell me things I couldn't respond to?   Is that some kind of interrogation technique?"

"We thought you were about to turn us down, so we created a difficult situation for you.  Women usually respond in two different ways, some keep having us buy them drinks and they get loud and obnoxious and finally tell us to go fuck off; the others stop talking, start listening and usually get with the program."

Anna thought about this for a moment before laughing aloud.   It was the first time Denon had heard her laugh, and he liked it.  He heard her stifle herself, though and it made him suddenly, inexplicably sad.  He turned away momentarily when he saw the pain in her face.

"I have not heard from my brother in nearly two years.   It's been over a year for the rest of my family.   The last time I snuck down during the dead of night only to find another family living in my family home.  That address was even temporary, as they had been forced to move out of the place where I was raised.   Don't you dare tell me you know where my family is unless you know this for a fact.   You lie to me I'll *never* work for you, none of you bastards."

Denon pulled a small packet of envelopes from his pocket and offered them to Anna in silence.   After a slight hesitation, she snatched the packet away, tearing away the jute tying the half a dozen letters together.   All were addressed to her from her brother, except with the slight change: *Mad. Anna Metzgen.*   Three to her old address in Paris; three to her parent's old family home in Aix.

"Jean Paul gave these to me when he found out I was being stationed in London. You know he escaped to England and joined the RAF after the armistice instead of de Gaulle's Free French Air Force. Many of our pilots did. RAF was transferring him to the Southwest Pacific to fly with the New Zealanders because of his experience with Boston light bombers. He never mailed the letters obviously, once he found out you were not at either address."

Anna clutched the letters to her breast and closed her eyes momentarily. She examined the envelopes one by one, fingering them like the precious documents they were, her hands trembling. Denon looked away again as Anna made a brief moaning sound. When he raised his head, he found Anna staring in cold fury. She shook the letters in her fist, unopened, in the air between them.

"You've had these, how long? *Who are you?* Why don't you answer my question? I don't know *you*. How do you know anything about my family? Did you serve with my brother? Where are my parents? Where is my sister? *Tell me*, you bastard! *Tell me!*" The fear, the vulnerability Denon had seen in her face before it was drained of color was gone.

# Chapter 2

*May 5, 1944. 30 miles off the coast of Bordeaux, France.*

The black-painted B-24 vibrated at certain power settings so badly some pieces of aluminum bracing hummed like a tuning fork. Without earplugs or earmuffs, the humming quickly gave Anna a terrific headache. It was a long ride, and her skull was numb from the noise. To ensure she and her radio operator could find their way if they had to bail out early over France, they learned the exact meandering route of the flight. They had poured over the aviation charts during the briefings, joining the navigator whenever they could. Anna, especially, realized their lives depended on the skill and precision of this air crew. They memorized the speed, altitude, checkpoint names and estimated times between each checkpoint. There would be no time for conference or discussion if the bomber was attacked by night fighters or damaged by flak. Every member of the crew and the Sussex team would have seconds to find their way out of a spiraling, possibly burning airplane, if they were lucky enough not to be killed or severely injured beforehand. If you cleared the airplane, you could only hope your chute was not damaged or burned, there was enough time for the chute to open, and that you were not bailing out over water.

Time moved slowly, the hands on her watch seemed to stop. Without a headset back here in what would be the bomb bay of a regular B-24, she was completely isolated from the cockpit. She kept glancing at her watch, mentally placing the airplane on course. Any communications came from the flight engineer, a burly young man coming by periodically to hand Anna a slip of paper from the navigator. *Approaching Bakerville in 2, descending, over Foxfire in 8.* At this point the bomber was pointed due South toward Bordeaux. They were 30 miles off shore, and in two minutes they would turn due east and began descending from their cruise altitude of approximately eight thousand feet to about 150-200 meters when they crossed the coast of France 25 miles south of Bordeaux, eight minutes later.

The small, single-engine Lysanders the SOE had used had Anna and a different radio operator sitting behind the pilot where they could see everything. The B-24 had no windows and you might as well be in a submarine. To stay out of range of enemy night fighters or flak guns, the specially trained and assigned squadron flew their B-24s off shore as long as they could. They crossed into enemy-held territory at the lowest possible altitude with a bright moon bathing the landscape below them, their navigation completely visual with everything happening very fast.

Most of the crews had flown dozens of these missions into France, so they chose well known paths with easily confirmed landmarks. Penetrating France in the south the pilots followed the big rivers, like the Gironde, the Dordogne or the Lot. All meandering snakes to the newcomer, but to a smart, proficient navigator who had memorized the intelligence photographs, the waterways were familiar, comforting roadways clearly marked for danger. They flew specifically to avoid anti-aircraft concentrations, fighter airfields and towns with eyes and ears attuned to the sound of low-flying aircraft.

Below Bordeaux, France is flat lowlands just skirting the Pyrenees at first, with small hilly rock outcroppings erupting higher and higher the further east you went until the land becomes one with the mountains again; stone outcroppings that were developed and inhabited at various times by tribes who found these hilltops easy to defend, especially if they were near one of the rivers. The tribes built walls and castles, *bastides* as they are known now, with communities raiding one another for decades, some thriving, some destroyed. But in these southern river valleys, where over thousands of years people from lands now known as Spain, Portugal, Italy, Germany, Scandinavia, England and France had fought, scrabbled, loved and bred with one another, there is barely a truce among them, and Anna had to wonder why she agreed to come back again.

In any case she was coming back and going home, although the vision and concept of *home* didn't mean what it used to. She was going back to France, southern France, a land she knew intimately, but a France of people she could not embrace as she once did. In a few minutes the four-engine monster she was riding in would be skirting over the rural farmlands of her homeland, the throbbing roar thundering over tiny, blacked-out farms with ancient, rock buildings inhabited by quiet, secretive peasants who could only dread what the machine was up to, or what it would it bring. They were, as those who lived before them on the same lands and perhaps in the same houses, victims of power struggles of which they had no say. She had learned not to trust them, these peasants, as honest as they may be, or pure as their hearts were in their support of what they understood would be best for them, and therefore the best for France.

The peasants, like the lower inhabitants of *bastides* long ago, found themselves the last to know when the community water supply was poisoned or a neighboring community had declared war on theirs. The first sign of imminent doom came as the castle doors were bolted from the inside, leaving the peasants working the open tier fields defenseless, soon to be slaughtered by archers and axe-wielding assault troops. This part of their condition, or situation, Anna understood. The peasant lives weren't considered in the grand design of warfare, conquest or even community survival. They simply didn't count. They had no education, connections, birthright or professional status.

Anna, once a rising member of the intellectual elite, was aware of this in a broad, philosophical way, saddened by it but did not give it great thought most of her youth and early adulthood. It was a fact with no bearing on her life or her future. Or so she thought. It was, as characterized by Congreve, *the way of the world*. It took direct experience of realizing, in the most personal way she was no longer a member of any elite, and that she too had been cast aside and disregarded as her family had, in exactly the same manner as the ancient peasants by entire communities of French citizens.

The loss of this lifelong trust her parents had instilled in her was the most painful to accept, because it swept away the foundation developed brick by brick of her confidence in herself, her family, her community and of France. It was swept away like the strong current of a rising river, a devastation so thorough and immense and coming so fast there was *nothing* to hold onto, a lifetime of building blocks cementing memories, small and large achievements, friendships and shared experiences crumbling instantly, dissolving into indistinguishable mud and lost below the surface forever.

It would not go away, this feeling of mourning, like the loss of an irreplaceable friend, one who linked with your soul so completely you first begin to suspect an outer world just beyond your vision or grasp, where everything, perhaps for a single, incredible moment, becomes crystal clear and whole. This person was a bridge. Anna refused to feel sorry for herself, because she understood she had survived for a reason, gave up what was to be her life's work because she had no other option. She no longer wanted to believe in the inherent goodness of the world. There was no such thing. The world is simply the world, it exists and men and women inhabit it. Like the *bastides* of old France, communities win or lose, thrive or die.

She had somehow landed on the losing side of a battle she could not quite understand, but did grasp she would never allow herself to blindly thresh the wheat outside the castle walls, never. She had a distinct enemy, but there were also many characters who she had once considered neighbors, friends and fellow countrymen that fell into other categories. One category included French citizens who waited to see which way the wind would blow; people, once trusted friends, who simply looked the other way or through her or her family as they were drawn out, separated and humiliated. Another category, the hidden haters, came out once they found themselves in relative safety and were quick to cast stones, separating themselves as true French, not outsiders, not foreigners. The distinct enemies, the Germans, the French police and Vichy officials she would deal with directly; the other categories would come later. In all categories there was no indifference in Anna's heart. Those who chose to sit on the fence and let her family suffer were no different than those who pointed them out and dragged them from under the houses. Those would never find the safety they sought— she would make sure of that if she had the opportunity. They were carrion.

The sadness in Anna's heart had a palpable density, one she could feel pull down inside her chest as though a lead weight was pressed under her breast. She managed to bury the emotion when she recognized it most of the time because it served no purpose. Her will was so strong she could find something to do to occupy her mind, forcing herself, as she would characterize it, not to feel sorry for herself or succumb to the weakness of the heart. The organ was the root of all pain, she determined, and she would not allow it to guide her mission. But here in the twilight darkness of the airplane bomb bay, there was nothing to do but to think.

She remembered the early weeks with the SOE, her naïve belief her short history in Limoges would somehow be unknown in England, her most difficult days in her young life as something she could flush from her memory, shred and discard because it was too painful, the fleeting but deeply imbedded memory of the scratching survival of a nearly drowned wild animal. It should be left alone to wither, no human being needed to be reminded of the darkness that is possible in life. But Captain Denon, French Air Force pilot who trained and flew with her brother, Jean Paul, forced her to retrieve it all, spreading out her carefully constructed identity into the light. Denon then peeled back every piece, casting aside the fiction, returning again and again to the surface of her hard bark, peeling and picking until segments came apart, revealing more layers and more pain.

"I think it was the fall of '38, September or October, when I met you at your apartment in Paris, the Marais." Denon scratched his face thoughtfully, as Anna stared at him hard, not believing him in the least. This information was available in her file, apparently, but it didn't mean anything.

"I told you, Captain, I don't know you, and I don't remember you."

"There were four or five of us—we had flown in together. Your brother had been one of our instructors in advanced flight training, and when we joined our first squadron after we won our wings, he was transferred to the squadron as one of our flight leaders. We all liked him and it was a great reunion. Anyway, we had some leave and he said he was going to Paris to visit his sister in the Marais, and you had a good-looking roommate. It didn't take much encouragement once he showed us some pictures. We found out you were starting your first year of medical school at the Sorbonne, and that was very interesting to one of the pilots, Guy Maurois, who left medical school to join the Air Force. Do you remember?"

*Guy Maurois.* Anna looked away, incredulous. It can't be. She was attracted to Guy the moment she laid eyes on him, and it seemed mutual. She didn't remember any of the other pilots, and couldn't even remember much about her brother during the visit, since she spent most of the time talking to Guy. Her roommate found all of the pilots attractive. In any case, there was correspondence between Guy and Anna for a few months but nothing came of it, as her medical studies consumed her time completely, and Guy never came back to Paris as the squadron was moved to the Belgium border.

"I met a Guy Maurois, yes. I—I was fond of him. Whatever happened to him?"

"He died the third or fourth day of the war."

"I'm sorry, I'm sorry for Guy. But this doesn't mean you and I have met, I still don't believe it."

"I remember your apartment. Rue St. Croix de la Bretonnerie, off Rue Temple in the Marais. I had some friends who lived on Temple when I was at the Sorbonne. Big, tall double blue doors to the street, couple of stories up for you on a really old, slick smooth wooden staircase. Red door for your apartment, all the others were green or blue. I remember because even though you ignored me for Guy, you made an impression. With the Sorbonne on the other side of the river, it was a hike for you in the rain, eh?"

Anna glanced up at Denon, her eyes wider, suspicious now as she searched his face.

"You were at the Sorbonne? Did you teach?" Denon nodded and smiled.

"I was a graduate student in engineering, but taught undergraduate courses as a teaching assistant. In the spring of 1937, I quit to join the Air Force like Guy."

"The Marais was cheap, and—I liked staying near—near the Pletzl."

"The Pletzl, yes. The Jewish quarter. You wanted to be close to your people."

"I had Jewish friends there, and like I said, it was cheaper."

"*Jewish friends.* Do we have to continue this ruse, Anna? Your brother's name is Metzgen. The day I went to visit you in the Marais, I went to see Anna Metzgen, Jean Paul's sister. I'm trying to establish an

18

identity here, Anna, yours.  I know who you are, where you came from, and your family history.    You are among allies here, Anna, you need to let go so we can establish a baseline of—trust."

Anna crossed her arms and sat back in her chair.  The door opened and Captain Ericson stepped back in, nodding courteously before finding his seat.  Anna said nothing, keeping her eyes on Denon.  Denon and Ericson made eye contact, and Denon signaled with his hand.  Ericson turned around, his face grim.

"Anna—if I can, I'll make this as painless as—possible, under the circumstances.  We have documentation, confirmed today as legitimate from both French *Vichy* records—*Milice,* actually, and German records, that your parents are deceased."  Ericson paused, although there was no reaction from Anna.  "I am so sorry.  We thought they had been moved from Les Milles, outside of Aix to Rivesaltes near Perpignan, or Recebedou near Toulouse, but apparently, they were sent to Drancy and then directly to Auschwitz within a week.    As French Jews, it was unusual that it happened so quickly once they were arrested, but it did, over a year ago.  It occurred when the Germans took over the unoccupied zone to speed up the transportation."

The only reaction Ericson and Denon could see was the color was drained from her face.  Unlike the episode in the bar, Anna did not pass out.   Her eyes, lifeless, drifted beyond Denon and focused on nothing.  Ericson gripped his knuckles on the table and shook his head slowly.  Denon sat down across from Anna and took an arm in each hand.   She did not resist, or make any motion.

"Anna," he said quietly, "We didn't know, we weren't going to use this information about your parents against you in any way.  We wanted to give you some good news.  We are so sorry.  But we can say this, your sister, Clara is still alive, and so is your brother.   You still have family, Anna, people who need you.  Your brother is flying for the RAF, but you know he is fighting for France.   Your sister, we believe, is in Nimes or Cahors.    She escaped the net that caught your parents and joined a Resistance group.  SOE has confirmed the name, Clara Metzgen shows up operating in the *Camargue* or *Aquitaine,* but there is a chance she is operating in the *Limousin.*   Age 22, formerly of the *Luberon.*   At this, Anna looked up, her eyes wide and boring into Denon with such intensity he could almost feel the heat.

"You seem to have it all, Captain.  Both of my parents died together?  They were arrested over a year ago?"

"The records show you father was arrested in early January, 1943 and he went to Les Milles alone, at first.   When he was transported to Drancy, your mother had joined him and went with him.  They were in

19

Drancy just a few days, and were transported to Auschwitz. They left Drancy in late January, 1943."

"My father was non-practicing, his father and mother didn't push it. They left Warsaw 40 years ago and moved to Paris, then Lyon, and then finally settled in Aix-en-Provence, where I was raised. My mother was a Catholic and my father converted. I was brought up as a Catholic, as was my brother and sister. I've never stepped in a synagogue. I just don't understand. He didn't practice, we didn't practice. I thought the proof burden was having more than two Jewish grandparents! My father was a well-respected lawyer, our heritage was not common knowledge. My father would not have volunteered this information."

It was old story and an even older argument. For Anna with her blond tresses, slim and small-boned Germanic features and a name like Metzgen, it simply never came up. Not even when she lived in the Marais, right on the border of the Pletzl, sharing her tiny apartment with another Sorbonne medical student, a French-Hungarian girl named Nina Rosenburg. Anna was just another struggling student, trying to make do on the small stipend her parents gave her for living expenses. Her small collection of Catholic paraphernalia, carefully displayed, stymied any other religious discussion. For Anna, it was better that way.

She was always in the position to move away from what was for many French, a sensitive subject. She was neutral in appearance and affect, and therefore safe from the occasional racist comment about *Juifs* among other students or faculty. Anna knew it was never so easy with her little sister Clara, who did not look like either of her parents, but very much like her paternal Polish grandmother. Slim and dark, with thick curly black hair, Clara's beautiful brown eyes scared young suitors with their intensity. Her full and wide lips were sensual yet foreboding, because her smile was rare and very selectively displayed. She looked like a gypsy, and as she grew older, the attention of men confused and angered her, which seemed to attract them even more. *Who am I?* She demanded of Anna when she was 15 and a male high school teacher tried to paw her breasts. *Why don't I look like you, Anna?* She pleaded.

"I need to go to my sister. Can you get me there?"

# The Beginning Journey

## Chapter 3

*June 24, 1940.   Paris, France.*

The phone call from her father changed everything.   Her father's sister, who also immigrated and lived in Toulouse, had informed her father his nephew had joined a radical movement a few weeks earlier, embracing his Jewish roots and the establishment of a homeland in Palestine.   Her Aunt, like her father was non-practicing and lived quietly. Her son was trying to trace the family tree, which she had revealed reluctantly, when he was arrested by French police because of his presence in a meeting attended by undercover agents.   He was only 16 and they eventually released him, but under rough interrogation he told them what he knew, including the family lineage in France.

"What does this mean for us, poppa?" She asked.

"No one was aware of our past, because it was buried for over 40 years.   Our religious history since we've come to France is all Catholic. My nephew, being the idiot that he is, has revealed new information that can be compared to immigration records traceable back to Warsaw. New information created suspicion.   The police always follow through on suspicion.   Hitler wants to isolate us and he will, then move us wherever he wants.   We've lost the war, Anna, and the Germans are here.   They will confiscate the French police records and it will be just a matter of time before the *Abwehr* comes for—people on the list.   They make a big deal about only going after foreigners, but you know what the Nazis want. They want all of us; foreign or French.   It will make no difference very soon.   Sweetheart, you're in the occupied zone in Paris, the Germans aren't counting on the French police to do their dirty work like they do down here.

"I read there will be a half a million Germans in France by spring, but at first they will mostly be up there in the north.   Don't go to class anymore; don't go anywhere.     There is talk about restricting the movement of residents of the occupied zone, so we need to get you out of Paris and home.   I'll think of something.   I'm so sorry, sweetheart, but the Armistice changes everything.   I'm afraid your medical education is over, at least for now.   It's too dangerous for you.   Our fine leader, Petain, shows no interest in protecting us.   In fact, he does quite the opposite.   It seems he wants to please the Germans, prove to them the French can still govern the provinces.   It is just a matter of making German policy French law! It's incredible! This new Commissioner General, Xavier Vallet, is no better!"

There was a long pause on the line, and Anna thought she could hear someone sobbing in the background. Her parents had a telephone in their home, but they knew Anna was on her landlord's line.

"Is Mother there?" She asked. "Can I speak to her?"

"No, Anna, she's too upset. This is a public telephone you're on, yes?"

The telephone was in her landlord's kitchen, but this was just outside the *Pletzl*, for God's sake, she thought, where boutiques are open on Sunday despite the fines levied for the rest of France. But Anna felt an ice-cold feather slide up her spine when she realized the landlady, *Madame* Clauser, was nowhere in sight. She had no idea if her landlord had a party line or not, or if there were other telephones in the apartment. She glanced down at her knees and found them knocking together against the small table like she had done as a little girl, waiting for her chance to solo on the clarinet. She had never felt this way here; her father called her every Sunday afternoon like clockwork. But they were Catholics, so there was never this sort of discussion before, thinly veiled at it was. France is a Catholic country, so Sundays were days of worship, days for the family. Not Saturday. The deception, if one could call it that, was complete in that Anna had never even gave her father's former religion and heritage a second thought, so telephone conversations were breezy, normal and involved *no code* words.

"Yes, poppa, it is."

"Say no more. Stay put, and stay out of sight. The Pletzl will be one of the first places they will come to. Listen, Anna…" She could hear the quavering in his deep voice, and sense his fear.

"Yes, poppa," she whispered.

"If you must sign your name on any list of any kind, remember your mother. It's a small thing, but there might be some protection in it. You understand what I'm saying?"

"Yes, poppa, I understand." It was a family joke. A simple typographical error brought Henri Metzgen and Simone Metzger together for the first time. Henri was a young law student teaching a night class on German literature and Simone a young woman undergraduate. The school administrators misprinted the last letter of her name from an "r" to an "n", changing it from Metzger to Metzgen. Henri called Simone's name, curious to this person with the same last name. Simone didn't answer at first, until finally coming forward flustered and embarrassed, approaching the handsome young instructor about the mistake. They were married almost two years later. Simone Metzger was a slim, beautiful blond whose parents were also originally from Warsaw. Metzger was a good German name, and Anna understood early how the small deceptions, based mostly on the truth, were the easiest to fall back on.

"I'll send instructions through the mail. That should resume now that we have the Armistice."

"Yes poppa, I love you and momma."

She never considered anyone censoring or opening the mail before, but it was starting to sink in France had lost the war, had capitulated, and Germans, Nazi Germans, were taking over France. Adolf Hitler was taking over France. She hung up the receiver and shivered. She felt utterly alone as she waited for *Madame* Clauser to appear so she could thank her for the use of the phone.

The apartment she shared with Nina Rosenberg wasn't just small, it was tiny, bordering on claustrophobic if it weren't for the tall windows that opened to the central courtyard, giving air and a passageway to the sky and the ground for four apartments on each floor. At about 400 square feet, no space was wasted. A small couch opened into a bed, but by mutual agreement they both found the double bed over the kitchen the most comfortable. It also allowed them to leave the bed unmade in the morning since it was above them and couldn't be seen. They were certainly not lovers, but Anna found a certain comfort when she awoke and heard Nina's soft snoring next to her. It made a lonely medical student's existence a bit more bearable.

It was nice in the early mornings, when all the blinds were drawn and the windows were closed into the courtyard. Anna, an early riser, would open her windows and lean out, looking up through two stories to the sky above before making coffee and beginning her studies. At night, especially right after supper, *Madame* Clauser's mother, who lived with her daughter in a large apartment on the ground floor, chained smoked cigarettes in the courtyard and soon began arguing with someone. These conversations were often quite loud and abusive. When Anna first moved in, she thought *Madame* Clauser's mother was arguing with her daughter. It took a couple of careful observations to realize the woman was arguing alone. After a few weeks of this, Anna found good reason to take an early dinner and then return to the Sorbonne libraries for evening studies. That was how she met her roommate Nina, and together they could safely make the trip across the Seine and the Ile de la Cite far into the evening. The smoke was dissipated by then, so the windows were swung open, the gauze drapes drawn across, and Nina and Anna would bring their dining room chairs to the windows and have a glass of wine in the twilight.

The weeks before the Germans entered France the anti-Semitic rhetoric increased, to the point Nina was becoming frightened and depressed. Nina was a year ahead of Anna in her medical studies and was almost never home during the day. She was a proctor in one of Anna's labs, and Anna was shocked when one of her fellow students openly mocked Nina after Nina scolded the student for not following safety procedures.

*Hell with the Juif bitch*, the young man said to Anna, his eyes rolling, his comment loud enough to be heard by a third of the class. Nina, who was close enough to hear him, turned her head slowly around and exchanged glances with Anna. Nina returned to her desk to correct papers and said nothing. Anna turned to her fellow student, a young man she had shared coffee with several times, and stared at him in disgust.

*She didn't do anything to you. It's her job to make sure none of us get hurt.* He looked over at Anna with equal contempt. *Hey*, he said coldly, *I don't listen to fucking Juif bitches. They don't belong in medicine, and if I had my way, the sons and daughters of Abraham would be kicked out of France. Don't get me wrong, I hate Hitler, but he's right about the fucking Juifs.*

Anna laboriously collected all of her notes and moved to another open lab station without a word. She never spoke to that student again, but she couldn't help but notice the smirks from a few of the other students who were close enough to hear everything they said. She clearly remembered no one else stuck up for Nina, and no one supported her either. It was a hard lesson.

Her protection, she thought, was something left at the Polish border 40 odd years ago when her father immigrated to France. His race, his religious heritage was in the records somewhere. Henri Metzenbaum was unacceptable to French immigration authorities so his name was changed forever to Henri Metzgen. *Juif* was the religion of record, but Henri, already non-practicing at the age of 19, was converted to the Catholic Church within weeks of his arrival in France. He understood church records stood the test of time, recording baptisms, marriages and deaths outliving monarchs, regimes or governments. He could do nothing about the immigration records of the past, but laid his future and eventual safety in the hands of the Catholic Church from every day hence forward. His safety, and eventually his family's, was the sanctity and solid record keeping of the Church, his hope the bureaucracy of government immigration authorities, based on rules established by fleeting governments, would collapse upon their own weight. Time, he felt, was on his side.

Nina never tried to hide her religion or race, although she was not particularly outspoken. Her black curly hair, olive skin and brown eyes were Mediterranean, but the tiny gold six-pointed star she wore at her throat glinted in the light for the world to see. When she and Anna first met at the library, they liked each other at once and it was Anna who suggested Nina move in with her. As fellow medical students it saved expenses, they could work late and return home in relative safety, and in both cases, it seemed, relieved a loneliness they both shared. Medical study is so intense and time-consuming few students had the opportunity to make close friends; or for young men and women, meet potential partners. Nina accepted Anna as a friend even as a gentile and a Catholic; Anna accepted Nina because Nina reminded her of her sister, Clara, and because she was a woman who knew who she was.

St. Croix de la Bretonnerie was a short street, running three blocks east to west between Rue du Temple on one side to Rue Vieille du Temple on the other. In the 13th Century when Paris expelled the Jews outside the city walls, the Jews found a new home in the Marais. As the centuries passed the Jewish quarter was established for a few city blocks, a small square of tightly packed tenements and shops known as the Pletzl, or "little place" in Yiddish. Rue Vieille du Temple was the established western border, with the short streets of Rue des Ecouffes, Rue Pavee and Rue Ferdinand Duval running north to south between Rue de Sicile and Rue des Rosiers.

Anna, who signed her lease with *Madame* Clauser two years before without any knowledge of the existence of the Pletzl, found it ironic she had chosen to live just outside the symbolic home of the exiled Parisian *Juifs*. The low cost for the apartment was a significant factor in her selection, of course, but the university counselors who suggested the Marais as a possible place to find cheap housing listed it as only one of several areas to consider. No one suggested or intimated it was a good place for *Juifs*, or was the traditional home of the Jews in Paris, or even called it the Jewish Quarter. It was simply the Marais, a long walk from the Latin Quarter across the Ile De La Cite and the Seine. It took less than 40 minutes to walk from her apartment to the Sorbonne. Anna, who loved to walk and explore, found the trip down Rue du Temple past the Hotel De Ville, and then across the island on Rue D'Arcole to view the grandeur of Notre Dame on her left exciting and inspiring. With the evening returns to the library she made the trip twice a day, but she never tired of the view.

As the months passed and their friendship deepened, Anna became quite curious and fascinated with the few Jewish artifacts Nina kept in the apartment. Anna displayed a small statuette of Mary Magdalene holding baby Jesus on her side of their shared bureau, but other than a small silver cross she wore occasionally she had no other visible displays of her Catholic faith.   She kept a bible in the bureau under her underclothing, next to her rosary beads.   She had joined no church, although she did occasionally step inside Notre Dame and attended mass on her way back and forth to the Sorbonne.   Her explanation to Nina, who was the only person who ever inquired about her religious affiliation and where she worshiped, was she was simply too busy as a medical student.   She was a member of a church back home in Aix, and wanted to retain that relationship.   This seemed to satisfy Nina, who attended a synagogue just a few blocks from their apartment.

Nina only had three artifacts but she treated them with such reverence Anna wanted to know where they came from, and what they were used for.   As she described them, Nina's eyes lit up with such intensity her affect reminded Anna immediately of her sister Clara.   She wanted so much to take Nina into her arms and hold her, but obviously she didn't, instead beaming warmly towards Nina, her heart wrapped tight inside with homesickness for her sister and family.   Nina had a small brass menorah on her side of the bureau, a candlestick holder for eight candles she lit every year for eight days to celebrate Chanukah.   The menorah was a gift from her father.   She also had a Kiddush cup, a beautifully carved silver wine goblet that was used for special occasions, but specifically was hers from her Bat Mitzvah at age 13.   It was a gift from her mother.   But her most cherished artifact was a simple little wooden spice box, given to Nina from her grandmother also at her Bat Mitzvah.

"If I were at home, I would fill it with cloves and leave it after reciting Haudalah. This is the prayer after it gets dark on Saturday night, closing the end of the Sabbath," Nina said, her eyes shining.   "I take it with me now to the synagogue, but I leave it empty inside."

Anna extended her hand and Nina handed the spice box to her without hesitation.   She smiled as Anna examined the fine craftsmanship. "It's beautiful, Nina!"

"It belonged to my great grandmother on my mother's side, and she gave it to my grandmother.   Her side of the family are all from Hungary— Budapest.   For whatever reason, she kept it and gave it to me instead of my mother.   It is built like a little violin, yes?"

Anna sniffed the box and closed her eyes.   She opened them after a moment and handed the box back.

"Fill it with cloves, Nina, it will make the apartment smell wonderful. I don't mind."

"You don't think it will be overpowering in this tiny space?"

"No."

Nina seemed pleased with Anna's interest in her family and religion, so when they went out shopping or decided to splurge a little by going out to get something to eat instead of cooking themselves, she began to take Anna to little delicatessens and stores where the shopkeepers didn't speak French to the customers, but Yiddish. Anna played the gentile friend perfectly, enjoying the special treats that were offered her, tasting and genuinely enjoying many Jewish delicacies she never had before. Nina enjoyed sharing these cultural specialties with her, that was obvious, but Anna couldn't help but detect Nina's distance and sadness at times. *She is so strong,* Anna noted to herself with admiration, *and is so proud of her family and her heritage.* As she considered her friend, Anna realized the incredible irony of what she was thinking. It was the first time in her life she felt true confusion of her identity. *My father buried his heritage on purpose, with all good intentions. He made me what I am, a free French woman. Why do I feel so confused?*

In early April, on the day Germany entered Scandinavia to begin its occupation of Denmark and Norway, Nina wanted to walk around the Pletzl and talk to Anna about something before dinner. It was a rare afternoon to have Nina not over at the Sorbonne, so Anna took the opportunity and was looking forward to spending some time with her. Some days they only saw each other for the walk to and from the campus. Once they walked the short distance to the Pletzl, Nina began by explaining casually how Rue Ferdinand Duval, a short little street between Rue des Rosiers and Rue du Roi de Sicile, was called *rue des Juifs* for about 600 years—*the street of Jews.*

"In the beginning, the Ile de la Cite *was* Paris, and the *Juifs* were exiled to the Marais, as you probably know by now. They herded all the *Juifs* in one place to keep them out of the city walls, out of the government, out of commerce and just out of the way.

"The next street over, rue des Ecouffes, was even worse in its reputation because of the horrible moneylenders. They robbed people so badly *Juifs* called the moneylenders Kites, like the little bird of prey, kind of like a small hawk. The street still has the name, Rue des Ecouffes, the Street of Kites!"

"Did they steal mostly from gentiles? Is that why they got the name?"

"Oh no, they stole from everyone, especially other *Juifs*. In those days the gentiles wouldn't come here. And no one would lend money to a *Juif*, so people in need of money had no choice but to use them."

"And they called them Kites? I never heard of them before."

27

"Nasty little birds, they kill without mercy. They have a big wingspan so they soar high above the ground, watching for their prey. Deception is its game, it can soar slowly and silently for hours and after a time the prey forgets about it and goes about their business. When it strikes there's a puff of feathers, and the Kite and the prey are gone!"

"The moneylenders were *Juifs* robbing *Juifs*?"

"Yes, Anna. In my culture and religion, there is no shame in wealth. Riches can be one of the rewards in this life. There can be excesses, but a rich man has so many more options than a poor man! The temptation can be very strong." Nina glanced at Anna with the sadness Anna had seen earlier, suggesting with a gesture they take an open seat at a street cafe.

"What does your father do, Anna?"

"He's a lawyer, but he doesn't practice anymore. He's a professor of Law at Paul Cezanne University in Aix. And yours?"

"He's a physician, a surgeon, but like your father he teaches now."

"He must be proud of you wanting to enter his profession. I used to sit through my father's lectures when I was a young girl since the University was just a few blocks from our house."

"You lived in Provence, in Aix?"

"I was born in Arles, but Aix is home. Do you know it? You're from…Lyon, right?"

"Yes, Lyon. But my parents have friends in Aix and we visited them a few times years ago. It is a very nice, pleasant city. I loved the climate and the countryside north of town. Where do they live?"

"It's in the old part of the city in a big, drafty building south of the Cours Mirabeau—practically a third of the block. It's actually quite nice and my father owns the whole building, but we only live in one part of it."

"I know the Cours Mirabeau! Incredible. We admired the beautiful buildings in the good neighborhood away from the heart of the old city! One of them must have been yours!"

"It is a nice neighborhood, but when I was a kid I didn't care, I thought the house was too big and old and wanted a regular house with a big yard! I had to make do with a couple of interior gardens and an old stone courtyard."

They ordered coffee and continued their small talk, but Anna sensed Nina was waiting for an opportunity to discuss something else. For just a fleeting moment, a cold fear crept into Anna when she considered perhaps Nina had discovered something, a link to Anna's family past. She felt both fear and guilt, then shame. These were all new emotions for her, and they made her very uncomfortable. The coffee came and Nina leaned closer, her beautiful brown eyes arched.

"Is something wrong, Anna? You look—upset! I wanted to talk to you about our situation, but if you are already upset about something, maybe we can talk later."

"NO! Of course not, I've been following the war news in the papers, and I heard the bulletins from your radio this morning. It does upset me, so please forgive me. I just wonder if we'll ever get the chance to finish medical school." Nina peered at Anna curiously, the thin line of her lips pursed into a grimace as she shook her head slowly.

"I have over a year to go, and I'll never finish—not here, anyway." Nina opened her bag and took out a cigarette, surprising Anna. She lit it with a match, inhaling and blowing the smoke away from their table. She smiled at Anna with a little embarrassment.

"I know you've never seen me smoke. I don't do it very often, and only when I'm nervous." She gently placed her hand on Anna's and used her free hand to point down at the table.

"Well, what I have to say involves the same thing, the war news, and what's coming to France, to Paris, to right here in the Pletzl. I'm a *Juif*, Anna, and like most smart *Juifs* in France I have my ear to the rail every free moment. We read the tea leaves, the papers, listen to the news, gossip, and what constitutes public opinion out there in the street."

She took her hand off Anna's, shifting back in her chair and crossing her legs. In the lengthening shadows from the fading sun, her face seemed older, yet even more beautiful. Her normally black hair had an arc of reddish-brown hovering and backing the curls, giving the wind drifted strands the depth and texture of a deep forest. Anna couldn't take her eyes off of it. Nina looked like a different woman. Anna began to speak but Nina stopped her with her hand.

"Please, Anna, hear me out, as I don't know how many more opportunities we will have to talk before I go."

"Before you go? Nina—what's happened?"

Nina lifted her hand again, and ticked off her fingertips with her other hand, one by one.

"Anna, you're a medical student! Apply your reasoning to what you are seeing in Europe. You're watching systemic failures of all the governments around us supposedly opposing the Nazis! Like the collapse and capitulation of Czechoslovakia over a year ago in March. Last September, the German Army took 35 days to put Poland on her knees. The Nazis just invaded two so-called neutral countries, Denmark and Norway. You can be sure Belgium and Holland will be next and put up one hell of a fight! It will be a hot knife through butter! I can tell you now as your physician, if Europe is your body, this disease has spread too far and is going to kill you, because *nothing* has been able to stop it!"

"I understand. You think France has lost the war already? Other than Poland, most of these other countries and governments didn't put up a fight, which probably saved millions of their citizens' lives. Perhaps the Germans just want resources, or are willing to negotiate to get what they want. Maybe, just maybe they will allow regular people to go about their lives. As medical students we offer a very positive contribution to society, we're not soldiers or politicians, we are just training to help people."

Nina stared at Anna with astonishment before slowly shaking her head again.

"Anna—do you have *any* idea what Adolf Hitler plans to do with the *Julfs* in Europe? Do you know *what he has done* to the *Juifs* in Czechoslovakia and Poland? Did you think the Germans would not stick to their plans, their *aryanization* of Europe? Us *Juifs* look to Czechoslovakia and Poland as a model of the future, the future of all *Juifs* in Europe, including France."

Anna did have an idea, as she had read the reports in disbelief.

"I do, Nina, I'm sorry I don't mean to sound so naïve. What are you going to do?"

"I will leave once the Germans cross the Belgian border. I guarantee you the Pletzl will not be a safe place for anyone, or any city for that matter."

"Then you're serious, you're going to leave medical school with only a year left. When will you tell the administrators?"

Nina again stared at Anna, shaking her head as if dealing with a child.

"Do you think I trust the Sorbonne administrators to not tell the French police where I went? Do you think Czech *Juifs* who were rounded up within days of the capitulation and transported like fucking cattle to Eastern Europe *volunteered* this information themselves? Or the half a million Polish *Juifs* now in labor camps or the ones who are now DEAD? Their own countrymen pointed them out, helped identify, isolate, transport and KILL THEM. Their own police, government administrators, teachers, bureaucrats and neighbors sent them to their doom. After listening to their rhetoric, there is no great concern for the safety of the *Juifs* in France with our own leaders, because they know the French public is indifferent. If France loses, French *Juifs* will encounter the same fate as all the other *Juifs* in Europe. I'm not going to wait."

"Nina, if you don't trust them, why are you telling me all this?" Nina, whose venomous and cold retort frightened Anna, softened visibly, although her eyes narrowed thoughtfully. She reached out again and touched Anna's arm, her fingers cool to the touch and gentle.

"Because I trust you as a friend, Anna.  But also, I wanted to warn you, since you didn't seem to understand the danger you are in by simply living near the Pletzl.  Being a gentile won't help you if the Germans are sweeping the Pletzl.  They may grab every person they see and you may not have an opportunity to get your papers.  You cannot assume you will be interviewed to determine your status.  Understand?  They will assume you are a *Juif*, and there may or may not be anyone to screen your papers to change their minds, even if you have them.  Your blond hair, your good looks might save you at a labor camp, but then it might not.  Why take the risk?  Get the hell out of here, Anna!  Find another place across the river, but get the hell away from us *Juifs*!"

# Chapter 4

*June 24, 1940. Paris, France.*

When Anna heard the news reports, running repeatedly on Nina's radio with increasing fervor and shrill, the numbers didn't mean anything but she assumed they were bad for France. The *Wehrmacht* crossed the Belgium border on June 5th, and the German Panzers arrived on the Seine River west of Paris by June 9th. *Where is the French Army? Where is the French Air Force? What has become of my brother and his squadron?* She tried to phone her parents on the 5th but *Madame* Clauser reported the lines were jammed, the switchboard full. There were also reports German spies or fascist French had cut the lines. Other reports, which turned out to be surprisingly accurate, stated categorically Germany had entered France with about 120 divisions. Anna assumed it was a big number, because whatever France had to counter the threat, it wasn't enough.

True to her word Nina left the evening of the 5th. What made it an especially hard departure was *Madame* Clauser coming to Anna early the same afternoon when Nina was out and insisting Nina needed to move. It wouldn't be until the 13th before Prime Minister Paul Reynaud would declare Paris an "open city" so the Germans would not destroy it, and not until the 17th before Petain, replacing Reynaud after he had resigned, petitioned the Germans for an Armistice. Anna, who was responsible for the lease, was asked by *Madame* Clauser to terminate any sublease agreements by no later than the end of the week.

*It would be best, Madame* Clauser said in a whisper, *with the Germans coming. Not that we've lost the war, but what if we do? I don't want my building damaged when they come looking for these people, you understand. I have the property and my other tenants to consider. I let her stay and a couple of others because I have complete faith in my good tenants, like you. But frankly, the police are informing landlords there are new rules for the Jewish problem and they will have to leave Paris. None of us property owners want to be holding unfulfilled leases when we could be filling them with good tenants, yes?*

Of course, Anna understood, and yes it would be taken care of. They both stared at one another for a long time before *Madame* Clauser smiled and disappeared down the well-worn steps of the stairs.

It was a tearful departure, but Nina was gracious and came through on a number of promises, some with hidden value Anna could not have ever anticipated. Anna did not discuss the conversation with *Madame* Clauser, but Nina mentioned other Jewish Sorbonne students who were given notice by their landlords to leave. Nina, whose worldly possessions only partially filled two medium sized leather suitcases, was leaving for Lyon. They exchanged information so they could correspond. Nina wrote out two addresses, one for her parents and the other the address of a young man Nina had never mentioned before.

"He's a cousin," she smiled coyly. "Living on a farm just on the outskirts of town. If things go really bad, and I think they just did, the country will be the place to be if you want to survive this war, Anna. There are a couple of telephone numbers too, use the last one, my parents, to leave a message. It'll get to me, believe me."

Anna was beginning to realize the magnitude of her loss, and couldn't control her tears as she kissed and hugged her only real friend in Paris.

"Whether the Germans demand it or not at first, Petain will follow through on his plans and all the *Juifs* on the faculty and certainly all the students will be kicked out. If they're lucky they'll have time to escape. If not, it's Czechoslovakia and Poland all over again. I don't know how stupid people can be, but there you have it." Nina smiled, holding Anna at arms' length for a moment.

"Pull yourself together, girl, I'm just going home!" Nina laughed, but Anna responded by crying louder as she sought Nina's arms. Nina held her tightly before stepped back again, looking into Anna's eyes with more seriousness.

"*Come with me*, Anna. Just pack your bags and get out tonight. When we get to the station we'll see if we can have your father wire you some money. If not, I might have enough. Or I'll have my father wire me some money! You can write *Madame* Clauser later. I don't trust her anyway. Getting you to Lyon is more than halfway to Aix. Get out of Paris! We're at war, and if the Germans get to Paris they won't be shooting *around* the Sorbonne because it's a fucking university! Don't stand here like a little fool waiting for your father to come get you like a fucking princess!"

But Anna was a dutiful daughter and her father had not given her any instructions. He knew what would be the safe way to get out of Paris if the situation got out of hand. Right now, *Madame* Clauser would be reporting Anna as just another Sorbonne medical student to the police.

Nina didn't want Anna to come down to the street with her and accompany her to the station. *I'm not the only one taking off tonight. A couple of us, not too many. If you're not coming, don't take the risk. We don't know what the hell the French police are up to, so we don't want to attract special attention. With the Germans at the border, there might*

33

*be a curfew I don't know about. Train seats out of Paris will be hard to come by soon. It's better this way, Anna.*

They embraced and Nina was gone. The minute she left Anna felt utterly alone and helpless, but worse than that was getting around the realization Nina had been absolutely correct in her assessment of the situation. Nina was strong, fearless and simply did what had to be done. She had offered Anna friendship and escape. Anna could not look at the tall mirror behind the front door because she was disgusted with herself. She was so afraid she couldn't think straight.

By the 9th when the panzers were at the Seine, Paris was in panic. Store shelves went empty. Nina left Anna her radio, and the shrill voices now repeated the procedures of getting water and emergency food rations. Just before she left Nina brought up several cardboard boxes of canned meats, cheese and bread.

"Where did you get this stuff, Nina?" Anna responded in delight. Mail was haphazard at best for weeks now, and Anna had not yet received her monthly stipend from her father.

"I've been saving up," Nina quipped, all out of breath. As she regained her wind, she started stacking the cans and boxes in the cupboard, which had grown bare. "You will need this during the next few weeks until the Germans allow the usual French supply systems to resume operations."

"How about you? Do you have enough to live on until you get to Lyon?"

"Plenty, I'll be in Dijon by tomorrow night, and I'll stay with family. I should be in Lyon by noon the day after tomorrow."

The water supply was now only available a few hours in the morning, so Nina helped Anna fill every available pot, jug and empty wine bottle with water.

"Just remember, Anna," Nina admonished, her face tired but serious, "stay out of the Pletzl! If you see Germans or French police come into this building when you're out and about, *don't come home* until they are gone. And if you see them start to round up people, don't wait around. Get the hell out of town, *leave everything, and always carry your escape kit!*"

For a week Anna stayed inside the apartment, the blinds drawn and out of sight. When she couldn't stand it any longer, she dressed in a long raincoat and hat even though it was a warm, sunny day. The day before Petain, now the Prime Minister, declared Paris an open city and the Germans marched down the Champs Elysees under the Arc de Triomphe, Anna ventured out like a spy down to the Sorbonne. She couldn't believe her eyes as she crossed the Seine and the Ile de la Cite, as the streets and boulevards were thronged with people.   They didn't behave like the working crowd she was used to, coming and going between the Marais and the Latin Quarter.    They wandered about like tourists, their meanderings seemingly without purpose, their attention upward and around them as if they were exploring the city for the first time. *Perhaps they feel just like I do*, Anna wondered.    *What will become of Paris? What will become of us?   What will become of me?*

What created a strange sense of normalcy to the day was the presence of the police.  They wore their kepis and neatly pressed uniforms as always, their backs ramrod straight and nightsticks in hand.    They stood or walked slowly down the street, courteous and watchful, singly or in pairs exactly as you would expect them to be on any sunny day in Paris before the war.  Only everything outside of the street scene was screaming something else.  She sensed the confusion among the other Parisians.    It was too much like theatre, the scene change vast and overwhelming. Anna considered in amazement the strident hand-wringing and despair she had heard on the radio for days, where the conquering German Army was a mile outside the city limits and the unreal image presented to her on Rue St. Jacques.

Anna entered the grounds of the Sorbonne cautiously, finding, like the streets of Paris, the buildings and courtyards packed with students. But it was very apparent regular classes were not in session as she found most of the classrooms had students milling around in them, but no teaching in evidence.  The students were talking, eating and in some cases sleeping in bedrolls shoved up against the walls.    She assumed like herself they were drawn to campus because despite the war they were students, and they had no other place to go.    As in centuries before Parisians bestowed a special status upon the Sorbonne and its students, and it was a status difficult to let go.

To Anna the unreality of the situation dragged her carefully controlled fear to the surface in a heartbeat when she saw the painted symbols on the outer walls of one of the faculty lounges, and then again in hallways and the walls of one her own labs.   *JUIF!!!*  The painted swastika and Star of David became more prominent as she explored the faculty offices.   As far as she could determine, no faculty members were on campus.   In any case her curiosity was satisfied.  The Sorbonne was no longer safe and familiar to her, and she felt a stranger to the halls, classrooms and her fellow students.   This had been her home for nearly six years and her strongest instinct was to turn and run away as quickly as she could.  Her sadness, the sense of unfairness overwhelmed her for only a moment, when the fear and confusion returned.

In the back of her mind Anna had thought she could talk to someone, a faculty advisor, an administrator about her situation. After realizing the staff and faculty were gone, perhaps for forever, and seeing the evidence of growing anti-Semitism everywhere on campus, she saw only an institution now ruled by the inmates. There was no one to talk to. The German Army, the *Nazi* German Army, was a day or two away from entering the city and imposing a new world order that could directly affect her life. *NO.* She thought firmly. It *would and will* directly affect her life if she let it. Without another glance Anna turned on her heel and headed north back to her apartment, knowing like Nina, her medical school days were over. Her future, her survival lay outside of Paris.

On her way home she became aware of the subtle change as she crossed the Seine and Rue de Rivoli. Fewer and fewer pedestrians were visible, until she turned right on Temple on her street, Rue Saint Croix del a Bretonnerie. She could see straight down the three blocks and not a single soul was visible. It was deserted. As she walked past the small markets the doors were closed, the stalls normally filled with fresh fruit and bread empty. She could not remember if they were closed when she left the apartment a few hours earlier, she had been so afraid. Stoking up her courage, she kept walking past her apartment for two more blocks to Rue Vieille du Temple, making the short turn up to Rue de Rosiers. The streets were also deserted, the delicatessens and shops all closed. She looked up and saw mostly drawn blinds, but a flash of movement caught her eye as someone opened and closed their drapes. *They are hiding. The Pletzl will be the first place they will come to.* Anna spun around when she sensed then heard a rumbling motion behind her. A man, mature, bearded and without a hat, whirred past on a bicycle. They both exchanged glances but there was no warmth or recognition. She felt very exposed standing in the street, quickly turning around for her apartment.

She checked her mail but there was nothing. No stipend check, no instructions from her father. She had frugally set aside a small amount for extra books that was spent on the monthly rent when the stipend check didn't come, so Anna was in good shape for the next two weeks. She could have been in trouble for food, but Nina's thoughtful cartons of groceries would get her through to the end of the month if she was careful. She had to send a wire to her father so he could wire her money. Sunday evenings she usually called her father using *Madame* Clauser's telephone, leaving a few *Francs* to cover the cost. Or sometimes, if it were arranged in advance, her father would call her. But the telephone lines seemed jammed or something since the Germans invaded, so there was no contact. With Nina gone and her father not available for advice, Anna felt both foolish and helpless as she wandered around the apartment trying to decide what to do.

Her association with Nina somehow linked her to the *Juifs*, and their fear and anxiety seeped into her psyche. What has she got be afraid of? She was a Frenchwoman, born in France, raised in the Catholic Church, and by all standards would suffer no more than any other Frenchwoman in occupied France. But as quickly as she calmed down by reassuring herself fear, totally unreasonable, crept into her mind and would not let go. It permeated her thoughts, emotions and dreams so thoroughly she broke down into uncontrollable tears several times over the next couple of days. Finally, in complete exhaustion, Anna fell asleep on her couch and slept nearly 12 hours.

The sound of vehicles, high powered motors, woke her up in what appeared to be the late afternoon. She slowly pulled herself up from the couch, groggy and confused, realizing finally after staring at it, the small clock on her mantle had wound down and stopped. The late sun crossed diagonally from the center courtyard, two floors up, a slit beam tracing through the drawn blinds onto the floor. Her brain registered the sounds of motors and she immediately associated them with military vehicles. Raw fear raced up her spine like a cat on a curtain, stopping to claw at her throat. She gasped for air, not knowing what to do. The apartment was an interior one, with no windows to the street for her to look out. She slid off the couch and crept to the door, her ears listening for the sounds of boots running up the steps. There were none. She retraced her steps back to the windows to the interior courtyard, and she cracked the windows without opening the blinds. She could hear voices, but nothing suggesting alarm or concern to what was going on in the street.

A couple of hours later, after washing up and getting something to eat, Anna cautiously opened her door and went down to *Madame* Clauser's first floor apartment. The *Madame* finally opened the door after what seemed an eternity, her face drawn and fearful. She seemed relieved to see Anna, but did not open the door any further than necessary to poke her head out. The *Madame* did have windows to the street, but only from the small apartment she also kept for herself on the second floor. Yes, she reported, the Germans drove up and down the street in small armored scout cars. This was the second time! They stopped and appeared to be recording information about the buildings on the street, but as far as she could tell, they didn't enter any of them or knock on doors.

*Like I said, Madame* Clauser stated conspiratorially, *they came to the Marais as soon as they entered Paris. They'll be back and they'll be looking for Juifs in the Pletzl, mark my words. I'm glad I got rid of mine!*

To change the subject Anna asked if she could use the telephone to call her father. *Madame* Clauser made a face and shook her head.

*The phone lines are still messed up, Anna! The Germans are in Paris, for God's sakes! Where have you been? Petain took over this morning, and ordered a ceasefire effective tomorrow! As if anyone was still fighting!* The *Madame* saw the look of panic on Anna's face, and softened. *Stop by tomorrow evening, Anna, we'll try then, okay? I know the lines are still down right now because I tried to connect with my sister in Orleans. She's worried sick about me and our mother. You can't even get an operator!*

Anna did not return the next day to try to call her father, but she did manage to get through to send a wire, and the day after that a large sum of cash was wired to her. Gratefully, she tucked the *Francs* away, hoping she would not have to make any rash decisions for a while. Her father did wire to say he would attempt to call her every night at five o'clock until he got through. Anna was reassured with this message, knowing her father knew her situation and would come up with a plan for her. With German Army units now carefully patrolling the streets of Paris, she felt the best thing to do at the moment was to stay in the apartment, just in case foolish patriots decided to shoot it out with the Germans.

The radio stations seemed to be taking a more conciliatory approach to the German occupation as the days passed, with repeated instructions to the listeners to remain calm, stay indoors and to wait for instructions. She searched the dial and came across the BBC late one night where a repeat broadcast from a former French Army officer, a Brigadier General Anna never heard of named Charles de Gaulle, pleaded with the French people to not accept the government surrender and to continue to resist the German invaders. As much as Anna wanted to believe in such words, it was easy to say from the safety of London. *How are we to resist?* She asked. The French Army and Air Force have simply vanished into thin air. The German Army is already in Paris, and not a shot has been fired in the city limits, as far as she knew. The only people who apparently have something to be concerned about are the *Juifs.*

On June 22<sup>nd</sup> the French government of Petain signed the German Armistice, ending all formal hostilities. On June 24<sup>th</sup> *Madame* Clauser knocked on Anna's door at five o'clock, letting Anna know her father was on the line.

Once Anna hung up, she waited for over five minutes for *Madame* Clauser to appear. The *Madame* seemed cool to her, but she said nothing beyond goodnight and would not accept any money for the phone call. In the morning a small envelope was slipped under her door. Anna stared at it in horror for several minutes before retrieving it, knowing what it must be. She was not disappointed. *Madame* Clauser wrote a very brief note on what appeared to be a standard eviction notice. The eviction date was June 30, five days away. No explanation was given other than what could be gleaned from the message in the *Madame's* flowery handwriting:

*You lied to me. However, you have been a good tenant these last two years. Leave immediately and I will not be forced to report you. If the authorities come before you have left, I will not lie to them and jeopardize my reputation or property.*

*M. Clauser*

Anna was overwhelmed by grief for what she felt was her own fault, not being careful for what she said with her father on the telephone, and her own foolishness on not listening to Nina and simply leaving when she had the chance. All she could say to herself now was it was a nightmare, a nightmare she could not escape from, one she could not have anticipated in a hundred million years. What have I done to deserve this? How could *Madame* Clauser listen in on the telephone and then tell me I was evicted, based completely on a private *conversation* I had with my father regarding long lost relatives? What is it about the *Juifs* that makes people treat them in this manner?

Any plan to try to reason with *Madame* Clauser was dissolved a day later when the *Madame* rang the doorbell. Without warning the *Madame* simply pressed her way beyond Anna with young couple in tow.

*They are here to look at the apartment, Anna. We don't have much time, and I have offered the apartment as of the first, and inquiries have been made. Please excuse us.*

That night Anna took a careful inventory of what she possessed, and more importantly, what she was going to take with her. Unlike Nina she had no idea if the trains were running, if the Germans and the French police would be searching out going passengers for any evidence of *Juifs*. She barely knew what the term meant, but by all important measures, somewhere it was documented she was one. There were all kinds of rumors, including the Germans shutting down all bus and rail traffic indefinitely, and the establishment of specific personal papers, carefully vetted, necessary for all French citizens within specific departments. What had been imposed, what was soon to be imposed, Anna had no idea. She didn't even have a valid passport with her, but as she sifted through her documents and possessions, she came across the small packet of documents Nina had produced for her. Nina had thought it out.

*Juifs who escaped Poland and Czechoslovakia said the Germans restricted the movement of all citizens immediately, especially Juifs. But certain categories of workers need to travel for their profession, so their documents allow them more movement. Physicians are one of those, and as almost physicians, we can bluff our way past the average German soldier, or French policeman! If they inquire what you're doing, say you're going home to treat a sick family member. In the packet is a half a dozen official forms, signed by officials for the appropriate department, and all you have to do is fill in the name and the date. Don't use them unless you have to! Get it? It's not a requirement, yet, but that can change tomorrow. You were attending a conference in Paris and got stuck there with the war, but now you're going home to Lyon, and then on to Aix to attend to your sick relative. The farther you get away from the Germans, the better it will be. But if for whatever reason you run into them, this is a story that works!*

Anna couldn't believe it would be that simple, but Nina seemed to have some remarkable connections in the Pletzl. They took Anna's picture and a few weeks later Nina gave Anna a slightly used, but currently up-to-date physician's identity card for a one *Dr. Anna Metzger*, of Lyon, France. Nina would take no money for the documents. The stamps and signatures of officials in the Lyon Prefecture were legitimate looking, but as Nina noted, everything would be changed in a matter of weeks when the Germans establish their own documentation requirements.

*These will be good for at least the first few weeks, Anna, enough to get you home. With these papers and your looks, no French policeman will get in your way. Just don't wait too long!*

Anna, fear seeping from every pore, stood in front of the mirror behind the front door and examined her traveling outfit. She needed to look like a young physician, a professional, so the casual outfits were gone. Her cupboards were empty except for cooking oil and flour, so it was time to go. She collected what she felt would be clothing appropriate for her role, yet light enough to fit in a smaller traveling suitcase. She hoped to be home in three or four days anyway, allowing for delays and train rerouting due to the war. Her eyes, green and grey, stared back in pensive concern. She forced a slight smile, pressing her breasts forward against the blouse and twisted her hips left and right. She was attractive enough, and had lost weight with her simple and bland diet. She was hungry, frightened and really didn't know what she was doing. Anna had received no instructions from her father. She couldn't expect *Madame* Clauser to let her use the phone again so she was on her own. She smiled sadly as she considered this would be the one and only occasion she would get a chance to be a doctor, at least in name only. *Well,* she said to her image, *you're going to have to be a little stronger from now on, Anna. Not a soul can help you now.*

# Chapter 5

*June 29, 1940.  Paris, France.*

When Nina left Anna's apartment that last evening for Lyon, she walked with her companions less than two miles to *Gare de Lyon*, the Paris station leading trains to the southeastern part of France.   Anna closed the door to her apartment softly in the darkness of a pre-sunrise bound for the same station.   The small apartment was clean after she had scrubbed it the night before, but she left two suitcases of clothing, books and small personal items too heavy for her footprint.   She had no idea what *Madame* Clauser would do with them, but she decided it was necessary to apologize in a note.   Anna was surprised how easily she discarded the paraphernalia of her medical studies and life of over six years.   A weight was lifted from her shoulders to be sure, but she was indifferent to it.   She knew fear had something to do with it, but there was also a palpable sense of separation, almost physical, from the Sorbonne, the Marais and even Paris emanating around her like a strange aura.   She simply wanted to leave and be gone.   Anna dropped her key into her mailbox and quietly stepped out into the street.

It was still early and fairly dark so Anna kept to the larger streets, walking down the center of Temple before turning east on Rue de Rivoli. Rivoli turned into Rue St. Antoine before ending at the Place de la Bastille.   No gasoline driven cars were about, only a couple of smelly, foul, black smoke-emitting charcoal burning delivery trucks gasped and rumbled by in the roundabout.   Anna kept her hat tight on her head and her eyes moving as she turned down Rue de Lyon on her way to the station.   When she was a block away, she could hear the noise of the trucks before they came into view.   She slowed her pace and eventually stopped, sitting down on a park bench under a street light, not knowing what to do.

Dozens of German Army transport trucks, the kind that carry men and equipment, were lined up in front of the station with what appeared to be hundreds of German soldiers disembarking from them.   The bark of non-commissioned officers reverberated across the coolness of the Seine, as men formed into groups before marching off towards the station.   It was obvious to Anna the *Gare de Lyon* was dangerous and off limits. Nina's radio, now abandoned back at her former apartment, had stated the Germans declared the *Societe nationale des chemins de fer Francais* (French railroad system), or SNCF, as theirs.   No surprise, since the SNCF was reputed to be the best train system in Europe, and was virtually untouched by the Germans during the invasion.   Gasoline was nonexistent, but the rail system had ample supplies of domestic coal on hand and the *Reich* had every intention of putting it to good use.

*Gare de Lyon* was the station for trains to Lyon and beyond. Her identity card listed Lyon as her home, but her travel letter thoughtfully prepared by Nina and her friends, explained her need to attend to a sick relative in Aix. *Again, only if it was demanded by the Germans.* There should be no need to explain her movement to French train officials or French police. Anna referred to her train schedule card knowing her next option was going to be *Gare d'Austerlitz*, the station half a mile away on the left bank of the Seine. *Gare d' Austerlitz* launched trains bound to central France; Orleans, Limoges, Toulouse and once down in the southern region, she could take the regional trains to Aix and home. She had formed a small hope that she would see Nina again in Lyon, but this route would be too far to the west.

As she watched the Germans, she became aware of her heart pounding in her chest, so much so she was gasping for breath. *You've got to control yourself, Anna! The mere sight of Germans cannot precipitate a panic. You'll create a scene. You'll get arrested.* Anna forced herself up from the bench, and as casually as possible, retraced her steps a few hundred feet back to turn south towards the bridge crossing the Seine, Pont d'Austerlitz. Luckily *Gare d'Austerlitz* had no line of Army trucks near the entrance. She could see German Army uniforms, but just a few small groups. She was dizzy from hunger and her brain was racing with fear, but she had no choice. She entered the terminal and got in line to buy a ticket behind two French businessmen and a group of three German Army officers.

One of the German officers, a tall, intelligent-looking *hauptmann* (captain), turned around when he spotted Anna. He immediately clicked his heels, bowed slightly as he touched his hat, motioning to the other two officers to give way to Anna. Confused and embarrassed at first Anna hesitated but the officer insisted, in excellent French, no gentleman could allow such a beautiful *mademoiselle* to stand behind them. Despite herself, Anna smiled and thanked them as she stepped forward gratefully, only to find the two French businessmen also stepping aside so she could purchase her ticket in front of them. With considerable nervousness now with five men close behind her watching, she asked for a second-class ticket to Toulouse. No tickets were available for Toulouse, but the train agent could get her a third-class ticket to Limoges thru Orleans, leaving in about an hour. Limoges was 250 kilometers from Lyon and over 300 kilometers from Aix, but she would be that much closer to home and a long way from Paris. *I'll take it.*

42

Anna smiled again to the two groups of men and walked quickly away, trying to get some distance from the Germans and to find a brasserie open for something to eat and drink. She was delightfully surprised to find a small bakery open in the terminal with a limited assortment of bread and coffee. As she sipped her coffee and nibbled her baguette slathered with cheese, the tall German *hauptmann* sauntered by and stopped by her table. He touched his hat again, and displayed a very neat row of white teeth with his charming smile.

"*Mademoiselle,* I couldn't help but overhear you were going to Limoges. My unit is going to Limoges, and like you, the best we could do is a seat in the third-class cabin! Do you mind terribly, if I join you?"

"Of course—*Herr*…I'm sorry, I'm not good with German Army insignia." The last thing in the world Anna wanted to do was sit with this man, but she was raised to be polite and did not want to create suspicion. The *hauptmann* smiled again, gratefully, carefully sitting down next to Anna before removing his hat. His blond hair was shorn almost to the scalp, with a small wedge of fur growing virtually straight up in front. It made him look like a little boy and she could not help but smile.

"Captain Berchtold—Karl, to you, *Mademoiselle*…"

"Metzger. Anna—*Herr Hauptmann*."

"Karl, please—Anna, if I may."

"You may."

Captain Berchtold, who had a cup of coffee in his hand, stirred it with his finger and took a sip before taking a seat. He glanced at Anna over his cup and nodded his head approvingly, then cocked his head in a youthful, boyish way.

"I have been in France for a week now, and I'm pleased there are French women willing to talk to us."

"Well, Herr *Hauptmann*—I can't speak for all of my countrymen, but this has come about very quickly. No one knew how it would be to have Germans in Paris. Still despite the war, we have an armistice. Lives have been lost, but with a truce coming as fast as it did, it could have been much worse." She felt at once she was talking too much, and stopped abruptly. Berchtold didn't blink or move, his eyes on her face.

"You also speak our language very well," she added.

Berchtold set his cup down on the table and brought his chair closer. He lowered his head as if to inspect Anna's face more carefully. This unnerved Anna but she met his gaze, which seemed to appraise her in a friendly way.

"Yes, many lives were saved, I agree, which is a very good thing. I spoke both German and French at home, strange as that may seem. I have a real—fondness for France. Lived here a few years when I was a

43

student.   I was born in Stuttgart with relatives living in Strasbourg and Nancy.   *Alsace-Lorraine* is Germany to Germans, and I suppose it will be again."

"I see.   Over the centuries the borders have shifted around, that is for certain."

"Have you been there, the *Alsace* region?"

"I have not.   But it must be like the *Aquitaine* and *Languedoc*, with their Spanish influence, or Provence with the Italians.   So many countries and tribes have lived and contested France."   Anna chose not to mention she also spoke German, Italian and English.   Berchtold peered at Anna with even more interest, relaxing a bit by slumping in his chair.   He nodded, apparently in agreement before retrieving some French cigarettes from his uniform pocket.   Anna shook her head to his offer.

"Do you mind, Anna, if I smoke?"   Anna shook her head again but at the same time, not in a secretive way, looked at her wristwatch.

"We have plenty of time before the train, fortunately."   He was careful with his smoke, but his eyes never left Anna's face.

"You are from, Paris, I presume?"   Anna had to think hard for a second, trying to determine her best response, when she remembered her identification card.   She lived in Lyon, it said, but the identification did not list her place of birth.   It wasn't a passport or a birth certificate.

"I've lived in Paris, but I was—attending a conference.   I actually live in Lyon."

"Ah, Lyon!   But you were trying to get to Toulouse!   Not to pry or anything, but I heard you request a ticket to Toulouse.   You weren't trying to get home, obviously.   Work?   Am I asking too many questions?"

He was asking too many questions.   She smiled thinly and shook her head no.   She was used to the brief questions of train agents and nosy French policemen in her travels, and had not anticipated a lonely, French-speaking German officer who wanted to talk about old pre-war times, or at least one she couldn't get rid of.   She decided not answering might somehow arouse his suspicions, so she decided to try out her cover.

"I live and work in Lyon, I'm a doctor, but I have a sick—relative in Aix I'm working my way down to.   The trains to Lyon and Aix were filled with German soldiers, so I figured I would get down to Toulouse and switch to a regional train."

"You're a doctor!   Oh my!   You're so young, Anna!"   He straightened up in his chair with an almost unbelieving look on his face.

"When did you start practicing?   I thought you were in your early 20s!"   She was in her early 20s, but Anna had prepared an answer, thoughtfully discussed in advance with Nina Rosenburg for just such a contingency because both of them were very youthful looking.

"I just got out of my residency last year—pediatrics. And no, Karl, I'm not going to reveal my age!" She said this with a wistful smile. Berchtold grinned back and bowed his head slightly.

"Of course, Anna, I didn't mean to pry! A pediatrician! Children!" He slapped his face playfully, once again with a charming smile. "What a perfect profession for a young *Mademoiselle!*"

Since most people knew very little about medicine, Anna hoped her declaration would lead to some simple conversation and then a change of subject. For Berchtold, his face just lit up.

"That is just too coincidental! I can't believe it. My father is a pediatrician—or was, I think he was retiring sometime this year. All those little patients wore him out, ha ha ha!" He laughed like a person who yearned to laugh, and hadn't in a long time. After a moment of inner panic, Anna decided she was dealing with a lonely man trying to make some kind of connection, but his motives were unclear. She was also very near the end of her prepared cover, so she needed to create some distance.

"Where did you do your residency? Paris?" He followed up at once, attentive and watchful.

"That is a coincidence! Not many doctors have the patience to deal with children all of the time." She glanced at her watch again, her mind racing. She remembered Nina talking about her dad's teaching hospital in Lyon, and made a mental note. She also needed to find an end to where she thought this might be going.

"I did my residency with the University of Claude Bernard in Lyon at the University Hospital.

"What do you do in the Army, Karl?" She added politely. Berchtold pursed his lips before making an unhappy face, his eyes bright.

"I'm a—logistician, I think that's the new term now. Logistics. The German Army wins its wars, if you don't mind my saying so, on our German propensity to plan things to the smallest detail. To move over 100 divisions of *Wehrmacht* assault formations, across a front from Calais to Metz; how many tons of cheese, 88-millimeter munitions, tank tread links, gallons of tank, truck and aviation diesel fuel; butter, bottles of Schnapps, bandages, blankets and toilet paper will we need? And how will we transport all of this material at the same time as the panzers race forward so there will be no delays from lack of fuel or ammunition? Where do we store this material to protect it from the weather and the enemy bombers and saboteurs?"

Berchtold glanced at Anna with a pained expression, as if he suddenly realized he was talking to a victim of his vaunted "*Blitzkrieg*". He need not have bothered to worry, as although Anna was inwardly horrified by his casual description of the German Army rolling through France, she was also grateful he was no longer asking her personal questions.

"I'm sorry, I was making light of my Army running halfway across your country. I sincerely apologize for my—rudeness."

"You're a soldier, it is what you do, but I accept your apology. How do you prepare for such a job? Are you an engineer?"

"No—not an engineer, I have no head for the mechanics! I'm a mathematician. I was an assistant professor at the University of Stuttgart, teaching mathematics to all those engineers, ha ha ha!" The same hearty, almost sad laughter. Berchtold looked down at his hands, his eyes leaving Anna for the first time since he sat down. He looked up and lit another cigarette, his eyes now hooded, introspective.

"I was at the Sorbonne in 1938, finishing off my master's degree in applied mathematics. The Third Reich reached out and began calling us home." He smoked and smiled at Anna wistfully, a sense of guilt and remorse in his eyes.

"I could have stayed in Paris, I loved it here. I had this little dump in the Latin Quarter off St. Germain, and could have lived there and maybe pursued my doctorate. But it was not to be."

"I'm sorry for you, Karl. You don't look like a soldier, and I realize now you really aren't one. You're an academic. You should be teaching your classes, and—going home to your loved ones, and enjoying your life. It's the war. I'm sorry." She regretted it the minute she said it, but it was heartfelt. Berchtold responded though, his eyes lifting to her face almost at once, bright and inquiring.

"If you don't mind my asking, Anna, how about your loved ones? I assumed by your age you were a *Mademoiselle,* and you didn't correct me. You are not—attached?" Anna, who was prepared, smiled warmly and simply nodded.

"My fiancé is also a physician—a surgeon, in Lyon. We met at the University Hospital."

"Ah—naturally. A lovely *Mademoiselle* such as yourself would of course be attached. A lucky gentleman in any case!" He smiled his winning, charming smile, his eyes sad and withdrawn. For a long moment he had nothing to say, and Anna almost felt a sense of guilt and remorse. He was a German officer and enemy soldier, the first she had met since the war began, but she had to admit she found him both attractive and charming. She had known many Germans in Paris, certainly at the Sorbonne, and she understood his loneliness and sense of displacement, especially since he really wasn't a professional soldier.

She had to close her eyes briefly and remember who she was, and the risk she was taking with such a man.

"Well," she said, "Karl, it's been a pleasure.    I need to see if I can call my relatives in Aix, check on my patient, and see how she is doing before the train leaves.    Let her know I might be delayed with my circuitous route."

Berchtold came quickly to his feet, and bowed slightly.    He put out his cigarette and carefully put his hat back on his head.

"Of course, Anna.    It has been wonderful talking to you."    His eyes were so disappointed despite his cheerfulness and smile, Anna reached out and took his hand.

"Hopefully we will see each other on the train," she said warmly. "I enjoyed our conversation, and for the record, you've eased some of my fears about our German—neighbors.    You don't strike me as a man we French need to be afraid of."

"Thank you, Anna.    I appreciate that, and you taking the time to talk to me."

"Best of luck on your—logistic assignment in Limoges.    I don't know why you would be going there, your Army is up here!"

Berchtold smiled and nodded, his head coming erect, his eyes watchful beyond Anna.

"I know, but my assignment has changed, I'm all about this wonderful French train system you have, the SNCF.    My little team is one of dozens carefully examining the little French towns and train yards for transport cars and locomotives.    You might say we are doing a survey. We'll look over Limoges, but we'll be all over Southwest France.    Your road system is a disaster!    No Autobahn in France, ha ha ha!    Our job is to find trains so we can move our panzers and our troops to face the British in the months to come, and inevitably, move our enemies in France to where they need to be."

"Your enemies in France?    You mean French prisoners of war? Where would you need to move them, Karl?"

Berchtold looked at Anna with a coolness not present earlier.    He hesitated for only a moment before responding, but by then Anna was stroked by an icy hand moving up her spine, lifting the hair from the back of her neck.

"Your *Juifs*, Anna, the scourge of Europe!    I know you French are no different than us Germans in this regard!    There are over 200,000 *Juifs* in France, and thousands upon thousands of foreign *Juifs* running across your borders to escape the inevitable.    You don't want them, Europe doesn't want them!    Only Germany has the strength, the will and the ability to do something about it.   So be it.   We will take them away, and they will no longer be a problem for France, for Germany, for Europe!"

# Chapter 6

*June 29, 1940. Limoges, France.*

Anna found the only way she could escape from her growing sense of hopelessness and fear was to feign sleep.  She could not bear to look at people, especially German soldiers.  Sometimes she actually dozed off, only for moments at a time, to be swept into terrifying dreams where faceless thugs in uniforms chased her down familiar streets.  Her legs were leaden and slow as the thugs surrounded her, pointed at her, reaching out to touch her just before she would awaken.  Her third-class car was absolutely packed with people, luggage and military equipment.  Many of the men, mostly young German soldiers, either stood or as the hours passed, sat or laid in the aisle on their equipment.  No one could move around much.  Despite her dreams the reality of her traveling companions was not so threatening.  The young soldiers were quiet, polite and gave their seats away if they came in first to French women or the elderly.

The trip to Limoges took all day instead of the normal six or seven hours before the war.  Passenger trains, even full of German soldiers, were obviously of lower priority than the freight trains.  Their train stopped frequently in switching yards or was diverted to a siding to allow freight trains to pass both coming and going.  Anna, like all of the French fortunate enough to find a seat on the train, was depressed and disheartened by the endless French flatbed cars filled with German tanks, trucks, tracked personnel carriers, fuel tanks and artillery pieces.  Everything looked new and clean as if the two weeks the Germans took to conquer the French and British Armies had required no serious fighting.  For a few frantic moments Anna thought about her brother, Jean Paul.  His squadron of light bombers had been based near the Belgium border and there was no way they could have avoided direct contact with the invading forces.  Her heart ached, wishing she could have spoken with him before the war started.  Not knowing was incredibly hard.  No one discussed the fighting or the losses anymore.  The French were too stunned.  Their only response in the early days was *where is our Air Force, declared just a month ago as one of the best and modern in the world?*  It was obvious to Anna none of the German equipment passing them in the freight trains had encountered much of the French air arm.

The German soldiers on the train were apparently on strict orders to not act like a conquering Army, at least not at this time.  Like Captain Berchtold, the soldiers pressed in like cordwood all around them behaved like civilized tourists, or at the very least foreign soldiers on leave.  She was impressed by their discipline and how quickly they responded to the direction of their non-commissioned officers, who did not disregard the French citizens and were respectful.    As far as Anna could see, the Germans had commandeered the train system but were attempting to be accommodating to the French populace and the government infrastructure.    She was certain Captain Berchtold and his team of logisticians did not have to pay for their tickets, but they received a ticket nonetheless.    The Germans understood the French well enough to bend to the primal needs of French bureaucracy.    *If the government was still running, perhaps things are not so bad...*

To Anna, it made for a very uneasy situation for her personally, as the Germans appeared to have crossed into France with a superior Army. The young Nordic soldiers were tall, tanned and fit, and to a young woman's perspective, quite attractive.    Especially as the soldiers wore their uniforms well, appeared to be healthy and disciplined, were polite and seemed to genuinely want to be accepted by the French as an occupying force they could work with.    However, Anna only needed to think of Nina and the look on her face when Anna had suggested the Germans may not mean to do harm.    Or the cold look on Captain Berchtold as he described how the French train system would eliminate the problems of the *Juifs*.    That meant the end of Nina and her family, and of the Metzgen family, all of them.    *That includes you, Anna.*    It didn't seem possible.  How could such attractive people want to kill my friends and family?

When the train reached Orleans, Anna needed to use the restrooms. She had no choice but to leave her seat and to take her small piece of luggage with her.    When she returned to her car her seat was filled and the middle-aged, short Frenchman sitting in the seat, who had been sitting in the aisle like many of the German soldiers, looked at her and simply shrugged.    Anna smiled and pointed towards the seat but the man simply held her gaze for a moment before rolling his head back and closing his eyes.  Anna, flustered, leaned over to touch the man on the shoulder when his eyes opened again and he gripped her wrist hard with a large workingman's hand, hurting her.

*Go away, Mademoiselle, it's my seat now, you understand?*

Anna's cry of pain was mostly a whimper, but nothing compared to the howl of agony from the Frenchman when another hand reached across his face and plunged two fingers deep into his nostrils, jerking the Frenchman half out of his seat, his head arched back in a very unnatural position.    He released Anna's wrist instantly as a strong hand pulled her aside.    She turned in amazement as Captain Berchtold gripped the Frenchman with both hands, his left-hand fingers still deep into the Frenchman's nostrils, lifting the man up and across the seat and into the aisle by brute strength.   Berchtold, who was almost a foot taller than the Frenchman, pulled his fingers out of the man's nostrils, which were now split and bled profusely, propping him up before turning him around.

"You do not know how to treat a lady and will be handled accordingly!"

Berchtold, even with the limited space of the aisle, cocked his right arm back and slapped the man very hard, twice, across the face.  So hard, the man's eyes crossed as he gasped in pain.   Berchtold pointed towards the closest non-commissioned officer as he released his grip on the man, who collapsed into the aisle.

"Throw this man off the train, *Unteroffizier!* (Sergeant).   If he has any luggage, throw it off too."

Berchtold wiped his bloody fingers on the Frenchmen's coat, and straightened his uniform.   He turned around, looking for Anna, who was still staring in absolute shock.   She had never seen such violence in her life.   She glanced up at Berchtold in both awe and fear, shrinking back as he drew nearer.   His face, red and flustered from the physical effort, softened as he approached her.   He clicked his heels and grinned, his hand out, searching for hers.

"I'm so sorry you had to witness such a thing, Anna, but I came in the car looking for you, as I saw you leave the terminal, and frankly, I couldn't believe the rudeness of this man.  He took your seat, I assume?"  Anna, still staring, finally nodded.   Every person in the car was also staring at Anna, and finally, she saw Berchtold's outstretched hand.

"Come with me, Anna, I have seats in another car.   Give me your luggage, I insist, please."   Anna glanced around at the dull, neutral faces of her countrymen and nodded, handing Berchtold her small case.   The German soldiers in the aisle instantly gave way to them as they left the car, and Anna, more than a little embarrassed about the incident, glanced down at her feet and numbly followed Berchtold.

On the way to Limoges Berchtold offered Anna cognac, which she refused, and some wonderful plums and brie cheese.   The car they were in was full of German soldiers, so Anna was given even more careful and polite treatment.   Berchtold carefully washed all traces of blood off his hands with a few drops of cognac, and smiled as Anna watched him, almost apprehensively.

"I'm sorry you had to see that, Anna.   It was a bit rough, I'll admit. I know I'm a mathematician, a lecturer of serious young people, but I was a collegiate wrestler in my day, a pretty good one."   He held up his hands, large, with long fingers for inspection.   Anna couldn't help but look at them, because she remembered what they looked like covered with blood.

Berchtold flashed his winning, boyish smile, his eyes bright and cheerful again.

"If you are quick, the referees can't see some of your moves during the initial maneuvers for a pin. They are all inside. A careful pinch of a nerve or muscle. Both opponents work for advantage, for leverage, you see. The referees can only see so much once we're down on the mat. We are all taught the little dirty tricks that buy you advantage. I have very strong hands, long arms. I can pull an opponent off his feet in a heartbeat if I can get a good purchase on his face! A quick thumb in the eye in the process! All disqualifying if you are caught! Ha ha ha ha!"

Anna smiled at his joke. Despite his early statements about the *Juifs*, Berchtold helped her when no one else lifted a finger, and she understood the strangeness of her situation. She was just a pretty French woman who would talk to him, and he returned the favor. She was safe as long as he had no access to police records, which may or may not reveal anything. He suspects nothing. Play along. It was still better to be here than in the other car. She was wary, of course, not forgetting for an instant how brutally he assaulted her countryman, even though the man was inconsiderate and rude. It was a lesson she knew every Frenchman or woman in that car learned about the Germans. Berchtold did not ask for permission to throw the Frenchman off the train, he just did it. That was assumed power, with full knowledge there would be no repercussions. He was a German Army officer, and whatever perceptions the French may have about how polite and gentlemanly the German Army appeared, they were a conquering Army. They owned the train. They owned France. Despite herself, she had to admit she was impressed, but there was no admiration. It simply made her more watchful and cautious. There was also something about his description of his wrestling technique to find advantage she found very sound and useful, and she noted it for her memory. Power is safety, and learning how to use what little she had to survive was now her number one priority.

The only problem now was Berchtold sitting with her with nowhere for her to go. The configuration of their car had every other pair of seats turned around. It was designed for conversation or perhaps to keep families together, but it was unnerving for Anna if she thought about it. Her brother, Jean Paul, was one to always find humor in what he called *outrageous circumstances*. For Anna to sit with three German Army officers specifically assigned to find French trains so they could transport *Juifs* to detention camps constituted just such a thing. It would be humorous in a sick sort of way, a good political cartoon, if it wasn't so personally dangerous in reality for Anna.

Berchtold's colleagues, like himself, didn't look the part at all. They were well-educated, good-looking young men comfortable with stacks of paper, formulas and statistics. Exactly the sort of young people she was so used to working with at the Sorbonne. Only they were chasing paper with the end result of the separation and murder of entire communities of French citizens because they were *Juifs*. They were polite, studious and very formal with Anna, which proved to be beneficial in that it kept the conversation down. Berchtold gave Anna the window seat, and she took advantage of it by either keeping her eyes outside on the passing countryside as if she was deep in thought, or she closed them and pretended to sleep.

Anna opened her eyes to find Berchtold watching her with an occasional sidelong glance. She had dozed for a few minutes, maybe longer, her thoughts murky. Berchtold shuffled some papers back inside a manila folder and closed his briefcase, balanced on his knee. He looked like an accountant with his fountain pen poised in his hand. The sun was lower in the sky, but filtered through the train windows in warm yellow rays. He capped his pen and primly slid it inside a pocket as he grinned and nodded her way.

"I trust you had a good nap?" Anna nodded and carefully stretched, noting the other two German officers, Berchtold's colleagues, were both asleep.

"I did," she said slowly, "I didn't realize how exhausted I was."

"I forgot to ask—did you manage to get in contact with your patient, your relative in Aix?"

"I did not. I could not get a line through. I'm sure by the time I get to Toulouse I'll be able to talk to them."

"This is a child, obviously. Hopefully nothing serious, yes?"

"A niece. A nervous child. She has chronic stomach and digestive problems. She has her own regular physician, and I suppose specialists," she added conversationally, "but my sister wants me to see her. The child likes me, and she is a reason to visit family."

"Oh course, always a good reason to visit with family." Berchtold set his briefcase down and lit a cigarette, his eyes glancing at Anna's hands, which Anna realized were ring less.

"Metzger. That is not a French name, if I may say so." He glanced over at Anna appreciatively, appraising apparently her hair, and smiled. "You have Germanic features, Anna, the very best kind, if I can be so bold, so as we know our history on this continent, there must be some Germans in your bloodlines, yes?"

Anna smiled and laughed, meeting his eyes directly.

"I'm sure there are but my immediate family, when it immigrated to France at the turn of the century, was Polish on both sides."

"Ah—Polish."

"I've never been there," she added casually, "and I don't believe we have any living relatives there anymore.　France—France is our home."

A concerned crease cracked in Berchtold's forehead, a darkness hooding his eyes as he watched her, only for a moment before it vanished. Anna, who was still recovering from her nap, came fully alert in an instant as a nibble of fear stroked at the nape of her neck.　*What did she just see? What thought just crossed Berchtold's mind?*

He leaned back, his eyes drifting off Anna towards the open windows.

"Then whatever idea you may have had about the old country, from pictures or stories from your relatives who have been there—leave it that way.　It would be unrecognizable to them now.　I assure you, the Poland of your ancestors is not the same, unfortunately.　It is gone."

"You were there during the invasion, Karl?"　Berchtold turned slightly and nodded, his face again dark with strain, his eyes sad and withdrawn.

"Afterwards.　When I was a boy my father took me to a medical conference in Krakow, then we took the train up to Warsaw.　I thought it was a magnificent city, as pretty as Vienna!　We had a spacious room in this ancient hotel overlooking the river, the—Vistula, if I recall.　I fell in love with it at once.　It was a city, like Paris, of so much history and past conquests.　Napoleon, the Tsars, even modern Germany captured it twice.　But I can tell you from first-hand experience those magnificent buildings, bridges, art collections and parks are gone, all rubble…sheer rubble.　My unit arrived after the last of the resistance ended, September 27th.　Between the work of our Luftwaffe and the mobile 88mms, there wasn't much left.　I couldn't believe it.　It broke my heart, especially since we Germans did this."

Anna, who had read the descriptions of the destruction and mayhem of the invasion of Poland and was as casually horrified as any distant observer would be, was much more touched by Berchtold's obvious distress and remorse of his experience.　He sighed and shook his head slowly, before looking for a cigarette.

Anna knew she had to keep him talking about himself, as she felt she knew him well enough to realize his highly organized, structured brain would return to her in a matter of time.　*He's a researcher*, she thought grimly, *a compiler of data, and he will periodically check his data for accuracy.　I just need to stay a step ahead of him until I can get away.*

54

"You were doing the same job in Poland?   Assessing their train system?"   His glance towards her was so sharp she felt an immediate physical reaction, a slight jerk of nervous fear she had overstepped her bounds.   His stare, penetrating and cool, slowly softened until he cracked a smile.

"I'm sorry the memory of Poland just brought me down.   I don't mean to be rude or abrupt."   He lit his cigarette and unbuttoned the top button of his tunic, and blew his smoke up towards the ceiling.

"It's no great military secret of our need for transportation, the whole world knows what we Germans are up to.   We are logical and analytical.   Although we move quickly, our long-term goals are obvious." He pointed out towards the windows, of the passing landscape of rolling hills, forest and farmland.   "We invaded Poland and Czechoslovakia for one reason only, to prepare the border approaches for our campaign against the Soviet Union.   Every bit of our magnificent war machine is based off the center of the hub, which is Germany.   You know the *Deutsche Reichsbahn Gesseschaft*, the DRG?   The German State Railway system?   It is the best in the world because Germans run it.   I was told to my face by a senior manager of DRG that the French system is better on paper, but a system is only as good as the people who run it!   Your unions are too strong!   Ha ha ha ha!

"Anyway, Anna, yes, we were assigned essentially the same task. My little team of mathematicians and transportation engineers ran all over Poland scouring the twisted wreckage of train yards trying to determine if the Luftwaffe left us *anything* to work with!   They did of course, but it was incredible to see the damage down by our Stukas and medium bombers in *three weeks!*

"Before the invasion we moved nearly 100 divisions on our own DRG rail system into position.   We did the same thing preparing for the invasion of France, but we learned our lesson and left your train system alone as much as possible!   It was an incredible effort and an amazing engineering feat for us to rebuild everything we destroyed in Poland by the middle of October! *Six weeks!* It was both luck and good planning most of Europe, and in this case, Poland, use the same standard gauge rail lines as the DRG.   We've got a system ready to support the campaign right up to the Russian border, but nothing yet to go beyond that.   Thank God I wasn't tasked to be involved in that—at least not yet!   Once they realized my entire team spoke fluent French we were sent to the *Western approaches*!   It is so much better to be here in France, Anna!" Perhaps out of his enthusiasm or because Anna was attentive and listening, Berchtold reached out and squeezed her arms as he smiled widely.   He held her only for a moment then retreated.

"Sorry," he murmured, when he saw the apprehension in her eyes. He looked again like a guilty little boy. "I got carried away with my story."

Anna, who possessed only the most cursory understanding of Hitler's desire to invade and defeat the Russians, tried to respond with a weak smile, her intent to keep him talking.

"I understand your happiness—you are glad to be here. It's hard to imagine what it would take to invade such a vast country. Russia is so large, so much land. I don't think we French had any idea of Germany's ambitions in that direction, although of course, we tried it ourselves and lost." Berchtold peered at her thoughtfully for a moment. He shifted in his seat, leaning in closer again but without touching her.

"It will be an enormous undertaking," he said quietly and gravely, "and absolutely the most risky step we will take in this war. I'm a mathematician not a historian, but I studied Napoleon out of pure fascination. You can be sure the *Wehrmacht* under Hitler's guidance has studied the huge distances in the Soviet Union with great respect, and kept those horrifying paintings of the French dead on the frozen wastelands in the back of their minds.

"Logistics will be the key and the only hope of success when you attempt such a thing. Logistics and a clear understanding of the timetable established by the Soviet winter!" Anna could see Berchtold was very concerned about the eastern campaign, with obvious reservations of its potential for success. It truly upset him, the furrows forming on his brow as he continued.

"The Eastern Front, as we call it, is the reason there are so few Germans here in France, even as we prepare for the eventual invasion of Britain. We are counting on our superior technology and our Luftwaffe to defeat the English, with an understanding the true manpower numbers will be used in defeating the Russians. Once we defeat the English, the *Wehrmacht* will strip half of our divisions in France and Britain and ship them straight to the Eastern Front. The DRG will need trains, train crews, and serviceable rail systems from the Normandy coast all the way to Stalingrad! And the Russians don't even use the standard gauge rail line, ha ha ha ha! The problems are enormous! Absolutely enormous!"

"Well, it looks like you don't have to worry about it, since they transferred you here." Berchtold snorted and slowly shook his head as he contemplated her statement. He hesitated before gently patting her hand with his own.

"Ah, Anna, you think like a rational, normal human being—but not a German! Every campaign in good order, and the only ones I haven't been involved in have been Czechoslovakia and the Scandinavian adventures. Couldn't be in two places at once! I suspect they will not need our services in Great Britain because their rail system is self-contained and doesn't link to Europe." Berchtold sighed heavily as he pointed his finger first at himself and then at his men.

"No, once we have completed our mission here in France, which should take a few months to assess, organize and implement—I have every reason to believe my unit will be back in Poland at the border, ready to roll across just a few kilometers behind the assault panzer divisions, trying to pick up the pieces of what will be left of the Soviet rail system…"

"Well, Karl, I hope you're wrong for your sake."

Anna, who turned to glance out the window, could sense Berchtold looking at her. She knew he was hoping for eye contact, some sense of a real opening, but she felt she had treaded along far enough for now. She sensed his eyes on her for quite some time, but resisted turning in his direction, appearing, she hoped, deep in thought as a Frenchwoman would be after a long conversation with a man who is, in every respect, a very recent enemy. In any event, Berchtold respected her gesture of gentle separation, and after a short time she heard the soft rustle of his snoring. She peered cautiously in his direction and with his eyes closed, examined his face. The growing strain she had witnessed earlier had relaxed under sleep, and he resumed his smooth, boyish, handsome jaw and cheeks. She looked carefully at his collar tabs, looking for the paired lightning strokes Nina had warned Anna to watch for. The strokes denoted a member of the *Waffen Schutzstaffel*. The SS. *They hunt juifs down like dogs, Anna. Stay far away from them.*

Berchtold's tunic had no such lightning strokes, only very ordinary embroidered parallel stripes on his collar, *litzen*, Nina called them. He seemed to have no other decorations to speak of on his uniform other than his rank as a *hauptmann*. He appeared to be exactly what he said he was, an academic pressed into service to serve as an ordinary Army officer. She resolved to say her goodbyes as quickly as possible the moment they reached Limoges. It was the end of the journey for him, but Anna needed to get on a train to Toulouse as quickly as she could. She realized she had learned a few things about the Germans, and for the time being, her faux identify was working.

When the train finally stopped in Limoges the sun was very low in the sky, the shadows long, the evening unusually cool for summer. Anna was hungry but declined Berchtold's invitation to join him for dinner before she departed. She wanted to get a ticket as quickly as possible, and she was hoping for an early train. He understood but insisted on joining her in the ticket queue.

"*Herr Hauptmann,*" she asked, returning to their earlier formality, "it's very kind of you to want to assist me in this, but don't you have people waiting for you here in the station?    I doubt there are any taxis with the gasoline shortage."

Berchtold smiled and laughed gently, nodding at her practicality.

"Of course, Anna, we do have some men waiting for us.  They had no idea when our train was going to arrive, so they've been waiting all day."   He grinned and brushed his insignia.   "I'm the unit commander, so you can be sure they are not going anywhere until I tell them to.  Now please, let me see if I can at least assist you in getting a ticket?"

There was short line at the ticket counter, but Anna was still afraid Berchtold was going to barge to the front of the line and demand a ticket on Anna's behalf.   Instead he stayed close to her as they quietly waited their turn.   When the ticket agent announced the earliest he could find her a seat to Toulouse was early tomorrow afternoon, Berchtold stepped up, nodded to the ticket agent to get his attention, and asked if there was going to be a night train to Toulouse that evening.   *This young lady is a doctor, and is on her way to see a very sick patient,* he said carefully, but without demand.

*No, Herr Hauptmann,* the agent offered apologetically, *there won't be a night train tonight because there is a problem with the track in the mountains just north of Rocamadour.    There was a collapse of the road bed and they need to reinforce it, and it's a tough part of the track, close to the river.   They hope to have the repairs completed by noon tomorrow. I'm terribly sorry.*

Berchtold asked for alternatives, but there weren't any.    Anna purchased the ticket for the following afternoon, and resigned herself to the reality she was spending the night in Limoges, and Berchtold not only wanted to take her out to dinner, but also take her to his assigned hotel.

"All separate rooms of course, Anna.  We're all ladies and gentlemen here!"   When she resisted the offer, he made the case there would be very few rooms available in Limoges because the German Army was coming in and leasing large blocks of rooms from every available hotel and apartment.

"And, Anna," he pointed out with a smile, "anybody who was going to be on that night train to Limoges is stuck just like you, and is looking for a room.   I on the other hand, can get you a room for a very decent price, I might add!"

Anna knew no one in Limoges, and she was tired and hungry from the emotional and physical strain of traveling under an assumed identity. Berchtold was handy in that she never got more than a wary glance from the few *gendarmes* they encountered in the rail station.   She sighed, knowing she would regret this decision, but finally assented to accompany Berchtold and his two companions.    Berchtold led the group, strolling rapidly towards the front entrance, attracting attention as they walked together; three young, tall German Army officers and a striking young blond Frenchwoman.    Anna did not like the attention, noticing for the first time the averted faces of disgust and distain in some of the citizens of Limoges as they passed, both men and women.    *They think I'm a collaborator.*  It raced into her head, and wouldn't go away.

A flat-green Army staff car was illegally parked practically at the front steps.    It was not very big, and made even smaller by the huge *unteroffizier* who apparently was their driver.    On their approach the soldier clicked his heels and saluted.

"Good evening, Sergeant!"    Berchtold boomed, "hopefully we haven't kept you waiting too long!"

"Nein, *Herr Hauptmann!*"

Berchtold stopped and surveyed the little staff car, and shook his head apprehensively.

"This is what they assigned us, Sergeant?  We're supposed to drive all over the French countryside in this little *stabswagen*?"

"It can accommodate four comfortably, *Herr Hauptmann*."    The *unteroffizier* glanced over at Anna with a quizzical look.    "And it sips diesel, *Herr Hauptmann*, *Herr Oberstleutnant* Korman insisted we conserve as much fuel as possible."

Berchtold grimaced and raised his hand in agreement.    "Fine, Sergeant.  We'll make do."  He turned around and introduced Anna to the driver.

"This is Doctor Anna Metzger, a French physician of my acquaintance who we are taking to our hotel, as she has no place to stay tonight, and later on, dinner.    Put her luggage with ours in the boot of this—*stabswagen*."

The only sensible thing was to put Anna in the back seat with two of the officers, and put Berchtold up front with the huge *unteroffizier*.  But Berchtold insisted Anna sit up front, and he squeezed in the small back seat with the other two officers.    This arrangement probably saved her from very serious injury, if not her life.

It was dark as the *unteroffizier* steered the fully loaded *stabswagen* into the surprisingly heavy traffic.    They crossed several blocks before encountering an endless procession of Army vehicles headed in a southward direction.    None of the vehicles were running full headlights, just assault slits allowing virtually no forward light at all.    Although it was cool, they rolled the windows down because of the heat of five people in a very cramped little staff car.  The noise was tremendous, as the truck traffic was all large, the engines and exhaust systems at or above the level of their little car. In between the troop transports there were armored staff and patrol vehicles, some half-tracked, grinding and clanking by, with an occasional motorcycle weaving in and out. It was a madhouse, made even crazier because they had approached a roundabout, and in the confusion of the darkness, vehicles were darting away or darting into the traffic circle without any apparent organized plan or direction.

"Which direction are we supposed to be going, Sergeant?" Berchtold demanded, after about five minutes of not moving at all. Vehicles behind their car, much larger, began beeping and honking their horns, until there was a cacophony of noise blending into one big, endless roar.

"Our way is across from this traffic circle, *Herr Hauptmann*! When I came through a few hours ago, it was a simple crossing!"

"Just get out there, Sergeant! Start weaving, make room, we have to get out there, or we'll be here all night!"

Reluctantly, as one of the smallest vehicles short of a motorcycle, the *unteroffizier* crept out. They quickly found themselves drawn into the inner part of the traffic circle and trapped by a wall of huge trucks. After five slow circuits around the traffic circle, Berchtold slapped the back of the front seat between the *unteroffizier* and Anna as hard as a pistol shot, scaring her half to death.

"Good God, Sergeant, get us the hell out of this turnabout! Get into the outer lane! The outer lane!"

The *unteroffizier*, his eyes wild with fear, simply turned the wheel into the traffic, which created more bleating horns, squealing brakes and somehow, a small space where the *stabswagen,* miraculously unscathed, remained for about ten seconds. Suddenly a hole appeared in the traffic and a clear path, perhaps twenty feet long, was visible with an exit.

"That's the one!" The *unteroffizier* gasped, down shifting and accelerating at the same time. They crossed the circle and were halfway into the exit when the big BMW motorcycle with a sidecar and passenger came out of nowhere and hit them broadside from the left at full throttle.

The only image that remained for Anna was the sensation everything was going in the wrong direction. A tremendous explosion on the left was forcing the car to the right, but she was hurled to the left across the seat into the *unteroffizier.* A solid, fuel spraying black mass flew past her and then everything reversed. The car hit something on the right and she was now hurled in the opposite direction to her side of the car. She felt a pinch of pain then blackness.

# Chapter 7

*June 29, 1940.  Limoges, France.*

Anna opened her eyes to growing dusk.    Something was between her and the sky, dark thin silhouettes—tree branches?   For a moment she was confused, because she realized she was lying on her back, not sitting. Not sitting in a car.   She turned her head and gasped from the stabbing pain from her shoulder, but was aware now of two things demanding her attention.   The first was the intense odor of diesel fuel mixed with a smell she knew well; blood, stool and the internal fluids found in human intestines and organs released to the air.   Sweet and foul, she could also feel the wetness all over her body.   The second thing frightened her even more because she didn't recognize it.   It was a *whirring* sound, so close she could feel the disturbed air near her head, *what is it?*

Other sounds slowly came up in her consciousness; idling engines, voices, so many voices now, many shouting.    A single moan from someone very close caught her attention and she forgot about everything else.   Her left arm seemed to work as she slowly propped herself up on her good elbow to see who was near her.    What she could see took a few seconds to register.   The little staff car had been slammed up and on a short rock retaining wall.   The car was only about two meters away from her, but was hardly recognizable.    The metal roof was sheared off, including most of the windshield.   The big BMW motorcycle had done that.   It also decapitated the *unteroffizier* driving the car.   Most of the motorcycle lay inches from Anna's feet, the tank shredded open and the handlebars twisted up like horns.   The sidecar was behind her somewhere, and she could not understand how all of this heavy, hurling metal had passed over her side of the car, tearing off the roof in the process, and miss her completely.   It was then she realized the still spinning wheel and axle of the sidecar were directly behind her head.   Everything was smoking, with diesel sprayed everywhere, but there was no fire.

Numbly, Anna looked at the car when she again heard a faint moan. She slowly crawled towards the back seat, dragging her right leg.    She found Berchtold with his eyes open, face pale as flour.   His body was half out of the car, his back stretched across the rock retaining wall.   His right arm laid at an odd angle with the lower forearm fully exposed, with the uniform sleeve sliced off as neatly as a razor stroke.   He coughed and a huge bubble of blood spurted from directly below his elbow, in direct rhythm with the beating of his heart.   She could see a deep slash with blood welling up, so she stripped her scarf from her neck and applied a tight tourniquet above the elbow, elevating Berchtold's arm as she did so. She quickly examined him and determined he had other possible injuries, but they appeared to be internal.   As other German soldiers started to come around and help pull Berchtold and herself from the wreckage, Anna pushed their arms away so she could examine the other two officers in the staff car.   Both had serious head injuries but she could feel pulses in their throats, weak but steady.

*Are you a nurse?*   One of the military policemen with a flashlight asked.   *No, I'm a doctor.*

She tried to push the soldiers away, but one look at her face, hair and dress, matted with blood and they carefully picked her up.   Her right leg didn't work, and as a soldier gently guided her out of the backseat, she slipped and he gripped her shoulder.   It was the last thing she remembered.

Despite her athletic youth Anna had never broken a bone.   She had snow skied the Alps, ice skated frozen ponds, water skied Swiss lakes and even tried mountain climbing with a one-time boyfriend, but never a fracture.   As a medical student it was always a sense of wonder of how people managed to actually *break bones*.   I mean, really.   It had to be hard.

The German Army orthopedic surgeon who set her broken clavicle and dislocated shoulder, repaired her fractured thumb and put the two pins in her broken ankle seemed too old to be in the Army.   Berchtold, who had survived the crash because of Anna's quick application of a tourniquet, had made her profession well known to anyone who would listen.   The surgeon stopped by every day to chat.   In fact, she was a small celebrity among some of the German occupation troops, and her picture was taken after a few days with the intent of using her for publicity. It was Berchtold himself who suggested it might not be such a good idea locally in France.   It was too soon after the Armistice.   French sensibilities needed to be considered.   There might even be retribution to Anna, or her family.   Luckily for her, the German Army had taken over the entire wing of the civilian hospital and her care was in the hands of the German Army medical staff.   The pictures and the story were published finally, but only in German newspapers.   The very thought struck Anna with sheer terror, believing any day now she would be interrogated by the *Abwehr.*

The medical staff did ask her if they needed to contact her hospital in Lyon, or her staff in her practice.   *No, no,* she said as casually as she could, *I'm on holiday, I was at a conference in Paris, and I was on my way to see some family in Aix.   I'll let them know I'll be delayed.   It's the war, you know. Once I'm up and about I'll send a cable, so they won't worry.*

It bought some time, but what really kept things at a distance and low key was Berchtold. Anna sensed there was a belief there was some kind of relationship between her and Berchtold, so she was handled with kid gloves with only the surgeon out of the loop. Anna had no choice but to play along for now, because despite her accident on French streets in Limoges, not a single French official or *gendarmerie* had approached her personally in the hospital.

"How old do you think I am?" Asked the surgeon, annoyed and hurt when Anna mentioned she was surprised he was still serving in the Army. A little flustered by his response, Anna tried to cover by saying she was only familiar with the French Army, and her friends who were called up for service tended to be—well, under 40 years of age. When Berchtold recovered well enough to walk around, he was stopping by Anna's room more frequently and after a few days, the surgeon figured it out and apparently gave up.

"What's with him?" Asked Berchtold, when the surgeon suddenly stood up and walked out of the room with a minute acknowledgement of Berchtold.

"Oh, he got bored with me. Once he found out my specialty was pediatrics, he had less to say. One of those men who doesn't care for children all that much."

"He's an old man anyway!" Berchtold sat down and pulled his chair closer to Anna's bed. He smiled, carefully scratching an itch on his arm in the sling. He held a small package in his hands but kept it low in his lap. He grimaced as he struggled to get comfortable in the bare hardwood chair, because like Anna, the accident broke bones. He had a dislocated shoulder, six broken ribs, a broken wrist, and a serious concussion on top of his deeply slashed arm. He smiled at Anna with what appeared to be real affection, and Anna responded in kind. He reached out tentatively and touched her cast gently.

"You saved my life, Anna." It was a quiet statement, "and I know you crawled into the car, full of fuel, to check on my officers, confirming they were still alive."

"I'm a doctor, Karl, it's what we do."

Berchtold watched her evenly, his hand still on her cast. He slowly pulled his hand away and shuffled around in his hospital housecoat until he found his cigarettes.

"Mind?" Anna shook her head, the hair on the back of her head lifting gently. She stopped breathing. She realized she knew this man very well and he had done what he was trained to do. Berchtold lifted

63

the small package from his lap and opened it, peeling off a single sheet of paper, folded in quarters. He unfolded it, glanced at it before offering it to Anna.

"What is this, Karl?"

"The MPs gave your purse and ID material to the hospital staff, who gave it to me for safekeeping. I told them we were friends, and I'd handle your effects. The MPs investigated the crash, and there will be more inquiries, as there were fatalities. Because it involved German Army vehicles the French authorities were not involved, although they were contacted as a—courtesy. There is the question of you, a French citizen. There was the interest in you at Headquarters because you saved my life, and you are a doctor. All of that. I—did the best I could to squash that. But I did take it upon myself to check up on you, do my due diligence, so to speak. I told our investigators we were recent friends—close friends, and I took the liberty to sort of—protect you.

"They will be back to fill in their little forms so the file will be complete. It's the German way, and in a way the French are the same! The local police did inquire when they found out you were French. Because you were with me, they chose to interview me, especially since I told them you were very upset and had been sedated. They took your name, but seemed less interested when I told them you were not from Limoges. They noted the particulars of the accident, and the extent of your injuries. I don't know what they will do in this situation, probably just file it since you're not from Limoges and you didn't do anything really inconvenient to a bureaucrat like die. We Germans are the controlling authority after all, so this might be the end of it.

"Thank you for what you did."

I do what I do, Anna, out of professional training, routines, protocol, whatever you want to call it."

"I understand, Karl. I'm a doctor and I'm trained the same way."

"I didn't use the usual channels to vet a French citizen. That is, I didn't approach the French police, our *Abwehr,* or the *Waffen Schutzstaffel* and submit your name for a background inquiry. Understand? I made a simple request to the German Army Liaison Office in Lyon to simply provide all the certified physicians in Lyon." His arm was still outstretched, proffering the paper which Anna had not reached for. Anna lifted her chin and met his eyes.

"You're not on this list, Anna. I know the French authorities, I understand French bureaucracy. They keep records for *everything.* How do you explain this?" He said this gently, without accusation, although his eyes were narrow, clear and focused on her face. Anna, in turn, examined his face with what she hoped was a confused, quizzical look.

64

She understood completely she had nowhere to go with this, she had no options. Absolutely no prepared cover beyond what she had on the table, right now. What she could see, what she believed she could see, was the hurt and dismay of this man who held her fate in his hands. He wanted to believe her, he wanted to trust her, she could see that much in his eyes. He liked her, enough to take a couple of precautions during his—inquiry, and told her about it. Why?

"I don't understand, Karl," she whispered apprehensively, her brow now wrinkled with concern as she accepted and scanned the paper. The list was handwritten and quite long. She could see the list was broken down by specialty, with a separate list with a code linking each physician with hospital privileges. Under pediatricians, listed in alphabetical order, there was a Metzger, but a Charles F. It was circled with a *question mark?* There were six other physicians named Metzger in Lyon, all circled, but none named Anna.

"You said you went to medical school in Lyon, and you have a practice there. I thought perhaps you were listed under another name, but then realized your physician ID card lists your name as Anna Metzger." He pulled her ID card from the small package and handed it too Anna as well.

"That appears to be a very legitimate physician ID. The signatures and names are correct. The stamp is correct and up to date." Berchtold's face remained neutral, almost consoling and empathetic. Anna simply shook her head slowly, examining the list again.

"I should be there on the list! I haven't been in practice long, but I have a very fancy certificate on my wall when I passed all my boards and examinations! The authorities certainly know where I work!" Anna knew she was burying herself deeper with every word, and not one she could substantiate. She simply grew angrier and more strident, which seemed to upset Berchtold. He lifted his hands carefully, one in a tight sling and other partially casted at the wrist, in a conciliatory manner.

"Do you have a partner in your practice? A senior partner, perhaps, someone we could contact?"

"No…I'm solo, I had to make a contract arrangement with another pediatrician to cover my patients while I was away."

"Okay, how about their name? Or a hospital administrator at any hospital you have privileges?" Anna glanced up at Berchtold in shock, staring at him for a long moment before she covered her eyes with her hands.

"Oh God," she sobbed, "*what* is going on here? Now even *you* don't believe me!"

It took twenty minutes to calm Anna down, she was so upset, and it was only after she was administered a sedative that Berchtold left her side. The attending duty physician, not the old surgeon, didn't ask what had upset her so much, assuming like the attending nurses it probably had something to do with Berchtold. Most everyone glanced at him with disapproving looks, noting among themselves the *fraulein was very young and still recovering from her injuries. He might consider that next time he chose to argue with her, or upset her with something, the fool.*

Berchtold carried away all of the documents he brought and didn't bring it up again until they were both released from the hospital, eight days later. The MP investigation found the driver of the BMW, who was killed, at fault for *driving too fast for the conditions.* The poor *unteroffizier* driving Berchtold's *stabswagen,* who was also killed, was exonerated by witnesses who noted he was simply trying to drive out of the roundabout and had a clear path to do just that when the *stabswagen* was hit broadside. Case closed. No French police follow up came regarding Anna, so Berchtold assumed the local authorities, knowing Anna was not from Limoges and not dead and in a German Army hospital, simply filed the information.

On the day they were released there was no fanfare or even anyone to greet them. It was an hour before a car from the Headquarters staff came to pick them up. His assigned railway engineers were still enroute from Poland, he last heard. Berchtold's only enlisted team member, the large, lumbering *unteroffizier* now dead, would have to be replaced. His two staff officers, his French speaking number crunchers, were still in the hospital with fractured skulls and numerous internal injuries. It would be two months minimum before their release back to duty. Even their *stabwagen,* wheels no doubt very difficult to get for an Army trying to occupy a country with minimal troops had to be requested again. His unit, for the time being, was practically out of commission with the exception of himself and the two arriving railway engineers. But they couldn't compile the data to save their lives. His meeting with his local commander *Oberstleutnant* Korman was brief, to the point and pretty depressing.

*Your mission requirements are still the same, Herr Hauptmann, Headquarters wants your initial reports within six weeks. Everyone in France is shorthanded, but I'll see about getting you a replacement driver and wheels from someplace. Maybe a good clerk to type up your reports, since we have no shortage of those! I can't do anything about your professional staff. Mathematicians? Pencil heads! I need a battalion of military police to restore order and they send me a company of clerks! As soon as your train people get here, develop a schedule and start working! I'll get you a driver and a car, don't worry! I said I would, didn't I?*

Anna had no choice but to accompany Berchtold to the hotel his unit was assigned. She had no place to stay and wasn't ready to travel. She wore a small cast on her wrist, her right shoulder was in a sling, and her right ankle was also in a large heavy cast. With crutches, she was lucky she could hobble 20 meters. Anna accepted a room assigned to Berchtold and attempted to pay for it, but Berchtold brushed it off. *Taken over by the Army*, he said quietly. *I'm surprised the proprietor was allowed to keep any!* It was one of the rooms set aside for Berchtold's staff officers, but they found the proprietor had temporarily let it to someone else. Berchtold created a scene and demanded whoever was in the room be evicted immediately, as he had injured staff straight from the hospital needing rest. The hotel clerk was apologetic to Berchtold, but his eyes leered at Anna coldly, taking in her injuries before lifting his hands in submission.

*Yes, Herr Hauptmann, we will clear the room immediately.*

Anna sat down on a lobby couch and waited. In about half an hour a couple, middle-aged and disheveled, were being led out of the lobby by hotel staff. They looked distraught and confused until they saw Berchtold in his uniform and Anna sitting beside him. Berchtold stood and stared at the couple, who began to speak among themselves before thinking better of it. They walked slowly past, their eyes on Anna the entire time. Berchtold, his hands on his hips, nodded at them, which seemed to frighten them, before he turned around and gently placed his hands on Anna's shoulders.

# Chapter 8

*July 13, 1940. Limoges, France.*

The summer and fall of 1940 were some of the strangest days in Anna's life. She knew her situation, at least part of it, was replicated a million times all over Europe. The days stopped, dragged, sped up or raced through in a whirlwind depending on so many things. Anna wanted to believe she was strong, her intelligence and youth assets of such advantage she would survive, somehow, to see her family again. Aix was only four hundred kilometers away but at times it seemed a continent apart. She was trapped and ensnared, yet the web now included her heart, wound like a plaited belt into the life of a man who on the one hand represented her enemy, and on the other did all he could to keep her out of the jaws of the *Third Reich*.

The little window that bought them time was the accident. They spoke of it in wonder and amazement from time to time, although it was always with a sobering silence as they considered not only the men who had lost their lives, but the suffering experienced by all of them, the survivors. Everyone would have permanent disabling injuries, and some, like one of Berchtold's statisticians who had part of a door frame punched into his skull, would never recover and be the same man.

Anna stayed in Limoges after being released from the hospital because she had no choice. She recalled her thinking at the time, and couldn't believe how naïve she had been. She was recuperating from her injuries and thought she needed a week at the most. Berchtold offered a temporary solution, as long as his gentlemanly background would respond favorably to Anna's distancing. She had felt only a little twinge of guilt in her manipulation of him at the time, justifying it whenever she considered why he was in France. Her intent was to leave for Toulouse and eventually Aix the minute she felt she was ready to travel. It let her sleep at night. Her cover was working, but she had stretched its boundaries to the absolute maximum, and she had to trust his willingness, *his desire to believe in her*, and keep him at bay for a few days. She really thought she could do it.

The accident temporarily destroyed Berchtold's unit with his staff either dead or in the hospital. Berchtold waited every day for some word of his railway engineers, and it became evident to Anna he didn't want to see them—not yet, not as long as Anna was around. The hotel was a good one and the rooms were large with windows looking out over a central courtyard. Berchtold's room was only three doors down from Anna's, and she realized quickly Berchtold had control of all four including hers. He used the one next to Anna's as an office, having the bed removed and two large desks brought in to replace it. They did have some equipment brought up, including a relatively large radio transmitter and two typewriters. Berchtold set up one of the typewriters on a desk but left the radio in the corner since they didn't have a radio operator.

For the first few days Anna accompanied Berchtold to the hotel dining room for their meals, but the staff made her feel so uncomfortable with their coolness towards her she stopped coming down. She still had money from the funds wired to her in Paris by her father, so she ordered her meals in her room. It was very painful to move about anyway, and Berchtold was kind and understanding. She went out once to the post office, a time when she knew Berchtold was not in his office, and slipped out wearing her hair under a scarf and without make-up. There was a telegraph office in the hotel, but Anna decided to not use it and hobbled nearly three blocks to the nearest post office. Her ankle was not healing properly and she couldn't put any real weight on it, but she stumbled on slowly, noting for the first time in her life how a disabled woman becomes invisible. There were no offers of assistance, courteous opening of doors. She thought maybe it was her lack of make-up, or her unattractive clothes. Whatever it was, she was frustrated and in severe pain when she sent her cable to her father.

*Sorry for no contact. Had an accident in Limoges. Not to worry, nothing serious. Be home soon. Love, Anna.*

She sat down on a bench outside the post office and closed her eyes, the tears of pain hard to conceal. *How am I going to get back to the hotel?* She wondered. She heard the squeal of brakes and opened her eyes to a door opening of a *Wehrmacht Stabswagen.* A tall, skinny *unteroffizier* popped out and opened the back door.

"Doctor Metzger!" Berchtold called out formally from the backseat. "We've been looking all over for you, although Sergeant Kline has excellent eyesight and spotted your cast and crutches!"

Anna, admittedly, was never so glad to see Berchtold. She smiled and was struggling to her feet when the young *unteroffizier* dashed over and helped her up.

Berchtold came out and walked over, touched his hat and clicked his heels, as he did the very first time he met her.

"Doctor Metzger, may I introduce our new driver and radio operator, Sergeant Horst Kline! I explained to the Sergeant how we met and of course, our tragic accident. Come, let's get you in our new wheels and off your feet! My Colonel has actually come through, I couldn't believe it! Back to the hotel? You were in the post office?"

"Nice meeting you, Sergeant.   I will take you up on the offer, my leg is killing me.   Yes, I had to tell my family the situation and I might be slightly delayed getting to Toulouse."

When they got back to the hotel Berchtold gave Sergeant Kline an extensive list of things to do.   Once he left Berchtold closed the door to his office and sat down next to Anna, no longer formal.   He looked at her with concern and reached down, touching her leg.

"You don't look well, Anna.   You were limping even more than normal."

"I know, it was a foolish thing to do, but I wanted to get out.   I didn't know it was so far away."   Berchtold leaned up and adjusted his own sling, sighing as he glanced up at the door.

"We need to find you another place to stay, Anna, my staff officers are still in the hospital but my railway engineers are arriving day after tomorrow."

"Well, it's probably just as well, I should be leaving.   My ankle is not healing right, but I don't want to wait around for your doctors to suggest I need another surgery.   I think I'll wait until I get home."

Berchtold looked at her sadly, his shoulders visibly slumping.

"Have dinner with me tonight.   We'll go somewhere else other than the hotel.   I know a new place.   We have a car available now.   I can drive myself."

"I'm really tired, Karl, I should rest."

"It's important we talk, I think—I think you need to hear what I have to say, and we need to do it away from the hotel, from these prying eyes."   Anna sensed something again, and a cool finger traced up her spine.   His eyes were clear and questioning, but caring.   She sensed it and knew she had to trust her gut.

He asked her to dress well for a special occasion, and she could only laugh at the comment.   She had one pair of nylons remaining but her right leg was in a cast.   She wore a nice cotton skirt, with a simple sleeved pullover flexible enough to poke her wrist cast through, and selected a large clean napkin to replace her somewhat dirty sling.   Pearls, she did have some pearls.   Berchtold showed up at her door in civilian clothes, a pre-war cotton linen sports jacket and a white dress shirt.   She realized she had never seen him out of uniform before, and she was very pleased with his outfit.   It fit him, and she knew at once he chose it on purpose.

"It suits you, Karl!   The only thing missing is a neck scarf and maybe a beret!"

"For a mathematician?   Anna, please!   A poet, maybe.   But I'm not a man of letters or paint!   I'm a numbers man!"   Obviously pleased with her comment, not even the dour hotel staff could take his grin away as they swept out the main door.

The restaurant was Italian, but Anna doubted Berchtold chose it because the proprietor was potentially fascist or pro-Axis. But Berchtold did converse with the owner in passible Italian, which Anna understood, and now it was her turn to be pleased.

*This is the beautiful young lady I told you about, Louis, and she is very special to me. Only the best, eh?*

Every restaurant has a special corner for lovers, and this one was no different. The table, set for two, rose a foot on a platform above the ground floor and to the side, but visible to any seat in the restaurant. The overhead lighting, subdued, placed the warm glow of the spot on the heads of the lovers. Anna, a bit embarrassed, brushed her hair away and laughed as Berchtold grinned and clamped his large, casted hand on top of hers.

"Karl, this is a bit much. If you have something to say to me you could have chosen something—less conspicuous, don't you think?"

"Anna, people think we are lovers and won't be listening to what we say, but would instead be wishing they were us or young again."

"Even the ones who hate the Germans and French women who fraternize? Even them?"

"Anna, I'm not in uniform. We could be anybody."

They ate well and Berchtold kept the conversation light. During the last course, a salad, presented family style, he poured himself another glass of Chianti and more sparkling water for Anna.

"Anna," he said casually, "I don't want to hurt you—hurt you in anyway, just know that." He sipped his wine and looked over the rim at Anna, who instinctively pulled her head back, out of the light. Berchtold leaned forward, his hand again looking for Anna's. He found it and she did not withdraw.

"I don't know who you are. There is no record of you anywhere. My Colonel has somehow got wind that I have a French woman in the hotel, and he was not pleased. I was angry, like any German officer or gentleman would be with such an accusation. I explained exactly what the situation is, and that you are a physician from Lyon. I explained the German Army had a responsibility in your recovery because you were in our vehicle when we crashed. You had no place to stay, and I had some space in the hotel because of the accident. But I also told him you were nearly recovered, we were moving you out of the hotel to make room for my railway engineers, and you would be leaving for Toulouse in a day or two anyway. That satisfied him, because he doesn't want any scandals and he wants me out there doing my reports."

"I need to leave."

"Yes, officially, you do. The world needs to see you leave. This is not like pre-war France, with the *La Surete Nationale* or the municipal police getting the hotel check-in cards for their records. We let the French police do what they want with their own citizens—unless they are in one of our rooms, like yourself. The German Army has this hotel, the German Army does not report their activities to the French, understand?"

"So—I leave officially." Berchtold sighed, his eyes hooded in the light, but his head was visible, nodding in affirmation.

"Yes." Berchtold gripped her hand firmly. His eyes suddenly out in the light and clear, focused and unblinking on Anna.

"There is no record of you, Anna. No record of Anna Metzger. *You don't exist.* If you—stay, unofficially, and the travel records have a one Anna Metzger leaving Limoges for Toulouse…you disappear." Anna was silent and simply stared at him with a blank expression.

"Anna—Anna," Berchtold seemed at a loss for words, "I don't know your situation and—frankly, I don't care. I just—want you here with—me."

"You want me to buy a ticket for Toulouse but not leave? What are you saying, Karl? You know my situation! I've got a patient—my niece—to attend. What do you mean, if I stay? Why would I stay, Karl?"

"Damn it, woman, don't play games with me!" He said this without raising his voice, but beads of sweat formed on his brow as he smiled pleasantly. "Yes! I'm saying right now, right this moment, we can make you disappear because the few who know of you expect you to leave, and leave for Toulouse. You will leave the hotel, which I will record, but it will be obvious to the hotel staff. We'll make sure of that. You will buy a ticket for Toulouse. My driver and I will escort you to the train station, a natural courtesy, and two witnesses. You can get on the train, be seen moving about in the cars. No one will notice while everyone is looking for a seat if you simply walk off. That will be the end of it. No one will check whether or not a passenger on a second-class ticket has gotten off or on. All the seats will be filled! The German Army has control of this railway, don't you understand?"

Anna, watching his eyes, tortured, trying to explain himself, found her own heart starting to falter, not really believing what she was hearing.

"Karl," she said gently, "why are you doing this?"

"I'm in love with you, Anna, isn't that clear enough?"

"Karl, please, we hardly know each other."

"Anna, I don't know how to say this, but… I don't know what you did, or what you are trying to hide, or run from, but—I don't care. Maybe I can help somehow. I just want to be with you. I will do whatever it takes to keep you safe, if—you want to stay."

There was a long pause of silence with Anna and Karl holding hands so the waiter took the cue and dashed in. He took away the salad plates and took their dessert orders, wistful as he glanced at their faces. So serious—*a parting?* To be young again. Such a pretty girl. The waiter, who was the owner's brother, knew Berchtold was a German officer and didn't care. A recent immigrant to France himself, he had served in the Alps 24 years earlier against the *Boche*. Severely wounded, it was the Germans who tended to his injuries after he was left for dead by his own retreating comrades. He would not forget he was given the same care and food as the German soldiers around him. This *Boche* was no fascist, he was a gentleman and spoke Italian and was respectful. He could not say the same for some of his own new French neighbors. *May you find some peace and happiness in the middle of a war*, he thought.

Anna didn't know what to say, but held on to Berchtold's hand as he squeezed it. So many emotions raced through her she could not think straight. She wanted to get up and run away and yet another part of her wanted to lean on this man, entirely, reveal the truth and trust him—trust him completely, a virtual stranger. Berchtold seemed to sense her dilemma and hesitation, deciding to reach out with his slung arm to gently lift her chin so their eyes met.

"I guess I tried to present myself as what I believe I am and hoped you would—recognize, somehow."

"I know, Karl. You're not a German officer, not like any I would expect. Not a soldier, anyway. I saw that the first day I met you. And I do recognize you. You are the kind of people I know. Academics, scientists, students and physicians. We're more comfortable with books, papers, labs, chalkboards and classrooms than with people, in many ways. We live in our heads, forget the outer world sometimes."

"Do you trust me, Anna?" Berchtold brought his other hand to her face, his fingers gently touching her cheeks.

"I don't know, Karl. I don't know. We're from—I just don't know what to think." Berchtold drew closer, slowly until his lips brushed her nose. Anna closed her eyes and lowered her chin. Berchtold brought his hands down and sighed deeply. Anna opened her eyes again, watching Berchtold.

"I'm sorry, Karl."

"Because of my assignment, I'm briefed daily on the latest regulations and roll-outs regarding the occupation of France, and particularly the issue of the *Juifs*. Your prime minister, the old general, is quite surprising. He's also quite the fox, actually, recognizing we Germans simply do not have the manpower necessary to implement many of the required *control factors* necessary to identify, isolate and eventually remove these undesirables from France and Europe. He knows what we want, and do you know what the old bastard said to us?" The moment of intimacy broken, Berchtold paused to light a cigarette.

"He proposes—he proposes for France—that the *Third Reich* let *Vichy* handle the *Juifs,* and he is proposing measures actually *above and beyond* anything we are doing currently in the so-called northern occupied zone! He stated in his proposal that France and Germany had the same goal in that regard, that is, getting rid of foreign *Juifs*, gypsies, some of these political prisoners who have caused you all kinds of grief down south, these veterans of the international brigades! And he's already implementing some of his plans by the most devious and most simplistic ways!"

"Petain is a bastard to many of us. You'll get no argument from me."

"I can see why you would feel that way! He said he would get the entire French government including all of the departments and the municipal administrators—the police, mayors, the prefects—the entire bureaucracy on board by simply changing French law! That makes being a *Juif* in France an illegal act, and legally protects all the bureaucrats as they enforce the new laws!"

"What has that got to do with me, Karl?"

"It means, Anna," Berchtold leaned in close, "It won't be the German Army who will be establishing all these regulations, which by the way, are already changing as we speak—it will be your own countrymen, Frenchmen, mostly, National or municipal police and petty bureaucrats who will continue to be paid even though we're occupying their country, and they will be doing our work for us because they have made it into French law. I find it incredible and somewhat, horrifying."

"We French are past masters at various times on turning on each other. It makes it somewhat easier if you make the offense against the current law." Frustrated, Berchtold stubbed out his cigarette, his eyes pained and confused. Anna watched him for just a moment before reaching out and taking his hand again.

"What are you proposing, Karl? I heard what you said. You know my story."

Berchtold clutched her hand with both of his, his eyes focused as he examined her face.

"I have some money, not a lot, but enough. I also have, right now, the influence to acquire rooms, apartments, or any type of space to establish my mission here in Limoges. My authority to requisition space is limited, but the occupation is just getting started and there isn't much paperwork required right now. The French authorities are tripping over themselves to be useful to us because they've been ordered to by their own authorities, so it's relatively easy for us to get an apartment for office space. I understand they just throw some *Juifs* out into the street when we come and demand space. In fact, I've already signed for a small place under the auspices of my job, but no one in the German Army knows about it, or will ever know about it. I didn't submit a requisition form to the landlord where he could hope to eventually get paid, I paid cash for the deposit up front and believe me, there were no questions asked. To the landlord, I'm just another source of steady cash every month."

"And you're proposing to move me in it after I've done my slight-of-hand at the rail station?"

"Well, it would be a place to stay until you heal up. And longer, if you wish."

"And who would know about it other than you? As you said, Anna Metzger gets on the train to Toulouse and that would be the end of that."

"Just me."

"I don't exist, you said so yourself. No trace or record once I leave Limoges for Toulouse. I don't live in Limoges so I don't have a ration card. You mentioned there would soon be a travel ban implemented so that people couldn't travel from department to department without authorization. If I stepped out of the apartment and got involved in anything at all, I could be arrested by the *Surete*. If it somehow got out who let the apartment, can't this be traced back to you somehow? You can't get me a ration card since I don't live and work here, so you'll be responsible for feeding me? How about when you're gone? That sounds like a fairly bleak prospect, Karl, and of course you would be disobeying your commanding officer's order. Why would you do this?"

"I'll be paying for this with my own money, not German Army funds. There would be no fraud involved."

"You've done this sort of thing before?"

"No! Anna, I told you, I—love you. I have a unique opportunity with my assignment, so I took advantage of it."

"And because of your feelings I should move in there?"

"No, but because I don't think you have anywhere to go to in Toulouse, or anywhere else for that matter."

"Now you're saying I'm a liar, Karl?"

"No, I said I don't think you have anywhere to go to in Toulouse, and that you're hiding something."

"From you?" Berchtold blinked hard as if he had been struck and Anna regretted the retort at once. She shook her head and squeezed his hands again.

"I'm sorry, that was uncalled for."

75

"It's okay, I realize how crazy this sounds to you. Like I'm setting this up for a concubine."

"Aren't you, Karl? Your mysterious French mistress?" Her attempt at slight humor failed completely as his face fell.

"I am so sorry, Anna. I am a fool."

"No Karl, I'm the fool here. But I can't tell you anything. I won't tell you anything. But if you can accept that and you have the key, perhaps we can see this mystery apartment."

# Chapter 9

*December 24, 1940. Limoges, France.*

Berchtold had chosen well, Anna saw at once when he pointed out the brightly-lit building in the darkness. Anna did not know Limoges at all, but the apartment was in the upper floors of a former department store in the business district. The first four floors were now small to medium-sized businesses, some retail, others small manufacturing. The very top floor comprised of the offices of the former department store, all converted to apartments.

"During the day the lower floors are full of people, so it will be easy to come and go unnoticed, especially in the morning and evening." He pointed out, watching her eyes. "This is a busy street, but there are actually three different entrances you can use for the building, on two different streets."

The apartment was a very small studio, but it had a side street view and was only two doors down from the stairwell, if Anna didn't want to use one of the two elevators. It was partially furnished with a small double bed set to the side with a privacy wall, a build-in bureau, a pair of overstuffed reading chairs, and a half-table with two chairs next to the tiny kitchenette. Nails still remained on the wall from pictures apparently removed in a hurry. Anna stared at the nails, thinking about what Berchtold had said about the landlords simply kicking some *Juifs* out to make room. Berchtold, reading her mind, opened a drawer or two aimlessly before shrugged his shoulders sheepishly.

"I don't know who was in this apartment before, Anna. It was empty when it was shown to me. The landlord stated this was his smallest one, which made it difficult to rent consistently. He said most of the other apartments are rented by professionals and they pretty much keep to themselves. I was vague but told him it would be used as an office and part-time quarters. The person who would be staying here would be typing up reports. It really doesn't matter as the landlord doesn't live onsite and will never see you. I doubt if he cares. He was most interested in my *Francs*. But if you choose to stay—it would be best to always come and go during the day with the workers. Dress like them, an office worker, that sort of thing. It's a zoo during the day, but very quiet at night, as you see."

Anna sat down on a kitchen chair and stared out the window where the drapes were partially open to the night sky. The view to the building across the side street revealed only the reflection of the single lit lamp in the apartment. The facing building was dark, deserted. Berchtold stood silently for several minutes before cautiously joining her at the table. He leaned forward and kissed the neat knot of her hair on the top of her head. Anna turned and lifted her chin, her eyes on Berchtold as her lips parted.

"You did this just for me, Karl." She reached for his face and they kissed once, gently. Berchtold sat down, his eyes expectant as he withdrew his hands.

"What do you think? Stay for a few days, see if you like it? For the time being I'm letting Sergeant Kline go to his barracks after six o'clock most evenings so I have the car to come visit, bring you things. No one will know where I'm going. I can park in different places, come up from any of the entrances. We'll begin our—surveys next week, once the doctors clear me for travel. I have a fixed deadline so I can't wait for my other staff officers to recover, I'll have to start alone with my railway engineers. I wanted to get you set up, because I don't know how long I'll be gone on these—trips."

Anna watched his face for a moment then looked out the window again. She knew what was coming, and also knew she had to give him something.

"Anna," he said quietly but firmly, "I have to ask you this."

"I told you, I can tell you nothing."

"What is your real name? Your physician ID is the real thing, except there is no Anna Metzger in Lyon. Did you lose your license, are you a physician somewhere else? You seemed to know what you were doing, our medics said. I—I just want to know, and I want you to know you can trust me."

Anna stood up and went to the window, closing the drapes and turning around staring hard at Berchtold.

"Let's go back to the hotel, Karl."

"I'm sorry, Anna, I thought maybe…"

"Karl, I'm taking you up on your offer—at least for a few days, or until you have to leave on your first trip. Let's go back and get my things, I suppose it's too late to get anything at the market."

"Anna, that is wonderful! But you need to stay in the hotel at least until we get you a ticket to Toulouse, remember? Hopefully the day after tomorrow. I want the hotel staff to see you leave, and your departure corresponds to the day your train leaves. And, if you don't mind, I did gather a few items from the market and have them in the trunk of the car— just in case you agreed to stay." Anna shook her head slowly and smiled at Berchtold's boyish grin. She came over to take his hand but he clutched hers instead, bringing it to his lips.

"Anna—Anna is your name?"

"Yes, Karl that is my name. I am not a physician yet, but I was a second-year medical student. It's a long story, and maybe someday I can tell it to you."

"A medical student! Remarkable! But where did you get that physician ID?" Her look told him he had received all he was going to get, so he nodded in affirmation.

"Okay, Anna, I understand, enough. Let's bring up the groceries and then return to the hotel. I don't want them to see me return you too late, it gives the wrong impression."

The next day Berchtold and Sergeant Kline drove Anna to the railway station to purchase a ticket to Toulouse. The earliest train with a seat was scheduled to depart at noon the following day, and Berchtold loudly ensured the railway ticket staff was well aware Doctor Metzger was leaving, and the German Army was apologizing profusely for both her unfortunate injuries and her travel delays. Late the following morning Berchtold brought Anna down the elevator in the hotel and informed the hotel lobby staff, unnecessarily, Doctor Metzger would be departing for Lyon, and her room would need to be cleaned and reconfigured for two beds immediately.

Anna boarded her train with a large group of other travelers and made a point of saying hello to the conductor. A French policeman had been stationed at the entry gate for the train, looking at the travelers carefully as he quickly scanned their tickets. She didn't see him detain anyone, but it frightened her. It was the first time she had ever seen *gendarmes* look at tickets before, and at first, she thought it had something to do with a criminal investigation. But it seemed too casual, no questions were being asked, just a glance at the ticket. It didn't seem right at all.

She remembered Berchtold's comment about *Vichy* France proposing to restrict citizen travel between departments without authorization. It was clearly designed to limit the movement of unwelcome foreigners and *Juifs*. If you can't travel freely, you are isolated and contained. What did Berchtold say? Once you identified, isolated and contained a population, then you can *transport them. Somewhere, anywhere.* She thought of the letter she carried in her pocket, which was just such an authorization, supposedly required by the Germans in Poland and other occupied countries. It had been twelve days since she left Paris. Everything she had, her physician's ID, her letter, her cover—all were designed for the first few days of the occupation, as Nina had warned. *What are they looking for? Were they making an exact count of passengers? Will she be missed? The gendarmes didn't ask for any identification, only her ticket. Was it just to get the population used to seeing French policemen at travel points?*

79

Anna declined the conductor's offer to take her small bag for storage and quickly found a seat in the aisle of the first second-class car. For a long moment Anna simply stared out the window as people jostled their way into a seat, knowing she could just sit still and ride away. This same man who was offering a place to stay and hide was the same man who was developing a system for such *containment and transportation.* A few hours she could be in Toulouse and then home to Aix. People were coming and going into the car from both ends and she knew she had to move now or attract attention. If she wanted to leave, escape—*just sit still.* This was her opportunity.

She stood up and walked slowly through her car and the length of the second before stepping off and searching for the platform bathroom. She walked with her cane across two sets of tracks while glancing as casually as she could towards the *gendarme* at the gate. There were two of them now to handle the crush of late passengers, but neither looked in her direction. Inside she changed into another suit of clothing including a hat and barricaded herself in a stall. With the *gendarmes* at the gate she couldn't just leave. She had to wait until another train arrived so she could blend in with the exiting crowd. Karl will pick up her up at the park next to the station at seven. Then she'll be safe. Karl just had no idea it would work out like this, she was supposed to leave the train, slip out of the station and walk the short distance to the park. She clutched her bag to her chest as panic slowly ebbed. *It's okay. You just have to wait.*

Luckily, she had studied the schedule thoroughly. There was a train coming north to Limoges from Cahors, probably originating from Toulouse that morning. Three o'clock was the estimated time of arrival. *Three hours. You just have to wait.* The public address system declared the last call for the train to Toulouse. Anna shivered and knew she was completely in his hands now. Somehow, she felt it was the right choice. Just for a few days, rest up and heal. Her ankle was still very weak and she couldn't put any weight on it for any length of time. If she stayed off heels, she could walk a block without limping if the pavement was level and she walked slowly with her cane. *There are pins in there,* the surgeon explained, but he was uncertain if they could be removed. *You're young and strong, you might not need them after several months. Young and strong.* For a few moments if anyone had been in the restroom, they would have been confused by the suppressed giggling and snorting of near laughter, followed almost immediately without pause by the sound of sobbing and sniffling.

Nothing it seemed these days worked out as planned, as far as Anna could determine. What she could say without reservation was that Karl

Berchtold kept his word for those things he could control.  Anna moved that first night into the apartment about nine o'clock.  Berchtold picked her up at the railway park in the *Stebswagen* in civilian clothes, delighting her by taking her to another small park near the Vienne River and presenting a basket full of food, wine and a blanket.   They had a wonderful feast, celebrating her departure from Limoges.

"I don't exist, but officially I left," Anna giggled, her eyes sad.  Berchtold, sprawled out on the blanket with a chicken leg in his hand, rolled over and kissed Anna softly on the cheek.

"You look very real to me, Anna," he growled as he examined her face with a wolfish grin that slowly turned serious.   He put his chicken leg down and wiped his hands with a napkin before he reached out and stroked Anna's hair.

"I didn't know if you would do it—stay, I mean.   You could have easily just ridden off on the train.   You had no reason to stay unless you wanted to.   It was a very long day for me.   When I drove by the park and saw your hair peeking out under that—ugly hat, you can't believe how happy I was—my heart just lifted out of my chest!"

Anna pulled his head down and held his temples between her hands.

"Karl, all I can tell you is I saw the *gendarmes,* found a soft seat and knew I was home free if I just stayed where I was for ten minutes.  But here I am.   I would rather be here."

For a couple of days, it was almost blissful for Anna because once she began accepting Karl into her heart, her fear and confusion were subdued to the point she could almost forget and enjoy the rapture and warmth of being in love.   She kept telling herself her time was short and she had to be careful about leading him on too much.   Not because there might be retribution on his part, but because she admitted to herself, she didn't want to hurt him.   The path to the railway station was her escape ticket, her back-up plan.   Her aging physician ID card and travel authorization letter the passage to safety when things were right.

Anna, in her heart knew things would never completely be right.  Her ankle was not mending property, but she could not see any doctors now, not legitimately.    For the German Army surgeons, she was long gone and history.   Her original plan, only a few weeks ago but seemingly months past—was to get home to Aix.   Join her parents.   And do what?  Were they hiding now behind closed blinds in their building in Aix like the *Juifs* in the *Pletzl* in Paris?   They resided in the unoccupied zone, the so-called *Vichy* zone, and now it appeared in order to keep the Germans out of the administration of *Vichy, Vichy* was creating their own rules for

*Juifs.* Building detention centers on French soil. Karl told her and she didn't believe him, that there were over 25 already existing in the unoccupied zone alone.

Berchtold brought her numerous French newspapers to read, which she devoured, and was appalled and horrified at the casual reference to the "foreign *Juif* problem" editorialized on the *back pages.* The actual articles, describing coming rules and immigration policies specific to *Juifs,* were small and hidden. The primary concern to the general population was the growing shortage of even the most basic food and living items in grocery store shelves. Milk was rationed only to nursing mothers and children in some locations, and eggs were impossible. Soap? If you could find it you would have to prove you had an occupation that was particularly dirty. The stories were extensive on how to make things stretch, or simply make do with something else. And of course, considerable detail expended on all the new rules and controls soon to be implemented by the French government to ensure fairness, and reduce the potential for a growing black market. Then she found it, right there in black and white serif type, the *Vichy* government was moving *undesirable foreigners* to these centers, implementation had begun already. *Where were these detention centers? Why were there so many of them?*

Anna found it both strange and perplexing she felt safer here with Berchtold than potentially home with her family, but then she had to remind herself she never revealed to Berchtold her situation. At home in Aix her family was waiting for the hammer to fall if German authorities examined Polish immigration records of 40 years past. It was totally unknown what would be revealed, but it was apparent what would happen to the Metzgen family if the *Juif* racial tag was applied. Berchtold may suspect it somehow, but she wanted to believe he thought it was something else. Her safety with Berchtold, in the beginning and as of now, was his trust and love of her. These were strong enough to keep his suspicions at bay. She had to believe this, and did. He was taking an enormous risk himself, keeping an undocumented French woman in hiding.

The fact was Berchtold made it easy to stay, he could only come in the evenings and remain for a few hours, but he revealed himself to Anna, as she expected, to be a kind and thoughtful man, and a gentle lover. His thoughtfulness was as thorough as his planning. On the third evening he arrived late, past ten o'clock, and could only stay for an hour. He explained he was leaving for his first survey of the train system the following day, oddly enough down to Toulouse, and then continuing on through the Pyrenees to San Sebastian by the Spanish border. He seemed exhausted, but more than that, concerned about Anna and what her intentions were.

"I don't know exactly how long I'll be gone, perhaps two weeks, maybe longer."

"Two weeks?" She stammered, knowing in advance what was coming, but the reality struck hard. She sat down as Berchtold joined her.

"Anna, will you be here when I come back?"

"Karl, I don't know. I can't just hide here for two or three weeks, what would I do?"

Berchtold nodded silently, then stood up and went to the small satchel he had brought. He carried it over and carefully dumped its contents onto the bed. He handed her a small envelope, two small documents and a key.

"In the envelope are 7,000 *Francs*. It's yours whether you stay or leave. If you leave, you'll need money to travel and find places to stay and eat. If you stay, you'll need it to buy food, clothing, books to read, whatever, Anna. So much is unavailable in stores now, but some things can be found on the black market if you have the money. I could be gone for weeks, or months. It's yours."

"Karl—that is too much! I can't accept it in either case!" She proffered the envelope back to Berchtold but he ignored it, pointing to the key and the documents.

"I have procured two ration cards for *Haute-Vienne*, valid to mid-August. I should be back by then to give you new ones. Don't ask where I got them. The key is for a post office box in my name at the main post office about three blocks from here, you know the one? If you stay, that is how I will communicate with you. I will mail you letters. When I come home from my surveys, I'll get you more money if you need it. But if for some reason I can't come home, I'll mail you more money. And don't worry about the rent or anything about the apartment, I have it for six months and have paid in advance for everything."

"What happens after six months, Karl?"

"I should be at the Polish border of the Soviet Union."

"And what would happen to us, to me?"

"I don't know, Anna. I don't think that far ahead regarding us. I'm thinking about the last half an hour I have with you tonight, which is probably the last time I will see you, yes?"

Anna tossed the items on the bed and rushed into Berchtold's arms, searching for his face and lips.

"Are you *really* a German soldier?" She asked playfully as she pulled him down onto the bed. "Not a bank robber or a thief?" He held her face gently in his hands and kissed her nose and lips before drawing back.

"No," he said after a moment. "I'm a German mathematician *masquerading* as a soldier who has accidently fallen for a beautiful French doctor."

"I'm a medical student, Karl."

"Okay, Anna, almost a doctor."

Berchtold stayed until nearly two in the morning. He would pay for it tomorrow, he said woefully. Anna made coffee but when it was time to go, Berchtold did not linger. They kissed and parted as though they would see one another tomorrow. His presence remained for several minutes however, to the point Anna thought he would come right back, but he didn't. What she could not forget was the sadness in his eyes as he blew her his last kiss at the door. It frightened her so much she could not sleep until long after dawn.

Anna didn't leave and Berchtold returned after 19 days, visiting in the evenings for two days before heading west towards Bordeaux. Their love affair was curiously balanced despite the communications being decidedly one-sided. Anna could not write Berchtold letters or send him cables, but she found her mathematician was a fine letter writer who wrote almost every day. Anna responded in kind by writing Berchtold letters of which she was never able to mail. She did get considerable satisfaction in the look of delight on his face when she first handed him a stack of letters.

"I will read these when I'm on the road!" He declared, "I'll treat them as letters from home!"

In the letters she was careful to not give away any particular details, describing instead the parks or museums she had explored, books she had read, or concerts she attended. They were, in every way, similar to letters soldiers receive from their wives and sweethearts all over the world. Light, cheerful and full of busy news and gossip. She did not reveal any detail on her personal plans for the future, or the fact she always left the apartment in disguise.

Berchtold's money was invested in several distinct suits of clothing. He was right, shops had few items for sale on their shelves, but a discreet inquiry often led to a much higher priced, quality black market item kept in the back. She used business attire to leave and return to the building during morning, lunch or evening hours. Most public parks and venues had restrooms so Anna used these to change into a disguise. She was growing accustomed to being alone, amusing herself by exploring different buildings and establishments while observing people.

84

Anna found she could exist on the street like a ghost if she was perceived as being of low enough status and made no demands. That was her first lesson. The higher up you are on the social ladder, the more attention you would receive because you demanded it. Lower, you could find pedestrians looking through you like paint on the sidewalk. Anna remembered her earlier experience out of the hospital, and how even a young woman disabled or injured becomes invisible. She felt physically stronger every passing day, especially after removing her casts by herself and discarding her crutches. She did keep the cane. It allowed her to practice, when she felt like it, the role of a crippled older woman blending into the brickwork on the busiest street. She knew instinctively she was learning a survival skill that would come in handy in the future.

Anna contacted her father by sending him a letter directing his response to Karl Berchtold and his post office box. Her father's response was immediate but guarded. Once he realized only Anna was reading his letters addressed to Berchtold, he wrote at least twice a week. His letters, sad, pathetic sometimes and full of self-pity, depressed her but at least she knew the Germans had not come for her parents and sister. Foreign *Juifs* were being rounded up even in Aix, he reported, and new laws were being established and enforced by the French municipal police. New restrictions were proposed for many professions such as law, medicine and teaching for foreign *Juifs*, but there was also discussion about expanding this to French *Juifs*. Foreign *Juifs* already had to give a complete list of all property, with the property to be held by a neutral party selected by the local prefect. The trend for French *Juifs* was obvious and not encouraging.

Even the definition of foreign *Juif* was starting to expand, possibly including *Juifs* who were already French citizens but immigrated after 1927, and who would have their citizenship revoked by law. *Too many variables, Anna! How can this happen?* This meant *Juifs* had to move, relinquish all bank accounts, jewelry, art, and virtually all personal property and possessions. *Oh my God, Anna. We have so much we could lose!* But despite this, her father remained her father, his letters still somehow ending with the little personal questions.

*Who is this man, Berchtold, Anna? Why are you staying there with him? It is a German name, yes? Is he a Juif? When can you come home?*

Anna could explain nothing and said nothing about it, other than she was safer where she was for the time being and would come home at the first opportunity. She had to admit it was strange now communicating with her father. She felt secure where she was and it was her father who seemed compromised, frightened and insecure. Anna was reassuring him in her letters, the words carefully selected regarding her situation. Her heart lifted though when her father reported he finally heard from Jean Paul. Jean Paul's squadron had been moved from Lille to Calais days before the invasion, with only a few of his comrades surviving the opening days of the war. Jean Paul was shot down and managed to parachute out of his bomber. He was captured by German panzers who were too busy to deal with prisoners, as he and two other Frenchmen walked away during the night. They joined up with British forces but ended up in Dunkirk and eventually England.

When Berchtold came home from his trips the homecomings were wonderful but heart wrenching because they were so infrequent and brief. He would write if he knew an assignment was near completion, with the code word "Holiday" included and a date range. His two injured staff officers, his statisticians, were finally approved to return to work. However, one of them, a young Berliner with a permanent metal plate in his skull, was suffering from chronic headaches and sleeplessness and was falling well behind his work schedule. Anna could not help but admire Berchtold for his loyalty to his friend and colleague, as he refused to request a replacement for the man because it was the equivalent of a death sentence. The *Wehrmacht* needed officers for the Eastern Front, and a privileged over-educated specialist hiding in France would be easy pickings for a transfer. *I will take up the slack,* Berchtold told Anna stubbornly, *Gunther is my friend.* It was the end of the discussion.

The work aged him, she noticed. His wheat-yellow hair was showing signs of silver on the temples, with crow's feet around his eyes and wrinkle lines on his forehead deep as trenches. His eyes, always so clear and bright when they first met, were often dull and blurred, bloodshot from sun and sleeplessness. The dark shadows below his eyes made him seem ten years older. His lovemaking was typically kind and gentle to her, his hands warm as he searched her curves and softness. But afterwards, exhausted, he slept deeply, the depth almost frightening at times as she tried to wake him so he could return to his hotel. He seemed so bottled up and Anna tried to help.

"Do you want to talk about it, Karl? Your trip? You seem so tired, and—well in intense pain."

Karl peered up at her and smiled sadly, rolling over, kissing her on the smooth deep curves around her buttocks and lower back. He laid his head on her hip and stroked the back of her head.

"We've been touring some of the detention camps to make sure we understood the requirement. They decided we didn't because we were organizing the wrong kind of trains, apparently. It's been quite an experience." He was silent for a long time, his eyes dark and vacant.

"These camps, as you said weeks ago, are in France."

"Yes, they're in France."

"When will they start using your trains?"

"They've been in use for over a month, Anna. I've been reprimanded because I was trying to find unused, discarded passenger cars and freight cars. We don't need passenger cars, you idiot, they told me. We need cattle cars! Freezer cars, storage cars, coal cars. We need anything that has a lockable, sliding door. I watched them, pack them in like sheep and then lock the door."

"Where are they going, Karl, these—people…"

"Poland, mostly, but we have—centers in Germany. I watched them. They packed them in and locked the door. They say the trip takes three days. There were no windows on those freight cars, no real ventilation at all."

"Oh, Karl, those poor people…"

It was the only time Berchtold spoke about the camps. When Anna tried to bring it out of him on later occasions, he brushed it off, refusing to discuss it. *I live this every day, Anna, I don't want to relive it with you! I want to relax and spend time with you and forget about it!* She understood he had his duties to perform whether he liked them or not, but she was concerned he would not discuss it with her at all, to let her help him. Instead he increased his consumption of alcohol. He was never drunk, but she worried about him in his exhausted state whenever he left the apartment to drive back to his hotel. The alcohol made him morose and reflective, never angry or abusive. It was a part of his character she admired and admittedly grew to love. He was a true gentleman and she could not call it any other way.

In early October it started to get colder and rained frequently, reducing Anna's long days walking the streets, parks and museums. One afternoon after several days of constant pouring rain the sun came out— bright and warm on the freshly scrubbed streets. Against her better judgment, mostly out of boredom or cabin fever, Anna fixed her hair, put on some makeup and dressed to go out. She enjoyed the attention she was getting from men, and as she sipped her coffee in a small open street bistro by herself, one or two tried to engage her in conversation. It was only when a young municipal policeman stopped and watched her for several minutes that she began to get nervous. She realized her dress was perhaps a bit too revealing of her legs, clad in her best nylons. A young, single woman attracting the attention of a lot of men in the business district could be streetwalker.

Anna instinctively knew there was only one thing she could do. She made a show of looking at her watch and left some money for her

87

coffee.  She gathered her things and walked directly towards the police officer, smiling brightly as she looked up at him.

*"Bonjour!"*  She said, adjusting her hat carefully on her head as she passed him.  He hesitated then smiled, nodding his head and touching his fingers to the brim of his kepi.

*"Bonjour, Mademoiselle!"*

Anna over did it, glancing at her watch again, feeling the eyes of the young policeman on her back all the way down the block.  She kept going, a bit too fast and her ankles began to hurt.  She slowed down, turning down a side street and stepped into another bistro, darker, with only a few tables.  She sat down with relief and closed her eyes for a moment.  As her eyes adjusted to the dim light, she started to reach down and remove her right heel when she sensed someone watching her.  She glanced over to the left, her head barely over the edge of her small table and met the eyes of two German Army officers, both watching her with interest.  She realized they were the only customers in the bistro, in the quiet hour between dinner and supper.  Their hats were on the table to one side; their bodies turned exactly the same way towards her.  She even noticed each man had his left hand cradled around a small glass of a neutral colored liquid.

*"Bonjour,"* she said politely with a slight smile.  Both officers nodded but the one on the left was the only one who smiled.  The other one stared, almost rudely, as if he was trying to place her face.

*"Bonjour, Mademoiselle,"* said the one on the left.  The waiter was just now coming out from behind his dark wood counter, but before he could take her order Anna made a great show of looking at her watch.

*"Pardon..."* Anna shook her head and waved him off, pointing at her watch suggesting she simply misjudged the time.  She grabbed her purse and left.  She could see out of the corner of her eye one of the officers was starting to stand.  Anna, despite the intense pain in her ankle, quickly retreated back around the block and onto the main street again.  She turned left instead of right, knowing she had a long, roundabout journey back to the apartment, but accepted the pain as due punishment for her foolishness.  She had been recognized, somehow, possibly from her publicity from her accident months before, or perhaps some place she had been with Berchtold.  *Never again*, she thought fearfully, glancing casually over her shoulder, *never again do you break your own rules if you want to live.*

From that day on Anna left the apartment in one of two basic disguises, a manufacturing technician or a low-level clerical office worker.  She saved the disabled older woman for special occasions.  She explored the medium sized manufacturing shops and noticed the technicians, all women, wore simple smocks and sensible shoes for staying on their feet all day, and scarfs for their hair. They also carried small metal lunch pails with food they brought from home, and most of them left their shops and went to one of the local parks for lunch. These women were ignored by the more well-dressed women in dresses and skirts from the retail shops and offices, and tended to keep to themselves. Men rarely looked twice at them, even the young ones because they were dressed for working lathes and drill presses, not perfume counters or selling office supplies. She could play either one. *What an actress I'm turning into,* she thought. *What role am I playing? But before she could smile or find any humor in the thought, she remembered her encounter with the two German officers, and Berchtold's description of the people jammed into the freight cars with no ventilation. The horror in the image was she could see her mother and father, and down between them, her sister Clara as the doors were slid shut.*

Her world had spun down from the intensely frenetic and exhausting life of a medical student to a world composed of boxes, angles and shadows. It was how she characterized her world of disguises and subtle deception. People were visual, and saw things in recognizable packages or relative association. The days were long at first because she was so used to planning and organizing every waking moment. If you weren't reading or reviewing notes, you were making notes to ensure you didn't forget anything. There was no time for daydreaming or casual reflection. If you didn't plan it and stick to the schedule, it wouldn't get done and the time was wasted. It was necessary for her survival in medical school, so much so it was a sad joke, mostly true, that medical students plan so many minutes for meals, so many hours for sleep, and if they were so lucky to actually have any relationships, they planned their romantic interludes to minutes and fractions of an hour. The days were hers to invent, and almost every waking moment was filled honing skills at living outside of the consciousness of others, invisible in plain sight. Like a female pheasant, she remained grey and blended, leaving the colorful plumage to others.

She missed her parents, sister and brother terribly, but was reassured by their letters that they were currently safe. For the first time in her life she had time to consider things, in depth without interruption, and she enjoyed the awakening of her own being. She felt stronger, more independent, and conscious that only she could truly ensure her own safety. This meant less mindless fear and confidence in her ability to work things out without involving her parents. But mostly she was aware she was secure and comfortable because of Karl and his confidence and trust in her. In her heart Anna lived her days in quiet motion until he returned. Nothing else mattered. The months had simply passed and only recently did they begin to consider what would happen when Karl was reassigned, as he believed he would, to Poland prior to the invasion of the Soviet Union. He came home twice in November for two days each, physically exhausted and depressed.

In mid-December Anna found a letter from Karl in their PO box. "Holiday" was prominent in the cryptic message, but no dates, only a "miss you and hope to see you soon" and a "Love, K". He had only written three letters in December, but intimated a grueling schedule where they were working every day of the week. Using one of the many black-market contacts she had developed over the summer and fall, Anna acquired a beautiful black dress for Karl's return, and a very expensive bottle of champagne. She cried after she slipped on the dress in the apartment, realizing the hopelessness of her dreams. He was everything she wanted in a man, she believed. He was kind, gentle, fun, bright and witty, and brought up in most ways exactly the same as she. After the war, he would probably resume his teaching duties in Stuttgart and have a fine career as an academic. If the world was a different place, she would marry him if he asked her and they would have beautiful children. She might even be able to resume her medical studies. Anna took off the dress carefully and sat on the bed, naked and limp, her head in her hands.

He knew nothing about her and loved her anyway, or so he said, and she believed him. And if he did know the truth, what would he do? Even if he accepted her for what she is, an enemy of the *Third Reich*, what could he do? What could they do? Anna turned off the lights in the apartment and opened the drapes to the dark sky as she approached the window. As usual there were no lights on in the building across the street. Only a slight reflection was visible to her in the glass, the darkness of her belly button and her nipples. She was willing to offer her body and her life to this man, who she felt wanted her in return. Her being was acceptable only if there was deception. Could she do that? Could she live like that?

Anna closed the drapes and turned the lights back on. Her tears slowly dried but the sadness remained. She felt she was beginning to understand the strength of a person like Nina. *She was not afraid, but simply adaptable. I am what I am,* Anna considered out loud, *and what we have I will embrace as long as I can.*

# Mon Cher Ennemi

# Chapter 10

*December 24, 1940. Ostroleka, Poland, west of the Soviet border.*

Karl didn't feel any guilt for what he did for Anna. How could he? He had never felt such a deep attachment and affection for a woman in his entire life. There were plenty of women he was connected to over the years, and some he felt he had been in love with. But Anna was different in that he was struck by her beauty and magnetism the very moment he set eyes on her. It was a magnetism of some immediate sense of familiarity, a reassurance of coming home, of rightness, *of being where you were supposed to be.* He knew that is how he would characterize it, but it didn't encompass all the other overwhelming emotions of *want, desire* and *happiness* that engulfed him when they were together. Karl couldn't quantify those and didn't try. He only knew what was lost. He was over a thousand kilometers away from her now, creeping along for the most part but now dead stopped in the middle of a frozen wasteland, freezing his ass off, waiting for the snow blowers to clear the tracks.

The guilt he felt was a concern he didn't do enough to ensure her safety and comfort. But at least he could hope to give her some freedom, a chance to escape. It somehow balanced out his other sense of guilt over a promise that was not kept. His small bundles, marked only with initials for a return address, would be arriving soon in staggered fashion. He had known all along his assignment would eventually end, as it would end for all of the other logistic teams assembling a transportation system in France. They scoured the countryside and sidetracks and put together as many trains as they could. Their mission reports, hundreds of pages now being compiled in Limoges, Lyon, Marseille, Nice and Paris, would eventually be bound and forwarded to Berlin. But Karl, who thought his team would be given a few weeks to work their reports and get a much-needed rest in Limoges, had been found out. An *Abwehr* counter-espionage team tracking suspicious French activities in the business district of Limoges, followed Karl when he returned from a trip. Their shadowing activity was based on a tip from a French waiter who was member of the *Milice.* The information gathered was inconclusive, but the *Abwehr* report suggested Karl was seeing a blond woman, a French national who could not be identified, and therefore a potential threat to the security of the *Reich.*

Karl and his team of two statisticians, an elderly *Wehrmacht* clerk-typist, the railway engineers and *Unteroffizier* Kline, were ordered back to Limoges. Karl was to report to his commander the minute they arrived. The interview was brief with *Oberstleutnant* Korman. Korman appeared drawn and grey, and as Karl was ushered into his office and saluted, Korman kept Karl at attention for several moments before peering up in irritation, his hands gripping a manila folder. He opened the folder and selected a document, holding it up prominently as a form of incriminating evidence.

"I thought I told you to get rid of that French woman, *Herr Hauptmann!*" He hissed in barely controlled anger. Karl had never seen the man so upset.

"What French woman, *Herr Oberstleutnant?*"

"You know the one I'm talking about, the French doctor, the pretty blonde who saved your life, you said!"

"Doctor Metzger? You must be mistaken, sir. She left in July, she had patients to deal with, *Herr Oberstleutnant!*" He responded indignantly, without disrespect. "You saw my report, I understood you were concerned and as soon as my railway engineers arrived, we thanked her for her medical assistance, apologized for the accident and her injuries, and escorted her out of our hotel and on to her train. I've forgotten where she was headed, but she is long gone. I have had no contact since, sir!"

"I saw your report, yes," Korman sighed. He passed the document to Karl, who lost some of his color when he saw the *Abwehr* letterhead. "You've managed to attract the attention of the *Abwehr*, apparently based on some tip from a waiter in a restaurant somewhere in the business district. What were you doing over there?"

Without permission Karl slowly sat down in one of the chairs in front of Korman's desk, reading the *Abwehr* report. He read it carefully three times, and it was clear the entire report was based on observations over a two-day period in early December. The agents shadowed him from his hotel to the building downtown, but they did not enter the building. There was no mention of a room number or any specific location details. The occasion was one of the very rare times he and Anna left the building to have dinner at an obscure restaurant not frequented by German soldiers. The photographs of Karl in civilian clothes and Anna were grainy and the lighting, thank God, was poor due to the late hour and the location. It was obvious Anna was a young blond, but it was difficult to identify her face, as Anna had taken lately to wearing scarfs that partially obscured her features when outdoors. There were three blurry pictures taken in a restaurant, but apparently the circumstances prevented the shadowing agents from getting closer. The images of Anna laughing and eating were what you would expect out of a very small camera probably shot from under a napkin, using high speed black and white film and the widest possible aperture setting. Considering the dark little corner table they must have had, it was a remarkable technological feat. Karl sighed with relief, but glanced up from the report with a guilty, apologetic look on his face.

"Oh, God," he stood up, dropping the report on Korman's desk and cupping his hands to his head. "What a fool I was!" He glanced down at Korman, who despite his glaring irritation seemed empathetic.

"Who was she, Karl?" Korman picked up the *Abwehr* report with obvious distaste and slipped it back into the folder before tossing it aside. Before Karl could answer Korman swiveled in his chair and glanced out his window, shaking his head.

"We're regular *Wehrmacht* officers with a very important mission, understaffed with impossible deadlines to meet, and these bastards have nothing better to do than sneak around and follow my officers on the rare occasion they return to home base!" Korman turned back to his desk, pointed to the chair Karl had vacated, and offered Karl a cigarette.

"I assume she was French, yes?" Karl nodded, sheepishly, accepting the cigarette and Korman's lighter.

"Somebody you picked up or a prostitute? I mean, you're gone for weeks at a time, just arrive back in town, and I'm going to make a fair assumption, Karl, because unless you have that woman doctor hidden away somewhere, patiently waiting for you when you return from your trips, which I highly doubt—this was a prostitute—an independent, who you see whenever you can? Tell me the truth."

"Yes, *Herr Oberstleutnant*, I've been seeing a prostitute. I know it was wrong, but I just…"

Korman waved away Karl's explanation with a brush of his hand, sitting back in his chair, eyeing Karl with obvious annoyance.

"Save it, Karl, I understand. The *Abwehr* report is what it is, and they will keep the file open and probably assign some spook to shadow you as long as you are assigned to my unit." He said this slowly and Karl, no fool, nodded his understanding.

"Yesterday morning Adolf Hitler issued his plans for the invasion of the Soviet Union. *Seven days before Christmas.* What a nice Christmas present, yes? I was informed about an hour after this was announced, that I was to begin transferring my transport logistic teams as soon as they completed their missions back to Berlin for reassignment. To the Polish border. Which means at some point not far in the distant future, I will be joining them in the frozen wastes of eastern Poland and

God forbid, the Soviet Union. No one seems to read history. I'm afraid, Karl, your team will be the first to go. Your assignment here in France is officially over, as far as I'm concerned. I'm sorry it has to be this way. Your team has done excellent work. The *Abwehr* doesn't seem to care, however, and I do not want any more scrutiny than necessary. Understand?"

"I understand, *Herr Oberstleutnant*. When do we leave?"

"I explained to *Abwehr* I believed you were foolishly seeing a prostitute, but your assignment was complete and you will have transfer orders to leave as of the 20th of this month. You and your team will be on a train to Berlin. That was satisfactory for the bastards, and they will close the file on your 'mystery' blond, I'm quite certain. Do you even know her name? That could be useful." Korman suddenly shook his head and waved the thought away with his hand.

"Forget it, don't even bother. I'm sure any name she gave you was a phony. Just get ready to leave."

"I see. Thank you for your assistance, *Herr Oberstleutnant*. Two days is not a lot of time, we haven't compiled your latest reports yet and..."

"Do the best you can, Karl. If necessary, I'll have other staff work the final report, it will soon no longer be your concern." Korman slowly got to his feet, a clear signal the meeting was over. Karl rose and clicked his heels turning to go when Korman's raised hand caught his eye.

*"Herr Oberstleutnant?"*

"Here's a bit of advice if you are fortunate enough to make it back here. The German Army understands the physical needs of its soldiers far from home. The French have some of the best *maisons* in the world, as you may know. Certain ones are specifically created for the ruling class, with the most beautiful women. They are by French law medically inspected weekly to eliminate disease. It will be just a matter of time before the German Army takes them over, but in my experience, which extends far back well before the war, the French already take it to a high level. I can't say I have much experience in Poland, but disease is always a concern, yes? Stay away from the independent prostitutes, they are outlaws, and are not regularly inspected."

Karl listened attentively and saluted. *"Herr Oberstleutant."*

Two days, he thought in growing panic. He needed to talk to Anna, but it was clear from the conversation he was an observed man. He could not see her before he left. He could not take the risk for her sake. *Abwehr* was apparently only aware of her operating somewhere in or near the building. Nothing in the report suggested the agents entered the building. Was she still under observation? Whatever he had to communicate, he had to do it through the mail, he decided. It was benign and he couldn't believe *Abwehr* had him as such a high value subject they would be opening all of his outgoing mail.

Karl thought hard, objectively examining what he knew. If they observed Anna for several days, they might see her visiting the post office regularly. If they examined the records, they would find the box under his name, and if they chose to, discover and copy anything in it. That would be the end. He closed his eyes as he considered the report. Nothing in it again suggested their surveillance extended beyond the evening observations of Karl leaving his office, driving to the building, meeting Anna and going out to dinner. It was, most likely, only the routine follow-up of a tip from a *Milice* informer. The watchers made the observations, wrote their report and submitted it. Had they moved on? Could he assume the mail drop was still safe? No official business was sent there and no German Army contact was aware of it. That was the key, no one knew about it. Did *Abwehr* have the manpower to search for such things based on a tip? Would they? Karl, in despair, realized he was thinking out loud in paranoia. How much of a threat was Anna and Karl to the *Abwehr?* Did they really suspect Anna was an enemy agent? Had his *oberstleutnant's* dismissal been enough to turn them off? In the end he realized he had no choice but to suspend any communications with Anna until after he was gone.

He had a couple of plans already prepared in advance to put into motion. He made numerous phone calls all day, strictly business, and avoided the telephone in his quarters. He knew *Abwehr* could not have taps on every phone in Limoges, and went out at lunch to a bistro not far from his suite of offices. He casually noticed everyone around him before paying his bill and leaving. He glanced at his watch and smiled as a man with extra time to kill would do, then sauntered down the boulevard towards a row of large old hotels. He moved quickly between the buildings before stopping to peer into windows of Christmas displays. He could see no one in the reflections as he turned abruptly into a hotel he knew had a bank of private telephone booths. Once inside he selected a booth with the light burned out, and sat quietly, observing the entrance of the hotel for several minutes. When no one suspicious came in Karl placed a call to the landlord of Anna's building, grateful when the man's secretary connected him after two tries.

Karl explained he was exercising his option and extending his lease for six more months. He would be leaving for a long assignment and could he assume the landlord would accept full payment in advance, in cash, *Reichsmarks,* of course? How he was going to handle this transaction in his limited time remaining, Karl admitted, he had not fully thought out, but he smiled to himself when the landlord, who somehow sensed Karl's problem, praised and noted *Herr Hauptmann* had been a good tenant and was trusted as a gentleman. The landlord gave Karl his own private post office box address, assuring Karl that as long as he received the money within the next two weeks the apartment was his as long as he needed it. The transaction, he explained in a lower voice, was completely discrete between the two of them. For a moment Karl hesitated, wondering if the landlord had seen them together. No, he decided, the man is simply greedy and wanted to reassure Karl there would be no *questions,* and therefore no one could give *answers*.

Korman was true to his word and quickly transferred the remaining paperwork to other logistic teams. It was obvious he wanted Karl's team on a train and gone yesterday. The others, forlorn and disheartened, couldn't believe their bad luck in being the first sent to Poland. At Christmas time? There had been rumors the high performing teams might get some leave to go home. We turned in excellent reports, did we not? Weren't we commended just a month ago? What did we do wrong, *Herr Hauptmann*? Karl had no answers. *You have done nothing wrong, believe me*, he reassured them. *Adolf Hitler has released the plans for the invasion of the Soviet Union and we all knew it was coming! It came earlier than expected. We are only the first to go, that's all. The rest will follow.*

Karl, in his last free moments, closed his office door and buried his face in his hands. It had been 16 days since he had seen Anna. He did not wire or write her of his return, only the earlier communication when he was sure he would be home for Christmas. The urgency of the message from Korman to return immediately sent alarm bells ringing, and Karl wisely, he hoped, decided to send out nothing to Anna that might be intercepted. Here he was, maybe three miles away, and in no position to contact her. To caress her, kiss her and comfort her in anyway. She was waiting, as she always did, as he imagined she was waiting for him—and he could not tell her he was going away, perhaps forever.

In his large stack of luggage there was a reinforced wooden case covered with leather, about a meter long, five decimeters wide, and four decimeters high at the peak of the curved lid. It was the only piece of his personal luggage that used two padlocks, one each for the latch on both ends, something he described to his staff and his batman driver as his rare book collection. It was not really a receptacle of rare books, except on the very top layer visible to view. Most of the weight of the case was the well-fitted black walnut frame, not the books. Under the books was paper— paper currency, once Polish *Zlotys* slowly and carefully converted over time to German *Reichsmarks*. Karl didn't know the exact exchange rate in the late 30s, but the current exchange rate was about .05 *Zloty* to a *Reichsmark*. In any case, the box once contained 38,000 *Zlotys* now worth about 19,000 *Reichsmarks,* minus what he had used for paying the rent for the apartment, living expenses for Anna, and the soon-to-be extension of the lease. He would mail the lease money to the landlord somewhere between France and the Polish border, as he would his correspondence to Anna.

With the discovery of the *Abwehr* surveillance and a file under his name, Karl realized his days of being an anonymous *Wehrmacht* leader of an obscure independent team far from Berlin were over. He could at any time be called in and interrogated, even arrested. His possessions, the personal possessions of a German Army officer normally protected by his rank and status, could be seized and searched. He knew this had not occurred yet, because there was no doubt in his mind he would already be in a cell. How in God's name could he explain the case full of *Reichsmarks?*

What would be the chances of the interrogators believing his story of the black walnut case being offered to Karl as a gift from a Polish railway engineer, a man saddled with the weight of his own guilt, who asked Karl to accept the case in a trade. The engineer was picked to accompany Karl's team as they rebuilt the Polish railway system after three weeks of constant aerial attack. But the engineer didn't want to have anything to do with trains anymore, and pleaded with Karl to accept the case and please select someone else. *What's in it?* Karl asked suspiciously. *The life savings of a family,* the man said with a straight face. The engineer was handed the case by the head of a Jewish family in a desperate attempt to save some of the children from the cattle cars. *Please,* the man had said, *save the children. It is all we have, Zlotys converted to Reichsmarks! Hide them, please! It was a confused switching yard*, the engineer said, *with three trains close together and few guards beyond the loading dock. It could have been done.* The engineer accepted the case and stowed it, the man was still standing near the loading coal bins and pointed towards his family and the cluster of children. The engineer made a decision and simply walked around to the other side of the coal bin. He stayed there until the cattle cars were loaded.

Karl had done what the engineer asked and noted on a form the man was unsuitable and selected another. The engineer dropped two keys in Karl's hand and disappeared, the case remaining at his feet. Karl had it moved to his quarters and forgot about it for nearly two weeks while the team crawled over the dangerous wreckage of the Polish rail system. One night he tripped over the case and pulled it out. He rummaged around to find the keys and was shocked when he opened it. It really was full of *Reichsmarks*. All converted from *Zlotys*, the engineer had said. Now Karl had to get rid of it as quickly as possible and there was only one obvious solution. The case, a product of a promise abandoned and of no further purpose of salvation to its former owner, had been given another chance.

# The Dark Passages

## Chapter 11

*December 30, 1940.  Limoges, France.*

Christmas came and went and there was no sign of Karl.  It upset Anna because it had been nearly three weeks since he last came home, and there were no other communications other than the letter two weeks before.  She left the apartment rarely, and a new sense of watchfulness came over her because of an incident a few days before Christmas.  She had reread Karl's letter a dozen times, noting the 'Holiday' code word, and decided he was trying to surprise her or was scrambling to get home by Christmas.  In either case she wanted to be ready so during lunchtime she visited a favorite butcher.

The proprietor was a jovial, middle-aged man who was captivated by Anna, and offered her black-market sweet meats for even less than he was charging others.  She was hoping to find something special.  The day was cold and blustery and she was dressed in her office worker disguise with a long wool coat.  She pulled out a scarf to cover most of her hair before slipping out the door.  She went down the hallway and used the stairs to get to the office levels, joining the throng of workers breaking for lunch, making small talk as they crowded into the number two elevator.  She had done it enough times she was always seeing a familiar face or two, and it felt good to be recognized and smiled at.  She admitted to herself she was lonely, and these small brief contacts with other human beings revived something in her.  She knew she had to keep her distance, however, and kept the chitchat breezy, turning down a rare lunch offer because she was "meeting her husband" or "have to pick up some things for the kids".  It always worked, because everyone was busy and 50 minutes for lunch was not much time…

Anna wore large sunglasses because even on overcast days, she spent so much time indoors any outdoor light was overly bright to her eyes.  The hair on the back of her head began to rise and she sensed eyes on her within a block of the building.  She crossed the street and looked both ways to check for traffic, noting the two well-dressed men thirty meters behind her stopping abruptly to stare at an empty storefront window.  Once across the street she turned in the direction she had come from, keeping the two men in her peripheral vision for a few moments.  One glanced over his shoulder at her before slowly turning his attention back to the storefront window.

With her sunglasses on Anna continued to turn unexpectedly for several blocks until she was convinced the two men were gone. She tried to spot other watchers but couldn't detect them. She decided they were not plainclothes *Surete*, but Germans. Something about the cut of their clothes or longer strides than typical Frenchmen. She wasn't sure. She continued to walk for hours before deciding, exhausted and hungry, her best course of action was to go home. She wore the wrong shoes for long distance walking with a resulting limp from her aching ankle. She approached her building as the temperature dropped and the shadows lengthened. She entered from the side street entrance when she could see no one on either side of the street.

The incident frightened her and she didn't step out of the apartment until her food was nearly gone. Despite her months of practice and preparation with numerous disguises she had somehow been recognized and somebody, most likely the Germans, were following her. But who were they following? Anna Metzgen, the *Juif* medical student or Doctor Metzger, the physician who collaborated with the Germans? What made it worse was her suspicion something had happened to Karl. It upset her so much she couldn't get out of bed for a couple of days. It reminded her of the time in her apartment in the Marais when the Germans first entered France, and later Paris. Those were long days and she admitted freely she was frightened. She hid then too, to no avail, as she was forced out into the street by her landlord a short time after Nina had been ordered to leave. This realization and the recognition she was quite alone finally dragged her out of bed. Your father couldn't help you then, Karl can't help you now. *Get up!*

The following morning five days after Christmas, Anna disguised herself as an old crippled woman, bent over her cane toting her wheeled shopping cart. She knotted her long silver and brown wig into a bun, covered it with a bland, tattered old scarf, and wrapped a thick shawl over her shoulders. She went down the deserted stairwell and entered the level with the small manufacturing shops, pecking along the long corridors with her cane until she made the elevator. Everyone was still working so she had the elevator to herself. As she slowly left the building, she swiveled her head on her neck turkey-like, her portrayal of an arthritic old women so effective she cut a swath through pedestrians like a bow wave. As usual, she was totally ignored by people trying to avoid her. Her head sweeps noted two men, similarly attired as her suspected German watchers, across the street reading newspapers. Anna headed straight for them, crossing the street against traffic and beeping horns, oblivious to the world as an old woman with a mission. She passed within three meters of the two men, both who were staring over their open newspapers in the direction of her building.    Neither gave her so much as a casual glance.

After watching for ten minutes for anything suspicious, Anna left the bench at the post office and pecked her way over to the corridor with the post office boxes.    The box was full and she quickly emptied it.    Her next stop was the butcher who only knew her as a lunch time visitor from a business office somewhere.    The jovial proprietor was cordial but did not recognize her at all, reminding the *Madame* her ration card would expire tomorrow and she needed to apply for a renewal.    He didn't seem to notice it was the same name she used under different disguises.    There was no connection to the young versus the old and infirm.    She asked about the availability of sweetmeats but the proprietor, sadly, had none to sell her.    *It's the war, Madame!*

Back at the apartment, Anna gladly removed her disguise and quickly made a meal out of her meager food supplies.    The ration card limits were based on what was considered a basic minimum, and not necessarily what was available on the shelves.    She knew she could go right back to the same butcher and get a number of fine items under the counter from the proprietor, but she would have to dress in her business disguise and she couldn't use that right now, maybe never again.    She would need to consider some alternatives if Karl didn't come home long enough to get her some renewed ration cards.    She sat down at the table in her housecoat and began opening mail.

There were eight letters and three parcels, large enough to nearly fill the post office box.    Five of the letters were from her family—three from her mother and father, two from her sister Clara.    As Anna had instructed, they used code names and abbreviated return addresses. Karl's letters were simply addressed to the same name used by her family to write her, Herr Berchtold.    Anna glanced at the calendar, realizing it had been six days since she'd last checked the mail.    Six days!    The parcels were all about the same size, about 15 centimeters wide and 30 centimeters long, padded and thick.    The handwriting was clearly Karl's, but the return address simply said 'KB'.    She was curious, thinking perhaps they were Christmas presents until she noted the stampings.    The postings were from Berlin and later from Warsaw, stamped eight to ten days ago.    An icy chill ran up her spine.    She dropped the parcels and tore open the first letter from Karl, one of three also posted in Germany and Poland.    *Oh no...* she gasped, *Oh my God, Karl...*

# Chapter 12

*August 5, 1941.  Limoges, France.*

When Anna thought about those days after Karl was transferred, she remembered the first month being the hardest.  His first letter, written late at night in his hotel room when they were only a few miles apart, gave Anna an even clearer picture of his love and thoughtful planning to provide for her.  The letter was meant to reassure her, she was certain of it, but he outlined in specific detail what the *Abwehr* had reported without realizing what a shock it was to her.  He omitted nothing.  When she considered the men who followed her from the building a few days before Christmas, her blond hair partially covered with a scarf, she was almost out of her mind with fear.

She wanted to pack and leave the building the same night, using every disguise she had at her disposal until she was far from Limoges.  At the same time, her highly developed survival instinct pointed out to her she was a cornered animal, currently safe, with the predators watching every escape avenue waiting to pounce.  *Stay where you are.*  She kept her blinds closed all of the time now, opening them only as necessary to carefully examine the side street for watchers or suspicious pedestrians.  Anna read his first letter again and again, where Karl explained what she should and should not do.   His orderly mind considered problems and worked out solutions, which in almost every case was resolved with large quantities of money—*Reichsmarks,* coming in the small brown parcels once or twice a week.  When Karl was still assigned to Limoges and was coming home, albeit infrequently, he had given her cash in small quantities in *Francs.*   But as the months passed and French merchants began accepting *Reichsmarks* from all the German soldiers because they were so many of them, their acceptance became commonplace and everyone had them.   The merchants really didn't mind at all, as the exchange rate was set by the German government and it naturally favored the *Reichsmark.*

By early January Anna's last two monthly ration cards expired.  Karl was in no position to acquire her others for the *Haute-Vienne* department, as he was far from France and his black-market resources.  Anna realized she would have to rely on her own black-market contacts for food from now on, easily tripling her food costs.  She considered whether she should inquire about possibly getting a bogus ration card through her contacts, but she knew this might create undue suspicion that she was an alien.   It was a risky move, as the *Milice* and the *Abwehr* were offering rewards for *Juifs* and other aliens who escaped the occupied zone and were not residents of the southern departments, and therefore not eligible for ration cards. She could trust no one in that regard. She was not known personally by anybody besides Karl, on purpose, and other than when she had to show her ration card to buy something, no one knew her name. By just buying some higher end food and paying black market prices she was simply demonstrating she had a little money, that's all, she reasoned. No one would fault you for that. But she had to choose her under-the-table sellers carefully and not overuse them. Right now, the only desperate people with money and no ration cards were foreign *Juifs,* cash rich if they were lucky enough to be paid for their confiscated property somewhere else. Luckily, she had easily a half dozen black market sellers to choose from, each only knowing her by a particular disguise. It would work. It had to work. She had no choice, she had to eat.

Ration cards were used for basics but were a must-have item if you didn't have money to buy from the black market. That was all the average Frenchman or woman had to feed themselves on. You simply could not buy food otherwise. Just as Karl had established some contact somewhere for the ration cards he gave Anna, probably at great cost, the best black-market cards were produced by true professionals who could duplicate the required stamps, inks and signatures as good as the original. Poor counterfeit copies existed though, and *Juifs* on the run were often caught attempting to renew a counterfeit. Anna was aware National policemen carefully watched the administrative offices where the ration cards were issued for just that reason. She had approached the office only once out of curiosity, frightened off when a policeman arrived to question a woman apparently fingered by local officials.

There was so much to worry about and she began to be concerned about her apartment and the on-going rent, but again Karl covered it all in his first letter. He prepaid the apartment for six more months, until the end of June, 1941. If Anna was still in the apartment then, he would extend it again. And continue to extend it until the end of the war, if Anna chose to remain there. She read this sentence several times and broke into tears, not only because of his kindness and thoughtful words, but because she could not conceive continuing to stay in the apartment alone without Karl.

The evening Anna received Karl's first letters and parcels she cut her hair. For some reason very little hair dye was available when Anna tried to buy some earlier, so she did the next best thing. She had two other high-quality wigs for her disguises, both dark brown in color. One was medium-long extending to her shoulders when she let it down and the other relatively short. By cutting her natural hair to about 12 centimeters in length she could wear the short one more comfortably. The mysterious blond in the business attire was no more. She would never leave the building without a wig again.

Karl could give no return address and he wasn't coming back to Limoges, so the communications were one sided. He wrote at least twice a week, sometimes more. Anna, who began to wonder where the money was coming from when she received her sixth or seventh parcel by the third week of January, received a cryptic answer in a long letter from Karl. He explained the money originally was part of a promise given by one person to another, and the promise was not fulfilled in time to be useful. The money was given to Karl as a trade from the guilty party who was not able to fulfill the promise. Karl simply stated the money was supposed to have given some people a chance, and now he was using it to give Anna a chance. That was all he said.

Anna dropped the letter to the table and knew intuitively where the money came from. Karl didn't say where or when he acquired it, but she remembered the *Francs* he gave her when he first installed her in the apartment, and now understood where the rent money came from. Poland, he came to France after the invasion of Poland. He brought it from Poland. She turned and stared at the nail on the far wall, a faint shadow of the picture that used to hang from it was still there. She never hung anything there. It seemed a sacred spot and she left it alone. She knew the former tenant of this apartment probably no longer existed, or was in a labor camp somewhere. She closed her eyes and clutched her hair, feeling overwhelming guilt and sadness. Pain, dull heart pain, deep inside. *My God... Oh God, Karl, my love, what have you done? How can I live like this knowing where this came from? How can I live with myself? If only he knew the truth...*

The weeks and months passed quickly when Anna finally accepted the apartment as the only truly safe option she had. The guilt she felt was subdued in time, for the simple reason she recognized he was saving her life. They both had discussed the possibly of the war ending by the end of 1942 if England would capitulate, the United States would stay out of the war, and the Soviet Union and Germany would come to some agreement before Germany invaded. These discussions all occurred before his transfer, and she no longer had any hope the war would end by 1943. She fell into a dull low-visibility and secretive existence where her days were filled with reading, cooking and occasional carefully planned forays out of the apartment. She slept poorly and never more than a few hours at a time.

After a few weeks the watchers simply disappeared. Their blond target no longer appeared from the building, and Anna could only hope the Germans decided the target had moved on.    All she knew for a certainty was one day there were no more well-dressed men pretending to be doing something else.    After two weeks she felt a weight lifting from her shoulders but she remained vigilant.    During the first three months Anna went out in either her old woman disguise, which was very slow and tedious but the most *invisible* and therefore most effective; or as a machinist in her dark short hair wig and scarf, slightly dirty coveralls and metal lunch pail.    She carefully nurtured and vetted her black-market contacts and eventually found one she trusted enough to sell her "extra" ration cards for her 'sister with twins'.    There were no questions, and she continued to use 'Anna Metzger' as her name on the ration card.    The ration cards were expensive but the real thing.    She was relieved she had at least one form of ID, and hopefully a long-term source for monthly ration cards for the foreseeable future.

She resumed writing letters to Karl that were never sent.    She wrote at least one a day, sometimes two, carefully storing them in order.    She never mentioned where she was or the disguises she used to go out in. She only described places she visited, like a tourist, but without naming locations, interspersed with her feelings about Karl's absence.    She knew they all sounded the same but he wasn't reading them anyway.    They were for her.    Writing them made her feel better and for a little while, gave her a sense of a conversation with Karl.    She understood any letter could be incriminating evidence for both of them, so the letters, if intercepted, would be the long-winded ramblings of a lonely young woman missing her far away soldier.    Karl had instructed her to destroy all of his letters once she read them, which was very hard to do, but despite his best efforts he did describe an incredibly barren landscape and the extreme climate.    He did not talk about his mission.    You would have to be a fool not to determine the writer was stationed somewhere on the Eastern Front, poised most likely on the Polish border waiting for the orders to cross into the Soviet Union.    She kept them longer than she should have, rereading them, often aloud until she could hear his voice, his inflections and pauses.    She kissed the letters when she could hear him, the tears and loneliness replaced, just briefly, by the joy of this small connection.

Her father's letters were becoming more infrequent and difficult to read.    In March, about the time the watchers abandoned their vigil outside of her building, her father's worst fears came to pass.    The *Vichy* government, not the Germans, was officially reviewing immigration records of French citizens suspected of being *Juifs*.    No one accused *Monsieur* Metzgen or his family of being *Juifs*, but as he related again and again about his sister's son, *his stupid son of a bitch* nephew who spilled the immigration truth under interrogation, *it was just a matter of time.* They would not be *suspected* of being *Juifs, they were Juifs,* converted Catholics or no, the Metzenbaums were Polish *Juifs* and it ran in the family veins right through Anna, Jean Paul and Clara. At his law school known *Juifs* were being forced out of professorships and tenured teaching positions. Those who are identified, her father described soberly, *lose everything.* They lose their profession and the right to own property, gold or bank accounts. The only option is to start the lengthy process to immigrate to the West; to England, Canada or the United States. There were limited quotas but the borders were still open. *My God, Anna, these people are French! And the French government is doing this! My God, what are we going to do?*

Her parents no longer pleaded with her to come home. They actually asked if she was in a position to take in her sister, Clara. Clara had been a student at university in Aix, but she dropped out just before the beginning of the winter term. Professors at her university suspected of being *Juifs* were also fired and students, including those who looked like *Juifs,* like Clara, were increasing becoming the target of verbal and occasionally physical attack. Anna only had to remember her own experience at the Sorbonne the days after the Germans crossed the border into France, and Nina's warning of what was to come. She shuddered and wondered if she could shelter Clara, then quickly shook it off. Who was she kidding? Her safety was her northern European features, even with her dark brown wigs her pale skin was Germanic. But it offered safety only so far as she didn't attract attention. Like her blond self. But mostly she survived because she lived in the peripheral shadows of peoples' daily lives, blending into the pavement and the background. Neutral and gray, unmemorable like her old woman. She survived because she was alone, moved alone. Disturbing a small wake like a slow boat, then gone. *Oh my God,* she thought, *I'm thinking of all the reasons I should push my little sister away...*

Anna responded to this guilt by engaging more often in direct correspondence with Clara. She was surprised and delighted how bright and insightful her sister had become. The petulant, self-centered, combative know-it-all teenager had matured so much in the year since they had last seen each other. Clara, by temperament and character was much stronger than Anna, Anna was convinced. Physically brave and athletic, Clara revealed her personal confidence by bold action when she was just a toddler. Always watchful without being the least timid, she was the first to pick up and examine an interesting object or interject herself into an activity she was drawn to. There was no holding her back once she decided she wanted in.

Clara really was in more ways than Anna could describe a younger version of her friend Nina Rosenburg. Like Nina, Clara's arguments were powerful and well supported revealing a sharp and structured mind. She never argued for argument's sake. Once she made a decision, she committed to it. Her passion for a subject would reveal itself in the intensity of her facial muscles; the eyes open and clear focusing like a light beam on an opponent's face. She was both intimidating and disarming. Despite the dire situation evolving in Aix, Clara managed to remain sarcastic and optimistic and openly contemptuous of their father's fearful concerns. One day she even challenged his position.

*If we are Juifs and there is no hiding it, why doesn't he just declare it and be done with it?* Clara wrote angrily. *He always talks about the immigration option, that France has abandoned Juifs, including French Juifs and we could make a new start somewhere else in the West. If we are unwanted by our countrymen and they are going to take our property anyway why not just leave? Why, Anna?*

Unlike her one-sided correspondence with Karl, Anna could answer Clara. She tried to be as diplomatic and thoughtful with her sister as she could.

*I'm not sure they will let us leave, Clara. There are labor camps and detention centers all over France, built by Frenchmen, not Germans, and the French government is assisting the Germans in developing transport trains to move Juifs from France to other detention centers in Poland. The Germans did this in other countries they invaded, Czechoslovakia and Poland for example. It is said the Juifs transported to these centers never come back, Clara.*

Clara was equally direct in her response. *How do you know about this, Anna? Are you living with a German? Father thinks so, and the German is protecting you somehow. Is that true? I told him I didn't think all Germans are bad, and he slapped me. And then he hugged me and apologized, saying he didn't necessarily hate all the Germans, but he didn't want to think of you staying with one. But then he said he can't trust his French neighbors anymore either, or his French friends. He says we Juifs are on our own, as we always have been.*

In May the parcels of cash stopped coming. Anna kept a record of them, estimating she received well over 20,000 *Reichsmarks* in five months. She slit a small slot in her mattress and stuffed the packets of bills in such a fashion they didn't lump or bunch up. Karl's letters were coming less frequently, the result of his overwhelming workload, he explained in a brief letter near the end of the month.

*Not much hope of any agreement, I'm afraid*, he added. *When it comes my team will be right behind the lead assault formations, so my letters may not come very often, my love. Not too many post offices on the wastelands. At least they are doing this in the middle of summer, with the hope it will be over before fall! You will always be in my thoughts, and your safety is foremost on my mind, believe me. I've renewed your lease for another six months, through December. You should have more than adequate funds to get you through any difficulties. I miss you so much, Anna. With all my love, Karl.*

It was the last letter she would receive from him for four months. She read in the papers Hitler had launched the invasion of the Soviet Union the first week in June. But no one had to read the papers in France to know something was drawing German troops away, because over the months preceding convoys were in constant motion to *the east*, instead of the west or south as before. Anna noticed it in Limoges, fewer tanks and mobile infantry on the streets. It wasn't comforting or reassuring however, as the French police or more alarming French *Vichy* troops seem to be filling in the void. It was French police, her father had complained bitterly, who were doing most of the hunting and arresting of *Juifs* in Southern France. *Shame!* He declared. *Shame on Petain and his government. Shame on him to be hunting French citizens down like dogs!*

Anna couldn't stand it any longer. Despite the risk she felt compelled to go home and visit her parents, explain her situation with Karl and reassure Clara, if only for a few hours. The dangers she faced were numerous but after months of her shadow life, Anna was growing confident in her ability to assume the role of what people expected her to be, and therefore attract no particular attention. Her primary problem was she was not an official resident of the *Haute-Vienne* department. She had no employee ID, only a ration card listing her as a resident. The rules for travel were tightening up all of the time, but there were no recent special declarations in the papers forbidding ordinary French citizens to travel she was aware of. For *Juifs* and other identified undesirables, yes—but for ordinary citizens, no.

She thought this out for several days, considering what Karl had told her about the confiscation and collection of railcars for transport trains. Anna had not been anywhere near the *Gare de Limoges-Beneditins* since her "departure" nearly a year before, so she knew she had to take the time to observe current procedures. She would not show up and attempt to travel blind. A traveler had to have a reason to get a ticket; for work or visiting sick or elderly parents, that sort of thing. She understood train seats would be difficult to get and anything out of the ordinary or suspicious activity would result in a demand for additional identification. Her only other ID, official and legitimate was that of Doctor Metzger of Lyon. She also had her unsigned and undated letter stating Doctor Metzger was traveling due to a sick relative in Toulouse. Both would probably work under normal circumstances, but Doctor Metzger was a blond on her ID. Would Anna be willing to risk it? Would her appearance at *Gare de Limoges Benedictins* result in her arrest because of the previous *Abwehr* surveillance?

Her honed instincts told her it was not a safe course of action, and she needed to heed recent experience and travel as a common worker. A laborer or tradesman would be expected to travel less and not be particularly sophisticated when it came to knowing all the requirements. Anna knew they were treated with disrespect and generally ignored, but usually waved through checkpoints as more of a nuisance than anything. She liked the idea of a doctor's letter declaring the traveler as a relative visiting a very sick or dying parent. She could draft that easily. An illiterate or less sophisticated traveler may not even understand half of the terms the physician would use to describe the patient's condition. This would frustrate train officials and the traveler even further, especially if some bureaucrat required some obscure form to accompany any letters. It was perfect. What she needed now was some basic identification of someone in a manufacturing shop in Limoges who looked somewhat like Anna, and their ration card.

In early May Anna noticed two of the small manufacturers adding evening shifts to increase production. The evenings when the corridors and elevators were quiet after five o'clock were no more, especially for the lower stories where the shops were. Something else was added too, more security. She didn't know why the work production was increased, but she did notice both of the shops produced high grade optics for binoculars, telescopes and some form of gun sight, and occasionally German officials in civilian clothes would show up. Anna used to come into the shops and walk around, mostly to determine the type of smocks or coveralls the workers used so she could match them for her disguises. But in May a security official of some kind set up a desk a few meters inside the door the workers had to pass through. His professional scrutiny was limited however, and he rarely demanded to see every worker's badge close up. Groups of ladies coming in from lunch, chattering noisily and encumbered with their lunch boxes and shopping items, were soon simply walking by and waving their badges. They looked the part, acted the part and after a few days the guard knew them all anyway.

On the night shift the security guard often left his post because there were less than half the workers on duty compared to the day, and few visitors or shippers delivering goods at the entrance door. Anna found this out when she opened the door about nine in the evening one night and peeked in. She could see no one in the foyer or in the locker rooms for the employees.  She crept inside and could see the security guard through a small window in the locker room.  He was having an animated conversation with an attractive girl sitting at a microscope.  Without hesitation Anna tried the lockers and found all of them locked except for one.  Inside the locker was a lunch box, a sweater and a spare smock was a photo ID with clip attached.  She couldn't believe her luck.  The ID was valid but the girl didn't look like her at all, but Anna pocketed it without hesitation.  It would get her through the door if she came in with a crowd during the day.  All she needed to do next is identify a few employees who looked somewhat like her and wait for her chance.

# Chapter 13

*September 15, 1941. Limoges, France.*

Once a day a yellow and green bus, a stinking, foul charcoal burning relic stopped in front of the building to pick up workers bound for *Gare de Limoges Benedictins.*    Anna didn't know it existed until she heard about it as she rode the elevator.   The bus made the seven-kilometer journey to the main station to arrive more or less promptly at 5:30.   Most nights there was a night train departing around 6:30 bound for Toulouse. Once the bus dropped off the workers it departed.   The day Anna went to get her tickets she knew there was no one to drive her back to her apartment and she would have to walk.   She estimated it would take her about an hour and a half to get home, and it would be dark when she approached her building.   She came well prepared, wearing walking shoes and carried both a torch and a paring knife in her small knapsack.

She stood in line with the other women, mixed with a few travelers hoping to find a seat on the night train.   When her time came, she knew what she had to say.   She was wearing her working smock and scarf, looking exhausted and emotionally drawn.   The train agent was middle aged, balding, and wore a trim green shade.   He too seemed exhausted and drawn.   As she walked up to his cubicle she hesitated, acted confused, then pushed forward her letter.   It was from a doctor in Aix describing her father's medical condition, advanced heart disease, and the immediate need for Anna to come as her father would probably pass within 48 hours. She then added her picture identification as Marie Broussard, working for the Plessix Optics Company of Limoges, and Marie's ration card.   The train agent wearily glanced at the letter,  worker ID and ration card.   He sifted through the documents again as if something was missing.   He peered at Anna with mild annoyance.

"Uh, *Mademoiselle,*"   he droned nasally, "where do you want to go?"

"What?"   She responded slowly.

"Where do you want to go?   Your letter says your father is sick, and he lives in Aix. Do you want a ticket to Toulouse?   I can't connect you on this ticket all the way to Aix.   But once you get to Toulouse you can buy a ticket for a westbound train to Montepellier, Arles and on to Aix.   I can't get you a seat on the night train, I'm sorry."

Anna closed her eyes, as if she could hardly believe what he said. She shook her head and stared at him, her eyes red-rimmed and near tears.

"What did you say?"   She said, hesitatingly, before getting louder and pleading.   *"My father is dying!   I need to get home!"*

111

"I understand, *Mademoiselle.* But you understand I can't get you on the night train. Not any night for several days. Completely booked. Most of the seats are set aside for the Germans, you know that. The earliest I can get you a seat—third class—would be the noon train, day after tomorrow."

Anna gasped and clutched the edge of the pedestal jutting out from the cubicle. She shook her head before pressing her face as close as she could to the small opening in front of the train agent.

*"You don't understand! My father is dying!* There must be something you can do for such an emergency! It will take all day to get to Toulouse! And I still have to get to Aix from there! If I don't leave Limoges until the day after tomorrow, I'll never see him alive again!"

Most of the people in line had moved closer and were switching their attention back and forth between Anna and the train agent. The agent looked at the growing crowd nervously and lifted his hands as if there was nothing he could do. He held up Anna's physician letter and pointed it towards Anna.

"Look, the regulations normally require the Prefect's authorization for medical emergency travel outside the prefecture. This new rule has been in effect for months now! Toulouse is 300 kilometers away! This really—his hand shaking the letter—isn't enough for the travel authority! I don't know what to say, *Mademoiselle!"*

Anna's howl of anguish was that of a wounded animal, her sobs racked her body as she bent over and wrapped her hands around the pedestal. Several of the ladies in line came up to help support her slumping body, comforting her. There was no question where their anger and disgust was directed to.

"Her father is dying, *Monsieur!* You heard her! There must be some contingency for such things!" Other voices were much louder and less polite, with some hands pounding on the agent's cubicle glass.

"Her father is *dying, you son of a bitch!* How can you be so cruel and heartless, you *bastard!* If I was your mother, I would be so ashamed! *Shame on you! Shame on you!"* The man glanced around the angry faces in surprise. He turned his attention to the paperwork on his desk.

"Yes—yes, of course…" the agent mumbled, nodding in agreement, his eyes wide with concern as the women crowded even closer and pressed against his cubicle. He heard the glass panels groan. "Where did you want to go, *Mademoiselle,* Toulouse?"

"Yes! Toulouse!" A woman called out, "have you got wax in your ears!" The agent shuffled several schedules before reaching for a thick journal out of his stack. He made a notation in the journal and pulled out his ticket book. He peered through his port window and looked directly at Anna, who despite her slumped affect, was paying very close attention.

"All right, *Mademoiselle!* Don't let it be said the railroad has no heart! I have a second-class ticket for you on the night train to Toulouse tomorrow at 6:30, will that be satisfactory? That is the absolute best I can do! I have waived the additional fee increase and it will be the same as a third-class ticket, due to your emergency travel. I also waived the additional document requirement from the Prefect's office, since there are special circumstances…" The rest of his explanation was drowned out by a short bout of cheering. The train agent's cubicle was pounded again, but not in anger. He seemed very pleased with himself. And relieved.

"I hope your father's condition was a mistake, *Mademoiselle,* and he will recover. My best wishes." Anna looked at the man appreciatively, and told him, heartfelt, she couldn't thank him enough. She paid for the ticket and scooped up her documents. Then she thanked the supportive crowd of ladies and other travelers, accepted their best wishes for her father, and headed for home.

The walk home was the longest journey she had made on foot in over a year, and despite her good shoes and slow pace her ankle ached terribly. It was dark when she approached the building. She stood in the depression of a doorway a half a block away and watched for several minutes for anything suspicious or unusual. With the additional evening shifts there were more lights on in the building, but other than the flurry of activity at five pm and then two am, the street was usually quiet.

Hot water was turned off two times a day now, but she made it home in time for the evening window. She drew a half a tub of reasonably warm water before it was shut off, grateful to slide in, slithering down as low as she could. Her earlier confidence in pulling off the trip had evaporated; she knew instinctively this was the most dangerous thing she could do at this point. She had her disguise down; she had no qualms about her ability to stay in character. She would travel like a semi-skilled laborer. She had examined many of them close up and understood their need to travel in their best clothes for their own sense of self-respect. The women wore little makeup, didn't own high heeled shoes, and embraced fashion only by what they could see in the magazines and worn by their betters on the street. They wore dated but clean dresses and liked hats. They could not afford manicures or hide the fact what they did for a living was hard on their hands.

Anna intentionally kept her nails short, a small line of grease or grime just under the nails that could never be scrubbed off because you were back in it the next day, even with gloves on. She could always spot a working woman by the way they made fists when their hands were out and displayed in public. It was a matter of pride and personal shame, and Anna adapted the same mannerism herself. She remembered her own mother's comment on poor women: You know where a woman comes from and what she does by the shoes she wears and her hands. In that her mother, God bless her, was trying to explain a woman with little education or means could not afford to buy well-made shoes, or did things with her hands that made lotions and manicures a waste of time. You don't want to end up like that, Anna, keep up the grades!

Out of the tub Anna dried off and dressed in her old housecoat. She had purchased a cheap suitcase from a second-hand store and was examining it closely for places to hide her cash. Her eyes spotted the little clutch belonging to the girl Anna had stolen the ID from on her bureau. Marie Broussard. Anna only had a second to get the ID material. She didn't mean to take the woman's purse, but she had no option and left the shop with the clutch under her apron. She unzipped the clutch again, dumping out the meager contents: 12 *Francs* and change, a tube of lipstick, a small key ring, a black book with addresses and telephone numbers, an almost expired *Haute-Vienne* ration card and a worn membership card of some kind. Anna turned it over and realized Marie Broussard was a member of the French Communist Party. There was no picture, only Marie's signature on one line, and the endorsement of some party official. She felt bad taking the woman's money, keys and address book, and hoped somehow she could return them once she came back from the trip. She thought about it for a few minutes before tossing the clutch into the luggage. She would consider taking it. It fit the character, added some depth. She was traveling as Marie Broussard, but if they questioned hard, what was her story? She knew nothing about Marie, so under hard questioning she had no alternative but fill in the blanks with her own history. They couldn't trip her up on things that were true. It would buy her time, but only for a few hours. This frightened her and Anna decided, for the fourth time, not to go.

Anna took a seat on the bus and it left promptly at 5:30. She smiled at two or three familiar faces but found a seat several rows back. If she had any regrets at this point, she wished she had written or cabled her parents she was coming. Girls of her class, that is, the class she was pretending to be, didn't own watches. Anna Metzgen owned a watch. Marie Broussard did not. She relied on the numerous clocks displayed throughout Limoges. Anna slept in and decided at noon she wasn't going to go after all, which was again an enormous sense of relief. She made a big lunch, re-read some of Clara's letters and decided she was a coward. She had covered this ground so many times and here she was doing it again. With her calendar spread out on the table, she counted out the months.  She had lived in the apartment for 15 months.  She had last seen her family 19 months ago.  She missed them terribly.  She was ready as she would ever be.  What could happen?

As the bus pulled into the parking lot, smoking and groaning, it was apparent something was going on.  The bus driver had to slowly pick his way through crowds of people, mostly young people, who were shouting and waving what appeared to be placards.  *Oh my God,* Anna thought irritably, *it's a protest.  A union protest.*

The bus driver tried to prod and edge his way to the entrance of the train station but the crowd wouldn't budge.  Instead they hit the side of the bus with the flat of their hands and Anna could hear the protesters shouting.

"I'm so sorry," the bus driver lamented, "I can't get through.  I'm going to let you off here if you don't mind.  My apologies for this, I don't know what's going on."

The entrance to *Gare de Limoges Benedictins* was blocked by a row of men and women, all young and many of them wearing the aprons and coveralls of workers, their arms linked as they shouted over and over, "workers unite!  Living wages for all!  Shut down the railroad, break down the wall!"  Travelers approached the row of young people and asked politely for them to step aside, but the young workers shook their heads, shouting their slogans louder.  In minutes there was pushing and shoving as travelers, their trains waiting, tried to get past the protesters.  Anna, just a few feet behind the front row, was hoping someone would force an opening she could take advantage of.  Instead she felt a blow to her cheek as someone swung a punch and missed.  Infuriated, Anna dropped her luggage and turned on the person, a young man, and shoved him as hard as she could.  She heard police whistles and was encouraged it would soon be over.  She had a train to catch.  Hell with these people.

The *gendarmerie* cordoned off the entrance and half of the parking lot with at least 40 officers.  They encircled the protesters and anyone within the cordon, and within minutes the *gendarmerie* batons were clubbing young people to the ground who resisted.  Anna put her hands up, holding her clutch, and was dragged forcibly aside with an arm painfully tucked behind her back.  The *gendarmes* ignored her painful cries of protest, especially as she was being separated from her luggage.  The next thing she knew she was handcuffed and led into a bus.  She was forced to sit in a seat across from a young man with a large cut on his face, his eyes closed as he bled profusely.  As she sat down the *gendarme* told her to sit still and be quiet.  Once the bus was filled another *gendarme,* a submachinegun in his hands, stood next to the driver and declared all the occupants were under arrest.

The arrested protesters including Anna, eventually filled three buses and not surprising, once the first bus was filled it took nearly an hour to bring two more. Anna could see her luggage in a pile of other traveler's belongings loaded on to another bus. She was seated with a young woman who looked vaguely familiar, but they didn't talk because it was forbidden. A few voices could still be heard whispering. The tall *gendarme* motioned with the skinny barrel of the MAS-38 for all the occupants to shut their mouths. He seemed angry, glancing out the windows nervously as if expecting the bus to be attacked. Some of the young protesters, especially the men, assaulted the *gendarmerie* with their fists. A few attempted to run away after appearing to submit to arrest. All were chased down and caught, their clothes torn and their faces bleeding as they were brought in. Once Anna's bus was filled the remaining protesters were ordered to sit down on the asphalt of the parking lot. They formed a tight group nearly invisible behind the heavily armed *gendarmerie* surrounding them.

During the wait Anna watched her train arrive and depart. She tried to breathe through her nose to squash her sense of growing panic. She was so frightened at first she couldn't control the quivering of her legs, clattering against the metal of the seat frame. Her companion on the seat noticed and with her hands handcuffed, placed her fists gently on Anna's, warm and comforting.

"It's okay," she murmured, her lips hardly moving. Her eyes, narrow, watchful and astonishingly blue, peered at Anna kindly with patient humor.

"There are too many of us, they'll take us somewhere to try to sort us out, get frustrated and let most of us go. It's late in the day, they don't have enough jail space and most of these officers want to go home to their families. That's why we chose the time! I've seen this before. The *gendarmerie* doesn't know what to do with us, and the Germans don't care as long we don't stop the trains…" Anna stared at the girl for a long moment, her breathing slowly subsiding to almost a normal rate. The girl looked at Anna carefully before she whispered out of the corner of her mouth.

"Do I know you? Where do you work? What is your name?" Anna, her brain racing, knew better than use her newly adapted name. This girl might know her. She might work in the same shop.

"I don't think we've met. I'm Anna. I was trying to get to Toulouse, but I missed my train." She whispered back. The girl grimaced and looked pained.

"I'm so sorry. I thought you were with us. I'm sorry we caused you to miss your train."

The girl looked over at Anna periodically but said no more. The other buses arrived and once loaded, the charcoal smoke swirling into the seats with the partially open windows choking the riders as the ancient machines chugged off. The shadows were growing long as the buses drove past the entrance to the main Limoges hospital and turned down a narrow alleyway a half a block away.

"See, what did I tell you?" Her seat companion whispered. "This isn't the main jail, they're taking us to the basement of the hospital annex." Anna noticed the girl stiffened as she said the words.

"Some of us are in for a hard time, I'm afraid, but they'll let you go once they realize you are just a train passenger."

The same 40 officers were waiting for them as they were taken off the bus. They separated the men from the women and ignored questions and demanded silence as the two groups were led single file into the building. The women, approximately 50 in number, were brought into a large room with neat rows of chairs and told to sit down and be quiet. A dozen *gendarmerie* spread around the periphery of the room. Some of the women asked if they could go to the restroom, but were told to be patience and keep their seat.

After a few minutes a senior *gendarme*, two civilians in suits who Anna immediately suspected to be Germans, and a severe-looking, middle-aged blond woman stood together at the front of the room behind a large table. The senior *gendarme*, looking tired and irritated, leaned forward on the table and addressed the women in a low, fatherly voice.

"Because of the size of the group—the group of protesters—which we didn't anticipate, we aren't processing you in the normal fashion. This isn't the Limoges courthouse or jail, as you can see." He seemed to be looking around the room expecting to find someone he knew, Anna thought. Well if he was, he was disappointed as he looked down at the table and sighed loudly. Two officers came in carrying a huge sack, turning and dumping the contents on the table. They included briefcases, luggage, rucksacks and purses. Anna could see her luggage and assumed her clutch was in the pile somewhere.

"This is what will happen, as we have to quickly determine who is who. I understand that some of you are travelers who got caught up in this—protest. If that is the case, I assure you we will have you out of here as soon as humanly possible." If there was going to be an apology, it wasn't going to come in the next few minutes, that was clear.

"We will call you up one by one, based on the identification information we have here, and you are to come up and claim your possessions, and follow the officer to a separate room for questioning. Those of you who do not belong here will be separated at that time, and

117

will be free to go." He did not ask for questions and no one raised their hands. Anna noticed the two plainclothesmen were examining the faces in the room very carefully. Her hands still quivered, but at least she was breathing normally. Six older *gendarmes,* the questioners Anna surmised, walked into the room and stood to the side. The senior *gendarme* waved them over, glancing up towards the women.

"Please come up when your name is called."

Anna, whose bladder was about to burst grew concerned as the hours passed and her name was not called. She squirmed in her discomfort but wasn't about to attract attention to herself. She saw her bus seat mate, whose name she did not recognize, get called in the first half an hour. Anna realized she had told the girl her real name, and that the *gendarmerie* would call her up as Marie Broussard. At this point she could only hope there was no one in the room who knew the real Marie Broussard and bring that to anyone's attention. *Oh my God*, she thought, *what differences does it make? I've lasted so long and foolishly got caught in the middle of a protest! My cover is so thin. Just stick to the personal stuff you know… stick to what you know…I should have stayed inside…*

After two hours there were four women left in the room. Anna noticed the two plainclothesmen were doing the actual selection of the women based on their examination of the documents. Her suitcase was still on the table, and she could see her clutch. The two men, who had examined her clutch earlier and set it aside, handed the clutch and ID to the *gendarme* who came into the room. The men seemed to exchange glances and Anna's heart fell. A stroke of ice slid up her spine as one of the two men looked up at Anna and held her gaze evenly.

"Marie Broussard?" The *gendarme* asked, holding up Anna's stolen ID card. Anna lifted her hand and got out of her chair, walking slowly to the table. She picked up her suitcase and watched the *gendarme* scoop up her clutch in his hands. He motioned her to follow him. She smiled at the *gendarme* and nodded to the plainclothesmen, her heart nearly stopping when they smiled courteously and followed her out of the room.

It wasn't a police interrogation cell but an equipment storage room with a desk for the attendant and two wooden chairs. The other interviews were occurring in similar rooms down the long corridor, and Anna could hear heated exchanges just out of earshot for understanding. She could see the waning daylight from an open door far down the corridor. They were still on the ground floor. Her *gendarme* examiner, a tall black-haired officer in his mid-thirties, removed her handcuffs and offered Anna a seat. He stood next to the desk, carefully opened Anna's suitcase with her key. The *gendarme* spread the two shells apart and expertly sorted through her things. He poked about but didn't dislodge or discover the pockets where Anna had stashed her extra money. The *gendarme* sat down in his chair facing Anna. The two plainclothesmen stood one inside the room, the other outside. At close range, Anna was certain she had seen one or both before. *Perhaps her previous shadows? Could they be Abwehr?*

"Please forgive us, *Mademoiselle,* for disrupting your travel arrangements. I've gone through your documents and discovered your ticket for the train to Toulouse—at 6:30 I believe, and your letter from a physician in Aix en Provence. You were eventually going to Aix? Unfortunately, you've missed it. Your father is very ill? And a second-class ticket, not easy to get! I was at first under the impression we had inadvertently swept you into this protest by accident." The *gendarme* said this with a sad smile, then opened her clutch and held up Marie Broussard's Communist Party membership card.

"But then we discovered this, *Mademoiselle.* Perhaps it wasn't such an accident, after all?" The other German stepped in the room, making the space very tight indeed. Anna stared at the card with a blank expression, glancing up at the *gendarme* now with a pained wrinkle in her forehead.

"I—I'm not really…" she stammered, but the *gendarme* leaned in closer and pressed the card up to her face.

"You are a member of the *Parti communiste francais,* the PCF? No?" The *gendarme* laid the card down on the desk next to Anna, who followed the movement and stared at the card.

"Here in the *Limousin,* there is no other, eh?" He leaned back and lit a cigarette, offering her one which she refused.

"You do not believe in Marshal Petain, eh?" Anna could not believe how quickly the interview was unraveling, but was surprised how clear her thinking was, only nothing came. Her tremors were gone, but she could not think of one single thing to say that would not incriminate her. The *gendarme* waited and she could feel the eyes of the Germans boring into her.

"Besides this—bit of information, there is the issue of your father's illness. The membership in the PCF—mere coincidence, perhaps? But as a Communist, surely you were aware of this protest action—known it quite some time, perhaps were even going to participate? That is, until your father suddenly became very ill?"

The *gendarme* slapped the top of the desk with the flat of his hand, hard. Anna jerked up in alarm from the sudden noise, tears beginning to well in her eyes.    She shook her head and cringed back from the *gendarme*, fearfully and in clear distress.

"*Mademoiselle*, you see where I'm going with this?  How unusual this can appear?"

"I—don't know what to say!   I'm not much of a member.   I joined out of friendship with people at work.   I rarely go to meetings.   I find them boring and too political."    Her eyes, pleading, looked from the *gendarme* to the two Germans, who stared at her coldly.

"All I want to do is get on a train and see my father before he dies."

"Where do you meet for the meetings?"

"*Pardon?*"    The *gendarme* put out his cigarette and crossed his arms.  He pursed his lips and lifted his chin, peering at Anna down his nose for a moment before reaching over for a pencil and notepad.   The two Germans were already taking notes.

"Let's start from the beginning, *Mademoiselle* Broussard.    We have some information about you of course through our employee record files, but I don't have those at my disposal at this site.   Where were you born?"

Anna knew this is where they would eventually get her, if they in fact had extensive employee records, but at least this will buy her time and if they believed her story they might let her go without confirming the information.  *Stick to the facts you know.*

"Arles."

"When?"

"1917, June 1."

"How long have you lived in Limoges?"

"Only a couple of years, three actually."

"What is your home address?"

She gave a street name and building number of a restaurant about five blocks from her apartment.   The pencils scratched noisily and the sweat was starting to drip down from her hair under the wig that was topped by a hat.   She still had her coat on, buttoned up and she was in intense pain with her full bladder.   She almost wet her underpants when there was a muffled scream from a woman followed by shouting down the hall.   The three men glanced at one another before one of the Germans stepped back into the corridor.   He shrugged his shoulders after a moment and returned to the airless cubicle.   The *gendarme* appeared concerned but then resumed his questions.

"We see where you work, at the Optics company.    What do you do?"

"I'm a lens grinder."

"When did you join the PCF?"

"Um, to make friends when I was new, I went to a meeting. They signed me up after an interview."

"Three years ago? Less?"

"Less, about two years ago."

"How often do you attend meetings? Who leads them?"

"I—don't go often, maybe once every couple of weeks. I don't remember who leads them, different people, most I don't know. I go to socialize and make new friends."

"I see. Where are they held?" Before Anna could answer, one of the Germans leaned in closer.

"Do you speak any other languages other than French?" Anna looked up at the German in confusion.

"*Pardon?* Which question do you want me to answer?"

"*Mademoiselle*, I have a hard time believing you." The German said in excellent English. "You are an English *saboteur*, probably have explosives under that baggy dress, eh? Is that not so?"

Anna's mouth dropped and it was all she could do to *not* respond in English: "*Absolutely not!*" She started to stand when there were more screams and shouting, now multiple voices spilling out into the corridor.

The two Germans produced small semi-automatic pistols from under their coats and ran into the corridor. The *gendarme* unbuckled the clasp of his holster and withdrew his revolver and turned to follow them. He stopped to face Anna and point a stern finger at her face.

"Sit down, *Mademoiselle!* We will be right back." Anna stood up as soon as they were gone to peek down the corridor. A dozen officers were struggling with several of the protesters 10 meters away, and some woman, out of Anna's sight, kept screaming at the top of her lungs. Anna looked in the opposite direction where there was some light and an open doorway. Her suitcase and clutch were still on the desk. No one was looking her way. It would take just a few seconds to get to the end of the corridor. Would they shoot her in the back? Where does the door lead to? A voice calmly spoke in her head: *Go Anna. Go now.*

The door opened up into a small courtyard facing a side street. There was no one in the courtyard as Anna raced through and down the street. The main hospital was somewhere behind her but she didn't dare turn around. She walked as fast as she could, ignoring her limp and the pain of her bladder, staying close to the buildings without having any idea where she was in Limoges in relationship to her building downtown. She turned down the first side street she came to and walked only a few meters before hopping into a doorway of a closed dress shop. The street was deserted and the doorway was dark. She could smell urine in the corners, and wished she had her paring knife with her.

121

She pulled off her hat and hesitated for a moment before carefully removed her wig. For this evening she was going to be herself. She discarded the hat into the bushes but stuffed the wig into her coat pocket; it was expensive and she would need it again. She brushed her hair with her fingers, regretting abandoning her suitcase and clutch with the only money she had with her. She had no choice, she did the right thing. There was more at home in her mattress. Nothing was lost with her name on it, only poor Marie Broussard... Marie—she was in trouble. Anna couldn't think about that right now, she had other pressing concerns. She was many kilometers from her apartment, it was now dark and she had no idea how to get home. At this moment she possessed no identification at all. She was a true alien. She sighed and closed her eyes. She would do whatever she had to do to avoid the *gendarmerie*. She was proud she escaped and had no intention to go through what she just did again.

The darkness was her friend tonight as she peeked around the doorway to see if anyone was looking for her. She saw nothing out of the ordinary. Her only saving grace she realized, was her now ingrained safety procedures to ensure she didn't lose her key. Because of her constant change of disguises, she never carried her key in a purse or in a pocket. She carried it in a small slot she made in her brassieres. She felt it against her breast and smiled. She vowed she would never leave the apartment again. The train station was history. That was too close. The Germans had to be *Abwehr*. They thought she was a *spy,* for God's sake. They would have shot her. She shivered and waited as her breathing slowly returned to normal. Not as a *Juif* or a French communist. They would have shot her as an English spy or anything else they decided she was. Anna stared into the darkness and wondered herself. *Who am I?*

# Chapter 14

*September 17, 1941. Limoges, France.*

Anna remained in the apartment all day before her sense of guilt overwhelmed her. She didn't know how she was going to do it, but she felt she had to warn her innocent double, Marie Broussard. The *Abwehr* didn't chase her last night because they knew where Marie worked. It would be a matter of time, perhaps hours before they came. After some thought she decided to tell Marie she had been caught in the protest, and was being interrogated with another person who claimed to be Marie Broussard. There was a commotion that caused the interrogators to leave the room, and the two of them managed to escape. The other woman admitted she had stolen Marie's identification and was leaving Limoges. Anna was going into hiding herself, but felt obligated to at least warn Marie, since they worked close by. Marie might not believe her story but Anna decided she needed to tell Marie anyway.

Anna considered her disguises and decided the best would be the one that would allow her to get close to Marie, and the one least memorable in the shop area. She selected Marie because they looked alike, and didn't want Marie to come to that conclusion too quickly. Anna dressed in the smock of the other machine shop that established an evening shift, and wore her blond hair naturally. She wrapped a short scarf on her head and hung a pair of protective goggles from her neck. She entered the second floor very carefully from the stairs, approaching the entrance 30 minutes after the evening shift began. She could see no unusual activity; no *Surete,* no men in suits. She opened the shop door and encountered the security guard, who looked up in surprise from the newspaper open on his desk. She stood half in, half out of the door and waved to him, even though he was only two meters away.

"*Mademoiselle,* may I help you?" He asked, after a pause. Anna shrugged in a familiar, friendly manner, almost apologetically.

"*Pardon!* Sorry to bother you, *Monsieur!* I work for—the other shop, the one down the hall, the other optic shop. I don't work here, of course. I forgot to give my friend, Marie Broussard, some information last night. Could I go see her...or could you call her to come up here? I don't mean to impose, but it's important to Marie I give her this information. It will only take a moment, if you don't mind?" Anna gave the security guard a broad smile and shrugged her shoulders again. He stared at her blankly and then slowly got to his feet. He looked at her hands and hesitated.

"Is there something I can give her? I can call down but if you have something in writing…" Anna shook her head.

"No, nothing in writing, *Monsieur*. It's personal, about a family member. Please, *Monsieur*, this is important!" The guard nodded in some irritation and walked stiffly towards the locker room and the telephone attached to the wall. He turned as he lifted the earpiece.

"Your name, *Mademoiselle?*"

*"Anna."* The girl would be confused with the name, but Anna could only hope she would come up anyway.

"Marie Broussard, you say?" Anna nodded and smiled gratefully when she heard the noise of numerous feet coming down the corridor behind her. She took a step back and peered down the hall, her heart freezing when she spotted the half dozen men marching directly towards her. Most were uniformed National policemen, the rest plainclothesmen. *Abwehr*. Without hesitation Anna stepped inside the foyer and closed the door. The security guard was just hanging up the phone as she moved backwards, carefully pulling up her goggles and placing them on her face. She opened the door just as the six officers approached.

"I'll come back with the drill," she said loudly over her shoulder towards the security guard as she turned away. One of the *Surete* policemen looked familiar and the two *Abwehr* plainclothesmen she recognized immediately.

"*Mademoiselle*," one of the *Surete* demanded politely, "is this the Plessix Optics Company?" Anna looked confused, before pointing quizzically towards the well-marked door she just left.

"This one? Yes."

"Do you work here, *Mademoiselle?*" Her goggles were starting to steam, but she kept them on. The two plainclothesmen studied her carefully.

"No *Monsieur*, I work for the other optic shop down the hall. We're loaning them some tools."

The policemen seemed satisfied with her answer and nodded, opening the door for the others. The two plainclothesmen stared hard now as they passed her. Anna smiled and turned on her heel and headed down the corridor without looking back. Out of the corner of her eye she had seen the security guard look out at her from the open door with a look of confusion. The minute the door was closed Anna ran as hard and as fast as she could to get to the other end of the corridor and the opposite set of stairs. She flung the goggles off so she could see, clutching them in her fist. There was no time for the elevator. She glanced once over her shoulder as the shop door flew open and someone shouted. She entered the stairwell and ran straight up to the fifth floor. She didn't hear the stairwell door open, gratefully, as her lungs neared bursting. She walked quickly down the entire length of the building to get to her apartment, meeting no one, looking both ways before entering. They couldn't have seen much of her face with the goggles, but they had a clear picture of her approximate size and weight and short blond hair. There would be a possible match to the blond in the pictures from months ago. Would they put them together? Had she reappeared? A prostitute none of the vice squad *Surete* was aware of? A new freelance operator the men who regularly frequented prostitutes couldn't identify? Or an enemy agent the *Abwehr* could not place? *Who was she?*

The sense of panic, the feeling she was a cornered animal being pressed farther and farther into a trap would not subside. Anna couldn't sleep or eat. Now that the *Abwehr*—the same *Abwehr* who photographed and shadowed her with Karl and waited for her outside on the street months before, was now in the building for the first time. She felt helpless and boxed in. They didn't know exactly where she lived but they suspected she lived in the building. It would be a simple exercise to shake down the landlord and request a complete list of tenants and knock on each and every door. What would stop them from doing this tonight? In the next half an hour?

The only hold up at this hour would be finding the landlord, as Karl had mentioned he lived somewhere else in the city. But they would find him, and the Germans would not wait for morning, not with such a fresh sighting. Was there a building superintendent? She had never seen anyone except the night cleaning staff. They could be conducting the room to room search at this very minute, with policemen blocking the elevators and stairwells. It may be too late already. If they came and pounded on her door, what could she do? If they didn't get an answer, the landlord or building superintendent would open the door for the *Surete* with a pass key, what choice would they have?

The danger of her situation set in as she considered the real legal tenant of her apartment on the lease. It was a German Army officer named Karl Berchtold. If the *Abwehr* came into the room and found Anna, Karl would find himself immediately in serious trouble because of the previous investigation, probably resulting in prison or worse. As a couple they knew this risk all along, but Anna was convinced the *Abwehr* didn't really know who she was and had lost interest. This new sighting would renew the investigation in a big way. It was getting very complicated and there was no way either of them could explain the connection with a known Communist. An agitator involved in a protest action ostensibly because of union issues, but a member of a political party overtly fighting against the Nazi occupation.

125

The toll of people in dire straits because of their association with her was growing. Poor Marie Broussard was suffering this very moment because of Anna, with a prison cell a guarantee but a very rough time and interrogation first and foremost. The *Surete* and *Abwehr* would have sensed a conspiracy, and Marie was their only living local connection to the mystery blond. Karl was in the Soviet Union, and even the *Abwehr* would have difficulty tracking him down. They would do it if they had to if they thought they had a big enough case, but for the time being they had Marie. There was no doubt in Anna's mind Marie was trying to explain that she *was not* at the train station protest, *had not* been arrested, and *did not* escape from the hospital detainment. Anna could hear the questions, the demanding pressure on the poor young woman who had no idea who Anna was, and was frightened out of her wits...

Why, she would protest to her interrogators, would she be so foolish as to come to work if she knew the police was looking for her? Then explain the blond, possible enemy agent—this *Anna,* who ran from us? Why was she looking for you, Marie Broussard? What information was she trying to give you? It was foolish of you to come to work, so it must have been important enough for you to take the risk! What were you two planning? Your escape back to England? A bombing campaign somewhere? Are you both saboteurs? You understand, Marie, if we determine you are an enemy agent, you will be shot.

The words were too real in her mind, and she knew Marie was suffering and had no recourse. *Oh God,* Anna cried to herself, *I am so sorry, Marie. I am so sorry to get you involved like this. Oh my God, please forgive me...*

Anna knew she had to leave as soon as possible before there was a room to room search. It could happen any moment. Tonight, it would happen tonight. They wouldn't wait to complete their interrogation of Marie, why should they? They know where Anna had been seen. She had to be in the building. Her only escape avenue was to leave now, if it wasn't too late. But she had so much to do. She brought out all of her currency and counted it. There were over 12,000 *Reichsmarks* remaining, and she realized she couldn't take it all, there wasn't room. She had to stuff everything she was going to take with her in her old woman's shopping cart and destroy or discard everything else. She had no idea where she was going, but it wasn't to any train station and she had to look her part. Her haven and warm nest for over a year was now a trap.

The trash for the building was collected on the side street in eight large containers, picked up twice a week. It would be the first place the *Surete* would look for evidence, but they wouldn't be able to link it to Karl if it wasn't in his apartment. The apartment would be clean, if she could

126

just get rid of all the evidence before they came. Somebody had lived in it, there would be no doubt about that, but they would glean little else from a search. She would take out what she couldn't burn in the sink in her old lady shopping cart and dump it tonight, within the hour. All of her or Karl's letters, anything that would link him to her would be burned to ashes. What goes in the trash would be the extra clothing for disguises she couldn't use anymore, and anything and everything that suggested a young woman lived here. She needed to get to work.

The house smelled of smoke but she couldn't do anything about it. Anna placed her largest pot in the sink and filled the sink with water before lighting her papers afire in the pot. She opened the windows in the living room to ventilate the apartment, cautiously reducing the light in the room as she carefully searched the side street below. All she could hope was by the time they searched the apartment the odor would be gone. It was completely dark, but there was enough ambient light from other sources to reveal no unusual activity. She had half expected to see *gendarmerie* near the side entrance for the stairwell by now, but there was no one.

She dumped the ashes in a discarded clothing bag and scrubbed the pot. Once she had her two piles on the bed, what was coming and what was going; it wasn't all that much. She would keep one set each of most of her disguises, discarding the rest with the exception of a rain jacket and a thick winter coat. She was moving to the streets of Limoges to live, and it was late September and getting cooler at night. The rain had already begun periodically. She had to find space for a couple of blankets and her pillow. She had no illusions to the life she was facing, she would be miserable. But all she had to consider was her alternative.

She was going to burn some of the currency but couldn't bring herself to do it. Money was the great equalizer when all else failed, she learned that much in her year in this place, and these *Reichsmarks* came at such great cost to those Polish *Juifs*. It could not be wasted. Anna only hoped she could work something out somehow and find another place. Karl may be dead for all she knew, but she was going to protect him anyway, just as he had protected her for over a year. It was the least she could do to repay him. To put the money promised for other's safety to good use. She tried not to think about it after that. She stuffed *Reichsmarks* all over her body in her old lady's disguise, padding out her curves, adding a bit more bulk to a bent back and drooping breasts. No one will care about the misshapen outline of a disabled old woman, and it kept her treasure close at hand. With that in mind, Anna strapped a short kitchen knife against her thigh, cushioned by a pack of *Reichsmarks*. A sharp paring knife was taped to her chest between her breasts, and a third knife was just inside the folding top of her wheeled shopping cart, out of sight but handy if necessary.

About 10 o'clock Anna stuffed all the discards in her shopping cart and cautiously worked her way to the elevator. Her floor, as usual was deserted. In her year in the building she had never seen a single person come out of one of the other apartments. Not once. Karl had said they were all filled, but the tenants kept to themselves. She had no qualms about that aspect of her neighbors. They would not be able to describe her to any one either.

This was the night for her best performance if there ever was one. If she was surrounded by *Surete* and the *Abwehr,* she would be at her wits end not wanting to drop everything and run. But the old lady disguise was her best and she knew it. If it came to it and she was in the position to escape when cornered, this would be the only disguise she had a chance with tonight. They were looking for a young woman. Anna had to assume the search had begun, and unlike some conventional search wisdom, they didn't block the exits on the ground floor and started on the top floor. She was putting out her trash if anyone asked, couldn't get to it earlier. Why is any of your business, anyway? She had the cranky old lady persona down well, especially one irritated by things out of the ordinary. She took a deep breath and took the elevator all the way to the ground floor.

The evening shift was hard at work so the elevator was empty. There were only two cleaning staff in the lobby. Anna, bent over her cane, pecked her way to the front entrance, pushed one of the doors forward and stepped out into the street with her shopping cart. The street was quiet, so she quickly turned down the side street and dumped off her load. As she worked her way back to the entrance, her head sweeping back and forth, she could see no sign of an impending raid. Was she just dead wrong? Are they still interrogating Marie and the others and are too short handed to deal with Anna yet? Or was her timing wrong, the landlord was finally found and the *Surete* and the *Abwehr* on their way? Anna focused on maintaining her steady bent-over cane pecking pace across the lobby. Not a soul looked her way as she entered the elevator.

It was nearly half past ten when Anna closed the door to the apartment for the last time. She was exhausted and wanted to go to bed, but she had to reconcile with herself she would never sleep in that bed again. The room had aired out for the most part and she was able to close and shutter the windows. Her shopping cart was packed full and heavy, making it a little unwieldly when towed with a single hand with her back bent over. If her back didn't hurt when she started, it hurt by the time she made it to the elevator. As she waited one of the apartment doors close by opened cautiously and a short, chubby man with dark, longish hair and a housecoat stared at Anna with surprise. He could have been a poet, a conductor or a professor.

"Good evening, *Monsieur*." She said hoarsely, just as astonished. The man continued to stare at her for a moment before nodding and giving her a slight wave of his hand.

"Good evening, *Madame*." He responded in a deep baritone. He took her in with a bent head, like a dog trying to sort something out that didn't make sense.

The elevator finally came and Anna carefully made her way across the threshold, struggling with her cart.

"It's late to be going out, *Madame*." The man said, offering no assistance. Anna finally got the cart inside. She felt no need to respond to him as the elevator closed. She was certain the man didn't see which direction down the hall she had come from, but by the way he looked at her he did find her out of the ordinary. The elevator stopped on the second floor by call and two young women, in the garb of the Plessix Optics Company and with metal lunch boxes, got in. They both seemed upset and stared at the floor, ignoring Anna.

"I've seen the girl in the picture somewhere, but I told them I couldn't remember where," whispered one to the other. "The cops are so nasty about this. They still have Marie downtown for questioning, and when I asked about her, they told me keep my mouth shut if I knew what's good for me!"

"I know, I said the same thing about the girl in the pictures," the other girl murmured. "I think I've seen her on the elevator once or twice, but the cops say she has short hair. I remember her with long hair, in a braid. Or maybe I saw her down by the park during lunch. But I never talked to her. But I don't like being told to go home when I need the money. That's the reason I signed up for this extra work at night. But cops are all over the building tonight, so they are cutting us loose early so we don't ask too many questions."

The door opened and the girls gasped and flinched involuntarily by the presence of four National policemen standing just in front of the elevator. All four held their nightsticks in their hands at the ready as if the girls were going to pounce on them.

Anna showed little surprise, and simply started to push her way through the girls to get off the elevator. The girls turned and stared with irritation at Anna's prodding, and one of them simply held out her hand to stop Anna's motion.

"*Pardon!*" Anna barked hoarsely, her turkey neck craning around the girls, as she tried to work around them. "Out of the way,

*Mademoiselles,* I need to get home to feed the dogs!" She wriggled past the girls and bumped into the line of policemen. One of the officers glanced at Anna for a moment and held out his hand to stop the two young women, while giving a signal to the others to let Anna past.

"Do you live in this building, *Madame?*" The senior policeman asked Anna politely as she pecked past. She stopped and hesitated, as if she didn't quite understand him, peering up at him with tired eyes.

"What was that you say?" She said, craning her ear. "I have to feed my dogs, *Monsieur,* I've been taking care of my sick nephew all day, who is old enough to take care of himself! My poor dogs!" She wailed. "Look how late it is! They will be starving!" She started to look around and take an interest in the police and activity. "What are you doing? What has happened?"

"Never mind, *Madame*, it's all under control. Have a good evening! Take care of your dogs!" He nodded towards one of the other policemen to give her assistance.

Anna concentrated completely on her cane, her pace and her bobbing head. There were at least a dozen officers in the lobby, and she noticed a very animated discussion between two senior officers and a tall, exhausted-looking gentleman in an evening jacket. He seemed quite upset and was shaking his head, clearly in disagreement. As she passed them, she picked up just a glimpse of the conversation.

"—it is much too late to be bothering my tenants, you have my list. Many of the owners of the businesses live out of town, and I don't feel it is right to just wander through their offices or apartments when they're not present—"

"These are our orders, *Monsieur*. You will either open the doors with your pass keys or we will break them down! We are looking for a very dangerous individual…"

# Chapter 15

*November 4, 1941. Limoges, France.*

One of the most difficult parts of being homeless and living outdoors in an urban setting for Anna was she could never be herself. Without Karl, she alone controlled any contact with other human beings when she lived in the apartment. A true recluse when she wanted to be, she was comfortable alone, willing and capable of spending days in preparation for her presentation to the world, to her audience on their stage. This intense, fastidious study of her characters was the major reason for her successful disguises and survival for over 15 months in the apartment, culminating in her escape through the arms of the *Surete* trap. She believed that and gave herself a pat on the back for her effort. She was equally capable of completely shedding the greasepaint and costumes of the roles to resume her place as herself, a 25-year-old woman with high intelligence and curiosity, but comfortable lying in bed, naked and vulnerable and doing absolutely nothing. She examined her youthful figure in the bathroom mirror to see what Karl used to see. Her curves, the firm skin and healthy bright hair promised youth, vitality and strength. It was, she realized, that promise being hunted by the *Surete* and the *Abwehr,* and what she was most successful in disguising with her disabled old woman.

An actor needs a back stage, a space to disappear and prepare. Rooms to store costumes, sets and props, and when necessary, bleed off the humiliation and pain of difficult roles. Anna felt like a traveling circus now, the set and costume changes occurring in virtual full view of the audience only they didn't know it. Smoke and mirrors, a drum roll and slide whistle for diversions to hide a head and shoulders shrug to discard a costume, and finally a sudden dip behind a painted panel preparing the audience for the illusion of a change. Public restrooms work when they're open and not crowded, and with winter coming on, they were always crowded. So she stayed in character because there is no Anna Metzgen walking the streets and parks of Limoges, it's Anna Metzger, the laid off lathe operator who bought the black market ration cards; or Anna Metzger the old woman with the poor hearing and the bad back; and occasionally, if she can get a good sponge bath and keep her clothes clean, it's Anna Metzger the low-level office worker who bought the newspapers and smiled at the butcher for the best deals in cooked meat.

Anna calculated, using a small desk calendar in the city library, it had been 11 months since she last saw Karl, and four months since she heard from him. It was from underground information, other women who listened to BBC broadcasts or printed illegal newspapers that she garnered the news about the Allies. Hitler abandoned his invasion of Great Britain and was throwing all of his remaining strength against the Russians. The *Wehrmacht* was stalled all along a huge line in the East. *Stalled. What does that mean, exactly?* Casualties were enormous on both sides, and the snow was beginning to fall. Panzers were buried in the mud during the fall rains, but now the tracks were freezing and the panzers were moving again. *What about the trains*, Anna wondered, *what about the transport trains to move all the equipment forward? What about those? What about Karl? Was he a frozen corpse left on the wastelands to rot like the smuggled pictures of hundreds of cordwood dead sent out by the Russians?* Her heart throbbed and she couldn't breathe when she saw the pictures. Pictures of the enemy, the captions said. Hun dead. German mechanized infantry. Dead Germans. *My Karl. Where is my Karl?*

Those moments, alone and cold, snuggled deep into her blankets that could never protect her from the chill of the hard ground, were the hardest. The security of the apartment, the warm bed and the temporary escape available from her small collection of books were all gone now. She was very careful where she slept and rarely stayed in the same place more than two days at a time. The days for the homeless are surprisingly structured, she found, from the first hint of light sweeping her reluctantly from the marginal warmth of her blankets, to the measured, steady progress of her feet as she traversed, kilometer after kilometer, her established pattern around Limoges. As evening progressed, Anna would always be in the disguise of the old disabled woman. She would make little eye contact with ordinary working people as they would not seek out her attention, or respond to her glance. She was invisible. Only other homeless would recognize her, sometimes out of cautious loneliness, or occasionally overt hostility. She would sense the staring eyes, the jealous glare of a mad brain, and slowly turn around to return the stare. It usually worked, the eyes would find something else to look at, and Anna would move on. Sometimes it didn't work, and she would sense the presence of a predator at a distance for hours. She would not stop moving until they were gone, with one of her knives secure in the palm of her hand.

Whatever her disguise, Anna made it a point to stay clean. She discovered a half a dozen locations in her daily movements she could sponge her body, brush her teeth and wash her spare underclothes. None of this was easy, requiring speed, planning and careful timing with people coming and going. Despite the fact she had slept outdoors in the thick bushes close to parks and municipal buildings, she kept her clothing clean enough to emerge on the street and pass for a young office worker. She got so good it was a point of pride to enter a large hotel lobby and make her way to the restrooms, coming out 10 minutes later in a new disguise. Anna knew which hotels had the largest stalls and privacy for her changes, but more importantly, hotels busy enough the staff would miss her passing. The trick was to keep moving, have an appearance of a purpose and under no circumstances attract the attention of men. Nothing drew staff and then police faster than a young woman in the same conspicuous location a bit too long, or two days in a row.

The prostitutes, dressed for the evening in the early afternoon, would use the same restrooms as Anna. Sometimes they would recognize her, but Anna never felt any threat from them. She would sense their stare and quick appraisal. Once they determined she wasn't competition, and that was easy since Anna rarely wore makeup or anything that could be considered evening or sexually *attractive* attire, they acknowledged her with a brief smile and departed. Anna noticed the police rarely arrested these women, but simply sent them on their away. This satisfied the hotel staff, which confirmed Anna's belief the underclass of French society was allowed to thrive as long as they remained essentially out of sight. This undercurrent, this unseen world supporting the black market, the drug trade and the sexual needs of Frenchmen and women who couldn't be bothered with the structure of the *maisons,* was nonetheless a dark and dangerous world where everything was allowed to happen as long as it didn't happen to someone important.

In November there was no getting around the falling temperatures or the wet. When it rained there was no place to sleep under deeply spun and rooted junipers, the torrents dropped by gravity for days at a time found itself into the thickest growth. Anna, who had the blessing of money, searched and eventually found proprietors of seedy, poorly lit hotels who rented their rooms by the day or the week and asked no questions when enough cash was presented. The police were required to review and make copies of the daily guest cards of the hotels in Limoges, which they did with routine efficiency. But like the black-market items hidden out of sight in every food market in France, many of the tired, worn down hotels far off the main track always had a few rooms they never listed. Anna knew who used them, but she had no such moral qualms when the wind, rain and cold battered her senseless, and she couldn't put enough layers on to fend off the chill. Sometimes the rooms were no more than cells just large enough to fit a slim cot. Once when she was sick for several days and didn't have the strength to get out of bed, she had to withstand the indignity of her wall, which her bed was jammed against, being hammered repeatedly by the bed on the other side from athletic endeavors.  This went on hour after hour as the prime inhabitant of the bed on the other side, a very popular whore and fine actress who seemed to thoroughly enjoy her work, was pounded hard by an endless series of men.

Once a week, always in the guise of her elderly disabled woman, Anna made her way to the post office to check her box.  There were always at least two and sometimes three letters from her family to look forward to, but in early November there was also a forwarded copy of a newspaper from her father, and a small letter with a return address of a *Wehrmacht* hospital in Warsaw.  It was addressed to the *Berchtold family*. She couldn't breathe and had to concentrate and not cry out.  *Karl.*  Under the printed hospital address was a neatly hand printed name and rank and ward number.  She read it several times.  *Berchtold, Karl.  Hauptmann. Neurology Ward 6B.*  She examined the handwriting carefully, and decided it had many of the characteristics of Karl's writing, but it wasn't Karl's.  Her heart pressed up in her throat and she wanted to tear it open, but knew this was not the time.  She closed her eyes, not knowing if she should accept this as proof of his being alive or not.  He was in Warsaw in a hospital.  The invasion of the Soviet Union occurred in June, when was he hurt?  *Who wrote this letter?  It was addressed to his "family", but his family lived in Germany.  Did he write it this way because it was being censored?*  She had so many questions, but she could feel her heart lifting, and she had to let it out, accept the hope.

It was a damp, blustery day and Anna headed straight for the library.  She found a desk away from others and carefully opened the letter.  It was written on hospital stationary.  *Oh my God, he's alive.*  The writer identified herself as a nurse's aide, describing Karl as "a sweetheart."

*My dear French Family-*

*I'm writing this letter for Karl Berchtold.  My name is Ilya Frohlich.  I am a nurse's aide in the neurology ward, and Karl asked me to write this letter for him, as he's been having some problems with his eyesight.  Karl was hurt in the Soviet Union in July, and he hasn't been able to write because he's been moved from one surgical hospital after another.  He's had a lot of surgeries, and each time it seems to take longer to recover from the anesthesia.  He asks for your forgiveness.  If he could have, he would have written sooner, as he knew all of you would be worried and possibly believe he was killed in action.*

*He almost was.  The Russians strafed his personnel carrier and killed all of his staff.  Karl wanted you to know that he was not blinded, although he did lose an eye.  I'm not sure of all of his injuries, but I believe he said he was hit in the head, arm, shoulder, and his right leg is*

134

*partially paralyzed. He says the doctors are hopeful the main nerve down the center of his leg will eventually heal, and he will be able to walk normally in a few more months. Karl is such a sweetheart, and I understand how much all of you would miss him! By the way, just so all of you know, his injuries to his face are not really all that visible. His skull injuries will be covered by his hair, and if we can find one that will fit, an eye patch will work nicely for his hurt eye. He's still very handsome!*

Tears came to Anna, tears that rarely appeared anymore since she abandoned the apartment. She didn't have much capacity for self-pity, as it had not taken her long to realize she was very fortunate to escape. But she cried out in relief of Karl's survival and sorrow for his suffering. She only hoped his head injuries wouldn't affect his ability to teach once the war was over, or his leg injuries not limit his ability to stand for long periods in the classroom. She did find herself smiling as she considered this, as she realized despite everything, she believed somehow, they would both survive the war and be together again. Is there anything wrong for a woman to think about what was best for her man? *Are you kidding?* A second voice chimed in. *That's the reason we do what we do, because there has to be hope in the future, of a time when the war will be over...* Anna shook her head and kept reading.

*Karl says he will continue to send his letters to this post office box since the family is so scattered due to the war. He wanted to especially say to Anna, the artist in the family, he was not able to contact the landlord of the studio for a renewal. Telephone connections for long distance are not very good here in Poland, but he will keep trying. He apologizes, but warns she may have to move her studio by the end of the lease period. His mission is over, as his men are dead and he cannot physically continue in his assigned role. He doesn't know what will happen to him, as he has a number of months of therapy to complete. He hopes to be home in Germany soon, and will try to make it out to visit his French family as soon as he can.*

*All of his love to his family who he misses so much,*
*Karl (Ilya)*

The letter was like a stone bridge suddenly appearing out of the darkness, it revealed a path and purpose beyond the daily survival and trudging goat trail of her existence. Anna knew she was strong, much stronger than she had ever believed she could be, but as the months passed without a word from Karl, a suspicion slowly evolved into the acceptance of his death that left her strength without purpose or meaning. She lived because she was smart, and using Nina Rosenberg as a guide, knew she only needed the will to find the way to keep on living.

135

She could not write him and had no idea when she would hear from him again, but at least he was safe and away from the front lines. There were so many ways for a soldier to simply disappear in a war. Injured, abandoned and left for dead to be listed as missing in action; wounded so severely his memory and the being known as Karl Berchtold vanished from the face of the earth; or captured and slowly starving or freezing to death in a prisoner of war camp on the Soviet plain. Anna knew she was one of the rare fortunate ones, especially since she was not a real family member, just a girlfriend. Instead of the dull ache of not knowing and trying to push the images of the frozen corpses of German dead out of her brain at night, she could envision him struggling with the limitations of his injured body yet know he was warm and no longer in range of the guns and planes. And every week he would be healing and that much closer to Germany and—somehow, someday back in her arms. It was enough.

Anna was inspired to try to contact Nina Rosenberg in Lyon through her parent's address as Nina had instructed. Anna knew it was risky but felt she could establish contact without revealing anything. And she wanted to. She missed Nina and knew Nina would be proud of her. Anna's father's letters were both distressing and annoying in his obsession with the coming family disaster, so Anna was curious to see if Nina's perspective and experience in Lyon were similar. Without telling her the particulars. Not in the first letter. She had always meant to keep up the friendship but here it was over a year and a half later. She felt guilty and fearful to make this first step, but was certain Nina would be especially careful in her communications. Anna explained how Nina should address mail to Karl's post office box, without telling her why. To cover for the months she remained in Limoges, Anna explained she worked office jobs waiting for the war to end. She had naively believed the war would be over soon and she would be able to return to Paris and resume her medical studies. The invasion of the Soviet Union made her realize nothing was going to happen for years. She planned on returning home soon.

As the winter months settled in there was no question of trying to live on the streets. In December it rained nearly every day so Anna moved quietly from one small, unrecorded hotel room to another as her short leases ended. She changed rooms constantly for security purposes, but also so she wouldn't go mad. The big problem with bad weather and having to stay indoors was she could not come out of character. If she rented a room as her disabled old woman, she had to remain in character the entire time she was there. It was difficult because the portrayal was hard on her physically. She had to walk slowly in short feeble steps, her back bent over, her focus entirely on staying in character. She was very good at it and was proud of her ability to maintain the character for days at a time, but it was mentally and physically exhausting.

The other problem with staying indoors in the "special" rooms was the attention of men. There was no question most of the tenants were men, and the few women who used the rooms tended to be prostitutes who lived elsewhere. This was the major reason she remained in the disabled old woman disguise, because most men would ignore her as a potential sexual partner. But even as an old woman, she knew she treaded a fine line on her personal safety. If she got to know a proprietor for a hotel well, they understood here was a person who did not want to be known by the police and had money. When one avoids the police at all costs and it is suspected one has money, it attracts attention. The wrong kind. There were many unsavory characters moving in and about these particular hotels, and for that reason Anna tended to do her sleeping during the day where there was more activity around. Men would follow her, even as a disabled old woman as she went to her room, and more than once she turned on a man with her larger kitchen knife visible down low near her thigh. Few words were spoken, but some men cursed her or laughed when they saw the knife. Some may have thought of it as a challenge, but in all cases they turned away. Not trusting the flimsy locks or the fact the proprietor might sell the key for a price, Anna made a couple of braces out of discarded wooden flagpoles to jam the door knob to the floor or to a solid piece of furniture. These safeguards worked well until Christmas Day.

The dark, solitary streets of the failing businesses away from the main thoroughfare of Limoges were deserted and dreary on Christmas. Anna felt lonely and sought company and a decent dinner at a Turkish restaurant, one of the very few eating establishments open. There was only one other customer, and Anna noticed the proprietor flipped over the sign to CLOSED and turned off the exterior neon lighting once they took her order. She came as a disabled old woman, but sat up straight and chatted amiably with the owner's wife in her rusty Italian. The wife spoke halting French, but conversed fluently in Italian with the other customer, so Anna engaged the women and the atmosphere livened up. Anna had ordered the lamb, and realized immediately her decision to speak Italian broke the barrier, and other members of the family came out to join the conversation.

The family had lived for many years in Taranto and Naples before immigrating to France. They lived in Marseille for a few years but found it too hot and dry. Anna described her early days as a child vacationing in Nice and Genoa, ascribing her gift with languages to her mother, and her fluency in Italian to her Italian nanny and housekeeper.

137

"You were rich!" They exclaimed in wonder, looking at her worn clothing.

"My father was a lawyer," she explained, "and made a lot of money. I chose my own path."

The owner and his family seemed to ponder this for a few minutes, as the conversation flagged until he opened another bottle of wine for Anna.

"We too had money—riches, but we left it all behind." He said quietly, his eyes sad but bright.

"But Poppa got us all out, and no one was left behind!" His wife said proudly, her eyes flashing at Anna and admiringly at her husband. "It cost him everything we had, but the family—all of the family got out!"

Anna, a little confused, nodded and sipped at her wine to be polite.

"We're Christian Turks," the husband explained in a low voice, "to stay would have been the death of my family."

"We're not Muslims," the wife said defiantly, her chin coming up. "To most Turks, we might as well be Armenians! No one cares if we've lived there for 20 generations!"

"We were accepted for all those centuries, but times change and suddenly a new regime determined we are undesirables—as you say in France, a disease, something to be eliminated, like rats, or cockroaches!"

"Yes!" One of the family members chimed in, "like the Jews! Like the Jews!"

Anna drank too much wine, feeling giddy and clumsy as she said her farewells to the family. At first, they didn't want her to pay for her meal, citing the gesture as a Christian thing to do—a Christmas gift. But Anna insisted; *you need to eat, pay your rent!* The owner's wife did press a large piece of wrapped lamb and a bun of sweetbread into Anna's hands, which she graciously accepted. The evening warmed her heart. It was good to be with people, good people, where she could almost be herself. Both of the adults were at least 10 years older than her, but because of her character role, they treated Anna as a respected elder.

Perhaps it was the wine or the sense of the good will from the restaurant, but Anna was not as careful as she could have been as she entered the hotel. The small, shabby lobby was almost deserted with the exception of two middle-aged men who stopped talking when she came in. The clerk was not at his post. The two men were sharing a bottle of wine, Anna recognizing them as sometime street vendors on market days.

"*Bon soir, Monsieurs,*" she said cordially. "Merry Christmas to you."

The two men, who she realized appeared quite drunk, stared at her for a moment before one of them, a tall thin man, waved to bring her over.

"*Bon soir, Madame,*" he slurred thickly, "come join us for a drink." He looked at the food in her hand and raised his chin in expectation.

"What is that you have in your hand?    Something to share, perhaps?"

Immediately wary, Anna, shook her head and pointed towards the small elevator without stopping.

"*Merci, No, Monsieurs.* It's a gift and I need my rest. *Bon soir.*" The tall thin man rose slightly from his seat and nodded, a simple courtesy, but to Anna, it felt odd and strangely threatening. The elevator was already on the first floor, the cage just barely large enough for two people. Anna stepped in and turned around, closing the door quickly behind her. She was alarmed when the tall thin man suddenly appeared next to the cage, his hands on the bars. Anna pushed the lever for up and selected her floor, intentionally choosing the floor above the floor she needed. The mechanism whirred and the counter weights started to slide up.

"*Bon soir, Madame.*"  The man said slowly, his hands still on the bars as the elevator started to slowly jerk upwards.  He was unshaven but his clothes were clean.  What made her most uncomfortable were his eyes, unblinking, large and yellow like a cat's.  They swept slowly over her body from head to toe as the elevator rumbled up.

Anna learned early she couldn't carry her entire stash of currency with her on a daily basis.  It made quick disguise changes impossible and besides it was uncomfortable and unsafe.  In October she acquired three two-kilo coffee cans with tight lids.  With a lot of effort, she managed to stuff 2,000 *Reichsmarks* in each can, hiding one in a ventilation grate and burying the other two near the roots of a huge, well-established juniper bush surrounding the entranceway to the public library, a favorite sleeping spot in milder weather.  That left her with nearly 2,000 *Reichsmarks* in 12 bundles she distributed in a variety of locations in her clothing, the bottom of her wheeled cart, sleeves sewn into her blankets, her winter coat, and even her brassieres.  Anna had found most homeless people in Limoges, the very few she allowed to get even nominally close to her, left one another's personal possessions alone.  No one really owned anything worth stealing, and there was a mutual understanding they were all in the same situation and theft shouldn't be one of their concerns.  Unless someone suspected you had money.

Anna entered her small room with the single electric coil the proprietor allowed her to heat water for tea.  She felt unsettled and nervous.  There was only one light bulb in the room attached to a small lamp with a fabric shade, and she turned it on.  It provided both light and warmth, but she felt cold and frightened in a way she rarely experienced once she was in a room.  The yellow eyes of the tall thin man seemed to follow her in the dark shadows of the room, so Anna pulled the big knife from her thigh attachment and kept it in her hand.

She'd been in this room nearly a week and had never seen the two men in the lobby before, and it bothered her she didn't see the clerk.  She braced the door knob with her makeshift poles, sliding the flimsy lock into the cracked slot in the doorframe.  It looked like it had been sheared off in the past and simply glued back in place.  She wanted to take off her dress and her wig, but it was cold in the room and something told her to keep her disguise on.  The door frame was not square and she could see spaces in the gaps between her door and the jams.  If someone came very close to the door, perhaps they could see inside.  With bits of newspaper she stuffed the spaces tight knowing it would fall when she opened the door.  Once she was done she settled down to read, her eyes occasionally drifting to the door whenever she thought she heard a sound or movement in the corridor.

She awoke with a start having fallen asleep when she tried so hard not to, but there was no overcoming the effects of the wine.  She wasn't used to it.  She almost never drank, but the Turkish family had poured for all and she wanted to share for a short time in their happiness.  Now awake, she heard the creak of the loose floorboards in the corridor, sensing the presence of someone just outside her door.  She was frozen with fear, not knowing what to do.  The lock in the door rattled gently with the pressure of a key, and as the knob turned there was a brief resistance as the unlocked door pressed against the flimsy slide lock and Anna's makeshift doorstop.  Anna gasped and realized her knife was not in her hand.  She leaned up out of the bed and spotted the knife on the floor where it had fallen just as the door failed.

The slide lock exploded out against simple plaster and Anna's poles skewed sideways in a shower of rotted wood.  Anna didn't have time to scream.  The two men were in the room in a flash, one throwing a pillow against her face and slamming her bodily back down on her bed, the other jumping on the bed to control her legs.  For a horrifying second Anna thought they intended to smother her, as the pillow was pressed hard against her face and strong hands sought to wrestle down her arms.

Whoever had control of the pillow slid his body across hers, his heavy legs kneeling painfully into her knees and thighs, his elbows pinning her arms to her chest.

"Get the door—close it and jam it with the stick!"  The man whispered hoarsely.  Anna, who couldn't breathe with the pillow pressed tightly against her face, recognized the voice of the tall thin man from the lobby.  This created panic as she struggled against the darkness and the pressure until it suddenly lifted slightly, letting in a clutch of fresh air. She sucked in a deep breath just as it was closed off again.

"Stop fighting, old woman!" She heard him say breathlessly, and her brain, registering for a moment he just might not mean to kill her, sent the message to quit struggling. After a moment the pillow was cautiously lifted off her face, and Anna, breathing deeply of the fresh air, gasped anew when the face with the yellow eyes appeared inches from her own, the cold steel of the kitchen knife pressing against her throat.

"This belong to you, old woman?" The man sneered, poking the tip of the blade just above her Adam's apple, puncturing the skin.

"Yes," she gasped, "what do you want? I'm just an old woman I don't have anything of value, *please!*" The man glanced over his shoulder as the other man stood next to the bed.

"Check her bag, her coat—it's got be here somewhere." His yellow eyes, so unusually large and clear, seemed to get larger as he leaned in closer, his brow furrowed with sudden interest. He was looking at her eyes and slowly drew back. Anna trembled as his fingers, large and rough with crusty tips, traced around her nose and lips. Suddenly his hand shot out and grasped Anna's wig, jerking it up and off her head, revealing her hair net and matted, damp blond hair.

"Well, well, *Mademoiselle,* what have we here?" The tall man waved his companion over. "Look at this, Claude." His companion's eyes grew large in surprise and then delight when he saw Anna cringing without her wig.

"I can explain," Anna stammered, "the *Surete* and the *Abwehr* think I'm an enemy spy and they are hunting for me, I have to use disguises."

"Enemy spy, *Mademoiselle?* Perhaps so… you have a very good, expensive wig here, and you seem to have an endless supply of money…you look well fed. You do a good job, you were well trained. We thought for sure we were robbing an old woman!" The tall man and his companion laughed, but Anna became even more afraid as the man pressed the knife tip up and into the flesh of her throat, making her whimper. The man's eyes compressed to slits for the first time and she felt his rough hand sliding inside her dress. It kept moving, down under her brassiere until he found a nipple. He squeezed it, hard, forcing Anna to gasp and cry out again.

"Shut up," he said coldly, "we want the money, the *Reichsmarks* you're flashing around. We thought we were dealing with an old woman who traded in the black market with the Germans, but looks like…" his hand traced farther down her dress, ripping the fabric and her slip underneath to feel her stomach and pubic hair, "we got ourselves a French girl who likes German cock." His hand withdrew and slowly pulled the

141

knife away from the skin under her throat. He brought the blade up where Anna could see it, the tip red with her blood.

"Is that what we got?" He asked, his eyes flaring open wide again, taking her all in with a sweeping glance. Anna shriveled inside, sensing his eyes looking at her body just as a predator would view a prey. "You a *Boche* lover *Mademoiselle,* eh?"

He suddenly shook his head and smiled, the coldness in his eyes sending fresh shivers of terror into Anna's heart.

"It doesn't matter to us, really what you're trying to hide. But we don't see too many *madames* or *mademoiselles* trying to pass as old ladies over here in this quarter, it's kind of—dangerous. You have something to hide from the *Sureté,* the *Abwehr*—whoever, we don't care. But you have money, *Mademoiselle,* and we want some of it. It's a simple thing for you, show us the money, or I'll cut those little cute nipples of yours right off your tits. No one is going to know, and no one is going to care what happens to you, so let's start right here and you show us the money."

Anna decided she had no choice and pointed out where she had created seams in her clothing to conceal the small bundles of *Reichsmarks.* They tore her clothing apart once they saw how ingeniously she had created seams in the folds. The two men counted the money and continued to rip up her mattress, her blankets, even the soles of her shoes. They removed every stitch of clothing from her, leaving her tied to the bed loosely covered with a bedsheet. Once they were satisfied they had searched and found every bit of her money, she prayed they would leave her alone, but she realized they considered her a gold mine and had every intention in returning.

"What are you going to do, *Mademoiselle,* call the police?" The tall man laughed. "I suspect you have more of it stashed away somewhere, so we'll be back tomorrow and help you find it, eh?"

The two men grew louder as the evening went on, and if there were other guests in the adjoining rooms, they were silent. Anna couldn't pull the bedsheet over her body as the two men gathered their loot and stuffed it into Anna's rolling cart. They picked up her wrapped lamb, sniffed it, and put it and the sweetbread into the cart. They exchanged glances and both started unbuckling their pants.

"Something to leave you with, *Mademoiselle,*" The tall one leered, as he rolled her over on her stomach, forcing her legs apart and pulling her hips up. "To remind you little whores we Frenchmen don't like our women fucking the *Boche.*" He leaned over and pressed his face close to hers, stroking her hair.

"We've been watching you, *Mademoiselle.* You're very good, you sure fooled us! But we know who you are now, and where you go when the weather is better. Don't try to run away, because we'll find you. And you know yourself you can't go to the *gendarmerie!* Limoges is a small town, really, when you must stay underground, eh?"

The two men finally did leave after an hour. The two took turns taking her, vaginally and anally, ignoring her cries and whimpering. When they departed, they left her only a cotton pullover and a thin pair of pants. They did this on purpose, she knew, because it was cold outside and she would not survive without any winter clothing. It was their way of keeping her in place. They promised to return by noon to "help her find the rest of the money." There was blood on the bed, but Anna rolled into a ball and cried. She cried in pain and her shame. They hurt her and didn't care and it made her feel small and worthless. After several minutes she cleaned herself up the best she could, and searched the room in vain for a pair of shoes and a weapon, but they took all of her knives. She tore a coverlet off the little side chair and fashioned a shawl out it, and searched the room again for anything they might have left her. They were very thorough and there was nothing. They took everything from her. As the minutes passed her shame slowly turned into anger because it was done by Frenchmen, not because she was a *Juif* but because she was a woman and vulnerable. She was hurt, physically and couldn't walk without a hobble, but she didn't care anymore, she was getting out.

She knew she could learn to hate men if it wasn't for a man like Karl, the enemy of her countrymen, a man who treated her with respect and kindness. She certainly hated two of the species, and there was no changing her mind or any sense of understanding or acceptance. They robbed and raped her, taking everything they believed was of value from her, and they would have possibly done the same to her alternative persona, Anna the old disabled woman. They would let her starve without giving her a second thought. The anger she felt slowly cooled into resolve, her recognition they had taken from her, but not all. And they want to come back.

The lobby was deserted when she crept through it. No one was behind the desk. She knew the clerk must have been in on it, or the proprietor. She thought just for a moment to set the lobby on fire, but she hurt so much she simply turned away. It wasn't raining outside, but it was very chilly. She wouldn't last long, they were right. Without her wigs or any disguises, she was a young blond woman entirely inappropriately dressed and would be picked up by the *gendarmerie* as a vagrant or mental patient. It would then be a matter of hours before her other identity would come up. Anna turned and started walking and realized she had absolutely no idea where to go or what to do. She could get to her stash of money, but she was afraid the two men might be looking

143

for her and might follow her. She sat on a bench shivering, her feet bare and dirty on the ice-cold ground. It was the only thing she could think of to do, the only place that might welcome her. She could acquire things through them and repay them once she was sure she was not followed. It was still very early and no one was moving about. Staying to the shadows, Anna headed for the basement with the Turkish restaurant.

# Chapter 16

*February 11, 1942. Limoges, France.*

When Anna opened her eyes she panicked because it was so dark. She must have screamed because a door burst open and within moments people gathered around her, the light coming up as she smelled sulphur from a match and burning kerosene.   It took her several seconds to recognize the owner and his wife, soon joined by other familiar faces hard to place just yet.  The owner's wife, whose name was Selin, came around the bed and gently smoothed the soft, thick comforter covering the bed while caressing Anna's hair.  It had been so many months since Karl last held her, she found the kind touch of another human being almost confusing.   Especially since the last contact was so frightening and painful.   Despite her initial fearful response, Anna quickly accepted Selin's warm fingers, turning gratefully towards her.   The family's kindness towards a complete stranger baffled her, especially since Anna had little recollection of her journey to the Turkish restaurant.  There was nothing to associate her with the family, and she didn't have a single piece of identification and very little clothing.  The last time she saw them she was in the disguise of an old woman with a gray hair wig.  It was a miracle she found the place, a miracle they chose to bring her in.  It was so cold that night she got confused trying to find the right street, her feet and hands numb as the frozen stones slowly infested her limbs and chest.  She knew she must have wandered for hours.

"Good evening, Anna," Selin said soothingly in Italian, "you're safe and warm and no one can hurt you now."  Confused, Anna stared at the woman.

"How do you know who I am?" She asked.  "How did you know I spoke Italian?"

"Because you told us!"  Selin smiled broadly, delighted to reveal the secret.   The entire family began speaking all at once before she shushed them with a curt wave of her hand.  "Be quiet, all of you!   Let me explain what happened!"

It was Monday and the restaurant was closed.   It was by chance Ahmet, the eldest son, came to the front entrance carrying two rounds of cheese and discovered Anna lying near the door.   He didn't recognize her, but being a young man nearly 18 years old, the appearance of a young barefooted woman with insufficient clothing unconscious on the doorstep was cause for alarm and more than a little interest.

"You were *blue,* and I mean *blue* like the sky, you were so cold. Your face, your lips, I thought for sure you would not survive the night!"

Selin said shaking her head as she leaned over and caressed Anna's face with both hands, a familiar, motherly gesture Anna did not miss.  Selin explained they first thought Anna was an escaped German Jew from one of the smaller internment camps recently established in Limoges, and they didn't know what to do.

"Are you going to just let her die of exposure, my dear husband asks?"  Selin said quietly, looking at her husband.  They brought Anna in and decided to call for a doctor, an unlicensed Turkish immigrant like themselves currently working part time as a butcher.  The doctor, a former surgeon, cared for the small Turkish immigrant population for low fees.  He could not prescribe any drugs other than what could be acquired through the black market, but the population had little use for them anyway.  He examined Anna and informed the family of her physical attack, prescribing bed rest with lots of warm hot water bottles and physically massaging her hands, arms, feet and legs to restore her damaged circulation.

Anna was delirious for nearly two days, Selin said, and it was while Selin was massaging Anna's legs Anna began speaking, first in French, then German and finally Italian.  She spoke of Karl, and Nina and Clara—of the loss of these people, and her need to hide from someone.  *Ambar? Amwar?*  She then started talking about Anna, then Anna Metzgen, which changed again into Anna Metzger.  By then, Selin said, they began to realize they didn't have an escaped German Jew, because they remembered Anna Metzger very well.  But this was not the Anna Metzger they remembered, this was no old woman.  It was Selin who looked at Anna's eyes carefully and decided this in fact was the same woman, only 40 years younger!  The clincher was when Anna began talking about the Turkish restaurant as her last hope, if she could just remember where it was…

Anna stayed with the family for nearly three weeks.  Ten days passed before she could stand on her feet for any length of time, her feet hurt so badly.  The doctor came twice to check up on her, explaining her toes were nearly frozen with the exposure to the cold stones of the street, and a certain amount of circulation loss would occur throughout her life.  He noticed her ankle scars from the car accident, and asked her to walk to and from him several times.  He was a tall, thin middle-aged man with piercing blue eyes that set his face apart because of his dark black hair and olive skin.

"You are a lovely young woman," he said admiringly, "you should have that ankle reset.  You have a slight limp that can be corrected easily."  Selin glanced at the doctor with irritation and had Anna sit down.

"She has other things to worry about, and you, Yusuf, should stick to business!" The doctor, offended, accepted the large portion of lamb Selin offered him and left.

"Don't worry about the doctor," Selin demurred, "he's harmless. He's married to my cousin and takes himself too seriously sometimes! But we're all here because we're Christians—but," she added with sadness, "we're *not* fascists. We have nowhere to go in Europe right now. Turkey doesn't want us. The Italian government is fascist and so is Spain. And *Vichy—Vichy* is a mess."

There was no way of explaining why Anna wore disguises and was living on the streets of Limoges. In many ways, at first, she couldn't understand their kindness and willingness to take care of someone who so obviously was trying to hide from the police. But as the days past she realized the Turkish community in Limoges, isolated from most of French society by choice, was living very much an underground existence like herself. Selin's husband, Ali, avoided paying taxes and restaurant fees by paying slightly less to certain city officials and one middle-ranking officer in the municipal police. The police, Selin explained, never come into this quarter unless there is a reported serious crime. When Selin asked her directly one day why she was hiding and didn't report the attack to the police, since, after all, she was a French citizen, Anna simply stared at this kind, warm-hearted woman. *You told us about your upbringing in Aix, remember?* Selin said, encouragingly. *Your Italian nanny and the big house in the city? Your father was a lawyer? Was that all true?*

*Yes.* Anna whispered. *All true. But not in the past, today. My father is still a lawyer. And I—I was a medical student in Paris until the Germans came.*

There was no one else in the room as the family was busy preparing for the evening opening of the restaurant. Anna stared at Selin with her eyes damp before glancing down at her new shoes. Selin slid her chair closer and as before, with a mother's touch, gently brought up Anna's chin before cupping her cool hands around Anna's face.

"I cannot begin to repay you for your kindness," Anna croaked. "But, I will. I have some money hidden away. You have fed me, bought me new clothes, paid for my doctor's bills and treated me—like one of your family." Selin nodded and said nothing, her warm dark eyes carefully searching Anna's.

"Sometimes children, maybe not ones you raised, come into your life for a reason, Anna. You came to us the other night for dinner as an old woman, and it was like having an old family friend around. Then you came back, hurt and abandoned by those animals, but we saw who you really are. But the two are the same, understand? Yes? I recognized you. You came here because you had no other place. This was your only home. You think we would push you away? There is something old world about you, Anna, I can't place it, but we are—what should I say—one and the same, you and me." Selin lifted her arms and stood up and so did Anna. They embraced for several minutes. They both cried then quietly resumed their seats. Anna smiled and wiped her eyes, her hands in tight fists in her lap. Selin waited patiently, looking at Anna's hands.

"Why are you holding back, Anna?" She said.

Anna insisted Selin and Ali tally up the expenses they ran up for her; clothes, medical bills and extra food, because she had every intention on paying it all back. Selin had somehow acquired a number of things Anna wouldn't have dared ask for without any money, including a new shopping cart, a small knapsack, a raincoat, warm winter boots, gloves, and an outdated but warm full-length wool coat. Anna made it clear she would stay no longer than what it took to get her well enough to walk a fair distance. Three weeks wasn't quite enough, but she felt she had taken their hospitality to the limit. She promised she would return with what she owed them within a day.

A few days before Anna was to leave, Anna met Kerem, the son-in-law. Ali, Selin and Kerem sat down with Anna and Kerem asked Anna to describe her attackers and the circumstances of their meeting. Both Ali and Kerem exchanged glances as Anna described the tall thin man with large yellow eyes. As Anna spoke her voice broke because she became visibly upset, and Selin suggested perhaps they should stop. *No, Anna insisted, I want to know who these men are!*

Kerem, who worked in a warehouse not far from the river, knew both men. Ali was familiar with the man with the yellow eyes. *Both are members of crime gangs, black market and extortionists*, he said. Ali shook his head, drawing his finger across his throat. *The bastard with the yellow eyes is named Maurice. He's a killer.* Ali glanced at Anna, regretting immediately when he saw the look of horror in Anna's eyes. He leaned forward, looking at her carefully.

"He was with a couple of other men a few months ago trying to extort a protection fee from the restaurant. They discovered it by accident and thought we would play along. I played dumb and couldn't understand his French. He got mad and frustrated, tossing some furniture around and finally grabbed me around the neck. I thought he was going to snap it, but Selin pointed my big MAS 73 pistol at him and he backed down." Ali looked over at Selin with a loving smile and nodded. "She would have shot him dead, I seen her do it in the old country when things were bad.

148

I thought we would see them again but we haven't. You want to stay away from them, Anna."

"The other one's name is Claude," said Anna quietly. She looked up at Kerem and Ali and Kerem nodded, his eyes widening.

"Yes, his name is Claude. He's not much better than Maurice, just a thief and thug. They live off of what they steal and extort. If they see you again, Anna, they will hunt you down. You're a known prey. Stay away from them, stay away from that part of town."

Selin helped Anna dye her hair dark brown, but that wasn't good enough for Selin. She fussed over Anna's face for several minutes before deciding to first dye Anna eyebrows, then mixed up a makeup base potion to darken her pale skin to a light olive sheen.

"Now, Anna, you could pass for an Italian, a Spaniard or even a Turk!" The men of the family came around and examined Selin's work, and both Ahmet and Kerem pronounced the result excellent. Ahmet, a shy boy, blushed as he looked at Anna perhaps a little too long. Selin glanced at the boy and slapped his shoulder with embarrassment.

"What's the matter with you, Ahmet!"

Anna turned and smiled at the boy and he blushed again. Selin produced a small hand mirror for Anna to see for herself. "You are beautiful either way, Anna! Those bastards will be looking for a pale blond and this allows you to move about in the quarter without being recognized." Anna stared at the image in the mirror and couldn't believe it. She spoke the words without thinking.

"My God, I look just like my sister, Clara…"

"Your sister looks like—this?" Selin asked cautiously. Anna put the mirror down and met Selin's eyes.

"Yes," she said. "My sister looks more like my father and her grandmother. I look like my mother. My mother is Polish with German and Russian roots. My father is also Polish, but…" she let the words drift off. "He has darker features, dark hair."

Selin let it go and put together a small package of makeup and hair dye for Anna to take with her. When Anna explained the first thing she needed to do was to get her money so she could pay the family back, Selin asked where the money was hidden and what time of day Anna planned on retrieving it. Anna trusted the family well enough to describe the canister under the heating grate behind a hotel. The best time to get it, would be late at night when there were few prying eyes. Selin was horrified and shook her head emphatically saying *no no no!* That is the most dangerous time, Anna! Especially for a young woman! Anna tried to explain to Selin she had lived on the streets for months and knew what she was doing, but Selin would have none of it. She enlisted the help of Ahmet and her son-in-law to go with Anna, especially since Anna insisted on doing it in the dark.  Ahmet would be a watcher at the end of the alleyway and Kerem would be her bodyguard.  Anna gratefully accepted, as she planned to bring the canister back to the restaurant with all of its contents, so she could repay the family and also purchase new items for her disguises.

Anna looked over Kerem, who was in his early 30s and strongly built.  Selin explained Kerem was actually a Spaniard by birth, but his mother came from both Italian and Turkish roots.  He had fought against the fascists in Spain, although he was not a Communist.  He had spent time in a prisoner of war camp in Spain and was briefly arrested and held by the *Vichy* at the internment camp at Gurs, near the Spanish border, because they arrested all the fighters escaping across the border.  He was eventually released with a large group of former soldiers in a prisoner exchange, but slipped back into France, knowing he faced a firing squad under Franco's regime.  Selin smiled and patted Kerem's shoulder affectionately, then gripped his arm muscle as if to test his strength.

"Kerem was a strong soldier, and he will protect you, Anna."  She nodded to Kerem as if to remind him of something, and he left the room. He came back a moment later with a small oil cloth and unwrapped the contents on the table.  The first item was a worn, well-oiled small automatic pistol.  He placed a spare magazine and a dozen extra cartridges on the table.  Then he unrolled a large but narrow folding knife next to the pistol.

"Do you know guns, Anna?"  Selin asked.  Anna knew a little about them and said so, as her father owned a small revolver and a shotgun.  She admitted she was not familiar with the little pistol, which didn't even have an exposed hammer.  Semi-automatic pistols were not intuitive as whatever happened in the mechanism was out of sight.  There was not a clear connection from pulling the trigger with the cylinder turning and lining up with the barrel, and the hammer cocking back like a revolver.  *I understand*, Karem said.

Karem carefully pushed the button releasing the magazine from the butt of the gun, then demonstrated the gun was empty by pulled the operating slide back and forth several times and showing the mechanism to Anna.

"This is a Ruby.  .32 caliber.  It holds nine bullets," he explained slowly.  He reinserted the magazine, which appeared to have bullets in it, back into the butt of the gun.  He carefully pulled the slide back and showed Anna how the bolt moved forward, picking up the first cartridge from the magazine and loading the chamber.

"Once you do this, Anna, all you have to do is pull the trigger, nine times until the magazine is empty. There is a safety catch, here on the left side, but it doesn't work all that well. The best safety catch is to keep your finger out of the trigger guard until you are ready to shoot. You try it."

Anna cautiously picked up the pistol, clumsy at first in determining how to hold the gun as she pressed the magazine release. Kerem, who stayed very close, helped her keep her fingers out of the trigger guard as he showed her again how to flick off the safety, then pull the slide back and ejecting the cartridge from the chamber.

"Check it again," he said firmly. "Never trust that a gun is unloaded." Anna fumbled with the pistol, but finally decided to hold the butt of the gun in her right hand as she pulled the slide back to check the chamber. She did this several times until it engaged quickly with a solid click. Kerem smiled and handed her the magazine.

"Now load the gun and eject every cartridge out of the magazine." This was a little harder, but if she held the butt of the gun firmly in her right hand, she was able to pull the slide back repeatedly until all eight cartridges fell onto the table. Kerem picked up the cartridges, examining them for any damage. He showed Anna how to load all nine into the magazine. He pushed them all out with his fingers into Anna's open palms, and had her load the magazine all by herself. This was difficult, but eventually she did it and put the gun on the table. Anna looked at the gun, the two loaded magazines and 12 extra cartridges before turning to Selin.

"Why did you show me this? You want me to carry this tonight?"

"No Anna, Kerem will carry the gun and knife tonight. But when you leave us, it's our gift to you. From Kerem."

"Don't you need it? Doesn't the family need a weapon?"

"Kerem has several guns he smuggled back to France from Spain. We have Ali's big MAS 73. This is a small gun, perfect for a woman." Selin smiled as she picked up the folding knife, which Anna noticed for the first time had worn burl scales, like a *Liguole*.

"Do you know what this is?"

"Well, a pocket knife." Selin turned the knife over in her hand revealing a large nickel button of some kind. She pushed the button up and the blade, double edged and a full 13 centimeters long sprang out instantly, locking in place. Selin held the blade up so Anna could examine it before expertly folding the blade at the lower end of the shaft, below the edged blades. She locked the release button and handed it to Anna.

"From Marseille, something no man or woman should walk the streets without!"

Despite the warmth of the family and their apparent acceptance of Anna into the household, she knew she was a danger to them despite their reassurances they too lived underground. She had to distance herself from them, but at first it was hard so for a number of weeks she returned every few days to get money, which she kept in their cellar, or change into one of her disguises. The family never asked again why she required disguises. It was almost as good as having the apartment in terms of convenience, except she no longer stayed at their residence behind the restaurant to sleep. Selin made it clear she was always welcome, but Anna sensed there was too much risk. She repaid the 100 *Reichsmarks* the family ran up for her and gave Selin 300 more.

She cautiously approached her good black-market sources, always conscious of any one following her or observing her, and managed to acquire new ration cards and some hard-to-get clothing items, like ladies' underthings. Wigs were still available at high cost at the higher-end department stores, and Anna was able to purchase used clothing for her new disguises at the numerous thrift stores popping up in Limoges. She kept her hair short and dyed dark brown, using the eye brow makeup and facial base much of the time. It was a mistake downtown. The thing she noticed now was the police did not look at her the same. With her blond hair and fair skin, she was an acceptable French citizen. With dark hair and olive skin, she was a foreigner. She learned from this and saved the facial base for when she was near the peripheral sections of the city. As she moved closer to the business district during the day, which was necessary to purchase the items of clothing she needed, she also noticed a much stronger presence of *gendarmerie* and *Vichy* troops. This alarmed her and despite her personal reservations, she decided to avoid coming downtown unless she was in the guise of her old woman. She avoided the post office for a little longer, remembering what the yellow-eyed man had said about "knowing all of your places."

In late February she was staying in an off-list hotel room because it was cold with snow flurries all week. She avoided the Turkish restaurant for several days, but she was getting low on cash. She had nearly 1,000 *Reichsmarks* in the canister in the cellar, and when the weather broke in the late spring, she planned to dig up the two remaining canisters under the bushes near the public library. Anna left the hotel in the early afternoon in the guise of the old woman; her updated disguise had the woman more upright, allowing a bit more speed, although she still used her cane. She toted her shopping cart with her and turned down the corner of the seedy street. She sensed almost at once someone observing her from behind, so she crossed the street and cautiously looked both ways, as would be prudent. She spotted the young man about 30 paces behind her, stopping to light a cigarette and turn his head away. Anna stared hard to determine if there was anything familiar about the man's profile, but she wasn't sure. But she was certain the young man stayed behind her when she crossed the street and resumed her journey.

It was afternoon, grim and gray, but there was daylight and if he was going to rob her, he would have to pick his spot carefully. Anna considered her options, and gratefully touched the pistol tucked under what looked like an old woman's drooping stomach. It was loaded and cocked. The knife was inside a small narrow sheath hanging between her breasts like a heavy necklace. The knife gave her a headache, but Selin told her emphatically it was the best place for a woman. She practiced and found she could pull it from the sheath and deploy the blade in less than a second.

Anna moved directly to the larger streets, away, unfortunately from the Turkish restaurant. As soon as it was apparent she was headed towards the central downtown area, the young man disappeared. She double backed on side streets twice, stopping often in doorways to establish a clear view of the street behind her. There were a few pedestrians visible, but nothing set off any alarm bells. She stopped for coffee at a tiny café, purchasing a newspaper and copying the example of her former *Abwehr* watchers, kept an eye out over the headlines. She could detect no shadows. After an hour she left the café and heading back towards the downtown before crossing the street two blocks up, slipping down a narrow alleyway and doubling back towards the restaurant once again.

When Anna got within a block of the restaurant she had to sit down, her old ankle injury and feet were hurting her so much. She found the steep steps of a former printmaking shop ideal, as there was a small retaining wall on both sides of the steps. When she sat down, she was not visible if she hunched forward unless the observer was across the street. The weaving through several kilometers of lumpy streets was nothing she was prepared for. She was not in very good shape, and the winter had restricted her movement even more. After a few minutes she got up and entered an alleyway she knew would allow her to approach the basement restaurant unseen. She stopped and looked up and down the alleyway until she was convinced no one was lurking about. At the end of the alleyway she stopped again and peered to the left towards the restaurant a third of a block down the narrow street, and was surprised when she saw the two police vehicles parked in front. She couldn't see any uniformed *Surete*, but she quietly turned around and retreated.

Anna double backed and entered a hotel she had used before for off-record rooms. She still had a couple of days left on her prepaid stay at the other hotel, but she needed a place to stay for the evening until the *Surete* left. The desk clerk looked familiar and acted like he recognized her, although her last use of the hotel was in early January and she was in the character of the old, disabled woman. The wig was about the same, but Anna was more upright and slightly more alert. She pushed the *Reichsmarks* across and the clerk simply nodded and gave her a key.

Anna examined the clerk carefully, knowing in her heart there was no way she could determine by looking at someone whether or not they would betray her. She trusted no one these days with the exception of Selin and her family, and she was worried sick something had happened. She decided to get some rest and then visit the restaurant after hours, when it was dark and the *Surete* would be gone. Once in her room she turned on the light and slid the heaviest piece of furniture, which was the single bed, right up against the door. She learned her lessons. Keys and broken locks would offer her no protection. A bed or bureau against the door would buy her a few seconds, and now she had both a gun and a knife.

It was scary and very dark when Anna approached the basement steps. There were few streetlights and the restaurant was dark on the front side. Anna, out of character because she was sure no one could see her, walked cautiously upright down the narrow street with the pistol in her hand close to her stomach. Not a sound could be heard except her own footsteps on the pavement stones. If someone had approached her she didn't know what she was going to do, but felt she had to see the family tonight. She could see dim lighting far back in the rear of the restaurant through a crack in the drawn blinds, but no one responded to her tapping for several minutes. Finally, she saw shadows moving about and a slat lifted from the inside, but the door remained latched.

"What do you want?" She heard what sounded like Ali just behind the door in his fractured French.

"It's me, Anna!" She whispered in Italian. There was no response until she saw more slats lift and another voice whispering behind the door.

"Go away, Anna! It's not safe for you to come here!" Ali's voice was muffled and strained, and he spoke slowly. Anna tapped on the window even harder.

"Please, Ali! Something has happened! You must tell me what's happened!"

There appeared to be an argument going on right beside the door, as another voice, female, grew more strident. Anna couldn't understand it, so she knew it was Turkish. The door unlatched a few centimeters, Ali's face close to the crack. There was something different about his appearance. The shiny barrel of his revolver was next to his chin.

Anna stepped closer but Ali held the door.

"Anna," his voice croaked and strangely muffled, "it is so dangerous for you to be here. They came looking for you this morning, and they forced their way in this time when Ahmet was bringing in bread. That bastard Maurice killed him! Killed my boy right in front of me!" His voice cracked and he moaned before taking a deep breath. The door opened wider and Ceyda, Ali and Selin's daughter and the wife of Kerem, pulled Anna inside.

"Come inside, Anna. Let me close and lock the door, I don't want anyone to see you coming in." Her voice was also strained and different, and she was having difficulty breathing. She put her arm around her father who couldn't stay on his feet, and led Anna through the darkness of the restaurant and into the living quarters. Once in the lit rooms Anna stopped dead in shock to see the broken furniture and total disarray of the house with every single drawer, cabinet and shelf dumped out onto the floor. From the floor her eyes were drawn to the dark pools of blood on the light tile of the kitchen, with blood spray and smeared handprints tracking all over the dining room wall. Her hand shot up to her mouth but she could only gasp in astonishment. The real horror came a few seconds later when she turned to look at Ali and Ceyda's faces under the lamplight.

The two men entered the restaurant about 10 in the morning, as Ahmet was carrying in the bread he had brought in by cart. They beat him senseless even though he had tried to defend himself. It was Maurice, the tall thin man with yellow eyes, and by his description, his cohort Claude. They were both armed this time and ready when the noise of the struggle in the entranceway attracted at first Kerem and Ali, and then Selin. Ceyda was in the cellar and thankfully, the children were at the Turkish school nearby.

Kerem was the biggest threat so Maurice shot Kerem point blank in the chest the second he entered the room. Ali was right behind him and stopped in his tracks until he saw Ahmet crumpled at Maurice's feet. Ali had no weapon but he was still a formidable man in his bulk and strength. He screamed and charged the two men directly, but for some reason Maurice lowered his pistol and clubbed Ali hard across the face with it, knocking him down. They proceeded to kick and stomp Ali repeatedly until Selin arrived armed only with a large knife.

"My mother has always been a fighter," Ceyda said both sadly and proudly "And she does know how to fight, with either a knife or a gun!

155

I was just coming up the cellar with all the noise and saw my mother bury her knife into the younger man's thigh! He howled like an animal. I think she stabbed him at least two or three times before one of them shot her…"

"Your *mother* is dead? *Selin* is dead?" The magnitude of what had happened was starting to sink in. "And Kerem? And Ahmet?"

During this early period of the attack, which only consumed a minute or so, the two men never said why they were attacking the family. When Maurice saw Ceyda run back into the kitchen, which he probably determined was where there might be a gun, he stopped pummeling Ali and chased Ceyda. Claude was going nowhere, as he writhed on the floor in agony. Ceyda was actually looking for a knife as she had no idea where Ali kept his guns and Kerem hid most of his firearms in the cellar. As she pulled a knife from the drawer Maurice was already upon her, pinning her arms down and slamming her against the counter until he disarmed her, screaming. He threw the knife in the sink and punched Ceyda twice in the face with his fists. Blood spurted from her nose and split lips, and she gasped in stunned pain. Maurice stepped back and slapped her very hard almost knocking her unconscious, then jerked her up by gripped her throat.

"Where is the money hidden, kitten, from your good friend Anna Metzger? Eh?" Ceyda's French was not very good, but she understood him. She was choking from lack of air as Maurice lifted her off her feet with his grip. Maurice dropped her when he heard the screams of his partner in the other room change to shrieks of pain and fear.

Ali had gotten to his feet and saw Claude on the floor moaning in pain from Selin's stab wounds. Selin was lying there with her eyes open, dead, and the knife she used to stab Claude was between the two. Ali looked at his beautiful wife who had tried to defend him before scooping up the knife and falling on Claude with all of his weight, plunging the knife deep into Claude's chest multiple times. He didn't think to look for Claude's pistol, lying under the body, but got up and stumbled to the kitchen with the knife in his hand, remembering the screams of his daughter seconds before.

He rushed into the kitchen like a bull with the knife in front of him, running headlong into Maurice with the pistol outstretched. They collided hard, their skulls slamming into one another, but not before Ali managed by accident to slash Maurice deeply in the forearm and superficially in the neck and face. Stunned from the collision, they both fell back, the knife and gun clattering to the tile floor.

Maurice got up first, dazed and dizzy. He held the corner of the wall and kicked Ali again in the head as he picked up his pistol, pointing at Ali's head as though he was going to shoot. After a pause he lowered the muzzle and booted Ali's knife to a corner in the kitchen as he looked around. He noticed for the first time the body of his partner, obviously dead, lying a few feet from Selin. Ahmet was coming around, lying where he was, holding his head and moaning. Maurice tore a thick dinner napkin from the cart and wrapped it around his deep slash wound. His face was bleeding and there was a large egg forming on his skull from his collision with Ali. He pulled out a dining room chair and sat down heavily. He looked around the restaurant and got to his feet again, looking carefully at Ahmet and Ali. He decided they posed no threat at that moment and started tearing the place apart.

Maurice was in the kitchen yanking out drawers and cupboards when he heard the crying and moaning coming from the front part of the restaurant. He discovered Ahmet on his knees with his arms around his mother, Selin, and rocking her body to some unheard rhythm. Maurice looked down at Ali as he passed him, his body still. He went directly to the boy and pointed the pistol at his head.

"Hey, quit your blubbering, you little wog! She's dead! You can't help her now!" It didn't take Maurice long to realize, like everybody else in this stupid wog family, nobody understood a word of French! Ahmet stared up at the bore of the pistol in uncomprehending fear, but he wouldn't leave his mother. Maurice had no tolerance for such sentiments. His own mother abandoned him before he was a year old. He knew orphanages and complete and total indifference to anything he might have ever wanted or cared for. So as an adult he would hardly be characterized as empathetic to his fellow man, or woman.

Without a sound, Maurice pointed towards his pistol and then pointed towards Ahmet. He used his index finger to give Ahmet a "come with me" signal. He pointed his finger at Ahmet again, and made the universal sign of no by shaking his head. Maurice made a sad face, then said "BANG" loudly. Ahmet got the message and slowly got to his feet. He made the sign of the cross over his mother as Maurice, who towered over him, grabbed him roughly by the arm and dragged him towards Ali's body.

He started kicking Ali in the abdomen, again and again until Ali slowly came to, his swollen eyelids carefully separating after being sealed with blood, serum and tears. Ali looked up at Maurice, the eyes growing thin and dark until they rested on Ahmet, tightly pressed against Maurice's chest.

"Ahmet..." Ali groaned, but it was a cry of relief. He had thought Ahmet was dead. He started to elbow his way up but Maurice pressed him down with his boot.

"Not so fast, wog!" Maurice jerked Admet's head closer to his and pressed the bore of his pistol against Admet's forehead so Ali could see it clearly.

"You understand French, wog? You understand what I'm saying?"

Ali kept to his original approach, looking up at Maurice questioningly as if he didn't understand. "No…" was all he said.

"Anna Metzger," Maurice said very slowly and loudly. "Anna Metzger. She lived here, still does for all I know. And Anna has money, *Reichsmarks*… lots of it!" Maurice rolled his fingers together in the universal symbol of cash. "You get that, right, wog?"

"Where is the…" Maurice again rolled his fingers and looked at Ali questioningly. He pointing his finger first at himself, then nodded, then pressed his pistol against Ahmet's forehead, and said "BANG!"

Ali closed his eyes and opened them again. He could sense the pressure on the trigger on the pistol against his son's head.

"I know nobody named Anna Metzger," he said in halting French. Maurice looked down at Ali in mock surprise, and shook his head.

"Really?" Funny, some of my—associates tell me Anna Metzger spends a lot of time here. My black-market contacts tell me she's been spending money. Let me try this again, wog, where is Anna Metzger's stash?"

"I don't know," Ali said.

"Well, your wife is dead, I think. I think I killed your son-in-law, and if you don't tell me the truth, I'm going to kill your—son? I suspect this young fellow is your son? And then I'll kill that other girl, who seems to have run away."

"She had gone to get the police. They will come get you!"

"Police. I don't believe so, wog. You don't want no police around here…" Ali shook his head firmly, as if he was through talking. Maurice sighed and nodded as if he was in agreement. He stepped away from Ali, pressing Ahmet away from him towards the kitchen.

"Last chance, wog!" He said, looking down at Ali. Maurice shrugged but turned in wide-eyed surprise when he saw the muzzle of the double-barreled shotgun. Ceyda had it shouldered and pointed directly at Maurice. In one motion Maurice swept Ahmet back into his grip, pressing his pistol and his own head very close to Ahmet's.

"Shoot me you shoot your—brother, right?" He could see the hesitation in Ceyda's eyes as she wondered what to do. Maurice looked down and carefully walked backwards out of Ali's reach on the ground. Keeping Ahmet close to his body, he backed half way into the restaurant, his eyes on Ali and Ceyda. Ceyda was moving forward slowly, confused, but not giving in. Maurice smiled and pressed Ahmet's head in closer before shooting Ahmet twice in the side.    Ahmet gasped in shock and pain, struggling now to stay on his feet, but Maurice kept him up.    Ceyda pointed the shotgun directly at Maurice's head but knew she couldn't shoot without hitting her brother.

Maurice dragged Ahmet up to the front door and opened it with his left hand.    When he was halfway out, he shoved Ahmet hard into the restaurant and ducked down as he turned and ran up the steps.    Ceyda wouldn't shoot with Ahmet stumbling and in the line of fire, not with a shotgun. At least he hoped not.  He disappeared into the night and nobody fired.    Ahmet staggered into the kitchen and collapsed.  Neither Ali or Ceyda could save him as his blood loss was too great.

# Chapter 17

*April 7, 1942. Limoges, France.*

It would be impossible to ever forget the pain and loss in their eyes as they recounted that morning. The sense of guilt and responsibility overwhelmed Anna, to the point she could hardly speak for hours. She simply could not form the words, or find words that had any meaning or purpose or explanation, some communication conveying the necessary level of comfort to replace the loss of loved ones in such a senseless manner. They didn't exist, it was impossible and she kept quiet. The three of them, with the three children were all that was left of their happy group of only a few months before.

The little ones, dark-eyed angels clinging to Anna like a favorite aunt, were still too stunned to even ask questions beyond *where is Nonna? When is Poppa coming home? Where is Ommy, Grumpa?* Their nickname for their uncle Ahmet. There would be time for that later. After an hour or two sitting together and holding one other, it was a collective decision to clean up, even at this late hour in the middle of the night. They ran around and lit every light they could find. Anna insisted on handling the mop and bucket to scrub the blood. *It's the least I can do,* she said. She didn't say it out loud, that she was the reason they were dead, but the congealed pools where Selin, Kerem and Ahmet poured out their lives was the last chance she would have to touch them, feel them with her fingers, to touch them as they had touched her.

At first Ali didn't want to call the *Surete* after the attack, but Ceyda insisted and prevailed. *We have four dead bodies, Poppa, what are we going to do, bury them all in the garden? Maurice needs to pay for his crime! He killed momma, my husband and my baby brother! Such a crime against people, even lowly immigrants, would surely create a strong response.* They said nothing about Anna to the *Surete* and reported the crime as an attempted robbery.

The *Surete* sent half a dozen officers to secure the scene, including two investigators. They questioned Ali, Ceyda and canvased the neighborhood for anyone who might have seen or heard anything. The two detectives were polite and one was fairly fluent in Italian. They knew Maurice by his description and there was no denying he was involved. His partner and fellow henchman, Claude, stabbed by Selin and killed by Ali, was no great loss to French society the detectives reported with straight faces. There would be no charges filed against Ali, as it was clearly a case of self-defense. Ali, as he listened to the officer, was stunned as he had never considered the possibility he might be charged for killing the man. When Ali reported no money was taken but there was a great deal of damage to personal property caused by their search, the two detectives closed their notebooks and made for the front door.

Photographs were taken of the bodies, the physical personal damage to Ali and Ceyda from the assault and the mess on the floor. The bodies were carefully rolled onto stretchers and the *Surete* allowed Ali and Ceyda a minute or two to say goodbye. They were both a little confused to where the bodies were going, but Anna, with her brief exposure to cadavers in medical school, explained to them later how a morgue functioned. It was during this discussion Anna realized there would be considerable funeral expenses for three family members, and vowed personally the family would not have to pay one cent. Especially after Ceyda explained the detectives had been informed by someone in the department that the restaurant was not licensed. The officers did not seem particularly concerned even though it was apparent the restaurant was open for business.

"I know nothing about the past, you understand," the Italian speaking detective concluded smoothly, "and this is not our line of business, but both the Department of Health and the Tax department will have to be informed if this in fact is an operating restaurant." Ali and Ceyda said nothing to the man after that, and he asked no further questions. As the bodies were led out to the waiting ambulance, Ceyda couldn't find either detective so she asked a uniformed policeman when they would hear something about the case.

"Soon, *Madame,*" he said, tipping his Kepi as he entered his car.

After the floors and walls were picked up and the blood scrubbed away Ali and Ceyda sat down at one of the small dining tables and stared at their hands. They had worked straight through the wee hours and it would be light in an hour or so. The work had exhausted them.

"We're shutdown." Ceyda said to no one in particular. "How are we going to pay the rent, feed the children and bury our family, Poppa?"

Anna heard this comment and went down into the cellar to retrieve her money canister, wrestling with the rusty lid and bringing the can to the table. She held up the *Reichsmarks* and pushed them between Ceyda and Ali. Ali looked at the money and his eyes softened, but his head shook to and fro.

"No, Anna. We have some money saved. Selin saved the extra money you gave her last time. You need the money. You're the one living on the streets!"

Anna pulled off 100 *Reichsmarks* for herself and tapped the remaining bills.

"About 900 *Reichsmarks.* I promise I will get some more. I have more money, so don't worry about me! You have no business right now, no way to make money. You have rent to pay, children to feed and three beautiful people you need to bury. All that takes money, Ali, and this is the least I can do for you and your family. Please accept it as a trade, if nothing else, of your past care and love for me when I had no one to turn to. I want to do this. Please."

Both Ali and Ceyda stood up and raised their arms for Anna and she joined them tearfully, as the only family she had right now.

The burial for Selin, Ahmet and Kerem occurred nearly three weeks later, although there was considerable difficulty in finding a church with an attached cemetery willing to accept non-citizens. The Turkish Christian community had established a place of worship but without their own cemetery. The funeral service for the community was held there a week after the burial. In the end it was a Jewish synagogue in the poorest quarter of the city that accepted the bodies, but Ali had to place all three members of his family under a single headstone. They were cremated as there was only a tiny space available. The cemetery was jammed packed with headstones, the older ones canted every which way, with Ali only allowed the small corner of the cemetery reserved for non-citizens.

Anna did not attend officially, although she watched from a distance in the guise of a window-washer. Ali and Ceyda understood her need to stay concealed, since Maurice had yet to be arrested and could be anywhere. She found it ironic that Selin and her family would only be accepted by a Jewish synagogue. Anna remembered Selin's expectation as she asked why Anna was holding back. Selin said it herself, *we are very much alike, you and me.* But Anna understood now just how hard she resisted in accepting her identity. And still did. But she was a part of it whether she accepted it or not. Selin saw right through it. Selin knew. Anna didn't have the courage to say it, that's all, didn't—couldn't trust Selin enough to say it out loud. I'll say it now, Selin, I'm a *Juif.* A *Juif* and then not. But an outsider, just like you. Now my people are taking care of you. Anna looked over her shoulder at the small gathering and closed her eyes. She still couldn't say what she wanted to say for some reason, then she thought of Nina Rosenberg and Nina's last words to her in Paris: *Shalom, my friend, Shalom,* she had said. *Yes, Selin, Shalom!*

Anna checked the papers everyday expecting an article describing the crime, a brief history of the victims and a picture of the hunted killer, Maurice. As Ali and Ceyda had said, the detectives were very familiar with Maurice and Claude. If he was a known entity to the *gendarmerie,* why haven't they picked him up yet? One thing Anna noticed, which made her suspicious, was the realization no reporters had ever come to the restaurant to interview Ali or Ceyda. They would have said something. Reporters work off daily crime reports submitted as public record. What has happened? Was a crime report submitted?

The family had held off funeral arrangements believing the papers would help inform others why there was going to be a funeral in the first place. But as the days passed, they knew they had to move on their own and take care of the burials. They reported to the small Turkish community newsletter the accidental deaths of Selin, Kerem and Ahmet in the course of a daylight armed robbery. This created a great deal of excitement and outrage in the community, but not a word came from the larger traditional newspapers.

It was Anna, sitting in a dark corner of a café watching her surroundings, who discovered the tiny article in one of the smaller Limoges newspapers. The article described a robbery that could have occurred the night before, because there was no date mentioned, involving an immigrant family at a Turkish restaurant in the Turkish quarter.

*Four people lost their lives, although it was reported no money was taken during the armed robbery in the late morning hours. One of the two purported perpetrators was killed, a known local gang member and petty thief with a long arrest record. A second perpetrator is reported as still at large, and is being sought by the municipal police.*

Anna set the paper down, incredulous. They didn't even bother to list the names of the victims, and certainly didn't care enough to list the dead robber, or bother to list the name of the "at large" perpetrator. Either the *Surete* didn't bother to provide the details or the newspaper ignored the details to fill the space, knowing the public wouldn't care.

This made Anna think about an elevator conversation she overheard months before when she lived in the apartment over the optic shops. One woman was complaining the newspapers gave too much space on the issues concerning *Juifs*, and another woman had retorted: *Come on, Suzanne, there's a war on! Got to say something about these poor people being sent to God knows where!* And to this her friend responded, which got a few guffaws: *But dear, we LOST the war, already, remember? Those are Germans out there in the streets! We don't have a say in this anymore, and besides Marshal Petain has made it clear he doesn't care about the Juifs!*

Anna made it a point to never bring up the article to Ali or Ceyda as she knew it would break their heart. But she suspected they already knew. Perhaps no one cared what happens to an immigrant Turkish family in an occupied city; certainly with little public outcry the authorities allowed Maurice continued freedom of the streets. Or the crime gang he belonged to paid off the *Surete* to leave it an unsolved case. She didn't know. *But I care,* she said out loud, ignoring the curious glance of a couple a few tables away. She paid and walked stiffly out of the café toting her cane and her shopping cart, her eyes full of tears.

In any case the *Surete* apparently couldn't figure out how to find Maurice. As Selin had explained to her months before, the *Surete* rarely came into the quarter. The murders of the family (Anna called it murder while the newspaper called it a robbery, reducing it to a secondary crime of mere property), but the event still triggered a police investigation and exposed the restaurant as *apparently* operating outside the city licensing and taxation systems. This was serious and required attention under the French system, because it broke a structured rule.

The fact the restaurant was previously allowed to operate under both city and municipal police payouts was irrelevant and ignored. The case was being investigated as a *discovery*. Because there had been a previous history tied to payouts there would be no penalty, of course. But the restaurant could not open nor could it continue. Everything just stopped for the family, their immense personal tragedy swept aside by the authorities and the media as though it didn't occur. All of it, the deaths and the loss of the business were completely attributable to Anna, but only she and the family knew this. Every bit of it was her personal responsibility. It was like the fallout from the situation she created for Marie Broussard, the unknowing optics technician she stole the ID from. Poor Marie was tortured, jailed and possibly even dead now because of Anna. Her sense of guilt was crushing.

In the case of Marie Broussard there is nothing she could do. This was history and the less she thought about it the better. Ali and Ceyda and the children were free and still alive and Anna could do something about their situation. She still had some money left from Karl's generosity, his effort to work out the guilt of another man. He helped Anna and now Anna had an opportunity to help this family survive since she took away their single source of income. She knew she had to be careful with what she had left, but she had to contribute as much as she dared. She could help them and at the same time repair something else. Retrieve something missing. Taken from her and she wanted it back.

It kept her up at night, the image of the yellow eyes that grew larger as her pain increased. Her hands shook and her lips trembled when she thought about it. To know he not only took from her but took from a family who had helped her infuriated her, the anger crystalizing into cold steely hate. He was still out there, watching and waiting. No one cared. He was a predator and this is what they do. She had something he wanted, money, and he planned to take it when the time was right. He could be watching her right now.  It was unnerving, frightening and for her, the sensation of fear bred self-loathing.  He butchered the family.  All necessary in his search for her.  Only she could make it right.

This wasn't like the *Abwehr* hunting her in the past, although she sensed they might be close by.  No, this was personal at a level Anna had never experienced before.  Claude was dead and it gave her no satisfaction, even though he raped her repeatedly and hurt her physically.  He was nothing to her now.  No, she thought, Claude was not only an animal but a dumb animal.  He followed the direction of Maurice.  Maurice hurt her intentionally and with malice.  He followed her to the family and hurt the family.  Killed Selin, Ahmet and Kerem.  Killed them because of Anna.  It made it personal.  She was afraid, the thought of being in the same room with Maurice again sent waves of nausea and cold shivers around her gut.  She remembered how poorly prepared she had been, how quickly they moved on her, pinning her arms and spreading her legs.  She closed her eyes and breathed deeply, her hand closing around the Ruby pistol and the other fingering the flick-knife.

Anna could wait for his attack or leave the quarter.  Those were the options she considered available to her just a few days ago.  As time passed a new option slowly formed in her mind.  It was oddly satisfying and warming, this sense of empowerment coming from the action of planning a trap.  She knew where he was or more accurately, she knew where he would be if she planned it right.  He would come to her.  A new voice took over and she listened carefully, no longer hesitant.  *No one can do this for you.  You set the time.  You set the bait.  Turn the tables, hunt him like prey.*

# Chapter 18

*April 26, 1942. Limoges, France.*

Anna sat on the bench and read her newspapers from cover to cover, her head moving slowly but her eyes never leaving the two well-dressed young men in the lobby. Uniformed *Surete* was an occasional sight near the post office but the sudden appearance of the plainclothesmen alarmed her. She settled down when they walked by and looked straight through her old woman disguise. If they sought Anna Metzger it was a different version. The young men were so obviously policemen or *Abwehr* even customers in line stared at them, at least momentarily. Everyone pretended to be preoccupied as the officers stood in a corner and waited. Something had alerted them.

Anna had not been in the post office for over two months but she followed her normal protocol and observed until she felt comfortable. The plainclothesmen were watching everyone and Anna had no idea if this was something very new, or had been going on for weeks. Her first instinct was to leave, but when they ignored her, she felt emboldened. She looked up every few minutes and peered at the entrance doors as if she was expecting someone. The ruse worked because after a half an hour the staff behind the counter stopped glancing her way. She looked up meaningfully at the large clock on the wall and slowly stood up. She tottered past the two officers and headed towards the foyer where the post office boxes were. One officer shifted his shoes slightly back to give her room for her shopping cart. She nodded her appreciation of his courtesy but he was already looking in another direction. She had become part of the furniture.

The key turned with difficulty but not because the box was full as she suspected. Since Karl stopped sending packages of currency, she only expected letters. Her nervousness was tempered by her anticipation, hoping to hear from Nina and Karl as well as her family. There was a letter from Nina and several from her family, but inexplicably nothing from Karl. She had no time to dwell on her disappointment when she sensed the two plainclothesmen were now in the foyer behind her. There was no one else in the foyer near the boxes. Fear clutched her heart and she stared into the empty box for what seemed a long time, but she knew it was only a second or two. She took a deep breath and let it out, focusing on staying in character, moving slowly and mumbling as she closed the box and dropped the mail into her cart.

As she turned to leave they were already walking away, so she decided to stick around and confirm what she was the most afraid of. She wheeled her cart into the line for others waiting to see a postal clerk, pulling the cart up close behind her forcing her to glance over her shoulder. She held her breath when one of the plainclothesmen walked back and leaned over to write down what she knew had to be her post office box number. Anna courteously stepped out of the line and headed for the entrance. She could never use the post office box again. She had to inform Nina and her family to stop writing to her.

In the hotel room she examined the letters carefully but could see no sign of tampering. She heard the *Surete* used steam techniques to open letters, but try as she might under the dim light of her reading lamp there was no evidence. Once satisfied the letters were un-tampered originals, she opened Nina's first. The return address was the same one Nina had given her nearly two years earlier, her parent's home in Lyon. It was a brief, one-page letter and like Anna's correspondence to Nina earlier, Nina was very conscious others may be reading. It was short and provided more than anything a confirmation her friend was still living, if not at home, somewhere in Lyon.

*Dearest Anna,*

*It was so good to hear from you, although I'm saddened to hear you haven't managed to get home after all this time, but I understand. We all hoped this war would end soon, but it apparently was not meant to be. Try to get home and see your family. Travel restrictions keep getting worse, even for ordinary citizens. It's important because although France has capitulated, there is still a war going on and nothing, and I mean nothing is guaranteed. For my family, to be French has been a temporary reprieve, but things are changing every day. My father's position at the University has been challenged several times, but so far French university authorities consider his contributions too great and have resisted severe Vichy pressure to remove him. I myself remain at a distance and am in a position to leave if this occurs.*

*Until we meet again, my friend!*

*Love, Nina*

Anna read the letter again, seeing between the lines the horror of what Nina's family must be going through, and recognizing what her own father feared was not only possible but already happening. Nina, as always had a plan and no intention of joining her family if they were rounded up. *Remain at a distance and in a position to leave.* Almost shamefully, Anna could see her situation was similar but not so well planned. Nina seemed to accept Anna's explanation of why she stayed in Limoges for face value because she saw Anna as an ordinary French citizen, not as a *Juif* in hiding. Nina wanted to survive, having explained in Paris her inability to accept the blatant, blind denial of her parents and other French, Polish and Belgian citizen Jews of the pointed evidence of Hitler's plans.

There were three letters from her father, confused and circumspect as he tried to explain his feelings of the choices he felt he was being forced to make. Anna glanced at the dates of the letters and found them all written in a three-week period, the newest now three weeks old. Perhaps when she didn't respond he became suspect of possible tampering, but his tone was so despondent, almost suicidal her eyes welled with tears because she was unable to console him in person. She could see him at his writing desk, so consumed with his grief he was unable to continue writing, his head down, his fists folded one over the other.

He was such a proud man he could come across as arrogant in initial meetings until he was formally introduced. Because of his considerable height he was usually among the tallest in company, a consideration he never took advantage of. He would be the first to smile and stoop his head surreptitiously to bring his face down to yours. It almost always worked, and certainly for little children lost in the forest of adult legs and hands. At faculty parties Anna would wander hesitatingly from one set of tall thin legs and black tails to another, until suddenly her father's large hand would arrive gently on her shoulder, one fleeting moment before his face, with his carefully trimmed beard, would appear from the heavens down next to hers, bent and folded like a crane, the grin always warm and welcoming. Anna read the last letter again and took a deep breath. He had talked himself into it that was apparent. She envisioned him as she had last seen him, tired but cheerful as he bundled her into her train bound for Paris. For a fleeting moment she felt a chill and the thought she would never see him again.

Clara's letter was like reading a political reporter from the opposing camp, the speech covered was the same but the interpretation between camps was fields apart. Clara had thrown caution to the wind. There was no reading between the lines necessary in her words.

*Father is convinced Vichy, the Milice or the damned Nazis will be coming for us any minute. He can't sleep, eat or focus on his work. No one has said a thing to him, but now he's convinced momma he needs to approach one of his friends, an assistant to the Prefect, and suggest a hypothetical, all in secret, of course. I think he's crazy, why let the cat out of the bag if you don't need too? No one has hinted all these months since our cousin was arrested and told the family tale! What if no one cares or was listening?*

*He's convinced momma we need to emigrate to the West, but you can't do it unless you declare yourself as a Juif. And it's so hard and so complicated! With the war, there's no simple immigration path for anyone in an occupied country, but there is currently a tiny quota for each of the few countries taking Juifs. Have you looked at what these bureaucratic idiots expect Juifs to do in order to simply apply? Everything requires a document signed by somebody, and each step has a time limit so if something gets delayed in acquiring a signature and goes over the time limit, the applicant has to start all over… It's insane, Anna!*

*Listen to this, Anna:*

*In order to leave you have to embark by ship from Lisbon. This is what the applications say you need to have just to get it started:*

*An entry Visa for the country of destination (I bet that's easy!)*

*Portuguese transit Visa*

*Spanish transit Visa*

*French exit Visa*

*As you know, Visas vary in their validity. It's apparent to me by the time you get the French Visa the others will have expired and you start over.*

*The French exit Visa has to come from the Prefect where we live, so the Prefect wants a Certificate of Good Behavior which has to come from the Commissariat of Police. On top of that all the arrangements for travel have to be made in advance. You have to have the ticket for the ship from Lisbon to wherever, and of course you have to arrange for the trips across Spain and Portugal. Father says it's all impossible to do, but what if we do nothing and they throw us into a detention camp!*

*I used to think immigration was the right path, Anna, but I'm not sure anymore. Father says the assistant to the Prefect is an old friend but he's not a Juif obviously, and the Prefect is under the control of the Vichy. What if he reports us? Father thinks his friend will listen to his story and make a recommendation, and that's it. They know how long these things take. He thinks his friend will be discreet and leave it alone if Father decides against it. Doesn't that sound dangerous to you? What do you think we should do?*

The last letter, from her brother Jean Paul, she set aside. She quickly wrote a letter addressed to the family and another for Nina, noting the post office box was no longer secure and should not be used under any circumstances. For the family she made no comment about the proposed meeting between her father and the assistant to the Prefect. She knew better, her father's mind was made up by the third letter, posted three weeks ago. If the assistant to the Prefect turned them in, Father might already be unemployed and the family homeless. Her mother was not a *Juif* but Anna knew where her mother would stand.

Letters from Jean Paul were always special to Anna because they were very close in the early years at home, and she still thought of him as a big brother even though they were only four years apart.  Once the initial relief of his survival of the German invasion was over, the knowledge he had escaped to England placed Jean Paul in a special category—safe and sound and out of the way.   The family had heard from him periodically, but Anna admitted to herself the last part of 1940 her world was all about Karl, and there was always a twinge of fused loyalties as her heart swept past her family and embraced Karl.   Karl was the enemy to Jean Paul, and briefly in the air over France and Belgium Karl's colleagues were trying to kill Jean Paul, as he tried to bomb *Wehrmacht* infantry and panzer formations below him.   It was all so confusing.

It all came in a heartbeat—his use of *sweet Anna* in his salutations rolled her back so many years, but she thought of his fearlessness and handsome back as he dove off the rocks into the warm Mediterranean in one of the Calanques out of Cassis a long-ago summer.   The small power boat bobbed off its anchor as a fishing boat trundled by, the fishermen waving at their father and mother, sitting down in the little cove.   Anna threw out the corn meal and the red fish, tame as gold fish, nibbled at the meal on the surface and at her hands and hair as she floated by the school.

"I'm going to be a fighter pilot when I grow up, Anna," Jean Paul declared as his head cleared the water.   "Up there, in the clouds, that's where I belong!"  He waved his brown arm vaguely towards a wispy little cloud, and Anna followed his motion.

"There's nothing up there but blue sky," she retorted.   "What are you going to do once you get there?  That sounds boring to me!"

"What!" He gasped, splashing her hard.   "You got to be kidding! Up there, you're the king of the sky.   You can turn and dive in any direction you want.   And if an enemy of France comes up to fight me, then I dive down and shoot them to pieces!"

Anna always secretly admired Jean Paul's ambition to be a fighter pilot, but you can't let a boy know you agree with him, can you? Especially your big brother!

Now as he described his airfield in Northern New Zealand as they trained to meet the Japanese in New Guinea, she could tell he was homesick for southern France, because of his comparisons of the neatly tilled farmlands of Whanganui and the lush green landscapes of the Northland.  What is a Frenchman doing flying for the Royal New Zealand Air Force on the other side of the world, she wondered.   But she had heard from her parents he was very disappointed with the leadership of the French Air Force during the German invasion, and chose to join the RAF instead of Free French forces forming in Great Britain.

*My mistake was I admitted to speaking English fairly well, and I had all this twin engine light bomber time including a couple hundred in*

*Bostons. I was hoping they were going to transition me to fighters, but no chance. But all of this is going to change, baby sister, because the New Zealand Wellington bomber group based in England needs replacement pilots, and I have requested and have been accepted for transition training on Wellingtons. I'm coming home, sweet Anna! They can't make up their minds whether I should do the transition training in Canada or England, so I'll have to see. But I hear in the eastern provinces of Canada they speak French...*

After a rainy beginning April revealed real promise for an early spring by the end of the third week. Four days straight of warm, brilliant sunlight convinced Anna the ground would soon be dry enough to dig up her last remaining canisters of currency. Soon she could go back to living on the streets with the better weather, allowing her, to her mind, better security. She was particularly wary of being followed by either the police or Maurice and abandoned all of her old street routines. Her health was improving as was her physical strength, allowing her to walk for miles and miles every day, meandering as she pleased, always conscious of location and potential threats. She changed her disguises frequently and avoided any of her old haunts for a few weeks, including the public library and the dormant restaurant of her Turkish family. It was a lonely time. With the loss of her post office box she was completely separated from her loved ones, the only thing that mattered now in her life.

She was confused at once by the construction blinds set up on the lawn of the library, bracketing the wide stone entranceway and steps into a single narrow temporary corridor. The public works sign proudly declared the construction project would only take five weeks to complete, the end product captured by an expansive and sweeping architectural image revealing all new landscaping and a much wider entrance. The first twitch of concern crossed her mind as she glanced over the stylized painting, realizing the new completed version did away with the thick, decades old junipers on each side of the steps. She waited her turn in the narrow corridor leading up the steps towards the building.

She could see nothing with the construction blinds until she crossed the top threshold. Clutching her shopping cart, she slowly worked her way up the steps, much to the annoyance of the young students directly behind her who could not pass. Once on the top she slid to the side, feigning exhaustion as a dozen people rushed past her. She looked down where there was once twenty meters of thick, impenetrable junipers to view concrete footings and steel tie rods. The original retaining wall was directly below her and had expanded three or four meters to accommodate the much wider, fan shaped steps. The base of the cornerstone juniper had been about two meters from the retaining wall, and her canisters were buried about 60 centimeters from the base. Her estimate of the location placed the burial site under a meter-thick slab of fresh concrete.

Anna was so stunned she could not accept the location as correct. For two hours she walked around the library to view the building from different directions, believing somehow she had become confused and this was not the real entrance. She had last slept under the junipers in the fall when the temperature dropped and the rains grew serious, five perhaps six months ago. The stylized architectural drawing finally convinced her. She oriented the drawing to the scaffolding and construction blinds for the umpteenth time and approached the steps again and found exactly the same thing. Her heart fell like a stone and the reality of her predicament seemed to shrink her lungs, her breathing coming in short little gasps. How could this have happened? The library was built in the late 1800s, the landscaping unchanged for generations. Who could predict the city government would fulfill a construction contract in the middle of a war, especially with half of the population unable to feed their families or heat their homes?

Her safety net all of these months had been the money, plentiful and available due entirely to Karl's careful planning. The 4,000 *Reichsmarks* in the canisters would have seen her through at least another year, although she had planned to give at least 2,000 to her Turkish family. Her generosity had limits, she knew. But she had to tell them the truth, because she had promised them more money and now, she herself was in serious trouble. Anna slowly got off the bench and headed off to see her other family.

The shadows were growing long when she decided she hadn't been followed and she could safely approach the street. There was no one about as she dragged her shopping cart down the steps. The entrance seemed dusty and deserted. No lights could be seen inside, which was easy to ascertain as the blinds were left open. She pressed her face hard against the glass to see to the other side of the restaurant where the living quarters were, but the rooms were dark and motionless. The chairs in the restaurant were all upended on the tables, and there were no lamps, candles, pictures or decorations of any kind on the walls or sideboards. She knocked for several minutes before she finally accepted Ali and Ceyda were gone. Anna only knew one or two of their neighbors well enough to approach them, and at first she thought they too had moved away. But finally, one responded to her knocking and on recognizing her, invited her inside their home.

She left after a half an hour, a small package from Ali and Ceyda safely in her cart, but nothing to fill the emptiness and loneliness she experienced as she trudged up the street. It was dark as she entered her hotel, her despair complete as she realized she had prepaid for five days and this was her last day.  She had some *Reichsmarks* left but she would have to be very frugal from now on.  A room only on rainy days until the money ran out.  Thank God Spring was almost here.  She would have to live on what she could buy with her ration card until that expired at the end of the month.  She would have to see if she could afford to get another one.

The hotel clerk looked up without expression or greeting as she crossed the small, dingy lobby, his cigarette so short it was a mere glow between his fingers.  Anna did not acknowledge him, her despondency so complete she felt as if she were wearing blinders, her view a small narrow porthole surrounded by darkness.  She did glance around the deserted lobby just before entering the elevator.  Her sense of awareness finally kicked in when she noticed the clerk making a telephone call as her elevator grinded its way upward.  She had no idea if the call had anything to do with her or not, but she had the Ruby pistol under the top flap of her shopping cart before she left the elevator.  She looked both ways on the poorly lit corridor, wheeling her cart along slowly her body fully upright, watching doorknobs on each side.  There was also a set of stairs at the far end around an "L" shaped bend.  She kept an eye in that direction as she inserted her key.

A slight shift in a shadow under the door stopped her dead in her tracks.  Someone was already in her room.  Her first response was *this was the wrong room.*  She looked at the room number, roughly painted in red on the door and it was correct.  Her second response as fear gripped her heart was *run away!  Run away!*

She took a deep breath and shook her head, *NO.  This must stop now.*  She started to mumble to herself as she retracted the key and attempting to reinsert it again.  The key shook for a moment in her hand, but she *willed* it to be still.  Anna slipped the Ruby out and pointed it at the door, keeping the muzzle close to her body.  She remembered how Maurice and Claude had pounced on her like cats.  She stopped again and slowly wheeled her cart around so it was in front of her, moving her body to the side.  Her finger closed around the Ruby's trigger as she brought it up tight against her breast so it couldn't be deflected or taken easily.  Kerem had taught her that.  She took a deep breath and turned the key.

The door jerked open suddenly from the inside, Maurice reaching for her with a big paw but his fingers slammed into the cart handle.  His big yellow eyes grew instantly larger and furious with pain.  He growled like a big dog and lunged at Anna as he tried to hurl the cart out of the way.  Anna gasped and stepped back out of his reach, aiming the pistol

173

at his face.  It was the face of her nightmares, large, twisted and red with hate.  She pulled the trigger twice.

The first bullet hit his right cheekbone, punching a small hole in the bone garnering a gasp and a grunt from Maurice, followed instantly by the second bullet, exploding and disintegrating his right eye on its way to his brain.    Maurice collapsed heavily straight down and backyards into the room.  Anna kept the pistol in front of her as she tried to control her breathing and excitement.    She pushed the cart aside and stepped cautiously into the doorway.  As she looked down her gun was gripped from the side and then twisted out of her hand, but not before a second hand yanked her painfully into the room.  Momentum had her off balance as she fell forward onto Maurice's mutilated face.  Anna turned her head just as a boot missed her forehead by a millimeter.  She looked up to see a young man, perhaps in his mid-twenties, mustachioed and already balding, trying to regain his balance and cocking his arm back.

Anna pushed herself off Maurice and used her legs to thrust upward, slamming her head into something soft.  The young man grunted in surprise and pain, retaliating instantly by punching Anna hard into her breast with his fist and again into her side, making her gasp and cry in pain.  He pummeled her again in the stomach, two or three times, stopping only when she collapsed at his feet.  He lifted her limp head slowly just before slapping her solidly across the face in a stinging, numbing blow. Anna, her vision and mind fading, lifted her right hand in surrender.  The young man laughed and lifted her straight up off her feet by her hair, now natural and half blond as the wig had fallen off.  He spun her around, oblivious to her whimpering, obviously surprised, pinning one arm behind her back as he came in close behind her.  He bit her ear before kissing her neck roughly, his hot breath in her hair.

Anna, remembering her last remaining weapon, reached up under her blouse with her free hand and retrieved the flick knife.  She stared straight down at her feet at Maurice, his undamaged eye open and still, wide with surprise.  His young accomplice seemed indifferent to the dead body, his hand now groping her breast as his face sniffed around her ear. She released the blade and gripped the handle unseen.  Anna moaned in faux pleasure, rolling her head away, stretching her neck in invitation and waiting until she felt his bristled cheek and breath brush against hers.  In one swift motion she swung the blade out and up, slamming the razor-sharp tip straight back into the sweating mass next to her head with all her remaining strength.

174

Anna couldn't remember exactly how she left the hotel, but she knew she somehow maintained the peace of mind to put her wig back on and to remove her blood drenched blouse and wrap. The young man had tried to scream, she could see it in his stretched jaw and gaping mouth, but his central nervous system failed him and the connections were not made in time before he died. Anna had rolled her knife arm up and back in an arc, bringing the blade down right under his ear just behind his left jawbone, straight through the thick muscle in the back of his throat and possibly penetrating the spine, burying the blade to the hilt in the process. His reaction was instantaneous, he gagged and gasped, gurgled and bubbled, the destruction so quick his arms simply fell to his sides and his legs collapsed. The spurting of arterial blood was enormous and Anna was sprayed and soaked even as he fell to the floor.

Anna left nothing in the room when she departed earlier in the day so there was nothing to retrieve. Once her breathing returned to normal, she backed carefully over the bodies into the corridor. Nothing moved. Two shots had been fired, loud, with an obvious struggle, and no one came out. Not one soul. Two people were now dead. She felt—nothing. There was no time for any sense of relief, she could only think of escape. She left the Ruby pistol wherever the young man had put it when he disarmed her, and the flick knife would remain in his neck. Her hands trembling as she dropped her blouse and wrap to the floor and went to her shopping cart for fresh clothes. She only had one thought at this moment. The room clerk had seen her and would see her leave, so this disguise had to go. There were no sirens, no immediate threat the *Surete* were on their way. Her arms and legs felt leaden, the sense of being separate from her body strange and unnerving. *This is no dream, Anna. You must go.* The voice was clear and she jerked into motion.

She carried one extra disguise but she needed to leave the area before changing. There was no sound now except the rushing of blood in her ear, a roar that could not be suppressed. She glanced one last time at Maurice and the young man, feeling neither guilt or relief or—triumph. She didn't want this in the end; they pursued her. What they didn't know was she was virtually penniless and there would have been no reward for them either.

When the municipal police arrested Anna ten days later, she was held by two brothers because she had attempted to steal a baguette of bread from a vendor stall. Her hair was mostly blond now, almost shoulder length. Selin's special dye concoction was long gone, as were the extra wigs and old woman accessories. The young *gardien de la paix* who took the report looked at her carefully and made a mental note, certain he had seen her before. She was obviously starving; thin, underdressed, dirty with no money, correspondence or personal items, and only a single expired ration card for identification.

Under his questioning the two brothers relented and decided not to press charges, but wanted her taken away. The police agreed, booking Anna at the police station as a vagrant and possible prostitute. Once inside the jail there was some concern about her mental health, but mostly they didn't know what to do with her because she also appeared ill. The young policeman who was going to follow up on his suspicions of her identity failed to do so. She was left in the hands of the women in her common cell, and when it was clear she was unable to even feed herself one of the women, a legally certified *maison* prostitute named Sonya who had an occasional drug problem, felt sorry for her and took over her care. When the time came for formal charging, Sonya admitted she knew Anna and Anna was a former prostitute but wasn't working because she was tubercular. Of course she was a vagrant, she couldn't work. Both were released almost immediately to the responsibility of *Madame* Marchand, who paid the minimum fines, signed the papers and waved to the judge.

# Die Frau nach der man sich sehnt

## Chapter 19

*September 10, 1942. Paris, France.*

The reflection in the pane of glass was smoky and dark, yet his features could be seen clear enough. It was getting used to the darkness on one side of his face and the much fuller head of hair that was taking time. The black eye patch was larger than he liked, but the Polish seamstresses who custom designed the patches over a year before noted the deep scarring extending beyond his eye socket onto the cheekbone, and made them bigger. It was quite an industry and in high demand, as Karl was hardly alone in his partial sightedness in the neurology ward of his *Wehrmacht* Warsaw hospital. The quality of the work was excellent, the patches carefully cupped to allow for the involuntary movement of eyelashes over a sightless glass eye. As an officer he could afford the custom work and ordered several dozen. Once the plaster skull helmet protecting his chipped and fractured parietal lobe was removed, he had to learn to deal with the freakishness of the right side of his head. It was like looking at two different people at the same time. The hair on his head slowly covered up the huge "T" shaped scar and indentation on his skull, and the patch went a long way in allowing him to accept the fiction of being almost normal looking. He only needed to visit some of the men silently inhabiting the beds around him to remind himself how lucky he was.

He found it ironic that even now when he had nightmares, the dreams of being unable to move, the smell of diesel fuel and the moans of the injured were often based from his much earlier accident, the wreck in Limoges where Anna had treated him and helped pull him from the wreckage. Karl accepted this because he knew the association with Anna was far more deeply rooted in his subconscious than those horrific first weeks on the Russian plain, culminating in an early morning strafing attack of which he had little recollection. His brain chose to spin confusion in his more distant past, finding a solution rooted in Anna's love and so many other positive things revolving around her; past, present and future. Karl had hope, he must have some belief in Anna's continued survival and eventual escape. The war couldn't last forever. As a couple they spoke of it in general terms at first, but as their love for one another grew they entertained the thought of an actual future together.

At least his subconscious considered such things. It had been nearly two years since he'd last seen her and held her in his arms, two years since they had spoken, kissed or made love. If she got his one letter dictated in Warsaw back in the late summer of 1941, Anna would at least know he was alive. But he had no real idea whether she ever received it. He could not contact the building owner in Limoges so she lost the apartment last year once the lease ran out. For all he knew she could be anywhere. If she stayed, found another place, then it would be a matter of waiting until the war was over. The thought depressed him thoroughly. Time was not on their side, although it changed nothing in his feelings for her. Despite the long absence apart he found even when he returned home to Stuttgart to spend time with his family, he wasn't nearly as happy as he might have been. He missed Anna, longed for her, but now he could never reach out for her even if he knew exactly where she was.

The invasion of the Soviet Union in June of 1941 raced over 150 divisions eastward on a 3,200-kilometer front. Karl's special logistics unit had expanded to a dozen men. They trailed four kilometers behind the lead panzers in two vehicles, a small reconnaissance utility car his engineers used to scout ahead looking for useable rail lines, and their Maultier Opel Blitz, a large, enclosed tracked transport that carried their radios, maps and mobile office. The Maultier towed a trailer filled with all of their equipment and personal gear. They were attached to the headquarters of a mechanized panzer division for support, but to all intents and purposes their mission was strategic and they reported directly to Berlin, but there was little for them to do at this stage.

For the first few days the lead formations were outracing their supply lines. The sky was filled with thousands of German aircraft pummeling soviet airfields and troop concentrations. The noise ahead was a constant roar, Karl had never seen or heard anything so terrifying and exciting in his life. He had no idea how a single Russian soldier or civilian could survive such an onslaught. Some of his staff, statisticians by training who were being fed the numbers, calculated the Soviet air force had lost over 2,000 aircraft in the first week alone. The Soviet Union would capitulate by September they beamed, at this rate.

The first real concentrations of rail lines were hundreds of kilometers in front of them, so Karl had the reconnaissance car hooked to the trailer to save fuel. The unit stayed back and out of the way, happy to remain outside of the fire ring of the Soviet artillery or seemingly ineffective air cover. They attached themselves to a small communications unit for mutual protection once they were warned roving Soviet mechanized cavalry units were close by. At night they circled their six vehicles like wagon trains in the old American western movies, and struck out eastward at dawn. Just as they loaded their vehicles and started moving on the ninth day of the invasion, someone reported aircraft, close to the ground, approaching out of the sun.

As was explained to Karl later, the flight of IL-2 fighter bombers was apparently looking for panzers and followed their normal pattern of approaching the front at medium altitude, then diving to ground level at high speed just before attacking their target. There was no other explanation why the Soviet air force's most heavily armed tank buster aircraft would attack a small column of transport trucks, although Karl's Maultier, with its metal tracks, might be confused with an armored personnel carrier. In any case the column didn't even have a single mounted machine gun to defend itself. The six IL-2s didn't make a second pass, realizing their mistake after destroying all six vehicles with cannon and rocket fire, leaving them twisted and burning. They saved their munitions for better prey and flew away.

A tank recovery unit came across the smoking wreckage fifteen minutes later. Of the 38 men in the six vehicles only two survived, including Karl, although at first the rescuers had reported no survivors. Karl's body was dragged from the wreckage of the Opel and stacked with other corpses and partial remains of crewmen. The recovery unit was ordered to continue on with their retrieval duties and leave the bodies for the grave's registration teams. It was the sudden weak cry of one survivor and the involuntary muscular twitching of Karl's leg that delayed their departure. Despite his enormous blood loss from a shattered leg and dozens of shrapnel wounds, Karl still had a pulse.

Eight months in hospitals in the Soviet Union, Poland and Germany resulted in a slow, painful recovery of his ability to walk and speak in a coherent manner. His hair grew out and covered the scars on his head, and as his dizziness, mental confusion, blurred vision and bone-crushing headaches slowly faded away, he rolled out of his bed first thing in the morning every day and tried to stay on his feet. He transitioned from wheelchairs to parallel bars to crutches and to canes as his right sciatic nerve, severed in a half dozen places, slowly grew together again to reform the connections. For two months he endured the daily agony of physical therapists applying car battery-powered electrodes to his leg muscles to stimulate them. He wore thigh and calf braces on his right leg until he felt he no longer needed them, a foolish mistake. Without a calf brace to keep his foot in a shoe at a right angle to his calf, he began to fall down as his still-numb foot tripped him up. He broke his right toe bones repeatedly as his limp foot curled forward in a phenomenon known as "dropsy". Instead of lifting the toes up, his foot rolled under and broke tiny bones under the weight of his impatient hurried forward stride. This impatience cost him his freedom as his doctors restricted him to his wheelchair. After the delay of healing bone fractures, he was forced back into physical therapy where he relearned to lift his right leg high enough to clear his dropped foot, in the classic old man gait he detested. But he was finally mobile and free of crutches or canes…

Depth perception was a problem at first, especially at night, but he didn't mind because his general vision, always excellent, returned and he could read for hours on end to his heart's content without headaches. It was his number one concern in his planned return to civilian life and university teaching, the ability to see and read the blackboard and correct papers. He became known as the "long walker" in his Berlin hospital, affecting much longer than regulation hair as he walked kilometer after kilometer through the wards. As the spring of 1942 brought early sun and blossoms, Karl was approved to walk the expansive grounds of the hospital unescorted, feeling a first real hope of a future, dreaming of Anna and a world postwar. His leg muscles, as the nerves regenerated bringing back the lift of his foot and the tactile feel of his toes, strengthened as they absorbed the weight of his body, hour after hour, kilometer after kilometer. He still couldn't run, he tried and always fell within five or six strides. The enormous complexity and circuitry necessary to transmit the weight and balance of his body back and forth at such speeds simply wasn't there yet.

When he returned to Berlin after his home leave in Stuttgart, he began to receive his first visitors where his future was discussed in oblique, subtle ways that annoyed and frustrated him. He expected to be pensioned off in a matter of weeks or months since he obviously could not do his former job, and his irritation and sense of confinement grew as the daily routine of physical therapy became boring and pointless. He was ready to leave. Abandon the hospital, the army, this incredibly painful phase of his life that he would just as soon forget as quickly as possible. That is with the exception of the only worthwhile element to come out of his experience, Anna.

One day in May right after lunch Karl was surprised to find two middle-aged men waiting in his room. That same morning, he had been awakened by two *Wehrmacht* officers he had never met before who informed him he had been meritoriously promoted to the temporary rank of *Major*. They presenting him a couple of formal documents, flowers and a bottle of champagne, stating his situation had come to the attention of some of the most senior staff in the *Wehrmacht*. Since his single combat achievement was to be the only man in his 12-man unit to survive the attack, his sense of unease was profound. When he asked politely who in the senior staff was interested, they demurred and explained he would be contacted soon. It was all very strange, especially to someone expecting to be released from service at any moment. He thanked the officers, who seemed just as uncomfortable as he was, and sent them on their way. Karl wondered if the promotion was a reward or a bad omen.

The two men waiting for him smiled and stood up immediately as he came in, not formally as military men would, but more like two accountants responding to the appearance of a new client. *"Herr Major."* They both said in chorus.

"Gentlemen," he nodded agreeably, "I'm at a disadvantage. How can I help you?"

One of the men went to the other side of the empty second bed in Karl's room, carrying over a spare visitor chair and setting it down facing their chairs. He pointed to the chair in invitation for Karl.

"Forgive us, *Herr Major* Berchtold, there was no time to inform you in advance we were coming today. This will not take much of your time, please join us and have a seat."

Remembering the visitors from the morning Karl nodded and sat down.

"I—was just informed this morning about my promotion— temporary, to *Major*. Which… which I did not expect at all. To be frank with you, gentlemen, I was under the impression I was going to be invalided home—permanently." The two men smiled as if he had told them a good joke, glancing at one another as they opened their notebooks.

"Well," said the taller of the two, "let us congratulate you again on your promotion! It actually had been approved weeks ago, but the machines of bureaucracy turn slowly at times, and the beneficiary of such grand tidings is often the last to know!" The two men grinned again before standing briefly, one at a time, to introduce themselves and shake Karl's hand. Although they looked like civilians and high-level bean counters at best, Karl was surprised and a little unnerved to find both of them were Army officers, both *majors* themselves, serving in the *Abwehr,* the German military intelligence organization headquartered there in Berlin. His response was visceral because the *Abwehr* had already established a relationship between Anna and himself back in Limoges. His immediate reaction was it had everything to do with Anna, because it was the *Abwehr* who had been shadowing her just before he was transferred, and he had assumed the case was dropped as his former commanding officer suggested. How naive he was. They might have been tracking Anna all of this time and finally caught her. They might have interrogated her and found out about the post office box and his packages of *Reichsmarks. How was he going to explain those?*

181

All of these thoughts raced through his head, but at the same time he grew cautiously and nervously optimistic as he listened to the two gentlemen—these friendly seeming accountants, who didn't come across as the hard-boiled enforcement arm one would expect if he was suspected of a crime.

"Have you heard of our organization, *Herr Major* Berchtold?" The tall one asked. Karl considered only for a moment to answer the question truthfully. He didn't know enough yet.

"I have heard about the *Abwehr, Herr Major.* Yes. In my work we were in Poland and in France right behind the assault troops, examining and generating reports about the status of former enemy transportation assets—railway lines, locomotives, transport cars—that sort of thing. Our job was to determine if they could be brought online for our own immediate use, or repaired so we could use them in future operations. In many cases our initial investigations were based on *Abwehr* estimates prior to our invasion, so there was both an understanding and collaboration regarding the role of the organization."

"I see. Are you aware of our organizational structure? Or what we actually do for the *Third Reich*?"

"Actually, not at all beyond the intelligence information provided my team. It was always very—shall I say, carefully handled. It was kind of a one-way street, we used the estimates provided and compared the two with what we discovered in the field. We turned in our reports and recommendations and that was that. I was under the impression the information came from the *Abwehr* and our information went back to *Abwehr*."

The two men, still smiling, listened to him attentively but when he stopped talking the tall one looked down at the open file on his lap, lifting out a single document. He held it to the light and signaled to his partner, who silently rose and closed the door.

"Forgive us, *Herr Major* Berchtold, but what we are about to discuss is of a rather confidential nature, and we need to ensure it remains so. Karl sat silent and watchful, finally accepting the fact he was promoted for a reason and was about to find out why.

The questions were seemingly random, but Karl picked up the pattern quickly. The housekeeping items were minimal: he lifted his right leg carefully, the 50-centimeter scar extending from the back of his mid-calf to halfway up his thigh was examined, and the 23-millimeter mole on the left calf was measured and photographed with a Minox mini-camera. The two men didn't ask him to lift his black eye patch, but one of them felt the indentation on the right side of his head.

"They didn't install a metal plate?"  No, he said, the doctors felt the bone would fuse together and they wanted to avoid the plate if possible.  The docs talked about residual problems with heat, cold weather and infections.

"You are an academic by training."  It was a statement of fact so he only nodded.  He assumed they had this information but the question he had for them was why?  But he remained silent.

"Our information reveals you have significant contact with extended family in the *Alsace-Lorraine* region of France.  You understand, of course, this region has been reclaimed as German territory, and the new rules have banned the speaking of French, sales of French literature, and of course, French Jews have been transported out of the region to detention centers elsewhere."

"Yes, I have family in both Nancy and Strasburg.  It's the primary reason I speak French so fluently."

"Yes, this was noted."  But the questions then turned, not to his time at Limoges as he expected them to, but his past prior to 1935.

"*Herr Major* Berchtold, please do not be offended by this question, but our—sources report you were approached a number of times when you were still a teaching assistant, where you were offered an opportunity to join the Nazi party.  You respectfully declined at those times, as you did later in 1936 after you received your teaching appointment, and again in 1938 when you were called up for your military service.  Am I being accurate in these declarations?"

"That is correct, *Herr Major*."

"Is there a philosophical issue driving this resistance?  You've been consistent.  The party has grown considerably in strength, and it might be said politically your position is the less popular one, yes?"

"I'm an academic—perhaps I'm more leftist than most these days, but philosophically, as you put it, I don't necessarily agree with many of the banner principles utilized by the party to subdue or subvert those who don't agree with them.  I'm a German citizen, I support the *Reich* and I uphold the oath I accepted when I became a German officer—but, I have my personal values I was raised on."

Karl glanced at the two men carefully.  Their faces were friendly, almost sympathetic.  The hairs on the back of his neck lifted slowly and pressed against the collar of his shirt.  He knew he was treading on very thin ice.  The taller of the two men seemed to sense his unease.  The man set his pen down and pulled out a box of cigarettes, offering one to Karl, who declined.  He lit his cigarette and said nothing, apparently waiting for Karl to continue.  When Karl shifted his attention to the sky outside of his window, the man addressed Karl in excellent, unaccented French.

"You will not find at the highest levels in the *Abwehr* organization many members of the Nazi party. And it was at these levels you came to our attention. It is the badge of the professional with integrity and scruples." His perpetual smile had disappeared to be replaced by the thin line of his lips, serious and with resolve. Karl nodded slowly, now intrigued.

"I see by your last assignment in France, in Limoges a few weeks after the invasion, you were specifically assigned to find functioning transport railcars and locomotives to move foreign and later French *Juifs* back to Germany and Poland." He shifted back to German.

"Yes, *Herr Major,* that was our assignment."

"You were commended for excellent work—although your unit was reassigned back to Warsaw to prepare for the invasion of the Soviet Union a few weeks early." The man's eyes would not leave Karl's.

"A small issue regarding a young blond woman you were seeing— a prostitute, a relationship that caught the attention of the Limoges police and one of our own counter-intelligence units, yes?" Karl let his shoulders slump and nodded his head guiltily.

"Yes," he sighed, "not one of my better decisions. I have no excuse for it. It was a matter of our constant travel and my personal loneliness at the time. My commanding officer put a stop to it and rotated my team to Warsaw ahead of schedule for punishment."

"I thought you never had any other contact with *Abwehr* other than the sending of reports back and forth?"

"I didn't, I never saw them. They approached my commanding officer."

"And you've had no further contact with this French prostitute," the man peered at his notes, "in—about 17-18 months?"

"None. I broke off the relationship, if you care to call it that, immediately. I was ordered to." The man closed the one file, but his notebook was still open and his pen was poised.

"*Herr Major* Berchtold, do you by chance remember this prostitute's name?"

"I do not. It was some phony French name anyway. I doubt very much it was hers."

The man put his pen away slowly, closing his notebook.

"You're a mathematician, *Herr Major* Berchtold."

"Yes, *Herr Major*, of course, since you know my education and work history."

"Forgive me my layman's ignorance of the higher orders of your field, but you taught a great deal of applied mathematics to the engineers

184

and scientists in your classes, but your interest and your advanced papers have been more in the order of mathematical theory, correct?"

"Well, yes, that is true—to a point." He sensed immediately it was useless to ask for clarification of the why.

"I'm getting the distinct impression I'm not separating from the German Army just yet." The two men smiled and the tall one shook his head.

"No, *Herr Major* Berchhold, the *Third Reich* desperately requires your services. Your teaching career must remain on hold for a little longer I'm afraid."


Karl spent the remaining months of spring and the beginning of the summer of 1942 in training courses, then later under the close supervision and tutelage of some of the best mathematicians in Germany. All assigned to special teams in cryptography, developing algorithms to make unbreakable code. Scholars who in recent years taught like himself at institutions of higher learning all over Europe, but were persuaded home. The *Abwehr*, like any intelligence service, was a secret society. Similar to a financial institution, an intelligence agency gathered and hoarded information instead of cash. Secrecy was king. The information was gathered, secured, sifted, analyzed and very carefully invested and used. He understood that like banks, intelligence agencies had lots of competition within their own countries, and sometime subsets of their own organization. Each agency was competing for scarce money, authority and political favor. Joining this secret society ensured the end of Karl's personal life that was obvious, as he realized how extensive the vetting process had been for even himself. There was no part of his life *Abwehr* had not examined or held up to the light. No part except his brief time with Anna. Once you're in the glass bubble you stayed in the light, there was no hiding anything.

In late August Karl's cryptanalysis team, which like his old logistic team in Limoges was comprised of fluent French speakers, was transferred to Paris. It was a bitter-sweet occasion, arriving in Paris this time without the pretense of July, 1940. He loved the city; the parks, museums and strolling the quais down by the Seine. Crossing the Pont de Sully to view the late summer light on the left bank and the spires of Notre Dame on the Ile de la City. After two years of steadily reduced ration allowances and heavy-handed administration from both the *Vichy* and German governments, Parisians were suffering and there was no doubt in any one's mind Germany was an occupying Army. The new brief for recently arrived German troops was quite different from the "try to win their hearts and minds" approach of 1940. Troops were prohibited from going out alone even during the daylight hours, and most were restricted to *Vichy* protected "safe zones" at night. Even officers were instructed to go out in pairs and to avoid any large congregation of French citizens. The term "resistance" wasn't showing up in the orders yet, but "agitators" and "insurgents" were.

All of it depressed Karl, especially since his cryptanalysis team was considered a military unit and they all had to wear uniforms and carry sidearms. When Parisians looked at them on the street, especially the men, the glances were sullen and resentful. They could read the papers. The losses in the Ukraine were not sustainable, the British were challenging Rommel in Africa and the American air campaign was striking German targets in France regularly.

In September Karl was informed he was being transferred to counter-intelligence, which besides alarming him, confused him. In Berlin his trainers had made it abundantly clear counter-intelligence was the purview of the *action* side, the *operations* side of *Abwehr;* espionage professionals best left completely alone. What he found instead was a sub-organization of *Abwehr*-Paris that had requested a mid-level unit manager to replace the loss of an officer killed in a car accident. The credentials for the candidate were fairly vague: *Adwehr* middle grade *(Major)* with command experience; intelligence professional, fluent French speaker, experience in French operations and experience with *Juif* support and communications infrastructure.

*What the hell does that mean?* He wondered.

"There are easily 20,000 *Juifs* still hiding in Paris." His new boss declared, pouring him a cup of coffee. "We just don't know who they are, and now that we're identifying and transporting French *Juifs,* the *gendarmerie* is dragging its feet. We must do the job ourselves. Berlin is screaming we are not transporting enough *Juifs* to handle the labor camps or the factories, and now that we're starting to draft Frenchmen for the labor camps, the French are impossible to deal with. So—here we are, intelligence professionals who should be hunting French and English bastards trying to blow up our trains and ammunition storage dumps, but instead we have this *Juif* hunting issue first. You know the problem, you built the transport trains. I saw your resume. I have only so many men to do everything Berlin expects us to do, so I'm assigning this jewel to you, *Major.* I know you are not an operations man, but at least you know the problem and you know the country. I can give you eight good men. Our target is at least 300 *Juifs* by the end of October. You have full authority to examine anything; birth records, church records, school records, anything that might give you a lead to where these people might be.     The Prefect would be the first step to grease the wheels for that information.     We're not murderers, though, we don't come at night and we don't summarily shoot people in the street.     The *gendarmerie* despite their lead feet, keep outstanding records.     If they balk, we go to the Prefect and set fires.     Good luck, Karl."

His chief lit a cigar and stood up, signaling the meeting was over. Karl reluctantly got to his feet and went out looking for his new staff.     He suspected everything his boss told him to do had already been done at least twice before by his predecessor(s).     It was the perfect assignment for a man new to *Abwehr,* and to counter intelligence.     He was beginning to realize nobody in the organization in Berlin really knew what the field units were doing.     It was the other side of extreme secrecy.     No one really knew or wanted to know.     He thought of all of those reams upon reams of paper his unit alone had produced in France regarding the train transport system in southwest France, and it depressed him even further.

# Chapter 20

*November 22, 1942. Lyon, France.*

The first thing Karl discovered was the eight men assigned to him were fluent French speakers as reported, but six were Parisian-born French nationals recruited by the other two, who were highly experienced *Abwehr* field officers. Karl's job was to direct and control the operations through his field officers; he would never meet the French agents. The six agents lived in five different quarters of Paris, and all had full time jobs and families to feed. All six were well-connected in their jobs, unions and communities, and had developed their own network of informers and sub-operatives. The agents were well paid for their services and in almost all cases, were recruited in the summer of 1940 as German forces rolled into Paris. Karl reviewed the agent files with his field officers and tried to understand the motivations for such individuals, who he found not to profess a particularly strong support of *Vichy*. If anything, the agents were generally indifferent to the politics, and were driven instead by the money and a fervent dislike of foreigners, especially *Juifs*.

In this first meeting with his field officers Karl confronted a stark reality.

"Is this the job you've been doing all along—hunting Jews?"

"Yes, *Herr Major,* since June of 1940."

"You two and these same six people?"

"No, *Herr Major.* One year ago, there were four field officers and 13 agents."

"What happened to them?"

"Our mandate is intelligence, *Herr Major,* and our senior officers here in Paris believed hunting Jews was more of an internal security issue, best left to security police, the SD. Half of our team was reorganized back to counter intelligence. Our arrests dropped significantly, which reduced the transport numbers. This caught the attention of both *Abwehr* in Berlin and unfortunately the *Oberste Fuhrer.* We are assuming this is one of the reasons you're here, sir."

"Adolf Hitler. There is a renewed emphasis on hunting Jews to provide the necessary numbers to fill the transport trains?"

"That is correct, *Herr Major.*"

"We need to increase the numbers—I believe 300 by the end of October was the target assigned to me, but they are not reassigning the two field officers and seven field agents back to us? I was told our eight is all I will get. *Impossible!* What are our numbers now? How many Jews are we finding per week? Per month?"

"It varies, of course, but we are doing well if we arrest 65 in a month. It's not like in the beginning when there were so many Jews in full view, like in the *Pletzl.* A typical tally will be 45 or 50. It takes time, and the arrests have to be coordinated with the *gendarmerie. Vichy* has insisted on knowing which Jews we were going after prior to arrest."

"From what I'm hearing it's *Vichy* and sometime the *gendarmerie* or the *Surete* who are tipping off French Jews we are coming—their friends or business associates. Why do we do this?"

"We did not want to offend the *Vichy* in the past, and we had counted on the cooperation of the police in the past as well. It has changed dramatically, the cooperation, when we started to go after French Jews. We also have the added complexity of our competition, the SD, which apparently has absorbed the German Army's entire police force. We heard they are also recruiting directly from the *Schutzstaffel*, so they will overwhelm our efforts by sheer force of their numbers."

"How are they handling this mission? Do they work with *Vichy* and the *gendarmerie* as we do?"

Both men smiled and shook their heads.

"No, *Herr Major,* they do not. That's why they absorbed the Army police force. They now have an enforcement arm. They don't go after Jews with *gendarmerie* supervision."

"And *Abwehr* will not concede this function to the SD."

"No, *Herr Major,* your presence confirms that."

Karl looked at the man over his fingers pressed against his nose like a steeple. There wasn't a hint of irony in his face. The man understood he was looking at another man given an impossible task with the same tools as before. He was forced to witness a one-eyed gimp of a temporary *Major* soon to be sacrificed when the mission fails.

"What can we do that we are not currently doing? As you said, SD will overwhelm us by sheer numbers, but we are required to give a strong showing somehow. Keep us in the game, I suppose. You two have been doing this for over two years now. What could we be doing we haven't done before?"

The two men, seasoned professionals, stared at Karl for a moment before exchanging glances. Perhaps they saw something in Karl, or knew Karl's eventual fate would be one they could share as *Abwehr's* fortunes drifted in the wind.

"In Germany we caught Jews with other Jews. We called those Jews *'Greifers'.* SD is now all SS so they use the technique, but *Abwehr* has been slow to adapt to the more—aggressive methods here in France.

189

Instead of tracking Jews through records, like we have been doing, we should force them to the surface with another Jew who can identify them specifically."

"Why would a Jew in Paris identify another Jew?"

"They won't *Herr Major,* unless you give them no choice. We have arrested most of the foreign Jews because no one knows them or cares about them. They are easy to discover because they have no connections, no one to vouch and lie for them. But the French Jews are often protected by both *Vichy* and even the *gendarmerie* and the *Surete,* as you know. These Jews have been here in France for generations, many have married non-Jews. Many are non-practicing. These are often the highly respected leaders in their professions and communities. The French don't see them the same as foreign Jews. They regard them as members of their family, personal friends or colleagues—and above all, they regard them as *French.*

"You see the problem? Denunciations are common place among ordinary Frenchmen towards Jews when there is a reason—competition in business or the perception Jews in power give favor to other Jews for jobs and contracts. This was easy to find when you're dealing with more recent citizens or foreign Jews from other countries. And we used those, but now our focus is shifting to French Jews and the doors are closing for us. With the necessary conscriptions of Frenchmen for our factories in Germany and Poland, there might even be a small amount of empathy for Jews now. To find the legally defined Jews who are also French citizens, hidden in plain sight, we must use other Jews because they know who they are! Many Jews have even hidden under the protection of the Catholic Church, converting through marriage and disappearing under the records of the church. One family knows another family. We capture one family, and put pressure on a weak member. We ask them to give us other names, other families under the promise of some—leniency for their own family. Jew against Jew. It works. It saves hundreds of man hours poring over old records. Give us a name and we won't transport your mother and father—this month. Anything, they will do anything."

"*Abwehr* has resisted this method?"

"Yes, *Herr Major.* When we identify Jews this way the French believe we are abusing their legal system. Abusing it because these Jews are French. They invariably will deny they are Jews, and even *Vichy* will defend certain ones because the individual's contribution to French society, and demand we establish proof. The *Abwehr*—the *Abwehr* does not believe it has the legal authority to countermand French law. That is our problem, *Herr Major.* I say this at the risk of sounding disloyal, but perhaps you recognize it yourself. You have read the *Fuhrer's* mandate.

The SD will be more successful because they are disregarding French concerns and operating on the principle it is the *accused* who must establish proof *they are not* Jews."

"If we start identifying Jews this way, you're saying we will assume the person doing the denunciating is telling the truth, and the *accused* have to prove otherwise? We have no man power to vet these denunciations. There are the three of us. Our agents, through their sources, provide us with names. We bring people in and persuade them it is in their family's best interest to give us other names. I'm no lawyer, gentlemen, but you are right, the French government will protest. The *Vichy* will not support us and the *gendarmerie,* as you stated earlier, will not cooperate as our enforcement arm. Without their help, explain to me how we would be able to arrest a single Jew?"

The other field officer looked grave and concerned, but when the lead officer glanced his way, he nodded his head in consent.

"I speak—frankly, for both of us, if you don't object, *Herr Major*. We are tasked, as you say, with an impossible mission. In *Abwehr* we are trying to operate in a gentleman's world, but this is not a gentleman's war. Our leadership believes we are an intelligence agency, which we are. We should provide information and turn it over to those who can act on it. It may have worked in the past, but our action sources are not working to our best interests. The French do not want us to go after French Jews, especially those who are highly placed in French society, academia, medicine or law. But our own leadership in Paris and Berlin— it may be less inclined to protest when you meet the *Oberste Fuhrer's* goals. Success will silence the concerns. We have strong association with a new group of fascist Frenchmen, the *SOL, the Service d'ordre legionnaire,* forming from ex-servicemen organizations. They have a much stronger presence in Southern France, but they have offered assistance in the past here in Paris. If we break contact with the *Vichy* government and the *gendarmerie*, I think the *SOL* will gladly step in and assist us in providing manpower for shadowing, arresting and interrogating prisoners. They are pro-*Vichy* but impatient with the French laws. Many of their members are out of work and blame the Jews."

Karl brought his hands down and met the eyes of the two men sitting across from him. They understood what was at stake and so did he. He had heard about the *SOL* and he shuddered. They were infamous for their extreme street violence and horrific and inhumane interrogation techniques used on their own countrymen.

"My orders are to meet my goals by all means available, presumably legal. However, I was given no particular instructions or restrictions in this assignment. You are authorized by me to do whatever you need to do to fulfill those numbers.  I will put this in writing in the form of orders for you this afternoon.  We are in the business of hunting Jews, and if we must turn Jews against Jews to find them, so be it."


Their success both surprised and horrified him.  His orders sprung hidden restraints off of his two field officers and they unleashed enormous invisible energy onto the streets of Paris.  Dark energies of fear and terror, he suspected guiltily.  Within three weeks they had managed to produce nearly 150 names and with the help of the *SOL* field associates arrested nearly 100.  The others were pending.  Karl hid in his office and reviewed the reports, astonished at the effectiveness of the campaign. The arrests were all of French Jews, many highly placed in government, finance, medicine and law.  The initial targets for questioning were all family members, often non-Jews, who had other family members in detention centers.  *SOL* provided interrogators and the targets quickly provided the names.  Protests were arriving daily from the Prefect and from the Chief of Police about the arrests, sent directly to the *Abwehr* Paris station chief.  Karl's name was never mentioned because he was unknown to the Prefect or the police.  What he did know was that his telephone remained quiet from his superiors.  His field officers were right. Success bred a different kind of silence.

Karl met his goals and was ordered to pack his bags for Lyon by the early part of November.  He found his success difficult to fully grasp because the action of arrest now seemed to guarantee a prisoner was declared guilty of being a *Juif.*  Virtually all of the arrested individuals eventually found themselves on a transport train to Auschwitz.  The arrest numbers and the transport numbers were the same.   He met his 300 for October and some and was rewarded with a letter from Heinrich Himmler, congratulating him for his success in meeting the goals of the *Third Reich.* A second letter, accompanied by a frightening SS *Obersturmbannfuhrer* (Lieutenant Colonel) who represented, he said, the *Oberste Fuhrer*, was a warrant confirming the promotion of one Karl Berchtold from *Major* (temporary), to the full rank of *Sturmbannfuhrer* (Major) (permanent). His superiors in Paris were impressed indeed, and gave him a beautiful, hand-tooled leather briefcase on his departure befitting a *Major* who would presumably not be a *Major* for long.

The incredible irony of his situation churned his bowels, as he understood now the guilt and shame he sensed from the railway engineer in Poland who had given him the suitcase full of *Reichsmarks.*  A man who had turned his own back on the same desperate people, choosing, out of fear or the simple inability to act, to look the other way and do his job.

It kept coming back to the trains, the transports and the impossible, unstoppable and seemingly inevitable machine drawing the unfortunate *Juifs* out of hiding, vacuuming them up like so many insects. His temporary success only guaranteed him more opportunity to find and lead others to their demise.

Lyon was the center of the French resistance movement, a new term he had never heard before. Terrorists, insurgents and agitators were the characteristics used in the Paris papers for Frenchmen who were anti-*Vichy*. The *Abwehr* had a large station in Lyon, large for *Abwehr,* but competition was forming again in a very big way, as a significant SD unit was coming. Karl Berchtold, recently promoted high producer in Paris, was taking over to ensure the *Juif* transport numbers were met, and to assist in the defeat of the so-called *French Resistance*. His orders were to cooperate with the SD to not only meet the end goals of the *Third Reich,* but to also ensure the *Abwehr* fulfilled its specific, mandated responsibilities. He took the time and studied the SD, his soon arriving competition, and understood SD had seven sections each with an area of responsibility in France. They were known officially as the KDS, or *Kommandos Sipo*. Six sections were coming to Lyon. Section Four was responsible for anti-resistance activities and would have a primary role. A section known as the *Gestapo.*

# Chapter 21

*March 12, 1943. Lyon, France.*

The only saving grace for *Abwehr* was Section Four was given the specific directive of destroying the resistance movement in Lyon, and had little interest in hunting *Juifs*. The newly arrived section head, a young *SS-Hauptsturmfuhrer* (Captain), was wholly focused on that mission alone. Karl invited him to his office in late November shortly after the *Hauptsturmfuhrer* had arrived, finding him polite but condescending. He congratulated Karl on his "success" in Paris, noting the SS had been using the technique for years. He considered *Abwehr* and its past approach to gathering intelligence outdated, borne out, he said pointedly, in post-war evaluations of their contributions in the Great War. *Abwehr* still had value, of course, he added, and there were some successes in the counter-intelligence side of the organization. Karl thanked him for coming, pledged complete cooperation and was glad to get rid of him.

He watched in awe as the *Hauptsturmfuhrer* established his headquarters in an old hotel and grew his organization to several times the size of the *Abwehr* detachment. The *Gestapo* was not only fully staffed, but it apparently had a large budget for indigenous agents. By spring there were dozens of pro-*Vichy* Frenchmen in the employ of Section Four, some volunteers and others fulltime, armed and issued with German Police SD identification. Many of these pro-*Vichy* French now working for SD were former informers or part-time agents for the *Abwehr*. They found hunting, arresting and assisting in the interrogation of their fellow Frenchmen more lucrative with SD. Karl was grateful the *Gestapo* in Lyon was more than willing to accede *Juif* hunting to *Abwehr*. There were only so many unidentified *Juifs* left in southern France and it was becoming an exercise in diminishing returns.

Karl now joined his field officers in reviewing the hundreds of files generated by *Abwehr* agents and informers because they needed every hand. They were also allowed to review some of the files produced by the *Gestapo*. The *Gestapo* made it a point to share the information gathered from interrogations when the subjects were *Juifs*. Karl recognized some of the files as originating from themselves, the *Abwehr*, as former agents and informers now in the SD introduced the same information to their new employers. It meant some of the individuals who had managed to be released by *Abwehr* were re-arrested by the *Gestapo*, and in 100% of the cases executed or transported to the camps. There was often new information, (i.e., names) based on the interrogations now requiring follow up.

Karl read these SD reports in horror and fascination because of the extreme detail of the record, but he was also drawn to the graphic nature of the files. Photographs were always included of the prisoners, at their arrest and during and after interrogation. Those that died did so violently. Only in rare occasions was there little evidence of repeated torture and physical mutilation. The final page of each file was signed by the young *SS Hauptsturmfuhrer* he met in November. He found it of special interest that in over half of these cases, the same *Hauptsturmfuhrer* was the actual interrogating officer. *How could that be?* He assumed there were hundreds of these files existing and the few sent over to *Abwehr* represented only a small handful. Why would the unit leader of such a big operation be involved in actual interrogations when he had so much to do? *Did he actually do these things to these people causing these horrendous wounds?*

Pouring through the *Abwehr* files made him realize how extensive the reporting was for the most simple of cases. For an *Abwehr* mission a six-man detail was assigned the task of shadowing someone. There were two men per eight-hour shift with the senior man on the shift writing the action report. They were excellent observers and watched everything with a keen eye for detail. Every human contact was noted extensively and the new contact photographed. In the back of his mind Karl thought about the late fall in Limoges when the *Abwehr,* the very same *Abwehr,* was shadowing Anna—his Anna. *What do they know? Is there a file somewhere?*

In early March one of his senior field officers approached him and closed the door to his office. Of all of his field officers, Karl trusted him the most.

"There might be a problem for you, *Herr Major* Berchtold in this file sent over from the SD last Thursday. It's part of a new group, all Jew interrogations, and you haven't seen them."

"This came from SD? What is the problem?" The man had the file in his hand, but he didn't open it. Instead he carefully laid it down on Karl's desk.

"This is a combined file, partially *Abwehr* and SD. Your name is mentioned in it—a personal post office box in Limoges, first noticed over a year ago by the *Abwehr* unit there, and then reported again during the SD interrogation of a Jew named Nina Rosenberg here in Lyon. SD had her family in Drancy and she was given the opportunity to buy them some time by providing new names. One of the names she gave SD is a medical student she knew at the Sorbonne who was hiding out in Limoges. They corresponded through this post office box, the one with your name associated. There is a note in the file stating your name needed to be followed up by the SD, but there is no record anything was done about it. Not in the file.   I think because it involves a Jew who has revealed some names, the SD passed it over to us without doing anything.   What do you want me to do with it, *Herr Major?*"

Karl looked at his field officer in the eye with mild surprise followed by irritation as he picked up the file.

"I used to have a post office box in Limoges when I was stationed there over two years ago!   Such incompetence!   I thought I closed it when I was transferred to the Eastern Front!"

"Easy enough to see what happened.   The French reassigned it to someone else with probably a phony name and the new owner, protecting their real name, discovered your name on an old piece of mail and had people mail things under your name.   Might even be an inside job in the post office, and they kept your name on the box.   No one looks at the name anyway.   The mail handlers just look for the post office box number."

"I suppose," Karl sighed.   "I'll get back to you.   Thanks for bringing it to my attention."   He stood up and then stopped his field officer with his hand.

"Did you follow up on the medical student in Limoges?"

"Yes, I tracked her through an old address of her parents in Aix, an address provided by this Nina Rosenberg.   I prepared the report, it's all there.   She's a Jew, on her father's side.   It's a strange story, kind of sad actually.   Read it, you'll find it interesting.   Let me know what we need to do with it."


It had always sat lightly in the back of his mind that she was *Juif* in hiding.   Her Nordic pale skin, blond hair and grey-green eyes could easily be from his family.   Her family, Catholic for over 40 years and knowing no other religion, might have remained undiscovered.   The report stated her father approached a family friend, the assistant Prefect and asked for guidance on possibly immigrating to a western country accepting Jews. He approached his friend with a hypothetical but had to admit he was a Jew, converted to Catholicism 40 years before.   The friend explained the process and the father started the arduous, tedious application.   In the meantime, the information was leaked out and he lost his job as professor at his law school in Aix, and shortly thereafter his family home and possessions were seized.   Karl closed his eyes as he started to read the paragraph again, because he saw the implications of his role in every word.

*The father tried to separate himself from his family, his non-Juif wife and his youngest daughter, who had run away from home a few weeks before. There are the other children, the daughter in Limoges, and a son reportedly in the French Air Force, believed to be in England. The father had been detained briefly at Les Milles, near Aix, under the pretext he was approved for immigration and was held for processing. His wife insisted on joining him near the end of the stay. This approval, apparently pending, never came. This was because of the November 10th declaration from Adolf Hitler stating Jews would no longer be allowed to emigrate from France. They were released temporarily but rearrested in January, 1943 by the Aix Police Commissiare, who refused to reconsider their case. Within a week they were sent to Drancy and on a train to Auschwitz a week later. They did not survive, according to records the first day of captivity. The status of the youngest daughter is still unknown.*

# Chapter 22

*April 15, 1943. Limoges, France.*

He couldn't explain why he was there, other than his need to be as close to her as he could. The *maison* was in the old part of the city, and he admitted during his time here he wasn't aware of it. He knew of course such places existed and were frequented by many *Wehrmacht* officers, but this one was a special one reserved for high-ranking French and German Army officials. A mere *hauptmann,* as he was in those days, need not darken the doorway. Not that he would get much better treatment as a *major,* his inquiries suggested he would have to be at least *an oberstleutnant* to get past the *Madame*—what's her name—Marchand. Besides he wasn't alone, he was assigned a driver. To the driver Karl had not actually given an address only a street. He had him stop the car a half a block away from the *maison* and pretended to be very interested in his notes.

Karl had granted his own travel authorization for a three-day trip to Limoges. Much of the time was allocated to train travel, but the *Abwehr* head in Limoges, an aging *hauptmann,* graciously loaned him a small staff car. The driver was a given, *majors* did not drive themselves, and this was the *Abwehr,* the driver would be debriefed about every stop they made. Karl's reputation preceded him as he was granted free reign of the records office. His explanation of following up on information revealed from interrogations was a free pass. A hovering clerk was quickly dispensed with a withering stare, and he started to search specifically for *Anna Metzgen* or *Anna Metzger* alone. It was encouraging yet frustrating at first because there was nothing.

He realized the SD file he had in Lyon regarding the interrogation of Nina Rosenberg, and all of the follow-up on Anna's father, Henri Metzgen, was never shared with the Limoges *Abwehr.* *Abwehr* had nothing official on Anna Metzgen. When he discovered there was not even a single piece of paper under Anna Metzger, he finally asked for assistance. He was looking for, he described in exasperation to the clerk, a certain type of evidence, as the name didn't exist in the files. He was trying to find counter-intelligence reports of suspicious individuals, possibly foreign agents, specifically young blond women contacting German officers or French citizens in the downtown area. Say, January 1941 to January 1942. How would you file such reports, *Obergefreiter* (Corporal)?

The clerk, a bespectacled and intelligent-looking young man Karl regretted being rude to before, stared at Karl in intense concentration. The clerk lit up and glanced over at a bank of file cabinets behind him.

*What you describe, Herr Major, are typical follow-ups our field officers do in response to tips from citizens, the French police and informers on suspicious activities. We handle hundreds of those and they rarely lead to anything. But I remember some cases of mysterious women who operated downtown, suspected British agents. There were also several reports on a young blond woman who used disguises and phony identification, but nothing ever came of it, because they never got a name or arrested anyone before she disappeared. Those sightings were occurring in the timeframe you speak of. Would you be interested in seeing some of those, Herr Major?*

Karl was distressed when the young man soon returned with several thick files covering nearly two years.

After sifting through dozens of reports for the fall of 1940, Karl finally came across a report he recognized. He glanced up from his reading to check on the file clerk, who remained in the room but at a respectful distance.

In late 1940 *Abwehr* responded to a tip from a French waiter that a blond woman frequenting a downtown restaurant might be a foreign agent seeing a German Army officer. This was followed up on and a small shadow team was assigned for a few days. The mystery blond was tracked to the building Anna lived in, and was observed meeting with a German Army officer (Karl) on several occasions, but she was never identified nor was her residence pin pointed. The watchers never followed her into the building, apparently. Karl was identified and followed from his office and quarters, but the team only saw Karl and Anna together in the evening, sometimes in local restaurants or cafes. The shadow work seemed sloppy to Karl, but it was obvious by the daily action reports the *Abwehr* watchers did not recognize Anna as a known enemy agent, and suspected her of being a French freelance prostitute preying on German officers. There was no record of *Abwehr* contacting the French Police to confirm their suspicion. In fact, much to his surprise, there was no reference to any coordination between *Abwehr* and the French police at any time.

Poor light conditions resulted in less than-useful photographs of the female suspect, identified mostly because of her slim figure and blond hair. In the end the result of the shadowing was referred to the commanding officer of the subject German officer. The file noted the subject officer was reprimanded for seeing a prostitute, and transferred. File closed.

A few weeks later the informant complained he was seeing the same woman, sometimes using disguises such as wigs and working women clothing, operating downtown. She did not operate like a prostitute but more like a spy. The informant, who was apparently pro-*Vichy* and used as an informant by the French police and considered reliable, felt she was not a smuggler or a black marketer. In his opinion, noted in the file, the subject woman seemed highly refined and too well versed in tradecraft to be a prostitute. *Abwehr* responded by establishing a 24-hour shadowing operation on her, noting her unusual but not illegal behavior. They were unable to identify her or catch her attempting to contact anyone once the subject German officer left the area. After four weeks her case was closed and the field officers reassigned.

Fascinated, Karl realized as he sifted through the reports, he was slowly developing a picture of Anna's existence after he was transferred. Months would pass and the sighting reports were routine, follow ups on tips but nothing relating to or pointing to the mysterious blond, or to Anna. In the chronology it wasn't until September of 1941 before he came across another thick file, stuffed with *Abwehr* and French municipal police reports. He read incredulously of the case of a Communist optics worker named Marie Broussard, who was suspected of not only labor disruptions at the main Limoges railway station, but having connections with a suspected British agent working under the guise of a French worker in another optics shop. Both shops were contracted to produce war materials for the German Government.

The suspected British agent escaped despite a huge police cordon around the building where she was believed to work and reside. She was actually seen by *Abwehr* officers and *gendarmerie* in the building attempting to meet with Marie Broussard. The physical description of the British agent was of a thin woman in her mid-20s of medium height with short blond hair. A German security guard and the Communist suspect, Marie Broussard, confirmed the British agent had used the name *Anna Metzger*, for identification. The municipal police confirmed there was no such person working at the other optics company, and the name was presumed to be an alias. The Communist worker denied ever meeting the subject, assumed alias name Anna Metzger. The record reported Marie Broussard was executed as an enemy agent when her case was transferred to the SD.

Karl put the file down for a moment, noticing his hands were shaking and his heart was racing. The *Abwehr* called her a British agent. And now there was a name associated with her, although the record seems to imply it, they disregarded it. There is no mention of it and there was no file on record, not even under known-aliases. Since they didn't have a true identity, he could see there would be no point in creating such a file. What they didn't know was it really was her name. Almost.

*My Anna. She was still living in the apartment in September of 1941, but somehow, she escaped. If Abwehr had caught her and transferred her to SD, she would have shared the same fate as Marie Broussard. The apartment was her only refuge. The decision to leave must have been immediate. How was she able to escape without leaving any trace? The lease on his apartment was under his name. Why no record of this in the Abwehr files? Did she manage to slip away without revealing where she lived? My God, where did she go? What happened to her?*

Guilt and fear clutched at his heart, but he couldn't explain why she was trying to meet with Marie Broussard. So much passed during those months he was not aware of. *Had they become friends somehow, since Marie worked in the same building Anna lived in? Had Anna joined the Communist party out of loneliness?*

The only file entry of interest, dated in the spring of 1942, was an *Abwehr* report attached from another investigation. An *Abwehr* shadow team was covering a suspected enemy agent who was using a Limoges downtown post office box for mail drops. A suspicious individual, an elderly woman, was observed hovering near the mail boxes for an unusual length of time. She was observed opening a box with a key and withdrawing a large quantity of mail. When the subject left, the *Adwehr* watchers noted the box number and confirmed the owner of the box from post office records. It was registered to a Karl Berchtold, a serving German Army officer who was assigned at one time to the Limoges area, but subsequently transferred to the Eastern Front. Follow up was recommended. The elderly woman matched the description of a suspected British agent, identity unknown, believed to operate in the downtown area of Limoges. The elderly woman's outfit was possibly a disguise, one of several she was believed to use.

There were no comments in the file noting anyone had seen or suggested any further action on this observation. How did the SD find this information then? Then he remembered his own field officer had followed up on the information reported by the *Gestapo* interrogation of Nina Rosenberg and written the report. The field officer must have called the *Abwehr* Limoges headquarters and asked about this information, perhaps spoke to this same clerk. Very possibly spoke with the post office officials on the ownership of the post office box.

Karl knew it would be unlikely there would be other copies besides the carbons. Most *Abwehr* reports submitted and filed, like police reports everywhere, were standardized. Prepared on carbon forms and these carbons were still intact with all copies. The carbons were for cross filing and each copy was supposed to be carefully recorded to placement, signed and dated. He learned that much in his *Abwehr* training. But there was no record of any copies sent anywhere in these files. They remained dormant and were simply collecting dust. Originals with all carbons attached unless someone had photographed them, page by page. It was done all of the time for important files but these were not important. They were routine follow ups.

The file clerk occasionally looked over at Karl, but seemed preoccupied with his own duties. Karl had his notebook for making some notes, but the file clerk wouldn't be able determine which files Karl was spending his time on. Karl looked down at the last file where his name was mentioned and knew he could simply unhook the original from the binder prongs. He could slip it sideways, fold it and slide it into his notebook. In the end he left them alone, undisturbed. He continued skimming the reports until he had read every file. He expected some follow up on Anna's abandoned apartment when she escaped, some mention of either the evidence found or the lease owner's name. A serious police cordon of the building would have entailed a room by room search. If she wasn't there, they would enter with a master key. What would they find? They would find everything unless she planned ahead, had time to clean the room of all traces of her living there for—how many months? But there was nothing in the record. Not a trace. *Abwehr* made no mention but the *Surete* was there too.

He sighed noisily and began stacking the files in obvious frustration, attracting the attention of the file clerk. He stood up and carefully approached Karl with a hopeful smile. He seemed genuinely sad as Karl shook his head and thanked the clerk for his assistance. *Not in these files,* he said.

Karl was already tired and hungry when he arrived at the National Police Headquarters, or as it was called, the Commissariat. He sent his driver out to find a late lunch for himself and asked to be picked up later in the evening. The Commissaire of Police was out of town but the Assistant Commissaire, on listening to Karl's apology on not calling ahead, was distressed that an *Abwehr* official of Karl's rank was handling an inquiry by himself. *It is a sensitive case,* Karl admitted, and left it at that, which did nothing to reassure the man.

He remained wary and clearly suspicious, especially when he heard Karl's excellent French and understood Karl had served in Limoges before. He insisted on assigning Karl two detectives to help in finding files, clearing a conference room of tired-looking, grumbling investigators for Karl's use.

*We are at your service, Major. Would you like some refreshments? Tea? Coffee, perhaps?*

The records, stacked in three neat files, confirmed what he had already known. *Abwehr* did not share information with the French police in any organized, structured manner, and the *Surete* returned the favor. It was unfortunate, as he reviewed the files, as the *Surete* kept excellent records of everything, that is, unless they were ordered not to by certain officials for a number of reasons. If they had taken the time, Karl noted, the *Abwehr* field officers would have found an extensive list of known operating prostitutes in Limoges by city quarter, with the primary list a breakdown of the prostitutes certified by the city because they worked in licensed *maisons*. A second list represented known non-certified freelancers who worked with pimps and or organized crime, and a third list of suspected prostitutes who worked independently without pimps or protection of any kind. Independents were routinely rousted and occasionally arrested, but payoffs at various levels of city government kept the actual arrests to a minimum. But Karl didn't even open the two latter lists. He found what he was looking for under the *maisons*. It was under this category of city employee Karl discovered a file for *Anna Metzger*.

When he asked for it the two detectives exchanged glances and returned, not with just the file, but with a man they introduced as their Chief Inspector. The Inspector was a short, husky man who appeared near exhaustion. His eyes were partially closed as he slowly stalked into the conference room, ignoring Karl to find the nearest available seat. He lifted his face and opened his eyes, which were brilliantly grey and clear, before proffering a large, puffy hand towards Karl. Karl stared at the man for a moment before leaning far forward to grasp the offered hand by the fingertips. It was an awkward introduction.

"If I may ask, *Major,* what is the reason for your inquiry?" The man seemed to sense the boldness of his challenge, and suddenly lifted his hand, perhaps in appeasement, as he searched his pockets, withdrawing a box of cigarettes. Karl's cold stare may have had something to do with it. It was the first time he realized how his appearance, status and rank could intimidate.

"I ask this in the spirit of *total cooperation, Major*. But the person you are interested in is the subject of a criminal investigation."

"I see. I can't tell you much Inspector, but *Mademoiselle* Metzger's name came up during the interrogation of a prisoner in Lyon, a *Gestapo* prisoner. The case was referred to us because of certain circumstances. She is an individual of some interest to us, and I would like to see her file to confirm some information we have. This should not interfere with your—criminal investigation. Agreed?"

At the mention of the *Gestapo* the Inspector's eyes widened perceptively, but otherwise there was no change in his expression. He glanced over at the detective holding Anna's file and waved him over. He took the file and gripped it in his large hands.

"Perhaps we can mutually benefit from the information we both seemed to have on this *Mademoiselle* Metzger, *Major*." Karl realized the Inspector wanted to bargain and he lost his patience. He slowly got to his feet. He towered over the Inspector and simply outstretched his hand.

"I don't know what type of criminal investigation you are undertaking, but I don't believe what we have in our files on this woman will be of much bearing. I must insist on the files, Inspector, right now. I do not have much time for my own investigation. If I must involve the Prefect I will, and I guarantee you will suffer for it."

"I'm hesitating *Major*, not because of a petty squabble over jurisdiction with the German Army, I'm no fool." The Inspector lifted the file and held it up.

"This is a very sensitive case, because it involves high-ranking officials of the French government and potentially—I say this with extreme caution, *potentially* a German Army officer. A colonel. An SS *Standartenfuhrer*." A shiver of fear ran up Karl's spine and his hand dropped to his side.

"An SS *Standartenfuhrer!* Is SD already involved? How is this woman—this Anna Metzger involved?"

"A SS *Standartenfuhrer* was murdered about six weeks ago in a hotel downtown. We started the investigation and it was taken over by the German Military Police, the SD when they were informed the victim was a senior German officer. There were no arrests and no witnesses. About six days ago Limoges had some high-level visitors from down south, the Assistant Prefect and the Chief Inspector of Police from Aix. They came for a conference and—well, they were entertained at the best *maison* here in Limoges, *Madame* Marchand's. Both were entertained by the most beautiful and exclusive prostitute in the *maison,* this Anna Metzger. That evening both men were somehow lured to the same hotel the SS-*Standartenfuhrer* was murdered in, and both men were killed in separate rooms at different times during the night."

The Inspector broke his narrative to light a cigarette, waving the smoke away. Karl sat back down, gripping the sides of his chair to control the trembling in his extremities. He could not believe what he was hearing, feeling separated from his body as if in a dream.

"There were two witnesses this time, both describing a slim woman with dark hair around these rooms about the time these gentlemen appeared. We became especially interested when we realized the two men from Aix were killed in the same identical way as the SS-*Standartenführer* five weeks earlier. So further investigation revealed, yes, the Colonel had frequented *Madame* Marchand's *maison*. We believe the prostitute he was with was Anna Metzger. In all three homicides the rooms were reserved in advance by the victims, and all three victims had other, official hotel rooms with luggage in them. It was obvious they were lured to the second hotel by a prostitute whom they had met at some point in their short stay in Limoges. Although it is highly illegal, it is not unheard of for *maison* prostitutes to meet with clients outside of the *maison* for a number of reasons. Because of this we wanted to question this Anna Metzger."

"You have Anna Metzger in custody?" Karl asked incredulously. The Inspector set the file down carefully on the table again and peered at his feet.

"No, we do not. She has disappeared. Vanished."

"You think Anna Metzger killed all three men?" The Inspector looked up and shrugged his shoulders.

"I don't know. It is interesting she left, however. The murder weapon was a knife, and our medical examiner believes the murderer was not very strong, possibly a woman."

"Have you told SD there may be some connection between the murders?"

"Not yet. As you can imagine when you are talking about senior public officials, you have to be very careful—and sensitive about the potential involvement of prostitutes. There are families and administrative reputations to consider. We wanted to make sure—and we didn't want the SD to take over the case."

"Is there anything new you can tell me about this Anna Metzger?"

"Nothing really, but of course we are looking for a motive. Some connection with this woman and the senior public officials from Aix. There is a chance, and it is based on our questioning of *Madame* Marchand and some of Anna Metzger's colleagues in the *maison*, that she may be an escaped *Juif*. It is all hearsay as we have no real record of this woman. We really don't know who she is. The name is probably an alias. She certainly doesn't look like a *Juif*. But why she would kill these three men is a mystery. The murderer did not rob them, none of them, but stabbed them repeatedly, so there is some prior contact, you can be sure of that."

The Inspector released his grip on the file, opening it and turning it around, revealing a top sheet with a grainy, black and white identification photograph of Anna. She looked tired and drawn, her full lips parted and eyes were wide open and looking hard at the camera. He couldn't take his eyes off of it. She seemed to be watching him. Her face was thinner than he remembered, unsmiling and accusing. Under the photograph was a number, a certification number. *Anna Metzger, alias.* PROSTITUTE.

Karl couldn't keep his eyes off the picture for a long moment, then let his eyes drift up and met those of the Inspector.

"A pretty woman." The Inspector said slowly. "A dangerous one. She lures these victims away from the *maison* and stabs them to death. They came along though, just to get her all to themselves. She must be very special." Karl sensed the policeman was probing him somehow, forcing him to look away. He examined the file again and noticed the folder had a code name typed under the file tab: THE KITE.

"What is the Kite?" He asked.

"I used to live in Paris, there is a street in the Pletzl—part of the Marias, called "Rue des Ecouttes." Karl stared at the Inspector.

"I know the street. The Street of Kites. Named for *Juif* moneylenders."

"I was thinking more of the bird, Ecouttes. A small raptor. Like a little hawk."

"You call this Anna Metzger 'The Kite'?"

"Yes. She is a bird of prey, yes?"

# Coming Back

## Chapter 23

*May 5, 1944. 30 miles off the coast of Bordeaux, France.*

If there was any envy in Anna's heart as she glanced over at her radio operator, slouched over the bench affair on the other side blissfully asleep, it was the total confidence she exhibited in any corner of her life. *Everything will work out, you watch, Anna!* Americans, with their short history and tendency to ignore the past and experience of other countries and cultures, blindly believe their arrival on the scene for the two WORLD WARS ensured triumph and success. There was no question in their manner: *we are going to win.* People like Melody, likeable and cheerful OSS officers who seemed to be sliced from the same loaf of American upper crust bread, had a confidence born of privilege and strength from an enormous continent, with natural resources and manufacturing power to back it up.

Melody Langdon, 24 years old, the only daughter of a former Massachusetts state senator and manufacturer of microscopes, presented this casual and astonishing world view without a shred of conceit. It was as packaged and admirably spun as a Hollywood yarn with Katherine Hepburn. As a European Anna could question the merit, but the package was bigger-than-life and the dazzle and pure confidence encouraged the suspension of disbelief. You wanted to believe in these people, embrace such a pure spirit. What the Americans presented wasn't arrogance or racism, not like the Nazis, but a clear, heart-felt belief America and the Allies represented all that was good and right in the world, and good and right would prevail. In the end, even Anna could not resist the temptation to join them, even when deep in her heart she believed them naïve and ignorant. They were, as power and tides ebbed and flowed, *going in her direction. They believed others thought like they did and in their enthusiasm for wartime expediency simply overlooked who she really was.*

As the Sussex teams were training, people started to pair up naturally. Most of the teams were men, serving military officers or civilians who had spent considerable time in Europe. There were only a few women assigned to the pre-invasion effort. Anna would have accepted a man as her radio operator, but the OSS protocol, similar to SOE, had women paired together. They hooked up and made the best of the situation, despite the differences in their backgrounds and personalities.    It was a difficult relationship to warm up to for Anna, as she disliked Melody almost immediately for the simple reason Melody found everything humorous, "a lark", as she characterized their parachute, escape and evasion training.

A product of private schools and Pembroke College in Rhode Island, Melody discovered New England urban life dull and predictable. She had lived with her parents for a few years in Brussels and Paris, so decided to return to Europe a couple of years before the war as a State Department clerk typist.    Like Anna, Melody was gifted with an easy fluency in languages.    She stayed in France even after the capitulation in 1940, protected for a time by American neutrality.    The Germans in Paris were friendly and respectful, the officer corps urbane and gentlemanly. Her youth, beauty and easy command of French and German made her popular with the German officers and she even dated a few, mixed with Frenchmen and fellow Americans until her superiors in the State Department abruptly put an end to it.

Anna was appalled as Melody happily described those early days, even as the German Army marched through the Arch de Triumph down the Av des Champs Elysee; it was so *historic, dramatic*—and, so *sad*. Melody's words exactly, her lovely head shaking slowly in wonderment as she carefully picked bits of cigarette tobacco off her tongue.    She appeared indifferent or ignorant to what the Germans demanded from the conquered, or the unspeakable horrors of their social engineering.    Anna remembered it clearly, wishing at the time she had a bat to club *this stupid fucking American* senseless.    Anna, who on the day the Germans marched under the Arch was four miles away in the Marais, hiding in her apartment as she had for days, hungry after exhausting everything in her pantry but too afraid to come out and be seen.    Melody, chattering on about her adventures, was clueless as Anna listened in silence, her fingers in her lap, clutched into tight fists. *How in God's name am I supposed to work with this bitch idiot?*

But work together they did.    After December 7th, 1941, American citizens, including non-critical State Department employees, were swept out of France across the channel to England.    Many of Melody's colleagues wanted to go home to the United States but a few, like Melody, accepted assignments in London.    On the strength of the recommendation of a romantically interested OSS officer, Melody was interviewed and hired a year later.    She joined the support branch preparing the phony documents to be used by real live OSS agents in enemy territory.    Her excellent work caught the attention of senior officers, who upon realizing her fluency in German and French and experience in France, asked if she would be interested in hazardous special operations work.

What kept Anna from refusing to work with Melody or requesting another RTO was Melody's demonstrated physical toughness, apparent fearlessness, coolness under stressful situations and her phenomenal memory. This became very apparent in field training as the bone-tired and exhausted student operative teams would somehow arrive at their designated target area after hours of grueling effort, only to be challenged by unexpected, overwhelming problems.

The training missions were specific, demanding accurate observations of troop formations, size, type, direction; possible identification based on uniforms, badges and equipment. All of it critical intelligence during the pre-invasion to determine what units were responding and where. The teams spent countless hours in training on equipment recognition, determining types of panzer vehicles, support trucks, towed artillery and tracked assault vehicles distinguishing *Wehrmacht* panzer divisions from a *Waffen-Schutzstaffel* panzer division. Despite their exhaustion and threat of capture, this information could be critical for invasion forces.

RTOs had to know constantly changing frequencies, call signs, codes and protocols or their communications would be disregarded as counter-intelligence work from the Germans. On top of this was the endless operational information they acquired as they made connections; map coordinates, addresses, telephone numbers and names. Most agents and RTOs carried critical, classified code books hidden all over their persons and equipment. If and when arrested, it was the most dangerous information they carried with them, as it was the key to mission success and agent survival. Used carefully, as the Germans did, it ensured for a time, the doom of dozens of missions and the arrest and executions of colleagues and Resistance members. The agents had no choice but to carry the books as it was too much to remember for most people. Not for Melody. No matter how exhausted she was Melody would remember most of those details. Despite her casual affect she *was* paying attention. Anna slowly realized what she had in her RTO and wouldn't trade her for anyone. Melody had no idea how quickly Anna planned to discard most of their equipment once they landed in France. Their only safety would be their speed, stealth and what was in their heads.

In the end Anna knew she came over to the OSS because the Americans didn't ask too many questions about the past, assuming her full allegiance with her SOE association. They had asked her what she was good at and she responded with no irony, *killing fascist pigs*. Something she never said to SOE, mostly because she suspected they knew too much about her already, and she wanted no history to be unburied by the police after the war was over. The SOE trained her well but her missions in the

209

fall of 1943 were in northern France; Brittany and Normandy, far from home. She assisted in the extraction of downed Allied pilots and sometimes other agents, and as her experience grew, she attempted to coordinate sabotage missions of German trains and facilities with local *maquis*. The reports leaked to her hinted her sister, Clara was serving with a *maquis* in the *Dordogne,* but Anna's missions were 200 kilometers north of the *Dordogne.* In her last extraction back to England she demanded specifically to be assigned a mission in the *Dordogne* but SOE turned her down. With the invasion of France only a few months away her skills were needed in the north.

Preparing for the invasions, both from the south of France and across the channel from Great Britain, the SOE was working with the OSS on numerous missions to prepare the French underground to disrupt the *Wehrmacht* infrastructure. Hearing from their SOE counterparts that Anna knew southwest France intimately, several OSS officers met with her ostensibly to question her about the physical lay of the land and the cultural history of the locals. They were very impressed with her in-depth knowledge of the transportation systems in southwest France, an almost verbatim overlay of the railways she had heard from Karl almost three years before, and her thorough understanding of the various *maquis* operating, in some cases against each other, from Limoges to Toulouse. When the OSS realized she wanted to go back there but was unable to do so with SOE, the meeting shifted to one of recruitment.

*Disruption* was the mission from the beginning, but she didn't know the OSS would take her initial comments about killing fascists so literally. Perhaps they didn't at first until her training supervisors noted her particular talents in field craft, hand-to-hand combat and small arms. Because she came from the operations side of the SOE and was already an experienced field agent, she moved through the training quickly. She learned the nuances of the American way of doing things, with different weapons and techniques, but there was no escaping the fact the OSS understood her desires and was preparing to fulfill her wish. All of the field operators were being trained in the .45 caliber service pistol, carbine and the various rifles and submachineguns carried by both the *maquis* and the German Army. Only a small group was given extra instruction, several hours a day, in close-in unarmed combat techniques, use of the garrote, the fighting dagger, small explosive charges attached to timers or plungers to be detonated as door knobs were turned or drawers opened, poisons and a small assortment of easily concealed devices that fired a lethal projectile at close range. Anna volunteered to go through the close-combat shoot house two dozen times until the instructors turned her away, explaining with a smile they had nothing they could teach her anymore.

The last phase Anna spent alone because it was mission specific. She was given several large books. The first was filled with the photographs of senior German officers. Head and shoulders, profile, with and without their uniform caps. Their name, rank, title and unit were printed under each image. They were battalion and regimental commanders, the assistant division commander and the division commander himself. Second SS *Panzer* Division. *Das Reich.*

The second book included the personal profiles of each of the same officers, listing where they were born, raised and educated, and the biographical details of their careers. She couldn't help but think of Karl as she read and absorbed the files. They were all young, handsome and intelligent looking men in the prime of their lives. Attractive, like Karl was to Anna so many years ago. Most were well educated with extensive combat experience. The Second SS *Panzer* Division entered France from Belgium in 1940 then fought for years on the Eastern Front. Now *Das Reich* was in southwestern France, based in Agen and Moutauban, fighting the growing insurgency presented by the *maquis* and other Resistance groups.

The third book included maps and aerial views of the same landscape, covering the area from south of Moutauban to just north of Limoges. The aerial views were the results of photo missions flown by Allied pilots at great risk. These always included *Das Reich* unit vehicles as they sortied out for a variety of missions. The sorties were dated and the photo recognition types tried to identify the origins of the sorties. By doing so a pattern was determined whenever certain units sortied, so a predictable path was mapped as the best choice for a unit whenever they headed north. The arrows on the maps marked the predicted path when D-Day was launched. Resistance groups and *maquis* would be waiting to attack and disrupt the panzer units as they headed north in response to D-Day, led and assisted with SOE and OSS teams who would provide additional weapons, ammunition and explosives. Anna and Melody would be among them, but Anna had an additional mission.

*Get close to the senior leadership anyway you can, Anna. Join in the disruption, use the maquis if you can, but this is a stealth job because the Germans, especially the SS, won't usually let civilians get close. Not now. But you have to. This is no suicide mission. You're a beautiful woman, be sure to bring a dress. We understand you're a master of disguises. You know what they look like, what their habits are. All we need is a couple of days delay. Slow them down. Take out number one and two. If you can't find them, go for regimental commanders or battalion commanders. But once they realize what's going on, they'll clamp down on the security. When that occurs, the primary mission is*

211

*over for you. Go to the secondary and hit them anyway you can. You cut the head off the dragon, it'll grow another head, but it slows it down.*
*What about reprisals?*

*Our job is to slow the division down, period. The local maquis will be flooding roads, blowing bridges, shoving explosives in the troop trucks and when they can, ambush and kill Germans. All of this activity is critical to the success of the invasion, so we can't think about reprisals.*

Anna looked up, Melody was awake and smiled. It was too noisy in the Liberator to talk, so their conversation was through their eyes. Melody, as usual, didn't seem to have a care in the world. This, her first mission, was so carefully planned, *what could go wrong?* The eyes seem to convey.

*You have no idea,* Anna thought, smiling back. As you have no idea my mission is to get as close as I can to a *SS-Brigadefuhrer* (Brigadier General) and kill him, using any means available to me including sacrificing you. The smile slowly faded from Melody, and Anna realized she must have seen something in Anna's face. Anna let it go, glancing down at her feet. *Well, OSS saw something in me, unless SOE told them the truth, which I doubt. I have killed five people. I don't know who knows it besides me. All for revenge. What did I get? Did it bring back Ahmet, Kerem or Selin? Did it bring back my mother and father?*

Tears didn't come to Anna easily anymore, but they came now and she closed her eyes, not caring that Melody was watching. She wished more than anything to have Karl's warm hands on her body and his face brushing against her neck. She had been alone for so long. *What have I become?* She thought. *Would Karl even recognize me anymore?*

Anna set up straight and as casually as she could, wiped her tears. Melody watched guardedly, sitting up herself, trying to convey confidence. Melody's safety, her life was in Anna's hands and Anna realized her responsibility. She looked up at Melody and gave her a long steady smile, followed with that American affirmation of mutual trust, a thumbs' up with her right hand. Melody responded immediately with her own, and a wink.

Anna sighed and glanced at her watch. *Karl was three years ago, my parents are dead, and I killed the people who sent them to their deaths. And now I'm parachuting into France to kill yet another man. It's all I'm good for now.* She examined her hands, hands once trained for another purpose.

*How will I justify what I have done? All I have for a reason for being is finding my sister. I am closer to her every minute that passes. That's all that matters now.* She closed around it in her heart, hoping it would be enough.

# This Matter of the Heart

# Chapter 24

*May 10, 1944. North of London, England.*

Jean Paul Metzgen landed his Lancaster after a grueling three-hour instrument check-ride. He was exhausted, his eyes red-rimmed and blurred. The night check-ride bounced the crew from Scotland to Ireland and back to London in a stomach-churning low-level round robin. Considering it was spring, the crew never saw the ground except for takeoff and 15 seconds in the climb out, and then again 30 seconds before landing when the flare pots on the sides of the runway became visible. Jean Paul's NZRAF squadron had once again transitioned to a new airplane. They left the Wellingtons' when they were re-designated a Heavy Bomber squadron in 1943, transitioning to the four-engine Short Stirling. With the coming invasion of France, all eyes were on Germany and the RAF wanted even more range for deep penetrations, so 75 Squadron was quickly transitioning the crews to the heaviest and best bomber in the inventory, the Avro Lancaster. Jean Paul passed the instrument check-ride and was slated to fly several milk runs before he and the crew were fully operational.

Jean Paul's squadron was now comprised almost entirely of New Zealanders. He was the last holdout former French Air Force pilot who chose to remain with the RAF, preferring the quiet New Zealanders to the squabbling infighting of the England-bound Free French, or whatever de Gaulle chose to call them now. His solid flying on combat missions made him popular among the other pilots so he saw no reason to change. He liked the mission, was glad to transition to four-engine bombers, and was taking a wait-and-see attitude on his future.

He entered the mess and found it closed for meals. After a quick shower he dressed in his robe and rummaged his quarters looking for something to eat. There was a knock at his door and he found a young officer, one of the Wing staff, looking for him. He needed to report to the Wing Commander's office at once. *Orders, old boy, sorry.*

Jean Paul was given 30 minutes to pack his bags and be ready to be picked up. The Wing Commander had taken the call from London personally and as Jean Paul surmised, there was no questioning of the lateness of the hour or whether someone should inform Jean Paul's squadron commander. A number of bleary-eyed senior officers in robes and other evening wear watched him go, wondering what about this very ordinary looking Frenchman caused all the fuss? He was guided into a dull-grey staff car and found himself in the backseat with the driver and a Royal Marine Captain in the front seat. The captain signaled the driver to go and peered over the seat to examine Jean Paul.

"Should be there in about 45 minutes, Captain, might as well get some sleep, mate."

"Where are we going?"

"Don't you know?"

"I just landed about an hour ago and was getting ready for bed. My orders were to get dressed and ready to go. And that was directly from the Wing Commander. Never met the man! Thought maybe you might know."

"Frenchy, eh mate? Well, your orders came from some of the higher offices of Whitehall, I can tell you that. But the boys who want to talk to you are the hush-hush boys."

"Is that why they sent along a commando?" Jean Paul could see the patch on the sleeve of the captain's blouse.

"Me? I'm just here to make sure you don't get lost, mate."


It was past midnight and Jean Paul had to wait patiently as the guard called down to confirm he was authorized to enter. The fact he was a captain in a NZRAF uniform made no headway with the British Army Military Police Corporal. The entrance to the estate looked regal and very unmilitary, with the exception of the small guard house hidden back behind a brick arch. There was no barrier other than what appeared to be the original wrought iron gate of the estate. The estate was brilliantly lit up once one made a couple of turns on the long entrance path, revealing a large rectangular main building of 18th Century vintage. Spotlights, very modern recent additions, were mounted on all visible building corners bathing the wide parking area.

The marine captain gave a short wave and left. Jean Paul was escorted through a series of narrow little passageways and suddenly arrived in a small office alone. He stared at a picture of a DB-7 Boston with the tri-color and recognized the tail number. He had flown that airplane many times. He smiled before he heard the voice behind him.

"It's been a long time, Jean Paul!" His old squadron mate, Jacque Denon, embraced him. There was so much to catch up since they had last met in England, nearly four years earlier.

"You are still with the RAF, Jean Paul! You like flying with the Kiwis, do you?"

"I do, and I see you're still with SOE."

"It's the best way for me to kick the Germans out of France." Denon offered Jean Paul a cigarette, which was refused. Despite it being past midnight, people were passing constantly in the hallway. Denon frowned and slowly closed the door.

"We knew you were switching over to the Lancaster so for once we could actually locate an operational squadron! You were flying tonight?"

"Instrument qualification. Instructor pilot had me all over the Orkney Islands at 2,000, scared me half to death, fog thick as pitch. Then out to somewhere near Galway, Ireland before he let me damn near kill ourselves on a tower in Birmingham on my approach back to London."

"You're dead tired, I understand. Anybody explain what was going on?"

"No, Wing Commander was tight as a tick and got a call from somebody out here that lit a fire under his ass. They snatched me with a Royal Marine Commando as an escort."

"Standard, sorry."

"Does anybody sleep around here?"

Denon smiled as he offered Jean Paul a chair. "After the war."

As Denon told the story, Jean Paul had to stop and interrupt several times. He could not believe they were talking about his sister, Anna. He grew angry and Denon took a break, asking for coffee and sandwiches. When they resumed, Denon continued the chronology of Anna's development as a SOE field operative, and her later recruitment by the OSS. This rekindled Jean Paul's anger, this time clearly aimed at Denon.

"*You son of a bitch!* You recruited her and trained her, and now you're telling me she was recruited by the OSS as a fucking assassin? *My sister?* She's a medical student, for God's sake! What the hell is she doing working for the Americans?"

"We kept her in the north to keep her from diverting from her missions and go looking for your sister, Clara. It happens all of the time with indigenous field agents. The OSS offered her the opportunity to work in the Dordogne, where Clara has been reported with a *maquis*." Jean Paul stared at Denon as if he were out of his mind.

"*INDIGENOUS*? You mean *French*?" He said incredulously. "I may be flying for the RAF, but I will *ALWAYS* be a Frenchman! What the hell are you talking about, Jacques!"

"I'm sorry. I'm so used to briefing Brits. I'm sorry, Jean Paul."

Denon came around his desk and sat in the other seat next to Jean Paul. They were so close their knees were touching. He gripped Jean Paul's elbow as their eyes met.

"Forgive me. We build natural distance with our agents, our people, because of the risk involved. The war—forces us to use people.

215

We're talking about your sister, one you haven't seen in—years, and there is so much to explain and there is so little time." He hesitated before bringing a hand up, palm forward, as a priest would in a blessing.

"Let me start again, Jean Paul. You need a better picture of what has happened here, and our—problem." Jean Paul grew rigid, staring at Denon with distaste. He tightly crossed his arms and shook his head firmly.

"You better explain yourself, Denon! Explain how my sister was recruited by you, denied the opportunity to look for our sister, Clara, and then—then HIRED by the Americans to become some kind of assassin? I can't believe you, Denon! That doesn't make sense, even for a dumb bomber pilot like me! *Why?* Why would the Americans, as foolish and as reckless as they can be, use Anna as an assassin? She's a medical student! Why would she be chosen for such a role? *She had no training for killing people!* She is a sweet, kind girl—you know her! It's ridiculous to even consider!"

Jean Paul started to stand but Denon gestured to stay seated. Jean Paul stared down at Denon in anger and contempt, but something in Denon's face brought him slowly back down.

"What? Why did you look at me that way, Denon? What have you done to my sister? Did you bastards train her to be an assassin?"

"No, Jean Paul. We didn't train her to be an assassin. When we recruited her, she had been living with an FTP *maquis* leader who worked with us, and we had determined he was a traitor and double crossing both us and the other *maquis* groups. We outed him intentionally and eventually he was executed by the other *maquis*. We had cleared Anna of any real involvement with this guy's treachery, but some of the other members of the group wanted her head. Our agents in France were very impressed with her background and language skills, so we brought her back to England and decided to use her. I'm pretty sure it saved her life."

"Anna was living with a *maquis* leader in the Limousin?" He said this slowly, incredulous. Denon nodded and lit another cigarette.

"There's more you should know—and it's worse. Before she joined the *maquis,* she lived in Limoges and worked for a *maison*. Not as a maid or housekeeper—but as a prostitute."

"*Impossible!* Where did you get such information! From the fucking *maquis?*"

"The *gendarmerie*—the Limoges Municipal Police, Jean Paul. Since she was a certified prostitute in the *maison,* they had her on file. She lived in the *maison* for almost a year, but she was listed as a tubercular for eight of those months. When she was medically cleared as an active prostitute, she worked for four months before she disappeared. When

216

we pulled her out of France, she had been with the *maquis* for only three months."

Jean Paul seemed stunned, his eyes wide and staring at his hands. He shook his head in disbelief.

"The Limoges Municipal Police believed Anna was responsible for the murder of three men, all customers of the *maison*, although the murders were committed at a nearby hotel. The first one was of a German SS senior officer. No witnesses to this first murder. Then the Assistant Prefect of Aix and the senior Police Inspector of Aix were murdered on the same night."

Jean Paul glanced up at Denon in total confusion.

"The Assistant Prefect and Police Inspector of Aix? Aix as in Provence, our hometown? And a senior SS officer? I can't believe what you're telling me! *WHY* would my sister, Anna, kill these people?"

Jean Paul had to stand this time, pushing his chair aside and walking about in the tiny office randomly. He clearly was not accepting anything Denon was telling him now. Denon let him be for a few minutes, knowing his friend even in his exhausted state would begin to realize what he had been told.

"The Assistant Prefect and the Police Inspector—both of these men were personal friends of my father. I remember both of them before I joined the Air Force. They came to dinner several times, especially the Assistant Prefect. I received letters from my father and Clara in the fall of 1942, my father was talking about seeing his friend about—well, immigrating. But only *Juifs* were eligible, but no one knew we were *Juifs*." His words trailed off, the impact of his own words visibly sloping his shoulders. He turned very slowly towards Denon, his eyes as black as coal.

"What happened to my parents, Denon? I have not heard from them in well over a year..."

"We checked the *Vichy* records; your father was in Les Milles waiting for approval of his immigration to the West. The November 10 declaration stopping all immigration of *Juifs* in France ended it. Your father was arrested and your mother joined him. They were sent to Drancy without delay, and then to Auschwitz. They did not survive, Jean Paul. I am so sorry."

"The Assistant Prefect turned my father in?"

"He didn't intervene in any way apparently. Sometimes French *Juifs* are given a chance to escape.

"And the Police Commissaire arrested him. Yes. The same opportunity for escape could have occurred, but it didn't."

Jean Paul collapsed down into his chair, nearly falling over. He didn't say anything or move for several minutes.

"My sister, Clara? Is she still with the *maquis* somewhere?"

"Yes."

"The Prefect and the policeman, why were they up in Limoges?"

"Some conference. Anna was the most desired of the—women in the *maison,* so they sought her out."

"And the murders occurred in a hotel?"

"The same one the German officer was killed in."

"And they believe all three were killed by the same person?"

"Yes. They have ways of determining that, I suppose."

"What was the story on the German officer? Why was he targeted?"

"According to the National police, the SS officer had something to do with the trains used to transport the *Juifs* from Drancy to Auschwitz. How the killer determined this we don't know. Perhaps the officer bragged about it. In any case the killer stabbed him to death."

"STABBED him to death? And the others?"

"Yes."

"And you just found this out?"

"No Jean Paul, we knew of this when we screened her. We learned of the suspicions of the police six months ago."

"Did Anna know about this? Know you knew about her background?"

"No not at all. She knew we knew about her time in the *maison* as a prostitute. She told us nothing whatsoever about any murders and we didn't reveal we knew anything."

Jean Paul stared hard at Denon, trying to digest all of this information.

"You believe my sister, Anna is the murderer of three men and yet you recruited her for the SOE. Doesn't that break some laws somewhere?"

Denon smiled and rubbed both hands through his hair.

"Jean Paul, I know you as a good soldier and French patriot. Your sister killed two Vichy officials who were directly responsible for the death of your parents. Five weeks prior she kills a SS *Obersturmbannführer* who must have bragged about herding *Juifs* into his trains. This is wartime, Jean Paul, wartime. Your sister was sleeping with the enemy, but I suspect she didn't do it by choice. She said as much to my face, and I believed her. And when she had an opportunity to kill the enemy, she did. So, there you have it."

218

"The OSS knows she has killed three men."  Jean Paul said this as a statement of fact.

"Yes, we informed them when we understood she was transferring over.  They may have found it out on their own, but I doubt it, they just don't have the connections.  But I thought they should know."

Jean Paul, obviously exhausted, screwed his eyes tight for a moment and sighed.  He opened them slowly as he placed his hands on his knees.

"Why did you bring me here in the middle of the night to tell me this?"

"You're going to find out in about ten minutes."  Denon picked up his telephone and had a brief conversation.  After he hung up, he sat back down behind his desk and put together a few documents in a manila folder.  His phone buzzed once and he identified himself.  He hung the phone up and opened the door.  He led Jean Paul to a small conference room where a large easel was propped up next to a wooden table, the contents covered by a large cloth.  An electric clock was mounted on the wall, revealing it was past two in the morning.  Jean Paul was exhausted, his head spinning with information that was just too much to comprehend.  He felt like he was in a dream.  The cloak and dagger night ride to a secret facility made it seem even more unreal.  Denon seemed to sense Jean Paul's confusion and said nothing, offering more coffee and some stale biscuits.  The door opened and two officers stepped in, one of them a very tall major.  Both Denon and Jean Paul rose to attention but the major waved them down.

"Please, gentlemen, stay in your seats."   He spoke perfect unaccented French, and Jean Paul noted the "France" tab on his uniform.  "Denon, this is Captain Metzgen?   Captain Metzgen, Captain Ericson."  The major, who had cold clear eyes, examined Jean Paul's face as they shook hands.

"There is a family resemblance Captain, I see it in your eyes."  He said this without a hint of humor or friendliness.  The major glanced over at his companion, Captain Ericson, who pushed a thick folder over to the major.  The major opened the folder, picked out a sheaf of documents and placed them on the table.

"You are aware of the Official Secrets Act, Captain Metzgen?  I don't think it's necessary for you to read all of the document, but what we're about to reveal to you involves some of the most closely held information in the world today, and some of the most important.  We're talking about the invasion of the continent, the retaking of our homeland.  Discussion of any part of this information outside of this room will result in your immediate arrest, imprisonment and possibly your death.  Is that understood, Captain?  We are not on French soil but British.  We are all wearing the uniform of the British Forces and are bound to their military and secrecy laws. I understand as a French Air Force officer you are also bound by duty and honor to protect military secrets, but our hosts insist on these rules and we are duty bound to follow them. Please sign where indicated."

With the preliminaries out of the way, the major opened the folder again and selected two full size black and white photographs. He studied each for a moment before setting them down on the table side by side so Jean Paul could see them clearly. Both were official pictures, one of a SS *Brigadefuhrer* (Major General) and the other was of Anna, unsmiling, in a British mufti uniform with no insignia. Nausea crept into his gut as he stared at Anna's picture. His sense of disbelief was so strong he was shaking his head slowly from side to side without even being conscious of it. He looked up to find the major watching him with narrowed eyes.

"Captain Denon tells me he has briefed you on your sister's recruitment by the SOE, a general scope of her missions in her brief time with us, and her subsequent transfer over to the OSS with the Americans."

"Yes, he has, Major."

"He also briefed you on what we discovered about her past in Limoges, information we received from the French National police? The prostitution and their belief she is the person responsible for the murders of an SS senior officer and two *Vichy* officials from Aix in Provence?"

"He briefed me, but I cannot say I have fully accepted these accusations as true. I know my sister, and these—behaviors—are not in keeping with her character. These are just not things Anna is capable of doing, in my opinion."

"I see." The major glanced over at Denon before lighting a cigarette. His hand drifted over to Anna's photograph, his fingers touching her hair. Jean Paul found the gesture somehow invasive and disrespectful. The major pulled his fingers back and stood up. He walked to the easel and carefully removed the cloth, exposing a map. There were no landmarks, airfields or boundaries on the map, just roads. No country, county, prefecture or sea coast for orientation. It could be anywhere, except at two meters Jean Paul could read the small dots for cities, towns and villages. He knew them all. Limoges was at the top of the map with Montauban on the bottom. To the west there was Villaneuve-sur-Lot in the *Aquitaine*; Cahors and Sarlot in the *Dordogne*. To the east there was Limogne, St. Cirq Lapopie and Aurillac in the lower *Limousin*.

The major stood next to the map for a moment before glancing up at the clock.

"Your reaction, considering you haven't seen your sister in years and only know her as a medical student, is perfectly normal. We won't dispute or argue this point with you, as we don't have the time. But these are the facts as we know them. The SOE and OSS use each other's operatives for various missions, some based on political considerations so the world will see the allies working together for the common goal. A good example is right here in this room. Three of us are French military officers and the other, Captain Ericson, is a serving British officer, but we came together in the SOE. The point is some of our SOE operatives are training for missions with the OSS to be dropped in the continent just before or right after the invasion. We have learned through one of these operatives Anna Metzgen was dropped into France with a radio operator on the 5th in *Dordogne*. Ostensibly their mission is to disrupt the movement of the Second SS Panzer Division based in Agen and Montauban when they determine the Allies had landed in France.

"The Second SS Panzer is a very special unit, used specifically for tough assignments often under the direction of Adolf Hitler. They were in the spearhead when Germany invaded France, and they spent years in the Soviet Union. Their current assignment is to destroy the French Resistance in southwest France. They are brutal and very effective. When the Allies land in France, the Second SS Panzer will be sent straight up a number of different roads in the *Dordogne* to Limoges and then straight through the Loire to Brittany or Normandy. They would be very effective against Allied forces if they are allowed to get in position to confront them. Anna Metzgen and numerous other teams are supposed to join up with *maquis* groups, equip them if necessary and coordinate attacks to slow down the Second SS Panzer."

The major lit another cigarette and stared hard at Jean Paul.

"But the fact of the matter is that is not your sister's mission." The major strode over to the table and pointed his finger on the photograph of the SS *Brigadefuhrer*. "This is her real target. Her mission is to get in as close as she can to this man and kill him. This officer, the OSS believes, actually runs the division. Kill this major general and the division commander will lose control and the division loses its momentum. Perhaps only for a few days but enough to ensure the success of the landing force."

Jean Paul stared back at the major waiting for him to continue, but he didn't. Confused, he glanced over at Denon and Captain Ericson, the Englishman.

"So—what's the problem?" Jean Paul asked finally, shrugging his shoulders. "I can't believe the Americans are sending my sister to kill this guy, which I guess is a suicide mission?" The major nodded towards Denon who simply pointed towards the map.

"I know you know where that is. Those are the possible routes the Second SS Panzer will use to move 20,000 men and vehicles north. They know the Resistance will try to blow up bridges, mine the roads and ambush their troop carriers, so they'll move north in dozens of directions. Can't cover it all. But somewhere out there your sister is getting into position to kill the assistant division commander, and we have to come up with a way to *stop her*."

*"What?"* Jean Paul blurted out, now totally confused. Denon nodded in understanding and leaned forward and pushed the photograph of the SS *Brigadeführer* closer to Jean Paul.

"Jean Paul, the OSS does not know this man is one of ours. He's not SOE, he's a Nazi, but something happened in the Eastern Front that turned him against the *Third Reich*. He approached us through the Resistance four months ago and we checked him every which way. He hasn't led us astray yet. We turned him and now he's a double agent. When D-Day happens, he will be instrumental in slowing the Second SS Panzer down, because he will have told us where his troops will be for the Resistance to hit. This gentleman is critical to the success of the landings. Do you understand what I'm saying?"

"What he's saying, Captain Metzgen," the major drolled with a bit of regret, "despite what you may feel both the OSS and SOE believe your sister is most capable of completing her mission. Our double agent is extremely deep and OSS was simply not brought into the loop for security purposes. We are going to launch a mission to stop her by any means available. If we can include you, Captain, we might find ourselves in a position where the only person she might respond to will be her remaining family members, your sister Clara or you. You may save her life, Captain."

Jean Paul slumped into the chair, his mind dull from exhaustion. He closed his eyes but all he could see was Anna's sad eyes in the photograph. He opened them to glare at Denon and the major, feeling used and manipulated.

"Who is going on this—mission?"

"Captain Ericson, an American OSS operative who will help us contact Anna, and we were hoping, you."

"But the OSS is not in this room, so I guess they don't know what the real mission is?"

"That is correct, and it will stay that way. Once he sets up the contact the OSS officer will be quietly removed from the operation."

"How will you do that?"

The major didn't respond but simply stared at Jean Paul.

"And the intent is to stop her by my talking her out of it?   And if I fail?"

"Captain Ericson has his orders, Captain."

# Chapter 25

*May 11, 1944. Harrington, former RAF air base, England.*

Jean Paul was shown to a small room with two beds and slept like a dead man for six hours.   He was awakened by Captain Denon and escorted to a mess hall that unlike a RAF station, didn't seem to have specific hours for meals.   Denon gave him a chit and he ate a wonderful breakfast of powdered eggs, greasy sausages and toast with preserves.  The coffee was strong and black, but there was real cream he couldn't pass up on the table.   The wartime shortages so clearly evident in London or even in the RAF messes didn't apply here apparently.   He savored the coffee and cream but a quick glance at his watch got him moving.

After a shave he was met by Denon who gave him a British Army battle dress uniform and beret to replace his flight officer togs.   The blouse already had his rank pips sewn into the epaulets and the "France" tab on the shoulder.

*Leave your bag in the room, and everything of a personal nature—your wallet, jewelry, pictures of family in the drawer.   Bring only your military identification, understood?   And Jean Paul, remember, take all of your cues from Captain Ericson; he's leading this one.   You're going to be surrounded by OSS at Harrington and they will be very interested in why you're going along.   Remember the mission.   They will be running on a different track.   Just go along.   Keep your mouth shut.*

By noon he was at Harrington, a former RAF base now used by a special squadron of USAAF B-24 bombers.   As a RAF pilot he had heard about this squadron that flew only at night with B-24s painted completely black.   The OSS flew so many missions into the continent where the only insertion method was by parachute, this squadron was formed to insure the long range, low level night missions could be performed routinely and safely.   As Denon explained, this specific mission was an SOE mission—therefore British in origin and British led, but because it involved an OSS mission in-country and an OSS officer would be included, the OSS offered SOE an airplane.

Once in a hanger guarded by US Army military police, the small light truck that carried them and their equipment backed in and shut down.   Several offices lined the side of the massive hanger and Captain Ericson and Jean Paul were ushered into the largest one.   It had no windows but several rows of high-backed chairs, obviously a former squadron briefing room.   Jean Paul was quickly introduced to a tall, very tanned and fit American officer named Sam McLemore.   He seemed enthusiastic but was wary of Ericson.   His face lit up when he met Jean Paul, quickly switching to flawless French.  He had lived for years in France and served with the Parachute Regiment in the French Foreign Legion before the war. He began questioning Jean Paul sharply about his duties in the SOE, but Captain Ericson interrupted and said, rather abruptly, *sorry, we have a lot to do, gentlemen!  Please take a seat!*  This visibly angered McLemore and Jean Paul wondered what exactly was going on between these two men.

Captain Ericson stepped up on the small raised platform and with the help of an assistant, unwrapped two large, flat wooden crates marked "FRAGILE – HISTORIC ARCHIVE PAINTINGS".  One box had several enlarged aerial photographs of the *Limousin* and the *Dordogne*; the other had detailed map overlays of southwest France.  Ericson began his brief and it was the first time Jean Paul heard the operation they were undertaking characterized as a *rescue* mission.  It was an elaborate overview to his mind, since there were only two people in the audience, McLemore and himself.  McLemore was the prime recipient and it was clear he was skeptical.

"As you know, gentlemen, we (meaning SOE) were not aware of the OSS mission with uh—agent Metzger and her RTO.  We became aware through one of our assets in the *Dordogne* that an Allied operative was in trouble.  You confirmed when we asked for clarification that a mission team, a Sussex team inserted—uh, May 5th—had not made any of their regularly scheduled radio transmissions.  Not one.  Uh—we obviously know Anna Metzger well as we trained her and inserted her in France previously, so we were concerned.  So were you, obviously, as this mission was critical for the success of our coming invasion of the continent.  You assumed the worst, as we would, that the two assets were either killed or injured in the insertion, or captured by the enemy.  We know now at least the prime asset, Metzger, is still alive, but our local asset cannot determine her exact location, only a general area between the Dordogne and Lot rivers as represented on this map with Highway N20 as our primary route.  Metzger has been reported in Cahors, in the areas of the hilltop *bastides* St. Cirq Lapopie and Rocamatour."

"This asset you say is not known to the OSS?  Where is the spirit of cooperation I hear bandied about so much, Captain?  Is this asset French or German?"

"I cannot say, Captain McLemore."

"Okay, fine.  Then I don't know why you feel the need to elaborate all of this unless you're trying to snow me somehow.  I don't give a goddamn, frankly.  I think I speak for my side to say you know and I know the OSS was going to deal with this issue.  People at a much higher pay grade than you or me made the decision to make this a fuckin' joint operation with SOE in charge.   Personally, Captain Ericson, I think this should be an OSS operation and I should be up there briefing you.   No offense to our French compatriot Captain Metzgen, but I just don't see how this is a Brit op at all."

Jean Paul was impressed how well Captain Ericson rolled with that punch, but he had learned Captain Ericson had been in and out of France posing as a regular German Army officer three times in the last four years. The man had to be a chameleon and have ice in his veins.   He did not disappoint.

"Captain McLemore we have an asset to protect, of which remains outside of your knowledge, and in the process, we wish to assist you in the retrieving—if that is the correct verb—of our mutual most valuable asset, Anna Metzger."

McLemore threw up his hands and sat up straight.   He glanced over at Jean Paul before challenging Ericson again.

"Let's get this straight, Ericson, mano to mano.   So we know where we stand."

"Okay, Captain.   I don't know how you were selected and briefed, but mine came directly from Whitehall.   But understand if we are going to go forward on this mission with you included, you need to accept who is in charge.   I don't mind taking a minute or two listening to your— opinion, but I'm leading this mission.   If you don't accept that, I will make a phone call and get you replaced as quickly as I can.   Do we understand each other?"

"And if something happens to you, Ericson?"

"Then the mission is aborted.   I'm the only person who knows the ground asset who is assisting us, and it will stay that way."

"I'm coming along as the RTO and we won't be communicating with your—asset—via radio?"

"No, we will use your radio only to inform our SOE controllers our situation, or to radio for assistance or extraction.   I'll communicate directly, that is face to face, with the *maquis* groups who will be waiting for us in France, and they will place me in contact with our asset."

"The asset is French."

"I cannot say."

"Holy shit Ericson."   McLemore sighed and shook out a cigarette. He glared at Ericson and lit his cigarette.   "Well—go on!"

Ericson stepped down from the platform and stood directly in front of McLemore.

"Are you with us, Captain?   That is, do you accept SOE leadership on this mission?"   McLemore stared up at Ericson and held it for a beat before nodding his head in the affirmative.

"Yes Captain, I do." They didn't shake hands like the Americans did at the drop of a hat, which Jean Paul almost expected, but Ericson did tip the front of his beret with his pointer and hopped back on the podium. He resumed his brief, stating, apparently at this point mostly for Jean Paul's benefit, where the various units of the Second SS Panzer Division were believed to be as of 0900 this morning, especially the headquarters and command staff. It was then Jean Paul realized just how dangerous their mission really was.

"If we are unable to find Metzger by any means, we have to consider her mission compromised and aborted." Ericson said quietly, glancing over at Jean Paul. "We may, if we find out she is injured or possibly detained by a hostile *maquis* group, be in a position to rescue her and extract her."

"Look Captain, I was brought into this about 24 hours ago and selected because I just happened to be in between missions. But there's another reason, which you should know. I was selected because I was trained originally for this mission *before* Metzger. *Before* they decided it would be a soft hit, and they were going to use a woman to get close and take him out. It was originally going to be a hard hit, commando-style operation. I was going in with a good-sized team and we were going to take out the entire command structure of the Second SS Panzer, really decapitate the tiger. But they deemed that too dangerous and likely to fail with so many experienced German troops around. These guys are supposedly very used to dealing with the guerilla tactics of the French Resistance and we would never get close. Okay. So now we've got this *cluster fuck* of a fix-it mission because this all-woman team gets lost, captured or whatever. Well I don't have my original team anymore, spread to the wind on other missions. All they have is me, trained, briefed on the target and ready to *go to the target*."

McLemore got up slowly to his considerable height and climbed up the platform. He pointed at the map, specifically the small town of Agen in the *Aquitaine*.

"I can tell you that our guy, the assistant division commander, is right there—*right now*. The division commander is a division commander, meaning he's called to meetings and conferences in Paris and Berlin all the goddamn time, so who knows where the hell he is. But really, who cares? But the assistant commander is always at HQ, because as we both know, he runs the show. Our lady wasn't dropped near HQ though. She was dropped close to the multiple routes the division would be taking when they get the word the Allies had landed in the north— somewhere. Metzger and her RTO were supposed to hook up the *maquis* groups in the *Dordogne* and prepare them for the day the Second SS

Panzer came clanking into town. Well, I'm here to tell you, and I'll take the heat for it, but our lady may have been dropped in the *Dordogne*, but I'd bet a month's pay—if she didn't just go underground and returned home to wherever home was in France—she backtracked to Agen or Moutanban and is watching our guy as we speak."

Ericson stared at McLemore for a long time without speaking. It was obvious to Jean Paul, Ericson was seriously considering what McLemore was saying.

"And why wouldn't she at least attempt to use the radio to check in, let you know she got on the ground ok?"

"She's a good operator and not stupid. She's French. We give our field operatives some of the best documents in the world—no offense to SOE. Even the most asstight bureaucrat in France couldn't spot the difference if we get the signatures and the stamps right. She's got French dental work, we use French stitches on the clothes, and she's a good looker. You know her past. She's a pro. She'll fuck any man she wants and they'll give her what she wants. I understand why she was a better choice than me. But she survives because she doesn't do the stupid shit field operatives do. The Germans have units triangulating radio signals every day, and she's right there in the middle of the highest concentration of French Resistance in France! With the best *maquis* hunters in France, the Second SS Panzer! If I was her and I wanted to survive long enough to kill my target, I'd dump the radio and turn my RTO into a spotter or dump 'em somewhere to wait out the war."

Jean Paul bristled with anger with his comments but kept it in check, unnoticed in any case by McLemore.

"You think we're wasting our time dropping in the *Dordogne*—that we should work our way south to the *Aquitaine*, where you believe Anna Metzger might be? How do you explain the reports of her sighting in the *Dordogne*?"

"I can't. Do you know when was she last sighted? She knows the approximate date for D-Day, but obviously she was not told the actual date, or where, that is known to only a handful of people. She could be working with the *maquis* to prepare for the sabotage mission, and would head south closer to the first of the month, but I doubt it. Knowing her methods, I would say she wants to get close to the target sooner. Fuck the *maquis* connection, which is a bullshit cover. Go light and go directly to the target now. No radio comms, nothing to draw attention to yourselves other than what is necessary to attract the target. Know where he is and never let him out of her sight."

Ericson and McLemore both stepped down from the platform and sat in the chairs next to Jean Paul. He was following his instructions and kept his mouth shut, which was hard. He was starting to realize these two men were speaking of two different missions as if they were the same.

"What is your understanding of our mission, Captain? And your role in it?" McLemore glanced at Ericson with the question before resting his eyes on Jean Paul.

"My orders are to assist your efforts in determining what has happened to our team. In the worst case, take over Metzger's mission and take out the assistant commander of the Second Panzer. My understanding is that you—and your team," McLemore acknowledged Jean Paul with a nod, "would assist me in performing this mission. We can't get close like the women can, but apparently, you've operated in Europe as a German officer for extended missions before, and come equipped with appropriate uniforms and documents. You must have a plan. We're simply not prepared to pull the trigger for a mission with our own people *right now*, so your offer was accepted hands down. Not that it's going to be a cake walk. The HQ is protected by an SS guard company who takes no fuckin' prisoners because the *maquis* tries to hit em' all the time. With just the three of us, it won't be easy, not anywhere near the HQ. But getting in will be easier than getting out, I can tell you that."

Jean Paul peered up at the map, avoiding looking at either man. *My God,* he thought in growing alarm, *they are both using each other to get close to the target. One tasked to kill a German commander who is in reality a SOE double agent; and the other tasked to protect the SOE double agent, and in doing so possibly kill my sister, Anna and McLemore—and presumably me if I fail in convincing my sister and try to intervene.*

His role as explained by Ericson to McLemore was one of pure fiction—Jean Paul was a French Air Force officer who provided the services of a guide and intermediary with the *maquis* groups in the area. With a Frenchman in the team, the *maquis* would accept them with welcome arms. Jean Paul was extremely familiar with the roads and *bastides* in the *Dordogne*, having been raised in southwest France. Jean Paul listened to this with barely concealed dismay, as he did know the area fairly well, but only as a youth traveling with his family or with friends as a student. He was raised in Aix, 300 kilometers away. In fact, Jean Paul suspected both Ericson and McLemore knew the area better than he did, and the *maquis* groups were as self-serving and distrustful of one another as only the French could be. And he personally was not Communist or a de Gaullist. He was as foreign to them as Ericson and McLemore.

Some groups were well led, others were not. Most were Communist oriented and financed by the Americans *and* the Russians; other, much smaller groups were ardent anti-Communists who supported de Gaulle and were financed by the British. In the past they sabotaged and attacked the communist groups at every opportunity. Ericson had briefed him about the uniqueness of the *Maquis du Limousin*. There were about 8,000 men in the *Haute-Vienne* department. Under the unification plan supposedly implemented by de Gaulle, the *Armee Secrete*, ORA and FTP were blended into one organization under the leadership and guidance of Free France. It just wasn't that easy, but the leaders being paid by the Americans, British and Russians said it was so.

Some groups were led by pure opportunists and criminals who simply took advantage of the chaos created by war. These were the most dangerous; they worked with anyone who offered them money and weapons. Jean Paul, who knew nothing about the Resistance or *maquis* groups because he had spent a year in the Southwest Pacific and three years flying out of England with the RAF, listened in horror as Ericson explained in detail the FTP *maquis* that would meet them at their drop zone between Cahors and the *bastide* at Rocamadour. If they encountered too much anti-aircraft fire or the drop zone didn't respond, they would back track to their secondary, a small field northeast of Villenueve-sur-Lot between the village of Fumel and the old Bonaguil castle. A second FTP group would wait for them there.

Ericson and McLemore argued about the FTP, as the Americans paid and worked with the FTP elsewhere. But OSS understood the British were openly opposed to working with the Communists. *What gives?* McLemore interjected. Ericson cut him off short, noting this was an SOE operation and the contacts had been established and the arrangements were done. It will be the FTP who will be waiting for them on the ground whether McLemore approved of the arrangement or not. McLemore flared and shook his head in anger, stating simply *this stinks to high heaven, period!*

Take off would be an hour after dark. Flying time was estimated at about three hours, with the Liberator departing south from England and staying well off shore at about eight thousand feet as it followed the English Channel and skirted around the Brittany peninsula. They would fly straight south until they were parallel to Bordeaux, then turn southeast to descend and cross the shoreline and follow the Lot river at about 150 meters. As they approached Cahors, they would turn northeast towards the rocky hill country between the Dordogne and Lot Rivers, descending to 120 meters and wait for the ground signal.

Jean Paul closed his eyes for a moment, realizing in astonishment Anna had performed this type of mission multiple times, first with the SOE and now with the OSS. He understood for the first time he really didn't know this woman at all, this version of his sister. Ericson and McLemore went over the details of the operation carefully, but with a routine acceptance of what was an extremely hazardous undertaking. Every component, including the low-level night flight into German-held territory was dangerous. Jean Paul knew this very well as a RAF bomber pilot, but this was just one part. He glanced at his watch. In about six hours he would have to drop through the *Joe hole* into the night and land seconds later onto French soil. He shuddered and accepted he was afraid. Very afraid.

*You are parachute qualified, Captain Metzgen?* McLemore asked his eyebrows arched high on his forehead. *Yes, of course. I've had to bail out twice, once in 1940 and again in 1943. First time was in Belgium after getting shot down. The second time we got shot up over the target and made it back to England but it was socked in solid. We timed and distanced and flew triangles over what we hoped was Scotland until we ran out of fuel and bailed out. We guessed right and all landed in a damp pasture about a kilometer from a sheep farmer.* McLemore seemed impressed, nodding in silence as their kit was stretched out on huge benches.

The enlisted British equipment fitters were all business, setting out specific equipment for each of the team members. Although Ericson had explained the need for German uniforms when the team approached the Second SS Panzer headquarters, it really didn't sink in until Jean Paul stared closely at the *Waffen* SS *Hauptsturmfuhrer* uniform laid out on the bench for him. It included a winter coat, polished boots, uniform hat, gloves, and a Walther P-38 9mm pistol in a highly polished holster.

*It should fit very well, sir.* The fitter said. *We have your uniform measurements.*

Ericson had smiled as he saw the look of dismay on Jean Paul's face. *Don't worry you won't be wearing it when we're dropped. That would be too dangerous if we get captured when we landed. We'd be shot as spies within the hour, if not on the spot. The uniforms, extra weapons and explosives are going in the equipment drop on the second pass. We have some extra weapons for the maquis too, part of the deal.*

Jean Paul examined his parachute carefully remembering Ericson's brief on their altitude on the drop. 120 meters above ground level. When he bailed out from his Boston in 1940, he separated from the aircraft at about 200 meters. When he looked down after pulling the ripcord, the ground came up so fast he had no time to think. He hit hard and the wind

231

was knocked completely out of him. The German infantry who captured him thought he was dead. Now he was jumping at night at even lower altitude. *God help me.*

His fitter explained the strange canvas attachment on his Sten gun.

*It's a suppressor sir. Very effective, about all you hear is the sound of your action cycling. But avoid rapid fire. Single shots if possible, as the suppressor overheats. Six stick magazines, 20 rounds each. We'll strap the weapon and the magazines to you, not stuffed in the equipment drop. Not much good if Jerry is waiting for you in the drop zone, eh?*

McLemore, who was sorting and checking his equipment, had brought some of his own. Jean Paul noticed the Colt .45 automatic pistol, but also spotted another thin, narrow, long-barreled semi-automatic pistol he had never seen before. McLemore was wearing two shoulder holsters under his field jacket, one for each pistol. He carefully wiped down the smaller pistol and was replacing it in the holster when he sensed Jean Paul's interest. He removed the magazine and opened the action, passing the pistol over.

*Something new in the OSS inventory. Silenced .22 High Standard. Suppressor built into the barrel, not attached like your Sten. Subsonic, about 20 decibels. Not much lead, but at close range, it penetrates one side of the skull and then sort of rolls around in there. Our kraut general will never know what hit him, I can tell you that.*

McLemore smiled and accepted the gun back, reloading it and dropping it into his holster. He didn't see the look on Ericson's face as he stared at McLemore, but Jean Paul did. It made his stomach churn and a ribbon of ice run up his spine. He had somehow fallen into a den of killers, and according to Jacque Denon and this Captain Ericson, Anna was one of them.

# Das Reich

## Chapter 26

*May 19, 1944. Paris, France.*

In the end after the purge, Karl was saved by his late recruitment and having had little contact with the so-called inner circle. In late fall of 1943 rumors were whispered nervously, circulating like fire among friends the *Oberste Fuhrer* himself no longer trusted the *Abwehr* because it was infiltrated by anti-Nazi sympathizers. This was seemingly confirmed as several *Abwehr* senior officers were relieved of their duties as they underwent thorough, if not harsh investigations that in many cases collapsed on-going counter intelligence operations. As an officer who had never joined the party, Karl was concerned and frightened as the investigations were being conducted by the Secret State Police, the *Gestapo*, the same organization he competed with while working in Lyon. He remembered distinctly his recruitment when he was still in the hospital, the *Abwehr* officers particularly interested *because he was not* a member of the party. Karl excelled at his assignment of hunting *Juifs* while in Lyon, supported by the *Gestapo* who continued to forward him names. When the end came for *Abwehr* he was absolved of complicity by the head of the *Gestapo* in Lyon because of his performance.

In February of 1944 the *Oberste Fuhrer* relieved the head of the *Abwehr* of his responsibilities and abolished the service. The intelligence service responsibilities were absorbed by the *Reichssicherheitshauptamt,* or RSHA (Reich Main Security Office). Karl's function as a *Juif* hunter was effectively rolled over to the *Gestapo* in Lyon. Since the head of the *Gestapo* section in Lyon was a *Hauptmann* and Karl outranked him as a *Major*, Karl was transferred to Paris to await a new assignment. Like most middle-grade officers in the *Abwehr* who were cleared of complicity with the anti-Nazi defectors, Karl found himself in a no-man's land where he had no allies or friends. There were only a few hundred of them and no one knew what to do with them. Some of these men found themselves eventually transferred back to *Wehrmacht* combat units in the Soviet Union and were dead within weeks.

Karl could not walk without the assistance of a cane after a hundred meters or so, and his rank was high enough to warrant both a small office and an *unteroffizier*. The unit where he had been temporarily dumped was a logistics support organization for armored units spread out from Calais to Cherbourg on the coast, facing the English Channel. It was run by an overweight reserve *Oberstleutnant* who took one look at him, gravely shook his hand and never spoke to him again. Karl's office, although quite small, was on the fourth floor in a rustic former government office building flanking the *Av Des Champs Elysees* with a wonderful distant view of the Seine and the Eiffel Tower. He had no orders other than those necessary to direct him here to Paris, and no responsibilities whatsoever for the logistics support unit. He was assigned a telephone and a system to ring the *unteroffizier* sitting at the desk in the outer office. The outer office was bare with the exception of a typewriter. He had no idea what the RSHA told the *Oberstleutnant* about him but the staff kept their distance. If anything, he felt sorry at first for the *unteroffizier* assigned to him, but a brief conversation one day revealed the man was an *Abwehr* refugee like himself, one very happy to survive the purge and not be on the Soviet plain.

Three times a day Karl and his *unteroffizier* spoke and acknowledged each other as they came and went. If anything since his days on the Eastern Front, Karl recognized the value of patience and time. He needed one to survive the passage of the other, but he knew every day was another day in relative safety and one more day closer to the end of the war. In the morning when he shaved, he found he avoided looking directly at his eyes. *Eyes were windows,* Anna used to say, and they had explored each other's in those long-ago evenings when they could lie together for a few hours.

*What would Anna see in them now? The view she used to say was one of a good, kind man. A man who loved without asking too many questions. A man who provided and took care of her during her time of need.* Karl sighed and wondered aloud one night if she had used him, played him the fool. But he didn't believe it, not in his heart. He saw something in her eyes too, and believed it was love. At one time, maybe still, but at one time this man, this German man who reached out for her, was accepted and she learned to love him. He believed it. This man.

*A man who was also responsible for, according to the reports submitted by the Gestapo in Lyon in his support during the purge, the detection and arrest of over 1,297 Juifs in his region in eight months. How could I look in her face when I can barely stand to look at it myself?* During those months most of his arrests came because of the interrogation of other *Juifs* by the *Gestapo.* Karl never interrogated a prisoner or was even present for an arrest. It was all done by others. *The detection and arrest* of people in hiding, people just like Anna. *Juifs,* like Anna.

One evening in late March he got a knock on his door in the hotel room that served as his temporary quarters. It was early after dinner and Karl was about to go for a walk. He had his raincoat and umbrella in his

234

hand when he opened the door. He came instantly to attention even though he was in civilian clothes, as his visitor was a man he only knew officially in the *Abwehr* as an *Oberst* (Colonel) who had survived the purge. There were those who believed he was among the *Abwehr* insiders who revealed the anti-Nazis to Himmler. He had transitioned very smoothly into the RSHA because of his SS ties and was now recognized as a SS-*Standartenfuhrer* in the *Gestapo*. He was a short, thin man with horned-rim glasses, and he smiled broadly, the glasses making his eyes appear large and friendly.

"*Herr Major* Berchtold, good evening. I—hope I haven't come at a bad time? Are you going out?"

"No, *Herr Oberst* Reinhardt, I was simply going for a walk. Please come in." Reinhardt nodded and stepped inside. It was an awkward moment until Karl turned on an additional light. He helped Reinhardt take off his overcoat and draped it carefully over a chair.

"May I get you something for a refreshment, *Herr Oberst* Reinhardt? I—have some brandy and some decent French wine, if you prefer."

"No—no thank you, *Herr Major.* I apologize for not calling at the office, but I wanted to have this conversation away from the eyes and ears." Reinhardt peered at Karl carefully before he gestured towards the two soft chairs in the room. "May we have a seat?"

"You obviously recognize me from your days before in Paris, *Herr Major?*"

"Yes *Herr Oberst,* of course." Reinhardt glanced around at the room casually, but Karl could see the man was measuring and seeing everything. The room was bare, spare and very obviously the domain of a single person.

"It's been difficult for you I'm sure, as all of us former *Abwehr* officers have endured during this—time." Reinhardt's placed his hands on his knees and leaned slightly forward, his eyes suddenly narrow and dark.

"Have you pursued your investigation on that Jewess prostitute— Anna Metzger, at any time since your trip to Limoges, eight or nine months ago?"

Karl reeled back from the question but he was certain he had not reacted visibly, although he almost suspected Reinhardt of reading his mind. He blinked as if in confusion.

"That was a follow up from an interrogation in Lyon, but the woman in question—*Fraulein* Metzger? She disappeared after what appeared to be a double murder."

"*Triple* murder, *Herr Major.* She is the prime suspect of the murder of a SS-*Obersturmbannfuhrer* about five weeks prior to that, I believe."

"You're right, I forgot about that linkage, because the killings were done the same way."

Karl became wary, noticing the long pause. Reinhardt was waiting for him to continue. He had the *patience.* Karl knew enough about interrogation techniques to know nervous people will invariably fill long silences with talk, incriminating themselves by blurting information that was not asked for. But this was not an interrogation cell, this was his quarters. He forced himself to remain still and silent, meeting Reinhardt's cool eyes with his own.

"What is the pleasure of your visit tonight, *Herr Oberst?*" Reinhardt didn't respond at first, his eyes dropping to the floor for a moment as if he were making a decision. He looked up and smiled warmly, clapping his hands together.

"On second thought, if you don't mind, *Herr Major,* I think I would accept a glass of brandy."

Karl filled their glasses and they drank to the *Third Reich.* He waited for Reinhardt to begin and it didn't take long.

"*Herr Major* Berchtold, you knew this woman, Anna Metzger before, didn't you? In Limoges?"

Karl knew policemen and intelligence officers often ask questions they already know the answer to. It was part of the cat and mouse to ferret out the truth. *Oberst* Reinhardt was with *Abwehr* before the war, he was a professional. The information was there somewhere. There was no evading the question or the answer.

"Yes, I was very curious when I came across the report in Lyon, but then I saw the picture taken by the Limoges National Police Brigade for her license for prostitution. I was shocked to realize it was the same woman. This woman had portrayed herself to me as a physician from Lyon, and that was easy to believe because of her grace and obvious education. It was reinforced again when she virtually saved my life when we were both seriously injured in an automobile collision. She had some medical training previously. We put her up in our hotel in Limoges for a week or so while she recovered, but then she had to go to—Toulouse I believe, to attend to the care of a relative. At least that's what she told me. We've had no contact since the summer of 1940."

"Yes, your memory is good. I was the Chief of the *Abwehr* counter intelligence unit in Limoges during those early years. I also recall a little trouble with another prostitute, another blond woman, which got you transferred, yes?"

"Yes, I certainly admit that. It was a foolish mistake to get involved with a prostitute, but at the time I was travelling a great deal and simply got lonely for feminine companionship."

"We're not talking about the same woman, are we?" Reinhardt's eyes grew narrow and dark, and for the first time Karl was truly afraid. His mind raced but physically he appeared perplexed.

"What same woman? Do you mean—Anna Metzger? She left for Toulouse in mid-summer and I never saw her again. This other woman I picked up in a bar."

"When Anna Metzger was in Limoges, did you have relations? Did you sleep with her?"

Karl slowly set his glass down and stared hard at Reinhardt.

"With all due respect *Herr Oberst* Reinhardt, what is this all about? You came to my quarters in the evening to interrogate me? Are you charging me with a crime? Why are you doing this here?"

Reinhardt put his glass down and raised his hands in surrender. He shook his head and smiled.

"I apologize, *Herr Major*. As I said earlier, the office is full of eyes and ears, and you're not currently assigned to a RSHA office. There is no security in your temporary situation, so I opted to come here so we could have this conversation. And *Herr Major*—I am not accusing you of anything. You have nothing to fear from me."

As if to reinforce this statement, Reinhardt stood up and found the brandy bottle, refilling both of their glasses. He sat back down, but before doing so he drew his chair closer to Karl's. As before, he sat with his hands on his knees as he leaned forward. He seemed to be seeking an intimacy even though there wasn't anyone else in the room.

"*Herr Major* Berchtold, I asked you these questions because you are one of the very few people who actually know this woman, Anna Metzger. Met her. Spent time with her. You've been away for years and have tripped across her again by accident because of your new assignment in the *Abwehr*. You're not an intelligence professional, you're not even a professional soldier—you're a mathematician, for God's sakes! *Yes?*"

Reinhardt waited until Karl acknowledged the question with a slow nod before clapped his hands again, loudly. He took another sip from his brandy and held up a single finger for emphasis.

"This *one woman* and we believe it was this Anna Metzger, operated in the Limoges area *for years*, certainly during the entire 20 months or so I was there, working with communists and other French anti-*Vichy* groups to develop networks and guerrilla cells to attack us, the German Army. She was obviously a British agent from the beginning, but she was so good in her movements and a master of disguises we didn't recognize we were dealing with a single person! We had so many field reports of various sightings but we were never able to get close to her, she was that good. We had reports of these blond women, brunette women and even old—disabled women, and it totally threw us off. They were treated independently. It wasn't until she escaped a huge dragnet that we realized we had her in our hands, but we were looking for a young blond woman and she escaped as something else." Reinhardt looked away for a moment then turned back to Karl.

"Well *Herr Major,* like yourself, when I was promoted and reassigned to Paris and then later back to Berlin, I had other duties and responsibilities and simply put the episode behind me. When *Abwehr* was done away with and I somehow managed to survive the purge—I accepted my blessings and my new assignment with the RSHA. Unlike yourself, RSHA considers me a professional intelligence officer and if I wasn't going to be shot as an anti-Nazi traitor, they wanted to put me to work. I still work counter intelligence, and my years in France brought me back here. My prime responsibility is finding the foreign Allied agents being seeded in France like popcorn prior to the invasion of the continent, and exposing them. The big differences being the RSHA action arm—the *Gestapo,* unlike our former organization, the *Abwehr,* doesn't trust the *gendarmerie*—or involve them in enforcement. It has caused some problems, as you can imagine, but with the RSHA absorbing the German Military Police we have adequate manpower."

Reinhardt sighed and shook his head, as if remembering something pleasant that was no longer available. He paused and watched Karl with a bemused look on his face.

"One thing we can say about the *Gestapo,* however—that is, between you and me as former *Abwehr* colleagues, the *Gestapo* and their heavy-handed *tactics* do provide quick results. I know you've benefited from them, all those months in Lyon working with Barbie, yes?"

Cautiously and respectfully, Karl nodded in affirmation.

"Well, we have again become the beneficiary of some interesting information garnered from a *Gestapo* interrogation of an indigenous SOE agent captured by the *Das Reich* in the *Aquitaine.* Your old friend Anna Metzger disappeared for some months, but she has reappeared again, this time working for the OSS. The timing is obviously designed to correspond with the expected new Allied offensive at the end of this month or early June. The Allies are sending all sorts of commando teams into France to organize the Resistance and are getting involved in direct action themselves. The information from the captured agent gives us the clear indication Metzger has landed with a radio operator, but there have been no transmissions—none. The SOE wasn't involved in the OSS mission, but knowing Anna Metzger and her skills, the SOE deduced her real OSS mission was not simply disruption, but *assassination*."

Reinhardt drained his glass and reached for the bottle, gesturing if Karl wanted his refilled as well. Karl shook his head, his thoughts confused, stomach churning. Reinhardt seemed to sense his growing discomfort, lifting his chin in mock concern.

"You read her police file in Limoges, examined them all. I saw the notes signed by the Police Chief Inspector. You saw what they called her. It's on the file folder."

"Yes *Herr Oberst*."

"The *Kite*. A bird of prey. What's the French term?"

"*Ecoutte, Herr Oberst*."

"Yes, that's right. *Ecoutte*. Did you know that in that category of bird, the birds of prey, the female is larger? More dangerous? Isn't there a street named after them, somewhere in Paris?"

"Yes, in the Marais. In the *Pletzl*. The Rue des *Ecouttes*. The Street of Kites."

"Correct, *Herr Major*. Well I have an assignment for you. The old Jew hunter of Lyon can't be left on the shelf forever, yes? I know your methods, *Herr Major*! Hunt Jews with Jews! Well, in this case, it's hunting a Jew with an old friend. This *Kite* is hunting the leadership of the *Das Reich*, this much we know, and as a master of disguises she will get close by all the means available to her. She is quite a looker, this Anna Metzger, yes? No sane man would turn her away from his bed, yes? Well, we're going to turn the tables on the *Kite* this time. She'll be using everything and *everybody* to get closer to the leadership, so we will arrange a transfer for you to the *Das Reich's* senior Intelligence staff, someone who works closely with the Assistant Division Commander for briefings. She will recognize you and will try to use you to get close. It will be a chance meeting and believe me, once she recognizes you—and frankly, *Herr Major*, you cut a rather dashing figure, she'll come to you."

"You'll set a trap. What will you do with her?"

"We'd like to take her alive, it would be quite the prize, but this woman—I doubt it. Don't worry, *Herr Major*. You will be safe." Reinhardt misread Karl's brief glance of concern.

"The *Kite* won't slip out of this noose. Not this time. You know her. You will point her out to us and get out of the line of fire. I would say it would go a long way in getting you back on the right side, *Herr Major*."

"When—when do I leave?"

239

"In about an hour *Herr Major*. The *Luftwaffe* will fly you to Montauban tonight. You'll have breakfast with the *Das Reich* senior staff. No one will approach you because they will fear you. Just operate like an observer from Berlin, you will be granted complete access. She may already be around. She landed in the *Dordogne*, but it makes the most sense for her to come to Agen and Montauban to get close to the leadership and stay close. Keep your eyes and ears open, *Herr Major*. She is a very dangerous one, this Anna Metzger, and I think she would sense a trap if you do anything but be yourself. Be surprised when she approaches you. Try to spend as much time as possible with her. You'll be new to the *Das Reich*, and finding a familiar face and staying close to her would be normal. You're lonely. She might see it as an advantage. When they come to take her, it will be a surprise, so no one will contact you in advance. Understood?"

But Karl was only half listening. He found his heart lifting and a smile forming on his lips before he grimaced and nodded his head. *Anna.*

240

# Chapter 27

*May 30, 1944. Cahors, France.*

Since his strafing experience in the Soviet Union Karl was never comfortable riding in an armored personnel carrier again, let alone a cramped staff car like the one that he crashed in Limoges, ages ago. They crossed the Lot River and entered Cahors in convoy; two armored scout cars, two light tanks, six transport Opels with 120 *Wehrmacht* of the SS Guard Company from the *Der Fuhrer* Regiment and three staff cars in the middle. As soon as they entered the narrow boulevard that rimmed around Cahors, he felt hemmed in and vulnerable.

Cahors is a small medieval city about 50 kilometers north of Montauban on N20, the major route the *Das Reich* Division used to cover its operational area and the primary route it would use to travel north towards Tulle, Limoges and further to Brittany and Normandy to oppose the northern Allied landings. Cahors represented the base of a tree with the trunk N20. Most of the 20,000 men in the *Das Reich* Division would be found over a 30-kilometer line spreading east to west from Valence d'Agen to Montauban. Southwest France is a mix of flat agricultural land and rolling, rocky hills with sparse forests and hundreds of major and minor roads interconnected by trails and goat paths not represented on any map. *Das Reich* was well dispersed and hidden away from the city centers under the trees in the forests. As a Panzer Division the *Das Reich* was all about mobility, and when it sortied to confront and destroy the *Maquis* of the *Limousin*, their numerous routes heading north to join at Cahors resembled the roots of the imaginary tree.

The city was established in a bend in the Lot River, protruding out like the top part of a fat thumb. Unlike the numerous hilltop *bastides* built on rocky knolls on the river, Cahors was once a lowland walled city that used the river as a source of transport and as natural protection. The high stone parapets were all gone now, but the shady, tree-lined but narrow little streets were perfect for the hit and run tactics of the *maquis* ambushes. When the call came to move north *en masse* the *Das Reich* would converge at Cahors on N20. It would be a perfect choke point and the Assistant Division Commander was more than aware of the vulnerability of the bridge on N20 leading into the city. He was personally inspecting the counter-terrorist preparations on the roads leading to Cahors, but also confirming the viability of alternative routes for the division.

With his black eye patch, cane and slow gate, Karl knew he cut quite the buccaneer figure. His new SS uniform notwithstanding, his temporary transfer to the Division Intelligence staff just before the expected Allied landings was not warmly received. His mission, as his orders so vaguely outlined, was to *assist in the identification of both known and unknown enemies of the Third Reich believed to operate in the Limousin, Dordogne and Lot areas at this time. Complete and immediate cooperation with his requirements for access to information and people is expected at all levels. Heil Hitler.*

The orders were signed first by SS-*Standartenfuhrer* (Colonel) Reinhardt, RSHA. His signature was counter-signed by some SS-*Obergruppenfuhrer* (Lieutenant Colonel), RSHA, a name he had never heard of. The last counter-signature was by Heinrich Himmler, *Reichsfuhrer* of the *Schultzstaffel.* Karl quickly got used to watching the faces of the staff officers as they read the orders. The Second SS Panzer Division was, above all things a *Schultzstaffel* division. The faces remained passive, almost perplexed as they read the brief statement, but the reaction was always the same as their eyes scrolled down the list of signatures. *It is as if,* Karl thought to himself, *God himself had spoken.* There was a slight straightening of the spine, a careful re-reading of the orders, then a cautious, respectful glance upwards towards Karl.

*Of course, Herr Major. My staff is at your complete disposal.*

In the end, as designed, Karl was left completely alone to do whatever he wanted. The *Das Reich* was assigned a small *Gestapo* contingent to work with the Intelligence staff as they encountered the *maquis,* and their leader, a young SS-*Untersturmfuhrer* (Second Lieutenant), made his staff and himself available to Karl. Like every other officer who read Karl's orders, there was no interest in small talk or asking any questions about his mission. He was introduced to both the Commanding General of the *Das Reich* and the Assistant Commanding General. As expected, the Commanding General immediately put the Assistant Commanding General at Karl's beck and call. The Assistant Commander, a relatively young man considering his rank, assigned Karl a SS-*Sturnbannfuhrer* (Major) from his staff to ensure Karl complete access to anything he needed.

*Where are these enemies of the Third Reich you are looking for, Herr Major?* Asked the Assistant Commander.

*They are all around us, Herr Brigadefuhrer. Seeing how you work, I suspect I merely have to stay close to you.*

The Assistant Commander laughed, and asked Karl if he would like to accompany his staff when they did a tour of the Lot Valley prior to the Allied landings?

*You'll see all the enemies you want in the eyes of the French as we tour our operating area. We are engaging the largest concentration of*

*Resistance forces in France, and with the Allies arriving with the new Front, it has emboldened the population. They no longer fear us. The gloves are off. Perhaps this is what the Reichsführer is trying to see. We'll show you, Herr Major! You be his eyes!*

There was no question this was not the southwest France of the summer of 1940. Then Karl and his logistics team had driven all over, from Biarritz near the Spanish border to Montpellier, a few miles from the Mediterranean. *Vichy* France that summer meant tentative smiles and hand waves from the French. They drove the little staff car thousands of miles into the French countryside with little concern for personal safety. As Karl recalled, the team carried personal sidearms but no rifles. They never encountered a problem or ever requested an escort. It was naïve, but it was 1940. The French had capitulated, the war was over, and to most of the French not much had changed.

*Hostile.* Karl remembered the Poles, certainly the Russians. There is no escaping the reality of being an occupying Army. He slid back in his seat and stared back at the faces of unrestrained hatred. He saw the look the women gave them, perhaps to him personally, as they slowed and made their way through the narrow streets. *How could she have loved me, the enemy of her country?* His sadness was so overwhelming it seemed to crimp his vision to a tunnel. He glanced at blonds in the crowds with furtive jerks. The curve of a hip, the angle of a cheek would catch his eye but it would never be satisfied. Anna would not be standing on some street corner watching us drive by. *If I stood next to the Assistant Division Commander would she still shoot? Would she trigger the bomb?* For Karl, his darkness rolled his vision inward and he no longer looked outside.

Like the rest of the *Das Reich* Division as evening fell, the command convoy of the Assistant Commander fell back from the small cities and entered the secure perimeter established by the panzer unit assigned to Cahors in a small neighboring village. The convoy's vehicles were draped with camouflage netting and the troops dispersed into defensive positions. The Assistant Commander was quickly moved into the mobile headquarters established in the largest house in the village. Karl was billeted in another house with some of the other staff officers, but keeping in mind his orders and open-ended authority, he left at once and strolled around. He quickly realized the difficulty Anna would have getting close to the Assistant Commander in the field. There was little sign of the previous inhabitants of the village or the confiscated farm houses. German soldiers were everywhere, and it was very apparent they understood the hostility they saw openly in the French civilians during the day could turn into a deadly ambush at night.

Karl knew what SS-*Standartenfuhrer* Reinhardt meant when he said Karl was safe, and all he had to do was to identify Anna. *Point her out.* He was not introduced to the operators assigned to the task and there was no further explanation. He didn't need any. A shadow team had been with him since he boarded the *Junkers* transport bound for Montauban. He had loaded first and didn't see all of the troops who followed. He regretted it at the time, but he finally recognized his shadows. Nineteen officers rode in the three staff cars of the convoy. Most were part of the Division Headquarters or Intelligence staff and he was introduced to all of them over the rank of *Oberleutnant* (First Lieutenant). All of the HQ staff stayed close to the Assistant Commander and appeared to have very specific duties. They either provided information to the Assistant Commander at his request, or they were *couriers* to communicate his orders. Karl noted two men, both SS-*Obersturmführers* (First Lieutenant), who didn't seem to have responsibilities with either the HQ or the Intelligence staff. Both were tall and extremely fit looking, like *fallschirmjagers* (paratroopers) he had encountered in Poland and the Soviet Union. He didn't always see them, but when he returned to his billeted farmhouse for dinner, he noticed they came in shortly thereafter.

The Assistant Commander's aide, the SS-*Sturmbannfuhrer* assigned to assist Karl, was waiting for him. The Assistant Commander had asked if Karl wanted to join him and his staff for dinner. Karl accepted, wondering how his two shadows would manage to wrangle a place in the Headquarters farmhouse. They didn't. The Guard Company took their responsibilities seriously, and there was no admittance without a recognized escort. During the formal, rather dull and quiet dinner that included a dozen officers besides Karl and the Assistant Commander, the conversation was stilted with a positive bent towards successes against the Resistance forces. Karl suspected the conversation was guided by the Assistant Commander for Karl's benefit. It was obvious his dinner companions were briefed on his orders as they were extremely polite, taking all cues from their boss. He was a pale, serious fellow, looking 10 years older than his reported age. Karl wondered if the man had been given any inkling of the mission launched against him personally. If anything, Karl decided, the poor man clearly didn't know what to make of Karl's role. There was almost an edge of fearfulness in the man's eyes when he engaged Karl in small talk, a deer-like wideness of his eyes Karl was certain was not characteristic of the man, given his reputation and responsibilities of what was considered one of the best panzer divisions in the German Army. He was afraid of something.

There were no cigars or *schnapps* after dinner; the staff went back to work. The Assistant Commander would be meeting briefly with the Mayor and some community leaders in Cahors tomorrow morning, and Karl was invited to attend. They would be discussing the responsibilities of the local authorities to assist the *Das Reich* in keeping N20 open, and to help identify the members of the Resistance who were openly defying the authority of the *Third Reich*. He said this without a hint of irony in his voice, although his eye brows lifted in surprise.

*There is no doubt in my mind, Herr Major. Although they will not be attending officially, the Resistance and the local maquis will be well represented,* he added with a wistful smile. *You will find it interesting and an opportunity to see what we are up against here.*

*Maybe tomorrow.* The Assistant Commander will be in Cahors where he would be the most vulnerable. Karl, back in his billet at the other farmhouse, looked down at the sidearm in his holster. As a special duty officer when he was called up, Karl was given only cursory firearms training. He had never fired the brand-new Walther PP in the black leather holster. He didn't even know if it was loaded. It felt heavy, and he did note the spare magazine built into his holster. Tonight, when he got to his room, he would examine it and make sure there was a round in the chamber. He was sitting at what was once the main dining room table in the farmhouse, sipping a glass of wine someone had handed to him. He peered around slowly but his shadows were nowhere to be seen.

His incompetence for this sort of task shook a sled of ice down his spine and his hands quivered. He knew what he had to do, but every scenario he envisioned resulted in his death. He would not let the two assassins kill Anna; he knew that much. They would assume he would finger her and get out of the way. But he couldn't protect her from the Guard Company professionals who would be protecting the Assistant Commander. If she attacked him in the open tomorrow, she might be successful in killing the Assistant Commander but there was no possible way she herself would survive if she attempted it at close range. *Would she accept a suicide mission?*

Karl had to believe she would not. Anna was a survivor. This was a professional mission, not a revenge killing. He closed his eyes and tried not to think of everything he had read in the reports, or had been explained to him as fact by the Police Inspector in Limoges, or by SS-*Standartenfuhrer* Reinhardt. But some images could not be brushed away, of her soft pale body in the arms of strangers. Those bore into his skull, probing deep into his heart. *Why did she do it? Was there no other option for her?* So much of it confused him, because the behavior was nothing he had expected or witnessed. The killings baffled him more, because she let them use her before she killed them—stabbed them to death, according to the police reports. In the end, he only knew that he missed her—he loved her, no matter what. He couldn't stop the tears and tucked his head into the crook of his arm when some of the Intelligence officers began coming in. A few of them stared at him for just a moment before they remembered who he was and who he represented. They quickly glanced away and went about minding their own business.

He wiped his eyes and put his head in his hands. If he could just somehow get to her before she attempted her operation, maybe they could walk away. Go somewhere and wait for the end of the war. Start over. He had to believe there was a chance. The Allies were coming, be here in weeks. They had to hold out. He had to be alert, watch for her, let her approach him as Reinhardt had suggested. But how? It didn't seem possible with the current circumstances, not here in the field. His best chance was to stop her before she tried anything. But how was he going to talk to her with his shadows on his heels? The minute they saw her they would close in for the kill; there was no mistake about that. Karl lifted his head and his eyes met one of the SS-*Obersturmfuhrers* who was shadowing him. The man lifted his arm in a casual salute as he walked past, his eyes nowhere as friendly as his voice.

"Good evening, *Herr Sturmbannfuhrer.*"

Karl ignored the greeting, staring at the man as he walked past. He would probably have to shoot this man—both men in order to save Anna.

*I'll do it. I'll do whatever it takes.*

# Hunt of the Kite

## Chapter 28

*May 30, 1944. Bonaguil, France.*

Like most pilots Jean Paul hated riding in the back of an airplane as a passenger. He found the Liberator to be just as cold, noisy and confining as a Lancaster, but the number one discomfort was not being up front and in control. He had thought he would work his way up to the cockpit and jaw with the pilots, but he was so overloaded with his parachute and other equipment he could hardly stand up, let alone walk about in the sealed bomb bay. Captain Ericson handed out earplugs to Captain McLemore and Jean Paul, pointing at his watch and displaying three fingers with his hand. Three hours to drop. He placed his hands together and folded them under his ear in the universal symbol of sleep, and motioned the two of them to take advantage of the canvas seats.

Jean Paul had paid extra attention to the pilot briefing, noting the pilots were trying to avoid flak concentrations near Bordeaux on the coast, and inland near road or waterway intersections, airfields and where German soldiers were garrisoned. Agen, Montauban and Cahors were on their route of flight and all along that corridor where the *Das Reich* was stationed. But what caught his attention especially was the prime drop zone area between the hilltop *bastides* Rocamatour and St. Cirg Lapopie, east of N20. He could read a topographical map as well as anyone, and the aviation charts revealed nothing but narrow, winding little valleys and corridors surrounded by high rock and straight-down fiords with meandering rivers at the bottom between the two *bastides* east of N20. The pilots, explaining their approach to the selected drop zone, would try to confuse observers to their whereabouts by flying, up, over and *down* most of these little valleys. After doing this several times it would be difficult for the Germans to determine exactly where the drop would take place.

With the planned seaborne invasion possible any day, the Germans were not shy about filling the sky with steel and high explosives whenever they heard airplanes overhead. But the special operations missions only flew on nights with at least a 50 percent moon exposure, allowing the pilots to navigate by the terrain features. The Germans forced the French to reduce lighting, and of course any or all aviation navigation aids or airway beacons were turned off. Without moonlight visual navigation, the black Liberators would never be able to precisely locate their drop zones.   But there was no denying the moonlight bathing the landscape beneath them worked both ways for those looking from the air or from the ground.

What woke Jean Paul up was the eerie quiet, the whistling sigh as the Liberator descended from its offshore cruise altitude as it made land a few kilometers south of Bordeaux with engines at reduced power.   He knew the pilots would stay at about 500 meters as they crossed the shoreline, staying high enough to be out of reach for any low-level flak batteries, and then continue to descend until they leveled near the Lot River at about 150 meters.   Something picked them up, as he could just hear the *thump thump thump thump* of the bigger guns, and the closer *crump crump crump crump* of the exploding flak bursts somewhere else, but close to their altitude.   He could feel the Liberator turn and the slight vibration as the pilot slowly brought up the power as they approached their target altitude.

The flight engineer and an assistant came into the bomb bay and spoke with Captain Ericson, then moved aft to unstrap the large aluminum cylinders of equipment to be dropped on the second pass.   Ericson woke Captain McLemore, and seeing Jean Paul already alert, signaled 40 minutes to drop.   The big airplane was twisting and turning constantly now, the crew keeping the river and landmarks in sight, but also avoiding flying over any areas of population or known flak guns.   Gunfire, at a distance, was steady over the roar of the engines.   Jean Paul didn't know if it was all aimed at their airplane or others in the area.   His Bomber Command experience with the RAF was always at night.   He knew full well how the sky lit up on the bombing mission's expected path and altitude.   He had to think, with the invasion imminent, there would be lots of aerial reconnaissance activity going on all over France, but the noise of a gun can be comforting and he could imagine many nervous gun crews tonight, no matter how disciplined they were.  Many rounds expended into empty sky.   He just hoped nobody got in a lucky shot.

As a pilot, even when the searchlights blinded him and the turbulence was so bad he couldn't hold an altitude or a heading, Jean Paul rarely felt sick.   But when the Liberator dropped its nose like a roller coaster for the thirteenth or fourteenth time, and Jean Paul knew they were down in some dark little valley with solid rock *above them* on both sides, he felt queasy in his stomach.   Then the roar as the Liberator pitched up, nose high, straining and moaning under full power to avoid yet another dark, impossible ridge of solid, unbending rock.

*Enough already.   Holy shit, mother of God...*

Somewhere down there the pilots were looking for the drop zone identification, usually three flashlights in a row with a fourth at 90 degrees showing the direction. This twisting and turning, diving and climbing continued for another 10 minutes or so, then the Liberator suddenly climbed back to 500 meters and leveled off, completely changing course, much to Jean Paul's relief. Ericson exchanged glances with the others and held up two fingers in a V: On to the secondary, apparently. No response from the ground.

They flew for 20 more minutes before Jean Paul sensed the Liberator descending with the power reduced again. The cabin grew quiet as they flew away from flak gun concentrations, and even the wind noise diminished as the aircraft slowed down. The howl returned as the flight engineer removed the large cover over the *Joe hole* in the middle of the bomb bay. He turned around and brought both of his hands palms up, signaling the three men to get to their feet. He glanced at the display panel on the fuselage and watched the large red bulb glow on and steady. As the men were helped to their feet by the assistant, the flight engineer signaled them to stand with their hands away from their bodies. The assistant quickly checked the parachute harness on each man and retrieved the tether attached to the pilot chute that would pull the parachutes from the packs. He moved the men in order and latched their tethers to the overhead bar that ringed across the fuselage. Ericson was first, then McLemore and Jean Paul.

The Flight Engineer signaled Ericson to come forward and had him sit down on the edge of the open hole, his legs dropping down into the gale of the 120-knot slipstream. Ericson gripped the handles on each side of the *Joe hole* and glanced at the Flight Engineer who had his hand up, his eyes on the display panel. McLemore shuffled right up behind Ericson but kept clear of Ericson's tether. The display panel switched from red to green and the Flight Engineer dropped his hand. Ericson released his grip and slid forward, the smooth sides of the hole designed not to snag the bulky parachute, and he was gone. McLemore stepped down to the hole, dropped his legs in and slid forward, and he too was gone. Jean Paul followed him and glanced down, amazed at how well he could see the moonlight bathed ground below, seemingly very close. He sat down and slid forward and dropped free. The Flight Engineer quickly pressed the ALL CLEAR signal to the pilot and began retrieving the tethers dangling down into the *Joe hole.* He held on as the Liberator began its slow turn to make its second pass, his assistant already sliding the metal equipment canisters forward on the bomb bay deck and hooking up the parachute tethers.

Because of the high rocky cliffs around the primary drop zone Jean Paul had spent a lot of his time, nervously, studying the terrain at that site. The secondary, 40 kilometers or so west of Cahors and northeast of the hilly forested farmlands surrounding the 12<sup>th</sup> Century Bonaguil Castle ruins, was examined only out of curiosity. As he cleared the airplane, he gasped with the parachute opening shock and the realization they had been dropped low, very low, perhaps less than 120 meters, and he was going directly into the edge of a dark forest. He pulled hard on his risers to arrest his turn towards the trees, but found he was descending straight into an ancient rock fence. He lifted his boots and cleared the top of the fence by inches only to slam into the hard bank of a dried-out creek bed on the other side.

There was no wind or he would have been dragged by his parachute on the cold ground. After a few minutes he cautiously got to his knees and slid out of his parachute harness, wrapping it up with the parachute into a large bundle. He carefully unstrapped his Sten gun from his chest pack, inserting a magazine and cocking the weapon. The moonlight made him feel completely exposed, but at least he was down in the depression caused by the creek bed, and behind him there was the rock wall. He remembered no such details on his examination of the drop zone. He poked his head over the edge of the creek bed and tried to orient himself to the dark forest he had seen moments before he landed, but suddenly a shadow brushed the ground around him and then there was the roar of an airplane. The equipment drop of course. He crawled forward and then clamored up the side of the rock fence in time to see an equipment cylinder hurdling towards his section of the fence at about chest height. It exploded into dozens of pieces on the ancient stacked rock.

"Well," Ericson said as they gathered on the edge of the forest to take stock, "look at the bright side. The radio and our costumes survived and nothing was destroyed." They were lucky in that regard. The canister that collided with the rock fence was the one with 80 Sten guns, 270 magazines and 12,000 rounds of 9mm ball ammunition destined to the *maquis*. The guns were carefully packed in cosmoline and wooden crates, as were the magazines and ammunition. The canister came apart as did some of the wooden crates, but the guns appeared intact.

Ericson and McLemore were not as fortunate as Jean Paul. They dropped a few seconds earlier and could not escape the forest. Ericson was certain he broke his left hand and a couple of ribs colliding with tree limbs. McLemore got the worst of it, breaking his right arm and fractured his cheek and losing a couple of teeth. Nothing was protruding out of the skin but the bulges, dark bruises and intense pain left no doubt to the seriousness of their injuries.

Unlike the expected large *maquis* reception by the *bastides,* the team was met by only four men in Bonaguil. None acted like a leader, and although all three of the team spoke excellent French, the Frenchmen of Bonaguil seemed wary, especially since two of the team were wearing British muftis. The seconds in the air did reveal virtually no lights on the ground, and the total lack of anti-aircraft fire once they flew over to the west side of N20 meant few German troops in the immediate area. Ericson considered having to go to the secondary a positive, because it placed them about 50 kilometers north of Valence d' Agen, where the SOE agents already operating in the region believed the *Der Fuhrer* Regiment of the *Das Reich* was based, and the Assistant Division Commander had his HQ. The problem at this point was transportation and some medical attention.

After some discussion the four Frenchmen disappeared for about 20 nerve-racking minutes. They returned with a half-dozen other men, all unarmed and apparently local peasants, to help move the canisters and their contents into the forest. There was some disagreement about the Sten guns as the Frenchmen wanted to take them immediately, but Ericson made it clear he expected to see a local leader to discuss their distribution. He kept asking about the whereabouts of two men who were to meet them, but the Frenchmen shrugged their shoulders. Ericson got angry and demanded to see the two men immediately, and for the Frenchmen to see about getting them a trusted doctor. Ericson produced what appeared to be a large quantity of cash, *Francs,* and proffered it without giving any of it away. The four Frenchmen, all armed, exchanged glances with one another and two of them fingered their weapons, but there were no side discussions as everyone present spoke French. Despite their painful injuries, it was obvious Ericson and McLemore had no intentions of aborting the mission.

Two hours later McLemore and Jean Paul were lying in the second story of a drafty hayloft. A physician from Fumel, a pediatrician, examined McLemore and Ericson and did what he could. He set McLemore's arm and devised a splint and sling, then wrapped a topknot head bandage to secure what turned out to be a fractured jaw. McLemore, who could only speak out of the corner of his mouth, was in intense pain and seemed very angry with Ericson. He waited until the physician finished wrapping Ericson's ribs and securing his broken hand in a splint. Ericson gave the physician some *Francs* and their thanks, but it was clear the man wanted to have nothing to do with them. He did take the money but was gone without another word. A new man who called himself the local FTP *maquis* leader, but wasn't one of the two men Ericson had demanded to see, arranged the temporary hideout and was waiting below.

"What the fuck is going on?" McLemore hissed in English, trying to whisper. "Who the hell are *these* people? Nobody seems to know who the hell we are! We're supposed to trust these fuckers?"

251

Ericson waved McLemore and Jean Paul closer until their heads were nearly touching. Jean Paul could smell McLemore's dried blood on his face and could see a piece of McLemore's scalp had been slit open. The physician had sewn it loosely together, with a mixture of dripping fluids forming around the edges of the wound. McLemore's eyes were open and clear and he stared unblinking at Ericson, who made the motion of cutting his throat with his free hand.

*"Quiet, they're right below us.* This is a secondary drop zone, remember? We're lucky they were here and heard the plane approaching. These people are FTP, Communists, so they don't trust us Brits. They don't know you, Mac, so they don't trust you either. But we need their help so we can get some transport down to Agen, and I need to connect with my SOE contact."

"What about Jean Paul, here? He's a Frenchman, why won't they trust him?" McLemore nodded irritably towards Jean Paul.

"They're FTP. Jean Paul is wearing a British uniform just like me. They assume he's a de Gaullist, and the FTP hate de Gaulle, you know that, just like you Yanks do."

McLemore shook his head and spat into the hay, disgusted and in pain.

"What a cluster fuck you got us in, Ericson. I thought all these people are French and on the same side and want to kill Germans. In a few weeks it won't goddamn matter."

"You're right, in a few weeks it won't matter. But we need help from these people tonight. The Germans must have heard the plane, so they will send out patrols in the morning. I didn't see any moving headlights coming down. First off, you're too hurt to manhandle the radio, so I'm going to get Jean Paul to help me set it up and let HQ know we're on the ground at the secondary. I think we'll be okay, as the *maquis* said they haven't seen any of the signal-hunting vans over here. Then Jean Paul and I will bury the radio out of sight of the *maquis.* After that I'm going to make contact with my local, and then be back by morning. The *maquis* say we're safe here for a day or two, but we need to be close to Agen by tomorrow night."

The two-way radio was built into what looked like an ordinary medium-sized piece of leather luggage. McLemore grudgingly handed over his code books, noting the appropriate radio code signs for the day. Ericson went below to the first floor of the hayloft and spoke with the *maquis* leader in low tones. Jean Paul joined him a few minutes later, keeping his Sten gun casually handy as Ericson handed the leader a sizeable wad of *Francs.* The leader looked at Jean Paul curiously as his men came in and started to cart off the Sten guns.

"Captain Metzgen, yes? You are from Paris? You are Free French, with de Gaulle?"

"No, I'm not with de Gaulle. I fly with the RAF. My home is in Provence."

"Provence? But you are not *Vichy*?"

"No, I'm not *Vichy*. I joined the RAF to get away from *Vichy*."

"You are a pilot with the RAF, but you are here with the British and the Americans on the ground."

"Yes, I'm here to help them clear the path for the Allied landings. Help them rid France of the Germans."

The leader watched him for a moment as he slowly lit a cigarette. He brushed his large, rough workman's hand across his brow in a brief salute. He swept up one of the last of the Sten guns and slung it across his body, stuffing three magazines into his belt.

"Good bye, Captain. And good luck." He nodded to Ericson and signaled him to follow him out. As he turned away, he smiled at Jean Paul, patting the Sten gun and his pocket where Jean Paul had seen him stash the *Francs*.

"Don't be in too much of a hurry, Captain. Most of my men have been out of work for nearly two years. They need the money. I need the money, yes? You, when the war is over, you go back to flying airplanes or back to being a lawyer, or whatever, eh? Many of us are not in much of a hurry to go back to the way it was before the war."

Ericson negotiated with the *maquis* leader for some food and drink, which was brought to them within the hour. Once the *maquis* left Ericson and Jean Paul set up the radio on the ground floor of the hayloft, and quickly established radio contact with the SOE in England. The report was very brief and they shut the radio down, putting it back in the suitcase and wrapping it in a waterproof tarp. They found some digging tools in the corner of the hayloft and stepped off a pattern so they could find it and dig it up when necessary. About three in the morning two men came for Ericson and he disappeared, promising to return by first light.

McLemore moaned in his sleep. Jean Paul woke up once very cold, gathering as much straw as he could for the two of them for extra warmth. At dawn Jean Paul crawled out from under his straw pile and peered out of the open window, realizing the second story was more like the first floor since the hayloft was built down in a depression next to the fields. It was an ancient stone structure with heavy wooden beam construction, well made, still in use but neglected. The old oak trees surrounding the hayloft were on the high pasture side, so as they grew older and the limbs stretched out, they enveloped the hayloft roof and structure and made it virtually invisible from the pasture or the road in front of the old stone farmhouse, half a kilometer away. It was a perfect hideout if you didn't know it was there. He rubbed his eyes to make out the hay cart that was on the road, slowly making its way around the perimeter of the pasture. It was coming their way, and he knew instinctively it would contain Ericson.

Ericson brought two closed ceramic jars full of hot coffee and a basket of hot rolls.

"We leave in about half an hour. My contact has made the arrangements for our transport and our accommodations in Agen. We need to get into our uniforms as we will be dropped off in a little village called Lauzerte, and a damaged German staff car will be waiting for us in a garage. Because of our injuries, our new cover will be as SS staff officers who were involved in a traffic collision on our way to Marseille, and we simply need a few days rest for recovery and possibly some new transport. I know a number of the officers in the HQ staff at *Das Reich*, so I'll ply their generosity. Jean Paul, your German is pretty good, and luckily for Mac, well, he has an excuse for not being all that talkative."

McLemore, who was up and trying to eat the rolls with his broken jaw, simply groaned and stared at them both.

"My German is pretty good too, Ericson," he slurred.

"How do you feel, Mac, still up for this? We could leave you here."

McLemore slowly pulled himself up and shook his head vigorously, his color and anger returning.

"I have a job to do. You know that, Ericson, if our little honey doesn't do it first."

McLemore looked hard at Ericson.

"Your contact say anything about Anna Metzger? Has she been seen anywhere near the *Das Reich?*

Ericson sipped at his coffee and returned McLemore's glare.

"She's there."

# Chapter 29

*June 2, 1944. Valence d' Agen, France.*

For the first five days on the ground Melody Langdon was never so frightened in her life. She calculated she averaged less than three and a half hours of sleep per night, perhaps less. If there was any question they were in enemy territory it was answered as soon as they landed. They were disarmed and painfully roughed up, their arms twisted and hair pulled tight to control their heads. After their hard landing on rocky, unplowed soil, the shadowy figures came out of nowhere, dozens of them, surrounding and throwing the women off balance before they got out of their parachutes. Anna spoke to the men sharply in French to complain but was slapped hard in the face and told to keep her mouth shut. Melody, stumbling and limping from an injured ankle, raised her hands in surrender, totally confused when she realized these people were all Frenchmen. For some reason, probably because they were women, they were lifted off their feet and carried by their arms and legs as if they were shot deer. They were carried in this fashion for a couple of hundred meters straight into an unlit barn, and then dumped onto the dirt floor.

The barn door was closed and latched behind them. Kerosene lanterns were lit, and soon both women found themselves surrounded by a circle of men who simply stared at them in silence. Anna, her bruised face glowing red, pushed her body off the ground, screaming at the men in French, telling them she and Melody were from the OSS—from the Americans. The huge coveralls they wore to contain all of their personal gear during the jump were partially torn open. Someone had already removed their .32 caliber Colt pistols, and Anna, rather boldly Melody thought considering their situation, demanded their weapons back. No one moved.

They could hear the roar of the B-24 as it made the equipment drop. The men glanced up as it flew overhead before returning their attention to their captives. The barn door rattled and one of the men unlatched the door and a single man, large and bearlike, entered and approached the circle slowly until it parted in deference. He was obviously a leader as the other men watched him carefully as he stopped and put his hands on his hips. Anna glared at him in contempt and pointed her finger at him accusingly.

"Are you the leader of this rabble? Is this the reception we receive when we are in the position to provide you with weapons and explosives?" She spat, peering down at her torn coveralls and touching her injured face. "I'm French, you son of a bitch, and I represent the American Army! The

OSS. Who are you? I know the leaders of the *maquis* here, and you are not the group who was supposed to meet us."

The leader nodded his head in agreement and sheepishly shrugged his shoulders. He sighed and glanced around at his men, a broad smile on his face.

"I think we got here first, *Mademoiselle.* You might say we're taking over." The humor left his face, and he nodded towards the fields they had just left.

"That was an equipment drop, yes? Weapons and ammunition? Where is your radio?"

"I asked *you* a question. Who are you? Are you FTP?" The leader ignored Anna and signaled to his men, pointing at the women.

"Take those coveralls off and search them. They say they are Americans but I believe they are British." He scratched his head and stared hard at Anna as several of the men stepped in and started to remove her coveralls. When Anna resisted, two of them gripped her arms tight until she gasped in pain. Melody quickly held up her hands in surrender and was still as her coveralls were roughly yanked down.

"You are French, yes? You lived here before, yes, *Mademoiselle?* What is your name?"

One man found a satchel of cash stuffed behind Anna's back, and he whistled when he tore open one corner to find it filled with *Francs.* The leader waved his arm and the satchel was passed over. One of Anna's searchers also discovered a second Colt 1903 pistol in a small holster below her waistband, his hand sliding down under her underwear as he laughed in her discomfort. She wriggled her body violently against her captors and spit in the man's face, whereupon he was preparing to strike her when the barn door burst open. Three men stepped in, all heavily armed and very upset. They were quickly joined by a half a dozen others, equally armed.

The leader of the new group, stout and darkly bearded, ordered everyone away from the women. No one moved, and the new leader raised his pistol and all of his companions did the same. The men around the women released their grip and stepped away, their eyes on their own leader, who was now shouting at the new group that they had arrived first. The bearded leader stepped in closer and cautiously examined Anna and Melody, his eyes apparently not missing a thing. He ordered the first group to return the money and the weapons back to the women, immediately. His pistol was now pointed squarely at the big man holding the satchel of money. The big man shook his head and demanded they split the money and weapons, and was promptly shot in the chest.

256

The others were surrounded and disarmed. They were searched for anything that might have been lifted from the women, and then they were taken away. There were two muffled gun shots outside in close succession, then quiet. Melody was so frightened she couldn't control her limbs or her bladder, her trousers soaking dark as she shook uncontrollably. She was aware enough to realize Anna and the new leader seemed to know each other, but she was appalled when she found out this new group was still not the people they had arranged to meet. Their pistols were returned to them as was the satchel of cash, wet and stained with fresh blood. Melody sat still trying to control her breathing as box after box of weapons and ammunition were brought into the barn. She listened in a daze as Anna negotiated with the bearded leader, offering him several dozen of the American made carbines, ammunition and hand grenades, plus a large sum of cash for some unspecified services. Anna couldn't give him all of them, she said, but she could promise more on another drop if she could get his help.

Later that night they were moved about three kilometers and found a warm bed in a farm house. About four in the morning Melody woke up, remembering with a shock she had not made her required radio check in. Despite all the months of practice and training, her first night in the field had flustered and confused her so much she forget her primary responsibilities. She was devastated at her personal failure and admitted it to Anna, asking where the radio was hidden. It was then she started to understand what she was dealing with when Anna explained very patiently that there would not be any radio contact with OSS—ever. Anna had destroyed the crystals and buried the radio. Their safety, Anna said soberly, depended on their ability to blend completely into the countryside and community. Leave no trace, no evidence of their presence or passing. My mission, she smiled, is not what you think it is.

By the fifth day, moving at night in the back of rumbling hay wagons or sitting up, fully exposed in smelly, foul, black-smoke emitting buses during the day, they had left the winding roads following the Lot River and bypassed Cahors. Briefly on N20 with a busload of other workers, the outskirts of Cahors was the first time they saw German troops in fair numbers. These were SS troops with hard, unfriendly faces and as the bus headed south on the small rural roads towards the farms, they were stopped often by road blocks. Melody had complained when Anna forced her to strip out of her British uniform and trade it for a dirty pair of dungarees and moth-eaten sweater. She also showed Melody how to carry her Colt pistol right down in front of her pants, pressed coldly against her pubic hair.

*German soldiers will not touch you there in a field search. Milice, SD or Gestapo will after they arrest you, but not regular soldiers, not even Schultzstaffel.*

The Germans would order everyone out of the bus and inspect documents, personal bags and satchels. Anna had insisted they discard everything they brought with them from England. Melody, her face dirty and smudged by Anna, also had her fingernails shorn short by Anna just before they loaded for the mission. Anna made her use rough soap for weeks to make her hands red and abused, then told Melody to keep them dirty, especially under the nails. The last road block was controlled by a tall, young SS *Untersturmfuhrer* (Second Lieutenant) who took his duties seriously. He was especially hard on the men, examining their papers minutely before pressing and probing satchels for false bottoms or hidden pockets. When he came to Melody, she smiled weakly, but his face remained impassive as he stared first at her papers then at her shoes. He suddenly gripped her hands and examined her nails. He dropped her hands and peered at her eyes and hair.

"What do you do, *Mademoiselle?*" He asked in French. Anna had drilled her on the answer and Melody was ready.

"I'm a baker's assistant at our farm cooperative, but I also help tend the grapevines."

"Ah—that explains why your hands look like they spend a lot of time in water!" He smiled, then turned and glanced at Anna, his hand out. Anna passed over her papers and proffered her small satchel, which he ignored. He flipped through her documents and returned them.

"Back in the bus, be on your way!" Turning on his heels he strode back towards the parked scout vehicles, waving his men along.

Anna and Melody joined the others and silently climbed back into the bus and returned to their seats. Anna casually glanced towards Melody and smiled, relieved when she smiled back. She appeared reasonably calm. There was no turning back for Melody at this point once she made her decision to stay with Anna. But Anna understood her RTO was frightened, confused and overwhelmed by the constant motion and uncertainty during these first few days. Anna had stripped away her personal mission, the purpose Melody had been dropped in France for when she buried Melody's radio. Melody had sat very still the morning Anna explained her real mission. Melody couldn't understand why she had trained for all those months as an RTO if Anna had no intention of ever using her services, but she didn't say it.

*I've already put you at enormous risk by forcing you to change out of your uniform,* Anna explained, *and I'm sorry about that, but it can't be helped if we want to survive. I know how dangerous it is out here on your own. We are strangers to these people, and we French are ridiculously suspicious of people we don't know. These villagers and countrymen are small-minded and selfish, and if there is any potential for gain in turning in a stranger, they'll do it. I use the maquis only because I have to. And don't kid yourself, the maquis work for us because we have money and weapons. I do not trust them and they do not trust us. As you have found out, they don't trust one another. Each group is a little kingdom, fiefdoms run by their chieftains for their own gain, not France. I believe the FTP is controlled by the Russians somehow, and the Russians don't want the Allied landings to succeed. I learned this when I was with a maquis up in the Limousin.*

*When this mission came up, I had to be prepared to go my own way. The OSS is—lacking in experience with the maquis, believing all Resistance groups have the betterment of France as their purpose, and that somehow the Allied invasion would bind these groups together. I had to plan on simply disappearing from the established OSS communication system and perform this mission my way. I could use your help, Melody, but make no mistake. If you stay with me and we get caught, they will torture us and kill us. With the invasion imminent at any time we will be treated as spies instead of soldiers, and they shoot spies. Once the mission is over, we can fall back and lay low until the Allies come through. But you, you have that option right now if you wish. I can arrange to have you hidden in a safehouse until the Germans withdraw or are defeated. It is up to you.*

Anna knew she had chosen her partner wisely when Melody reached out and gripped her hand with both of her own. *I'm in, Anna.* Anna did not tell Melody who her actual target was in the *Das Reich,* or how she planned to execute her mission. Nor did she divulge her intention to abandon the OSS once the mission was over to find her sister. If they were captured or separated Melody Langdon would give very little useful information to her captors about Anna Metzger.

The *maquis* hid them a few kilometers outside of Valence d'Agen. The local *maquis* leader listened carefully as Anna explained her intention to assassinate a *Das Reich* senior officer, not naming anyone. He was very familiar with the layout and functions of the *Das Reich* Headquarters unit stationed in the outskirts of Valence d'Agen. His family business provided the bakery goods required for the Assistant Division Commander's HQ staff, which numbered nearly 120, not including the Guard Company that accompanied the HQ staff wherever they went. Two times a day a small contingent from his bakery drove a truck to the heavily guarded compound and delivered bakery goods. At the same time, another vehicle delivered a small team of domestic staff who cleaned the quarters of the Assistant Division Commander every morning.

"Your family provides the domestic staff too?"

"Yes, as a matter of fact, we do. *Das Reich* trusts us. I personally am held accountable."

"What are the ages and sexes of your bakery staff? And your domestic staff that does the cleaning of the Assistant Commander's quarters?" The *maquis* leader stared hard at Anna and shook his head violently.

"*Absolutely not!* I just told you, I am personally responsible. *Das Reich* believes in reprisals for *any* German casualties. They will take it out on the civilian population of the closest hamlet. If anything happened and it could be proved the killers got in the compound under the guise of being my staff, I will be taken outside and shot, and perhaps all of my family, perhaps everyone in the village! *Absolutely not!*"

It took some serious convincing and nearly 70,000 *Francs* to persuade the *maquis* leader to let Melody replace a member of his bakery staff for a few days. The baker's assistants were all female and young, and Melody could easily pass as the sister of one of them. It took another 50,000 *Francs* to let Anna replace one of the three aging domestics. She promised nothing would happen, but they needed to get inside the compound and look around. They would carry the exact same identification as the people they were replacing, counting on the *Das Reich* staff to not really notice the difference.

Anna, who carried her disguise kit with her at all times including two wigs, spent the evening with the domestic she was replacing, ostensibly to learn the job, but really to study closely how the woman walked, dressed, wore her hair and spoke. Melody spent the evening at the bakery learning her new job, and was requested to show up at 3:30 in the morning to assist in baking the bread she would be taking over. She also quizzed the young woman as to where she lived, where her family came from and the exact duties she would perform when she arrived at the compound. It was the first time Melody had been separated from Anna in six days, but she took it in stride. Her French was a little too formal for the countryside, but she understood that and said she would keep her ears open and learn the idiom.

*Play dumb, Melody, if there are any questions from some HQ staff member or from a SS German soldier,* Anna explained carefully. *German soldiers are conditioned not to expect much from women outside of their traditional roles. That's why they searched the men on the buses so thoroughly and we only had a cursory examination. You noticed they tore the men's cases apart but left ours alone. Stay in your character and your role, and they will leave you alone. Be what they expect you to be.*

*You won't be there long. You're just delivering baked goods. Act like a delivery person. Once you do this twice a day for a couple of days, the staff will get used to you. Look without appearing to. Pay attention. Notice everything. You're delivering, I assume to the kitchen. Look at places where someone might hide if no one was looking. Learn the layout of the place—and be able to diagram it. Be conscious of who is watching you. And how carefully they are watching. Are they more careful in the morning or the afternoon before the evening meal?*

The following morning Anna was informed by the *maquis* leader the Assistant Division Commander was returning after a quick tour of Cahors and some of the N20 approach routes.

*Whenever the Assistant Commander returns*, the *maquis* leader noted *security steps up and the requirements for the bakery jumps through the roof. He loves our bread! The BBC has informed us the invasion may occur any day*, he said candidly, *and when this occurs Das Reich knows the Resistance will double their efforts to try to disrupt their movements of reinforcing the defense of Brittany and Normandy. They will head north in a variety of directions and we must delay them anyway we can. But whatever we do, we will try to do it away from the villages and towns so there will be fewer reprisals. Understand, Mademoiselle?*

*If we wait until they have left, then they will no longer be a threat to you*, Anna thought, *or your family. Das Reich will not be coming back.* She nodded gravely, however, conscious of the watchfulness of the *maquis* leader.

There was no doubt in her mind he understood the risk he was taking by simply having Anna and Melody replacing his staff for a couple of days. Yet he took her 120,000 *Francs*. He trusted her to keep her word. The man and his family already lived a dangerous double life. If she assassinated the Assistant Commander in the compound, she knew she could not escape. The repercussions would be immediate and the *maquis* leader was absolutely correct. None of the locals would escape either. He and his family, all of the staff involved and most of the village of Valence d'Agen would pay for it soon enough, many with their lives. The OSS in their cavalier way, didn't believe the reports of the *Schultzstaffel* executing civilian prisoners in reprisals for the killing of German soldiers. Your mission is *strategic,* Anna. Don't worry about reprisals.

There may be an alternative, another opportunity. But she knew she would not have many more chances to get close to him once the Allies land on the beaches. *Das Reich* would respond and once on the road

261

north, *Das Reich* will turn into a true panzer division with a combat mission. There was no pretense of civility with a panzer division on the move, and there would be none with the Second SS Panzer, the best in the *Wehrmacht*. Anna remembered the briefings binders very well. They would crush the Resistance in their path and confront the Allies. For the Germans, *Das Reich* was the first team. They would complete their mission because they were very well led.

For the first time in many months Anna realized the immediate importance of her mission in the support of her country and the end of the war. Right now, in front of her, it was there. It was a small part, but her opportunity and the ramifications were crystal clear. All of the talk of the second front in England had seemed distant and academic, just like the uniformed academics who bandied the discussions, hundreds of kilometers away from the fighting. But here it was, in her hands. He was only one man and his loss would be temporary but the timing was the issue. On one hand if she pulled it off just as the chaos of the invasion unfolded, *Das Reich* would potentially flounder. But if she did it this way, she and many other French men and women would die.

Anna had survived four years of the war on her intelligence and willingness to do anything because she wanted to live long enough to bring something back into her life. Once it was to see Karl again, and her family. Or was it something else? Her will to live was so strong, but she risked so much in her revenge for Ahmet and Selin. Then for her parents. She struck out against those who took without remorse, or who like the Assistant Prefect of Aix and the Police Inspector, betrayed their friendship with her father. She had no regrets.

For the *SS-Standartenfuhrer* who liked to be dominated by a beautiful blond woman and bound to a chair with leather straps, he would have lived to continue to rise in the ranks of the SS organization if it wasn't for his penchant interest in describing what it was like to witness the raping of Jewish girls in Poland before they were loaded on the trains. He laughed because he liked to use the biggest brutes for the assaults. The girls, mostly schoolgirls he said, were so ashamed they would cover their heads with their skirts. Anna had smiled despite her horror and laughed at his joke as she screamed inside. She invited him to a private session outside the structure of the *maison,* which he accepted. Strapped up, his penis hard and at attention, he died gagging in his own blood, his throat and chest punctured a dozen times. Only the police report and the crime scene photographs revealed the swastika carved on his chest and forehead.

# Chapter 30

*June 4, 1944. Valence d' Agen, France.*

Before Anna buried the radio set, she had carefully slid out a small flat box that was taped inside the case. It contained an oil-clothed bundle with a .22 pistol and 50 rounds of low-velocity ammunition. The suppressor was built into the barrel, so all she had to do was to load the magazine and charge the chamber and it was ready for use. Anna kept the piece of tape, a very strong canvas-backed industrial tape used to keep electrical wire in place on practically any surface, for reuse. Once she committed to her plan her first concern was getting the weapon in position.

By the end of her first day on her bakery deliveries Melody had spotted a small cleaning closet next to the pantry large enough, she said, that someone could hide in it if some of the shelves were rearranged. Anna asked her to determine how low the shelves were. Melody already had the answer, stating the lowest shelf filled with cleaning fluids, was about 40 centimeters from the floor.

*How do you know?* Anna asked, surprised.

*I saw a kitchen worker open the closet to get a broom and a dustpan. It's a tight fit in the kitchen and the pantry is a kind of afterthought, stuck around the corner in the hall. The closet is at the end of the hall.*

*Are you out of sight at any time you're there?*

*It depends. When we arrive in the morning the kitchen staff is pretty busy and once the guards let us in, they only watch us as we come in the door and as we leave. We're only there for a couple of minutes. There are four of us carrying all of this bread, and they seem to take note of that. They smile and always comment on the smell of the fresh bread. I think I can put a package on the lower shelf unseen on the way in if I'm the last one going in.*

*Okay, but what about taping the package under the shelf? It must not fall off. Understood? The tape is very strong, and you'll have maybe five seconds to secure it.*

*What is it, Anna?*

*It's a gun.*

*What if there's no time?*

*How high is the tallest shelf? Can you reach it? Is it dark in the closet? You could simply slide my package in on the top shelf as far back as you can. Hide it from sight. Would that work?*

Anna asked for and received that evening a very large round of freshly-baked bread, and carefully slit it open on one end, sliding the pistol inside completely, and pressing the tape, sticky side out, against the soft bread fibers.   The bread crust was exceptionally thick and strong and easily distributed the weight of the gun.  She resealed it and laid it on the bottom of the basket for the morning delivery.   That first morning Anna and the cleaning staff had to wait outside the compound with the bakery staff, watching the guards examine the bread.  She noticed the guards spent more time looking under the basket liner and the cloths and paper wrappers than the bread loaves themselves.  As long as they didn't try to lift it, the larger loaf sat at an angle like the other loaves, and it was easy to see around it.

The next morning Melody was the last of the bread carriers to be examined.  She joked with the German soldiers as they picked around her bread basket, playing their daily game of sniffing and feeling the heat of the fresh, still hot baguettes.   Once inside the big farmhouse Melody turned towards the hallway leading into the kitchen, letting the cleaning staff get past her.   She carried her basket into the hallway until she was opposite the closet, sitting the basket down as though she were adjusting the load.  She watched the hallway out of the corners of her eyes as she picked around the bread to ensure it was clear.   Melody lifted out the heavy loaf and opened the closet door in one motion.   The loaf of bread was dropped on the top shelf and pushed back out of sight, the closet door swung shut silently.

The instructions for the cleaning staff were to never disturb the Assistant Division Commander for any reason.   If they arrived and the outer door to his quarters was still closed, they were to wait in the small conference room adjoining his quarters until his staff opened the door. The open door usually meant the Assistant Commander was already out and about in the outer offices, or more likely, sitting at his small desk with his uniform jacket off, sipping coffee as he glanced over the night reports. Anna had only seen him for a moment, but she recognized him at once.

At the entrance to the compound their cleaning cart was very thoroughly examined, and the three middle-aged cleaning women had to submit to a daily pat down of their aprons, coats and hats.   Anna, who trimmed and dyed one of her wigs to match the woman she was replacing exactly, enjoyed the sense of being invisible again in her portrayal of a tired, older peasant woman.   She held up her photo ID pass like the others but there was only the short nod from the guards.   The young German solders did not joke with them or casually look over their rumps and legs like they did the bakery assistants.   It was all business, and once they determined there were no weapons in the cart or on the old ladies, they

264

waved them through and never looked back. There were always three of them, all in the field utility uniforms of the SS Panzer carrying MP-40 submachineguns. They looked experienced, tough and very fit. There would be no escape coming in this direction.

To help ensure the silence and cooperation of the bakery assistant and the room cleaner, Anna insisted the women continue to receive their normal pay from the *maquis* leader and gave them each a few hundred *Francs* extra. The money would be additional evidence against them if there was a trial of course, but more likely they would be executed, along with the other staff, within a few hours of the completion of her mission. She tried not to think of it, considering instead the words of her OSS trainers who admitted, sadly, the Allied invasion of France would involve directing artillery, naval gunfire and aerial bombardment onto French homes and cities. *We will in the commission of this mission, have to kill individual French men and women in order to take France back.* Anna understood. She knew French history. It didn't make it any easier. But she refused, after consideration, to risk Melody any more than necessary. The *maquis* leader would be informed of the invasion when it happens by the BBC. When it occurred there would no longer be any need for room cleaning or baking bread. To Anna, it came down to opportunity. *Das Reich* could be called any moment and the Assistant Division Commander would be gone forever.

The weather had been poor for days so there were few Allied overflights. They increased daily until the skies turned gray and wet. *Das Reich* was staying under the camouflage netting during the day so they would not be caught out in the open and strafed. With the weather keeping the skies safer, *Das Reich* patrols resumed. What would it take to move an Army across the English Channel? Would they only go if the weather was clear? No one knew, certainly not the OSS. Anna was briefed only to be ready by the first of June. If she waited until the last minute, the chaos of the invasion and the loss of immediate leadership might be enough for many of the *maquis* to escape. She knew the Commander of the *Das Reich* was headquartered in Montauban, but he was rarely seen. How quickly could he re-establish leadership? Anna knew these townspeople, the villagers who had lived in Valence d'Agen their entire lives wouldn't just up and leave. Where would they go? There were always a few who had never ventured outside of the department in their entire lives. They would slip down into their cellars like they did centuries before and hope it would be enough. Sometimes the very same stone cellars their forebears had hidden in. And like before, many would be dragged out and persecuted, tortured, hanged or shot. Casualties of yet another war they barely understood.

Anna decided she could not wait another day and planned to execute her mission in the morning.  She noticed there were several additional *Wehrmacht* staff officers arriving, with attending activity planned for evening meals.  Was that because the Assistant Commander was back at his headquarters, or were they here for another reason?  What she could gather from the *maquis* leader was the Assistant Commander rarely stayed at headquarters more than a few days at a time.  Tomorrow would be day three.  She no longer needed Melody in the bakery assistant role; Anna needed to brief her on her escape plan.  It had to be tonight.  Let her know Anna had not actually destroyed the radio crystals, and give her an exact diagram where the radio was buried.  That would spin up Melody's energies.  The rest was up to Melody and her wonderful memory.  If she couldn't make it back to the *Dordogne* or the OSS wouldn't accept her radio calls because she got the call signs and dates wrong, then the best Melody could do is stay low and wait.  Anna accepted she would never see Clara or Jean Paul again, but she couldn't help that, not now.  At least she knew they were safe.  But she could save Melody from certain death.  She could do that much.  That lifted her heart for a short while.

# Chapter 31

*June 5, 1944. Valence d' Agen, France.*

As a military pilot Jean Paul had known cold fear many times in his career. In-flight emergencies, night approaches in bad weather and as a bomber pilot, the gut-tightening fear as his formation approached the target at night, level and straight to create a steady platform for the bomb aimers. German 88mm flak guns peppered the sky in front of them, behind them and occasionally when the gunners guessed the altitude right, all around and through them. Punching holes through thin aluminum with big red-hot shards of steel that sliced fuel lines; control cables and surfaces; human bone and muscle, and bomb bays loaded with high explosives with equal impunity. But he had to admit sitting at a dining table in a German uniform having dinner with the staff officers of the Second SS Panzer Division was a new experience entirely.

No one wants to admit fear or show it so air crews joked, focused on their job or manufactured something to do—anything, to take their minds off what they knew was happening all around them, or to other crews. But Jean Paul, Ericson and McLemore could do no such thing. They were portraying the roles of war-weary SS staff officers and victims of an automobile accident, and were now the temporary guests of the *Das Reich* until they could find some suitable transport. With the Allies strafing French trains and vehicles from dawn to dusk if the weather permitted it, there weren't many options for them. If there was any concern on the part of the other staff officers about what they were, it was alleviated by Ericson, who was well known and apparently popular with several of the *Das Reich* staff officers. It was a real Godsend for Jean Paul and McLemore, who's briefing on their individual characters was adequate for brief contact and small talk, not for serious conversation.

McLemore wore a large, thick bandage on his jaw, thanks to the kindness of a *Das Reich* surgeon, and was forgiven as not being able to hold his end of a conversation. He was fluent enough as a German speaker to understand all that was said, responding when appropriate with the odd nod and smile of understanding. Jean Paul, on the other hand was not injured at all. His German, although excellent, had a French accent that was picked up on by several officers, including a tall, crippled SS *major* with a black eye patch. He was reputed to be a *Gestapo* Jew hunter from Paris with direct Himmler connections. He seemed friendly enough, but Jean Paul avoided him. He had to respond after a direct inquiry from the *major* about his accent. Jean Paul explained he was originally raised as a boy in Nancy, in the highly contested *Alsace-*

*Lorraine* region between Germany and France. He spoke both French and German at home as the result. The *major* lit up, stating he was born in Stuttgart but spent many summers with relatives in Nancy, and he too was a bilingual speaker because of it.

The *major* wanted to reminisce but Jean Paul had to admit, sadly, that all of his recollections about Nancy were when he was a mere toddler. He remembered very little. The brief years his family actually lived in France were in Aix, in Provence. They had enjoyed their time there before his father, a lawyer, had to return the family back to Munich. It was the only German city Jean Paul knew well because of the travels he had made with his real father. He felt he was talking too much and apparently so did Captain Ericson, who was looking uncomfortable. Ericson did his best to guide the conversation away from Jean Paul, but Jean Paul noticed the SS *major* watched them carefully.

Despite the expected invasion within days, wine and some spirits were available to the Assistant Commanding General and his staff, and it was poured easily prior to dinner. Jean Paul excused himself to use the restroom, stopping in the hallway to allow several attractive young French women to carry in fresh bread towards the kitchen. It suddenly occurred to him that Anna may use such a ruse to gain entrance into the house, and he couldn't risk the shock of her recognizing him in public. She might scream or do something else to draw attention to them both. He turned away and examined some old painting on the wall, waiting until the women, four by his count, had trundled their loads down the hallway into the kitchen. There was only one blond, but his colleague with the SOE, Captain Denon, had said Anna was known to use disguises. Jean Paul came out of the bathroom and noticed the SS *major* with the black eye patch was peering down the hall. He turned and saw Jean Paul and smiled. He had obviously noticed the women too.

"Well, we will have fresh bread tonight, eh, *Herr Hauptmann?*" The four young women scurried back down the hall, their heads down avoiding the *major's* glance. They closed the door behind them and the *major* stepped over and looked out the window.

"I'm surprised they don't use an escort when they come into the house." He stated almost to himself, shaking his head. "But I guess they check them out as they come into the yard."

Jean Paul shrugged and returned to the dining room, but not before he noticed the SS *major* making his way towards the kitchen. This one seemed suspicious of something. They said he was *Gestapo,* but what was he looking for? *A Juif hunter.* Jean Paul stopped and stared hard at the wooden floor before returning to the dining room. *Was he somehow aware of Anna's mission? Was he looking for her too?*

Jean Paul accepted a glass of red table wine from an enlisted soldier server, but Ericson, the senior officer in the room since the Assistant Commander had not yet appeared, waved him over.

"Join me for a cigarette outside, *Herr Hauptmann?* Bring your wine." He signaled to McLemore to remain at the table with the universal sign of a "V" between his fingers for smoking. McLemore nodded and stared at them in irritation. Outside they lit up and strolled slowly away from the house and prying ears.

"Did you see those young ladies bringing the bread?" Ericson whispered to Jean Paul in French. "I didn't see Anna in the group, but I didn't get as close as you. What do you think?"

"I looked pretty closely, and Anna wasn't with them."

Ericson smiled as if they had shared a joke and blew out his smoke as they sauntered along.

"That doesn't mean she won't be here tomorrow. The guard detail says they deliver the bread twice a day. About an hour before breakfast and the same before dinner. They're gone now, so we should watch very carefully tomorrow morning. We need to be up early and rooting around the kitchen looking for coffee or something."

Ericson stopped and stretched, flicking the ash from his cigarette, surveying the area and waving casually to someone behind them. Jean Paul instinctively turned his head slowly in that direction and saw the SS *major* with the black eye patch staring at them at the entrance. Ericson turned his head away and spoke out of the corner of his mouth.

"That bastard suspects something." He sighed and dropped his cigarette, looked at Jean Paul carefully.

"I think because the Assistant Commander will be in the house in the morning, this might be the time Anna will strike, although I don't know how she would escape. Our only hope is one of us seeing her in time and stopping her." He saw the look of concern on Jean Paul's face and nodded, keeping his own face turned away from the house.

"I know, Jean Paul. This is going to be pretty dicey. We can only hope you see your sister first and you can somehow—dissuade her without causing an alarm. McLemore is hoping she succeeds, of course but if she doesn't, you can be sure he might try something on his own. *That is his mission.* I have to deal with him tonight. Leave that up to me. If we can do this and no one knows the better, then we all get away free. I don't want a shootout if at all possible. With the Guard Company all around and Mr. *Gestapo* there, we'll all be dead men." He smiled casually, watching Jean Paul for a moment, letting the message sink in. He leaned in closer, old comrades sharing a joke, bringing his arm around

Jean Paul's shoulder and tucking his head down. He patted Jean Paul's back for the audience and spoke very slowly.

"Jean Paul, we have to think of the invasion. Of the quarter of a million men who will be landing on those beaches in a couple of days. We're talking about bringing an end to this war. The end of the German occupation of your own country. It's more important than any one of us. Do you understand what I'm saying?"

Jean Paul stopped and stared at Ericson, his face passive but his eyes turned as dark as coal.

"I hear you loud and clear. We're talking about my sister. You take care of McLemore and I'll take care of my sister." Jean Paul remembered Denon's parting words about Ericson having his orders. Ericson seemed to sense what Jean Paul was thinking. He pulled away and crossed his arms.

"Walk with me," he whispered, guiding Jean Paul back to the house.

"I will take care of McLemore, but I will need your help, Jean Paul. Your sister becomes our only concern. I have a plan."

That night after dinner the staff officers of the *Das Reich* returned to their planning work. The Assistant Commander, who seemed very preoccupied, said little during dinner and excused himself after just a few bites of his meal. The three guest officers from Paris returned to their quarters, a small house in the compound. After walking around the house to confirm there were no lurking eavesdroppers, Ericson came back inside and the three of them discussed a plan of action for tomorrow.

Ericson and McLemore agreed there was a high probability Anna would make her move in the morning while the Assistant Commander was still in his quarters or in the house. If not, McLemore believed they should be prepared to do the job themselves, although there was only a small probability of any of them escaping capture or death. Ericson disagreed, stating emphatically their mission was not a suicide mission. If they could have coordinated an attack from one of the *maquis* as a diversion to draw most of the Guard Company away, that would have given them more of a chance here in the compound. But they understood the *maquis* hesitation to mount such a bold attack. It would guarantee immediate retribution to the local civilian population. Better to wait. Ericson told McLemore to be prepared but to hold back to let Anna do her work. If she didn't show, they should lay low, stay out of everyone's way and wait until the invasion news arrived. They were accepted by the headquarters staff and Guard Company. Wait for the invasion. This alone would create significant excitement and general chaos. They could act and disappear before anyone would notice.

McLemore was not happy with the decision but begrudgingly agreed to wait. He had no choice. As it was his shooting hand and arm were now in a cast and sling, courtesy of the *Das Reich* medical staff. Jean Paul knew many shooters who were ambidextrous and certainly could see McLemore was more than capable, but it still created a disadvantage. McLemore had no way of knowing Ericson would not allow any harm to befall the Assistant Commander, and assumed he would get whatever assistance was necessary to complete his mission. They were all tired so they went to bed early. McLemore and Jean Paul shared a bedroom but McLemore was not communicative and was asleep in minutes.

There was a barely audible tap at their door around four in the morning. Jean Paul was already awake, slipping out of the covers as Ericson entered. As planned, Jean Paul stood by to help restrain and muffle McLemore as Ericson went directly to his bed. Ericson was very careful and efficient, keeping the hypodermic needle behind his back as he silently waited for Jean Paul to join him. Without hesitation Ericson injected the solution into McLemore's shoulder through his shirt and gripped the big man's elbow, pressing his body weight down on McLemore's arm, controlling it. Jean Paul had covered McLemore's mouth and gripped his head as McLemore awoke with a violent start. He groaned and started to fight them but it was too late. Within three seconds his eyes closed and his struggles subsided, his head and limbs falling limp.

"What is that?" Jean Paul demanded uncomfortably. "Is he—dead?"

"Pentobarbital," whispered Ericson. He carefully searched around McLemore's pillow and found the silenced .22, slipping it under his jacket. "Double the dose he would be dead. As it is, he will sleep for about four hours. By that time, we will have come back and got him, or you and I will be long dead."

They stayed in the room for a half an hour. It was still dark, but Ericson peeked out the window facing the main house and reported the lights in the kitchen were on.

"Okay, put your uniform coat on but don't button the top two buttons. It's four-thirty in the morning. The duty day hasn't started. There won't be many people around except the guards on duty, the officer on duty in the communications room and the kitchen staff. We'll saunter across and let the guards know we're going in the kitchen on the ruse we couldn't sleep and need coffee. The guards are used to seeing us around so there shouldn't be any problem. Once inside we'll stick around and wait for the bakery crew to show up. When we hear the bakery truck, you go into the hall and wait for Anna. You have to catch her attention without alarming her, understand? She won't expect to see you here, and not in a German uniform. You don't want to get killed by your own sister. But understand you must stop her. Don't let her deliver her bread, have her just put it down. I'll stay in the shadows so she doesn't recognize me. "

"You'll be in the kitchen?"

"I'll be close by and watching. I don't expect her to go in the kitchen, I expect her to go looking for the Assistant Commander."

The rest was left unsaid between the two of them. Jean Paul had no doubt if he failed to persuade Anna, Ericson intended to kill her. Because of his deep cover Ericson would be able to explain his actions and suspicions. Jean Paul felt for the butt of his Walther in its holster and took a deep breath. There was no sticking a hypodermic in Anna and pulling her aside; that was not an option. His inadequacy for this job gripped his stomach and he felt physically sick. He had not seen her in four years. She was a trained—agent. An assassin according to the SOE and OSS. He would have just a few seconds to attract her attention and if she didn't instinctively kill him first, persuade her to believe he was, in fact, her brother Jean Paul, and not a German officer. Once she overcame that shock, he was to then persuade her to believe the Assistant Commanding General of the Second SS Panzer Division, her mission target, was actually an SOE double agent. It struck him like a wooden mallet. No trained assassin would believe it. He was just a man who looked like her brother. Anna would most likely kill him on the spot. The outrageousness of the entire plan overwhelmed him and his knees almost buckled. *Impossible. How did he get involved in this? How did Anna? My God,* he thought, *what if I don't recognize her because of her disguise?*

He heard the door latch close behind him in the dark and sensed Ericson beside him.

"Okay, here we go." Ericson whispered, walking noisily towards the big house, his boots crunching small pebbles, knowing it would alert the guards on this side.

"Well," Ericson said loud enough so that the guards could hear him, "since we can't sleep, we might as well see if we can get some coffee!"

They knew something was up and out of the ordinary as the lights were going on all over the big house and the rest of the compound. As they approached the guards, they could barely make out a squad of soldiers, shuffling and yawning, coming out of one of the big garrison tents in the compound and falling into formation. It was a full hour before normal reveille.

272

# Chapter 32

*June 6, 1944. Valence d' Agen, France.*

Because of Himmler's endorsement on his orders Karl was allowed full access to the coding and communication room at any time. Unable to sleep he rose very early. There was no sign of his two shadows but he knew how well they were trained. He had to assume they were there. He glanced through the code-translated flimsies as the operator typed them as quickly as he received them in his headset. The operator looked up at him wide-eyed as he handed over the latest. It was a series of reports, not yet fully confirmed, from as far north as Calais and as far south as the Brittany peninsula suggesting the long-awaited invasion of Europe had begun. BBC coded message streams seemed particularly active during the last 24 hours. Aircraft reports were numerous, as well as flashing lights at sea. Parachutists were also reported landing in Brittany and behind the beaches in Normandy. *Das Reich* was ordered to alert status like every other operational unit in France, but no movement orders.

Karl knew the division's standing orders, which were to counter the efforts of the *maquis* in the region to sabotage and slow down armored units once they receive their orders. But Karl had listened carefully as the Assistant Division Commander had explained the *Das Reich* would move north immediately, taking on the *maquis* whenever they chose to engage the *Das Reich*. Resistance would be met with overwhelming force and with no mercy. But this was a side show. Their true enemy was landing on the beaches and *Das Reich* intended on taking them head on. Karl handed the flimsy to the communications duty officer, who read it and quickly picked up the telephone to inform the division Chief of Staff and the Assistant Commander. It was the Chief of Staff's responsibility to inform the Division Commander in Montauban. The switchboard started to light up and within minutes Karl could see troops running around in the dark finding their place in various formations. *Das Reich* was waking up. But this was not an ordinary day. It might be the last day they spent in Valence d' Agen. Karl glanced at his watch. It was just a little past 4:30 in the morning, nearly an hour before reveille.

Karl had requested information about the three SS officers from Paris who were involved in an alleged motorcar accident, using his *Gestapo* authority and channels. Several of the *Das Reich* staff officers seemed very familiar and friendly with the SS-*Obersturmbannführer* and they vouched for him, but Karl didn't like the looks of the tall one with the broken jaw and arm, and the *Hauptmann* with the French accent seemed very evasive. All he knew was there were Allied special operations people all over France and he trusted no one. Nothing had come through from his request, so he decided to go to the other side of the house where the kitchen was. He would wait for the young women who would bring the bread. It was a slim chance, but it was one way to get in the compound and inside the house.

The headlights of the truck circling the driveway caught his attention. He glanced at his watch, surprised to see the bakery truck so early. It wasn't the bakery truck. Three older women in aprons and smocks unloaded two small carts and trundled their way to the guards. Karl stepped aside and found a place in the shadows where he could view the walkway through a window. The carts and the women were searched thoroughly and the guards waved them on. Karl could not see the women well in the dim early light. They were middle aged and hunched over, the result of too much labor and bending over for years. The guards ignored them once they completely their search, hefting their MP-40s and turning their attention back to the darkness beyond the driveway. The women pushed the carts up the steps and entered the house, turning immediately towards the hallway that led to the Assistant Commander's quarters. Karl was in an alcove in the same hallway so he slid back farther in the shadows, but not before he noticed the last cleaning woman hold back, and after a moment, turned her cart toward the hallway that led to the kitchen.

Karl couldn't move without exposing himself, so he waited until the other two cleaning women passed his alcove. After a minute or so he heard the squeaking of a cart and the third woman passed him, moving slowly. He remembered the cleaning closet in that hallway and decided the woman had retrieved something from there. She was slimmer than the other two and as she pushed past Karl's alcove, she was sliding a large baguette of bread under the cart. Her hair, light brown but grey streaked and wrapped in a tight bun, matched her heavy cotton dress and heavy shoes, but her slim legs and the brief profile of her face was youthful and immediately familiar. Karl's heart raced and he almost called out, but she was gone.

He crept out of the shadows far enough so he could see the front courtyard through a window. Headlights swept around again and he heard the roar of the bakery truck. At the same time lights were flashing on outside in the compound as men started moving about. Karl wasn't sure what it was all about, but immediately suspected a diversion. *Maquis?* In support of Anna? He glanced down at his holster and hesitated before he pulled out his Walther PP. With his thumb, he lifted the safety which cocked the hammer. He lowered the small pistol and pressed it close to his leg and looked both ways down the hallway. His two shadows—the assassins, may already be in the building. Would they wait to see if he would kill her or take over from here? He saw the young women with the bread baskets approaching the guards and knew there would not be much time. Standing erect, he marched purposely down the hall towards the Assistant Commander's quarters.

The doors to the quarters were open. Karl started to knock then realized his folly, deciding to use his rank and special privilege to gain and explain his entry if he was challenged by anyone. The quarters for the Assistant Commanding General were two large bedrooms connected by a small hallway and a master bath. The door to the master bath was open. One of the cleaning women was visible, wiping down the sink. The double doors to the first bedroom were open and another woman was making the bed. She glanced up at Karl and stared for a long moment before looking away, fear in her eyes. His eye patch and gaunt looks were menacing to some, and he had gotten used to the stares, but the woman wasn't staring at his patch. She saw the gun he held close to his leg.

As he walked slowly towards the back bedroom, he sensed motion and turned to catch the back of the woman who was making the bed running away. Karl stopped and pressed his back to the wall when the woman collapsed in her tracks. He had heard nothing, but there was now significant noise outside with NCOs barking commands and more vehicles driving up. A moment later one of his shadow assassins, a suppressed pistol in his hand, drifted silently down the hall. His partner joined him a moment later, both of them extremely alert and watchful, their weapons out.

"Is she in there?" One of them hissed, nodding towards the last bedroom. Karl didn't respond, but the soldier noticed the pistol in Karl's hand and shook his head. "Too much noise, *Herr Major*, we have it from here."

"I'm not sure she's in there—or the *Brigadefuhrer* for that matter!" Karl whispered, not knowing what to do. The two soldiers slipped around him and began carefully walking towards the last bedroom. Karl raised his Walther and aimed it at the back of the soldiers. He couldn't let them do it. Not his Anna. None of them heard Ericson as he slid up behind them. McLemore's High Standard barked three times, the sound like someone slapping a table top firmly three times in succession. All three were head shots, and none missed their mark at three and four meters.

Ericson glanced down at the bodies but didn't stop his approach. The doors to the last bedroom were open. With a firm two handed grip on his pistol, Ericson stopped only long enough to listen for a second or two. When he heard no voices, he figured he was too late. He spun into the room and rolled to the right.

Jean Paul had raced out of the kitchen despite being told by Ericson to stay put. Ericson had already ordered the kitchen staff to leave out the side door. They were long gone. He had seen the two German soldiers with suppressed pistols sneaking down the other hall. Ericson and Jean Paul had held the bakery girls in the kitchen at gun point, as Ericson pulled at their hair and clothing looking for phony wigs and disguises. Jean Paul stopped and returned to the kitchen. He found the young women still in the corner where they left them, too frightened to move.

"Go home!" He ordered in French. "Get out of here before you get hurt! Go!" The four of them hesitated only for a second before they rushed out of the kitchen and down the hall, leaving their baskets and boxes.

Jean Paul turned down the hallway that led to the other side of the house. Once inside the Assistant Commander's quarters, he gasped when he saw the body of one of the cleaning women lying on her side in a pool of dark black blood. She had been shot in the chest. There were bloody footprints from her body running all the way down the hall. He peered nervously into the first bedroom and saw another body near the bed. He stepped inside and glanced around the room, expecting to find the Assistant Commander's body, but it was another cleaning woman. He quickly backed out and nervously poked around the doorway. It was then he realized there were more victims down the narrow hall. His hands trembling, Jean Paul paused to pull the pistol out of his holster and put a round in the chamber. Three dead German soldiers, including the *Gestapo Major* with the black eye patch, were sprawled to one side of the hall. All three looked like they had been shot in the back of the head. He crept up on the last bedroom and stopped to listen. Every instinct told him to turn around and leave immediately, but he couldn't do it. He steeled himself to see the body of his sister and stepped around into the bedroom.

The room was neat and tidy, the bed made and all the lights were on. It was a large room and there was a desk and telephone on one side, obviously used by the Assistant Commander. It appeared deserted until Jean Paul cautiously approached the bathroom. The door was closed and only opened halfway before something stopped its free travel. The fresh blood was still spreading like reaching fingers on the old tile. With his pistol in hand Jean Paul pressed against the door and peeked inside.

Ericson was dead, shot once in the side of the temple with a small caliber bullet at very close range. Jean Paul had heard nothing.

"*Anna?*" Jean Paul whispered, his voice weak and nervous. After a deep breath, Jean Paul peered into the shower and the rest of the bathroom.    There was no one else there.    The Assistant Division Commander of the *Das Reich* wasn't here.    If this was his sister's work, she too had disappeared.    Jean Paul could hear voices outside but no one had approached the quarters yet.  Of course not, the Assistant Commander was over at Plans or was not even in Valence d'Agen.    No one was in the quarters except the cleaning staff.  With Ericson dead and McLemore still knocked out in his bed in their little house, there would be a lot to explain and it wouldn't be very long before he would be arrested.  Out of uniform.    He would be shot within hours.    After many hours of interrogation.  Jean Paul holstered his pistol and took a deep breath.    It was getting light and it was time to get out.  He couldn't help McLemore because he was still drugged.  He would be interrogated before he was taken away or shot, but he would not have much information about the real mission.  Jean Paul brushed his uniform straight and carefully picked his way out of the quarters and out of the house.

Outside in the compound area there were now hundreds of troops in various formations preparing to leave.    The small park and center square were filled with vehicles of every kind.    Tracked and multi-wheeled transports were departing as quickly as they were loaded because of the risk of air attack.  The morning was threatening to be clear and beautiful.    American P-47s and British Spitfires could come over the horizon any minute.  Allied troops were apparently landing on Normandy beaches, and Resistance forces were attacking *Wehrmacht* forces all over the *Limousin.*    The *Das Reich* was rolling to meet them.    No one questioned Jean Paul because no one cared a whit for a stranded SS *Hauptmann* who was not part of the *Das Reich.*  He went looking for their old damaged staff car and simply took it, as no one asked or offered him a driver.    Jean Paul wanted to drive into the countryside out of sight of the *Das Reich* and dump the car and the uniform.  He was a Frenchman after all, and somewhere in the *Limousin* was his sister Clara.    He was done with the SOE and the RAF.

# Chapter 33

*June 6, 1944. Valence d' Agen, France.*

Her heart sank when she realized the *Brigadefuhrer* wasn't there. The bed didn't even look like it had been used. Anna had no time to ponder her options when she heard the three quick barks in the connecting hallway. The suppressed .22 has a unique signature and she had certainly practiced with it enough to know it when it was fired from five or six meters away. She glanced at the bathroom but the bunched floor length drapes were closer. She silently made it in two quick strides and slid her slim body completely behind the drapes, tucking her shoes in. Her High Standard was up and pressed against her breasts, her finger on the trigger. Whoever it was walked very carefully into the room. It took a good ear to sense the heel to toe movement of a professional, but he or she was there and Anna breathed ever so slowly through her nose. There was the slightest creak from the transition from the hardwood in the bedroom to the tile in the bathroom and a hesitation. From a narrow gap in the drapes she watched a dark form cross the threshold and disappear.

Anna peered left towards the bedroom door to ensure no one was behind her before lifting the drapes slowly aside. She crept along the wall to the edge of the bathroom door, her pistol fully extended and her body flat. Her only warning was the slight movement of the door hinges and suddenly the slow appearance of a suppressor and barrel of a pistol and the sleeve of a German SS Army officer uniform. Her pistol was already at head height and as the head appeared, she squeezed the trigger.

She stared down at the slumped body in shock and confusion, because as she fired, she recognized Ericson too late. The bullet had caught him an inch in front of his left ear, killing him instantly. So many thoughts raced through her mind they blurred. Some stuck. She remembered he said once he had slept with her several times as a guest at *Madame* Marchard's *maison* in Limoges. She had no recollection. As she had no recollection of those days—and nights. And the men who pressed against her and used her body. She did what she had to do. But she wasn't going to take time to remember any of it. She looked at him dispassionately, noting instead the OSS-issued High Standard, identical to hers, close to his hand.

*What the hell was he doing here? Was he here to kill the Brigadefuhrer or to kill her?*

As Anna stared at Ericson, she heard a creak in the hallway. She slid around and slipped back behind the drapes, her heart pounding. The pistol was still warm and ready. This person hesitated before entering the room. She could hear the footsteps and the creak as he or she entered the bathroom. There was an audible gasp. Anna could just see the dark shape of the German uniform as it came out, but there was no hesitation this time, the German scurried out.

Anna waited no more than a few seconds. She moved the drapes aside as she heard shouts outside. She threw her pistol under the bed and slipped quickly to the bedroom door to listen. Whoever that was had left, but she could hear a great deal of movement just outside. She peered down the hallway, stunned again by the three dead German SS soldiers, two apparently carrying suppressed pistols. Not standard *Wehrmacht* issue. The third was an SS officer, lying on his face, a black eye patch covering the eye and half the face that was visible. *Who were they? Who were they hunting? And who killed them?* Anna considered Ericson for a moment then shook the thoughts out of her head. It didn't matter. Her mission was blown. She needed to move at once, they would be coming inside any second. She gasped when she saw the bodies of her temporary cleaning service colleagues. One was shot in the chest and the other in the head. Somehow someone got the message there was going to be an assassination attempt. *What else could it be?* Out of the side window Anna could see guards running around the house in the direction of the front door. She had to move now.

The front entrance door slammed open hard and there was a lot of shouting as men rushed up and down the hallways challenging anyone inside. Most of the activities were at the opposite end of the house where the quarters were. They must have discovered the bodies by now. Inside the closet Anna crushed her body into a tight ball. When she entered the closet, she had lifted the two lower shelves and moved then aside so she could slide in. She clutched her hands and when she heard multiple voices outside the closet she started to moan and whine, shuffling her feet around so things began to fall down in the closet. The door was yanked open roughly and Anna screamed.

*"Please—Please, don't hurt me! Don't hurt me!"* She screeched hysterically as she covered and clutched her wig carefully so it would not be detached.

*"Come out at once! Come out of there!"* Some soldiers yelled at her, brandishing their MP-40s. She cowered when they touched her arms and legs and screamed again. All of the soldiers were from the Guard Company, but she stared at them wildly without recognition, her eyes filled with terror.

*"Please—Please..."* she begged in French, *"don't hurt me..."* One of the guards dropped to one knee and placed his hand on her arm gently. He looked at the others and shook his head.

"She's one of the cleaning staff. She must have run away when they started shooting and hid here. Look at her, poor thing, she scared to death. Help her up!"

The soldiers tried to get Anna to talk but she simply babbled about men shooting her friends. *Why*, she asked, staring at them wildly, *Why?* There were now dozens of soldiers and officers milling around the house, and Anna was led outside and was shown a bench near a tree.

"We'll be back," a soldier said, "you rest. Stay right there."

Anna sat, sobbing, and waited until a large group of soldiers entered the courtyard and blocked the view from the house. She stood up carefully, wiping her tears. Walking slowly towards the entrance where there were no guards at their post, she turned left towards the village. Once out of sight from the main house she turned again down a side street and removed her apron and smock, discarding them behind a bush. No one took notice of her at all as anyone out in the streets had their attention towards the sky. Dive bombers were dropping high explosives and strafing in the direction of the forests where all the *Das Reich* vehicles were parked. Anna remembered her briefings. Corsica-based American P-47s and B-25s would be hammering railways, roads, trucks and any *Wehrmacht* vehicles caught out in the open the minute the weather opened up, and the invasion had begun.

She turned down an alleyway and pulled off her wig, shaking out her blond hair. With a handkerchief she wiped the pancake makeup off of her face. It was risky because she had no phony ID with her, only the real ID of the cleaning woman she had replaced. But right now, they were looking for a middle-aged woman. She threw the ID into a trash bin because the woman wouldn't be working for *Das Reich* anymore anyway. Anna had not given too much thought about what she would do after the mission because she didn't think she would survive. But she sent Melody away and hopefully she was halfway into the *Limousin* by now. If she could find the radio and OSS would accept her coded messages, she might make a pickup. Most likely she would just have to stay low until the Allies arrive. At least Melody has a good chance. She was smart and wanted to live. She would have interesting stories to tell her grandchildren someday back in New England.

Anna had left a small bundle at the *maquis* leader's house, including all of her remaining cash. If he hadn't already been arrested by the *Gestapo* on the suspicion of his involvement in the debacle, Anna could retrieve her things and escape. The invasion was the ultimate diversion for them both, but if he chose to remain in Valence d'Agen there could be some risk of retribution. The mission was a failure because the prime target escaped. But what other missions were going on at the same time she was not aware of? What was Ericson doing? Who were those three German SS soldiers apparently killed by Ericson, two holding suppressed pistols? Why were the other maids killed? None of it made any sense.

But Anna felt she had to ensure the woman who she replaced understood what happened and would be able to handle her role. She was an innocent party, but under interrogation would she reveal Anna's role? Anna had to impress on her that if she played dumb and afraid, she would be okay. She saw nothing except her dead friends. She hid because she was scared out of her wits. The guards could attest to her behavior at the time they found her in the closet. She was hysterical, half out of her mind. To attempt to escape or simply hide would create suspicion of her possible involvement. Anna felt guilty for what she had done. Two women were dead already, innocent of anything, and the least she could do is to explain to the poor surviving woman her options, as bleak as they were. And they were bleak. The more she thought of the poor, simple-minded peasant woman the more she realized the best thing for her was to run away. *She was not a sly, lying, thieving, murdering whore like me*, she thought.

It was obvious the *maquis* leader heard about the shootings as his house was deserted. He was no fool. Everyone was gone, including all members of his family and the dog. Good, Anna thought with relief. But it meant her only contact for the cleaning woman was gone. She could only hope he had persuaded her to leave too. She had forgotten her name. As was typical for French village homes at the time, the backdoor was unlocked. Anna listened for several minutes and watched from a shady alleyway to ensure there were no shadows. She approached from the neighbor's yard and slipped in the backdoor. She found her bundle of things undisturbed under the loose board by the bed she had shared with Melody the first night they had arrived in Valence d'Agen.

In it were the false ID papers of a traveling nurse from Beynac in the *Dordogne,* about 50,000 *Francs* in varying denominations, the short hair wig of a brunette, and a .32 Colt automatic pistol and 20 rounds of ammunition. The *maquis l*eader had a young daughter in her early 20s, and from her room Anna took both a small backpack and some clothing that would fit. She scoured the house for some food, and discovered a stale baguette and a quarter round of cheese. She lifted a very sharp paring knife and wrapped it in a cloth, before leaving a few hundred *Francs* tucked into the knife drawer. They still might return when *Das Reich* was gone. If OSS wanted a complete accounting, they would have to come see her after the war, but for now she was a French woman taking from other French citizens and she wanted to repay them fairly.    She didn't give a damn where the money came from.

She stayed hidden across the street from the house until noon, and when no German troops appeared Anna decided the invasion and other events had simply moved things along.    She hoped it would remain that way, but she felt her obligation was over.    In all regards.    She felt so empty.    She would never contact the OSS again.    She wished she could say she was going to go home, but her home was gone.    Jean Paul was in England somewhere, flying for the RAF.    But somewhere, perhaps within 100 kilometers, her sister Clara was with a *maquis* in the *Limousin*.    So much was history now.    Her time as a medical student, the days with Karl in Limoges, her time on the streets and her months with *Madame* Marchand's *maison*.    Since her fate was not to die in the assassination attempt of some *Brigadefuhrer*, perhaps she had a future.

Somehow, she had to deal with what she had become and what she had done.    She knew she was still numb with shock with the realization of her survival.    She was through with killing, the fire was gone.    Her fury was spent.    So much was taken from her but something still remained.    She still cared.    She was going to find the only family she had. She was a good hunter, this she knew.    It was time to find her family and some peace.    Perhaps they would understand, accept what she had done. Perhaps she could learn to accept it herself.

# Chapter 34

*June 9, 1944. Tournon d'Agenais, France.*

In some ways Jean Paul felt he had returned to France as a complete stranger. The years of occupation increased the natural tendency of the French to tribalism beyond his comprehension. He wasn't there to share and endure the humiliations of the occupation, or the suffering brought about by food and fuel shortages. He wasn't drafted to serve Germany in the labor battalions, and certainly didn't suffer the loss of everything he owned including his life, like his father and mother did because they voluntarily declared themselves as *Juifs*. He certainly understood the dangerous grey areas that now existed between those who sided with the *Vichy* and those who passively or actively resisted the Germans. Retribution and payback were soon coming for parties who chose the wrong side. The winds had changed with the arrival of the Allies on French soil, and the acts of violence and the public denunciation of those who served the *Third Reich* and turned against their own countrymen had all the trappings of kangaroo courts and an earlier revolution on French soil.

Jean Paul, having no identification other than that of a Free French aviator in the RAF, knew his situation was more tenuous than most. Out of uniform he would be treated as no more than a spy. If the Germans caught him, he had no question about his fate. Alone and in uniform, his fate around the FTP *maquis* could be the same. He stole his ill-fitting clothing from a clothesline before discarding his SS uniform, and he wore the too-small rubber boots lifted from a shed. He stopped shaving and hitched rides on hay wagons on his journey north away from Valence d' Agen, spending some of the last of his money to purchase some bread, cheese and sour wine from a farmer's wife. He remembered the expected routes the *Das Reich* would take when the invasion came from Ericson's map, and tried to avoid those roads. If a road block was spotted ahead, the hay wagon would stop for a brief moment as several of the riders dropped off the wagon, slipping away cross country. There was always the threat of air attack, but generally the Allied fighters flew low over the hay wagons, rocking their wings when the riders wildly waved.

Any other form of transportation including the farm worker buses, were fair game to the fighter pilots. Jean Paul didn't know if the pilots could distinguish between *Wehrmacht* vehicles diving down at 300 knots, or they were ordered to shoot up anything with an engine. It only took a strafing or two to discourage the French from driving around in the open, because there were few survivors when six .50 caliber guns converged on a car or a truck. It was obliterated into a cloud of flying pieces seconds before the fuel tanks exploded.

He knew the FTP didn't trust anyone associated with the British because they chose to back de Gaulle, but the last reported location of Clara was in the *Limousin*, with an FTP *maquis*. He heard Ericson when Ericson explained the FTP was trying to slow down the Allied advance, but it was hard to believe. Could they actually be controlled by the Russians, with the Russians trying to delay the Allies in France until the Soviet Union could advance farther and retake their own borders? This just meant to Jean Paul that France and most of Europe were once again pawns between the clutches of great powers, all struggling to take the most spoils once the fighting was done. Jean Paul shook his head, flushing the political considerations from his mind. It won't matter what the FTP did in a few weeks. Once the Germans were out of France, French men and women would begin picking up the pieces and weld them together as if nothing had happened. It was the French way.

Twenty-five kilometers east of Villenueve sur Lot there is a jutting promontory with a medieval *bastide* across the top. Like a pale, stone man o'war at full sail, Tournon d' Agenais was surrounded by rolling farmland as far as the eye could see from its high walls. Unlike many of the *bastides* in the Lot and Dardogne River valleys, Tournon d' Agenais was not built on a river. The *bastide* took advantage of the natural protection of the steep promontory sides, adding its own vertical stone to totally enclose the community. A deep central well ensured protection from siege. Because of its enormous view and prominence at the time, Tournon d' Agenais became a crossroad of sorts, with thin ribbons of undulating roads, all former cart trails, converging from Agen, Moutanban, Valence d' Agen, Villenueve sur Lot, Fumel and Cahors. Because of it some might expect the *Das Reich* to have the crossroads covered with armored vehicles. But they didn't and Jean Paul knew they wouldn't because the intelligence reports and photo reconnaissance demonstrated *Das Reich* stayed east and mostly on N20.

As it grew dark a group of people who had ridden with him in the back of the hay wagon dismounted below the curving approach road under the *bastide*. Jean Paul knew none of these people, and tired and hungry, wondered what he was going to do next. A large woman with red hair noticed him holding back near the wagon and walked back towards him. A man, bearded and hunched over from apparent fatigue, joined her.

"What is your name, *Monsieur?*" She asked. Before he could answer the bearded man pointed towards Jean Paul and shook his head.

"I saw your hands, *Monsieur.* They don't fit your clothes. Tell her the truth." Jean Paul, exhausted and weary, stared at them for several seconds.

"My name is Jean Paul Metzgen. I'm not a farm worker. I'm a pilot, a French pilot."

"You were shot down, *Monsieur?*" Their eyes widened.

"No. I arrived by parachute from England. To help with the Allied landings." They continued to stare at him for several moments as they pondered this. The woman looked at the man and he shrugged.

"Where are you from, *Monsieur?* Why is a pilot here to help with the Allied landings?"

"From Provence. Aix. We came here to slow down the *Das Reich.*"

"Were you successful?"

"Partially. But I have yet to connect with the *maquis* in the *Limousin.*"

"You were part of the disorder in Valence d' Agen? We heard there was an assassination attempt on the Command Staff. Is that true?"

"I cannot say."

The woman stepped in closer. Jean Paul could smell onions and garlic on her hand as she reached out and touched his face. It was an intimate gesture and he was taken aback.

"You are from Provence? And you say your name is Metzgen?" She glanced over at the bearded man and again he shrugged.

"Come with us. There are fewer German patrols near Tournon d' Agenais these days, but with the Allied landings, anything can happen. *Das Reich* rarely comes up this way. We have a place for you. We hid *Juif* children there once, under our shop. The building is built over a stone cave, and the wooden floor covers it completely. The Germans searched the building from top to bottom in 43' and missed all of it. Once *Das Reich* gets on its way, no one will bother us. You must be hungry. And you want to go to the *Limousin?*"

Jean Paul felt the warmth of the woman's hand and nodded. The man, who turned out to be her husband, smiled and placed his large paw of a hand on Jean Paul's shoulder.

"I think we have someone here you want to see. One of your— team members. She was in Valence d' Agen with you, I think." He looked at his wife, who nodded.

"She has the same name as yours, *Monsieur.*"

# About the Author

Jerry Coker is the author of two other historical novels set in World War II, *First Among Men* and *Into the Wet*. A former United States Marine rifleman, the author is a historian and researcher who earned degrees in English Literature from the University of California, Davis and Brown University when he returned from Southeast Asia. He lives in Northern California with his wife. For more information visit http://Stories of Jerry Coker.com.

41160020R00168

Made in the USA
Middletown, DE
06 April 2019